THE LOST GUIDE TO LIFE AND LOVE

Born and brought up in Wales, writing is all Sharon has ever wanted to do. After grammar school, she read English at the University of Bristol, then worked for the BBC and later for ITV. Among other journalism Sharon now writes five newspaper columns a week. To find out more about Sharon visit www.sharon-griffiths.com

By the same author:

The Accidental Time Traveller

SHARON GRIFFITHS

The Lost Guide to Life and Love

AVON

AVON

A division of HarperCollins*Publishers*
77–85 Fulham Palace Road,
London W6 8JB

www.harpercollins.co.uk

A Paperback Original 2009

Copyright © Sharon Griffiths 2009

Sharon Griffiths asserts the moral right to
be identified as the author of this work

A catalogue record for this book is
available from the British Library

ISBN-13: 978-1-84756-091-9

Set in Minion by Palimpsest Book Production Limited,
Grangemouth, Stirlingshire

Printed and bound in Great Britain by
Clays Ltd, St Ives plc

Mixed Sources
Product group from well-managed
forests and other controlled sources
www.fsc.org Cert no. SW-COC-1806
© 1996 Forest Stewardship Council
FSC

FSC is a non-profit international organisation established
to promote the responsible management of the world's forests.
Products carrying the FSC label are independently certified
to assure consumers that they come from forests that are managed
to meet the social, economic and ecological needs
of present and future generations.

Find out more about HarperCollins and the environment at
www.harpercollins.co.uk/green

Acknowledgements

There is, sadly, no such place as High Hartsone Edge, which exists only in my imagination. But if you go to the top of England where the high Pennine Dales of Durham, Northumberland and North Yorkshire soar up and meet the fells of Cumbria, you will find places very much like it. To find out more try the centres at Killhope (www.killhope.org.uk), Reeth (www.swaledalemuseum.org) and Nenthead (www.npht.com/nentheadmines), all of which helped me in the background.

Many thanks to all those who let me pick their brains during the writing of this. Special thanks to my agent Laura Longrigg – always so encouraging – and to the enthusiastic team at Avon – Maxine Hitchcock, Keshini Naidoo and Sammia Rafique.

And to all the brilliant food producers of the north, whose products have sustained and inspired me and added immensely to the pleasure of life.

With love to the Amos men –
Mike, Owen and Adam – who
filled my life with football.

Chapter One

Suddenly, the photographers stopped slouching and snapped to attention. They threw their cigarettes into the gutter and hoisted cameras into position, jostling for space and a good angle as the limo glided right up to the red-carpeted steps.

Dazzling flashes of light filled the autumn air alongside shouts of 'Over here, Clayton!' 'Give us a smile, Tanya!' 'This way, darling!'

Before the limo pulled away, two taxis arrived. More shouts, more flashing lights. A glimpse of the top of a blonde head, a sparkle of jewellery, a protective male arm. Then a glimpse of expensively cut jackets and a fluid athletic movement as more men sprang from the taxi almost before it had stopped.

Our queue pushed forward, straining to see. 'Who is it?' I asked Jake, as I put my hand on his shoulder and tried to jump up and look. My view was blocked by the huge presence of the security man, whose massive head seemed to grow straight out of his shoulders, his broad chest straining the seams of his jacket.

'Clayton Silver and some other footballers, I think,' said Jake, over his shoulder, 'and a couple of those girls off *Hollyoaks* or *EastEnders*.'

'Oh, I hope we get in!'

The footballers and their glittering girls went in through the canopied entrance, shielded from view by a phalanx of security men and the tubs of trees on each step. The taxis sped off, the cameras stopped flashing, the photographers went back to slouching and the queue pushed forward, impatient to be in. A beautiful young man in an impossibly tight shirt was checking names off on a clipboard. Ahead of us a group of girls – all long legs, long hair, huge eyes and glossy, scarlet lips – were pleading with him, but it was no good. He shook his head. The security men motioned them away out into the dark. The rest of us watched, fearful that we too would be rejected. It's probably easier to get into heaven than Club Balaika.

When Jake had said he knew someone who knew someone who could maybe get us in, I was first of all stunned that he'd suggested it. Not normally his sort of thing at all. But things hadn't been too good between us. We had hardly been out together for ages, so I guessed this was his way of making up for being so offhand lately. I'd agonised over what to wear – my bed had vanished under discarded outfits – and had finally settled on a chain-store knock-off dress, but adding a bit of class with my funky rainbow earrings that had cost me a week's wages on a working trip to Paris. I'd treated myself to a whole load of new smudgy eye make-up too, not that anyone would really see it in there . . .

Now at the Balaika, the people before us were allowed in. Did that mean that we were more or less likely to be? We were at the head of the queue now. I tried to look cool, above it all, as if I wasn't bothered whether we got in or not. I fixed the beautiful young man with what I hoped was an ironically amused glance as Jake gave him our names. He checked us on his clipboard list, looked me up and down in a totally uninterested way, then gave a brief nod and we were in. I tried not to yelp in glee.

The club was hot, dark and crowded, a lot smaller than I'd imagined and way smaller than our usual haunts but it certainly smelled more expensive, swirling with perfumes and colognes that were tantalisingly subtle. And the people, oh they were definitely more expensive. No chain-store knock-offs here. Every inch of flesh on display – and there was a lot – was honed and toned, polished and glossed. Every strand of hair gleamed. Every smile dazzled. There wasn't an ugly girl there. Each one looked as though she had spent the whole day, her whole life, getting ready to come out. Bet they hadn't had to rush home from work, dive into the shower and dash to get ready. These girls had all the time in the world. Time to acquire expensive tans, perfect hairstyles and stunning bodies, and, above all, a careless confidence, almost boredom. The men with them had all the assurance that money brings and something else – reflected pride? Ownership?

Jake and I made our way in to the bar, trying to look as though we belonged, Jake's journalist eyes flitting here and there, noticing everything, his eyes blinking as though he were taking rapid instant-camera shots. I was busy looking down – so many wonderful, wonderful shoes. Just slips of leather in jewelled colours, leopardskin, gold and silver – sometimes even all together – narrow straps, towering heels, exquisite decoration. All miniature works of art and engineering that these girls wore so casually on their elegant, narrow, bony feet. You just knew that they had at least twenty more pairs at home.

There was nowhere to sit down. Well, there were plenty of tables in alcoves where laughing groups sat round ice buckets full of champagne and bowls of strange-looking drinks. But to get a seat you had to reserve a table and you could only reserve a table if you were going to spend serious amounts of money. Not hard, as Jake muttered, going pale as our two drinks took a huge chunk from his credit card. We were definitely out of our league. But we could pretend for a night.

As my eyes got used to the dim but changing light – an icy blue made everyone look like ghosts, almost green, like aliens from a cheap science-fiction film. I thought I could recognise some of the people – someone from a boy band perhaps, or the guy who played Hugh Grant's little brother in something. But maybe it was just a look. *All* the guys looked like Hugh Grant's little brother. *Handsome is as handsome does*, as my mother used to say, quoting her fearsome Granny Allen; but handsome is still very nice to look at. Everyone seemed to know each other – lots of shrieks and greetings and extravagant air kisses. I couldn't see the footballers but there was no VIP area – the whole place was a VIP area – just a series of booths leading off the main room, and I guessed they were in one of those. Then I stopped looking, made the most of the music and leaned into Jake for a dance, surrounded by all the beautiful people.

This was all for work, of course. For Jake, everything revolves around work. Clubbing isn't his first choice for a night out. And such a club . . . I spotted Kit Kenzo, who does that late-night music programme, all over the girl who does the football reports. Then that earl who's a model, and I couldn't help gazing at him over Jake's shoulder. This was beginning to be fun. Then a tall elegant girl with the most perfect shoulders gazed with interest and a hint of envy at my earrings. Good.

As the night wore on, the music grew louder (great DJ), the atmosphere looser. Even the beautiful people looked not quite as beautiful now and not quite so bored. I wanted to keep dancing, but Jake was standing by the bar, watching people over the top of his bottle of Asaki.

'Come on, Jake, let's dance,' I said, putting my glass back

on the bar and taking his hand, trying to encourage him onto the dance floor. I wanted to make the most of this.

'Yeah, OK, Tilly,' he said, kissing the top of my head, a rare show of affection these days. I glanced up happily to meet the warmth of his gaze, but instead I could see he was watching someone on the other side of the room. I turned to see a couple of middle-aged men in expensive suits coming in and going round to one of the booths. I recognised one of them – Simeon Maynard, a billionaire businessman who had come from nowhere to buy Shadwell, the premiership football club that Clayton Silver played for. Presumably that's who he was drinking with. A few minutes later a waitress went over with ice buckets of champagne.

Of course this was why we were here. For weeks Jake had been researching some big story. Not quite sure what it was about – he didn't talk about work so much to me these days and we were increasingly like ships that passed in the night – but it was hard not to notice all the newspaper cuttings about Maynard piling up in the flat.

I danced close to Jake, my arms round his neck, but he didn't bend into me, the way he usually did. Somehow it felt as though he wasn't there with me at all. Or didn't want to be. After a while I gave up, stood back from him, let my arms drop to my side. At the same time, the two actresses who'd been drinking with the footballers and Maynard were coming out of one of the private booths and heading rather unsteadily across the floor.

Now Jake took my arm and whispered in my ear, 'Try and listen in to their conversation. See if they say anything interesting.'

Excuse me? He was definitely beginning to lose it. I looked at him and shook my head, and then followed the actresses downstairs to the Ladies. At least I'd get a sit-down. My strippy-strappy shoes were beginning to give me strippy-strappy blisters; there's a limit to what party feet gel insoles can achieve.

In the Ladies, there was a whole different party going on. Small groups of girls giggled round the washbasins. I didn't look too closely at what they were doing, but I don't think they were sharing their holiday snaps. A girl with a face straight from a Pre-Raphaelite painting lay slumped across an armchair, her eyes shut, her minuscule handbag dropped on the floor. She groaned slightly. I must have looked alarmed because a blonde with the sort of tan you only get from sunbathing on the deck of mega-yachts said dismissively, 'Leave her. She's always the same after too much of the house hooch . . .' she paused . . . 'on top of everything else.'

Other girls in their tiny dresses, as leggy as storks, leant forward into the mirrors, pouting provocatively at their own reflections as they brushed back manes of expertly highlighted hair.

The actresses I had followed had already emerged from the cubicles, swaying, laughing loudly. They joined the girls at the mirror.

'Not sure about this lip gloss. Too red, I think. What do you think?' said the dark one, peering at her image.

The fair one looked at her through the mirror and concentrated hard. 'No, you're probably more of a reddish pink. Me, I always prefer a pink. My colour consultant told me it brings out the warmth of my skin tones.'

'Yeah. I can see that.'

Riveting stuff. They snapped their handbags shut and tottered off. This was what I was supposed to be listening to? What had got into Jake? What had it to do with any story he was working on? Of course, if he talked to me more about what he was doing, then I might have more of an idea.

6

Suddenly the room emptied, instantly, magically. 'The princes?' one girl breathily asked another. '*Both* of them? Oh, yes please. *Such* good fun. And I just *so* adore the bodyguards.'

Out they all swarmed, a mass attack that would strike terror into even a prince. All except the girl slumped in the armchair, who was now at least sitting up and looking less green.

I was about to follow them. A chance to dance with a prince – well, within a few yards of one, at least – was too good to miss. I was just drying my hands on one of the neatly rolled little towels when the door suddenly burst open.

The girl who charged in wore a short sparkly dress that was definitely not a chain-store knock-off, but she could have worn a bin liner and looked stunning. Six feet tall with red hair piled on top of her head, she had the sort of cheekbones that make the rest of us just want to give up hope. She glanced quickly around the cloakroom, gave me the briefest of nods and raised her eyes to examine the high windows. Then, while I watched with my jaw dropping, she took off her shoes, stepped up onto the marble surround of the washbasins, reached up to push open the narrow window, then pulled herself up, wriggled through it and dropped out into the night.

I pulled a chair over and jumped up, twisting my head to peer down through the window. The girl was loping easily down the back street, past a surprised security guard, towards a taxi rank. Her hair had come loose and my lasting image was of her in the light of the streetlamps, her copper-coloured hair streaming out behind her, shining, dazzling.

Chapter Two

'So, Tilly, did you get to dance with a prince?' asked Bill, my godfather, the next day when I called in to his bistro. He and his kitchen staff were prepping up for lunch and I stood by the door of the kitchen, out of their way. While Bill talked to me, he was still keeping an eye on the chopping, slicing, searing, stirring going on all around him. I always loved watching him, cooking with him, tasting, experimenting. His restaurant kitchens had been a second home to me, and it was all down to him, really, that I was working for *The Foodie* magazine.

'A prince? Sadly, no,' I laughed, helping myself to a deliciously sweet cherry tomato. 'It was impossible to get near them – and seriously uncool to try. So I don't think I'll be the next princess.'

'Shame,' said Bill, kissing the top of my head as he came past me with a tray of prawns. 'You'd be a perfect princess. And it would be good for business too. The princess's godfather! Everyone would want to come and eat here.' He grinned at me. 'Coffee?'

'No, thank you. Actually, I've come to ask a favour.'

'Ask away.'

'Jake and I are going up north for a sort of holiday.'

'*Sort* of holiday?'

'Well, yes, he's got some project he's working on. And

I thought I could do some stories up there too, so we're renting a cottage for a couple of weeks. I've got the names of some really interesting food producers – cheese-makers, chocolatiers, and a monk who makes cider from the monastery apples, but if you know of any more, it would be really good. And as long as I keep sending them plenty of articles, the magazine's OK about me being away.'

'Sure,' said Bill, 'I can give you some contacts. If you're staying for lunch, we can sort it out then.'

'Sorry. Can't. I'm lunching with Mum.'

'Ah,' said Bill with a sigh, 'your mother. How is she?'

'Don't you know? Haven't you seen her recently?'

'No. She has, she *says*, been far too busy. Too busy for anyone as frivolous as me.'

Bill looked sad for a moment and I felt sad for him. He'd loved my mother for years. Hopelessly and helplessly. There was a small silence. I helped myself to another tomato.

'These are really very good,' I said as the juice spurted sweetly in my mouth. 'They taste of sunshine.'

Bill's face brightened. 'Yes, they do, don't they? They're from a new supplier. Tell you what . . .' He picked up a generous handful of the tomatoes and popped them into a paper bag. 'Give these to your mother, with my love. And I'll email you some suggestions for those foodie pieces.'

'Right. I'll give them to her and I hope they bring you luck.'

I gave him a hug and a kiss and set off with the usual mixed emotions to meet my mother, Frankie Flint . . .

Yes, *that* Frankie Flint, Fairtrade Frankie, the one who set up the chain of coffee bars. You'll probably have heard of her. She's always in the papers. There's even talk of making a film about her.

About how Frankie Flint and her husband Theo started a tiny little restaurant making delicious food so even though the chairs creaked and the tables wobbled it was quickly a huge success. Critics enthused about it, famous people 'discovered' it. Their friend Bill came in as a partner to help them. The day they had their first rave reviews in the colour supplements they held an impromptu party at Theo and Frankie's house. In the middle of the afternoon, Theo popped back to the restaurant to get some more food and wine. He took Josh, their two-year-old son, with him.

And in the middle of a sunny Sunday, on an almost deserted road, a drunk driver, just nineteen years old, jumped the lights and rammed straight into their car. If Theo himself had not had a couple of glasses of wine, he might have seen it coming and avoided it. Maybe. Maybe not. But he didn't. Theo and the other driver died instantly. Baby Josh lingered on before he, too, died three weeks later. I think my mother would have liked to have died, too. But she had her daughter, me, aged five, to look after.

Years later, probably when I was about ten, I came across a photo tucked into a book at home. It was a typical holiday snap of a family sitting around a café table in the sunshine. Father with a baby boy perched on his shoulders, a small chubby girl in big sunglasses reaching up to drink from a straw in a perilously tilted glass, and a young woman with long flowing hair laughing at the camera, eyes slightly screwed up in the sunlight, nothing more to worry about than the chance of some spilled orange juice.

'Who are they?' I asked my mother, who had gone pale at the sight of the picture.

'That's you,' she said, pointing to the chubby toddler. 'And your dad, and Josh, the year we went to France.'

'But who's *that*?' I asked, pointing at the laughing woman.

'That's me,' said my mother. 'You won't recognise me because I wore my hair long then.'

But that wasn't why I didn't recognise my mother laughing

in the sunshine. It was because in the five years since the accident, I had never once seen my mother laugh.

After my father and brother died, I think my mother must have had some sort of breakdown. Understandable really. But somehow she emerged and set up a new business. Energised and determined, she wanted to give people an alternative to pubs and bars, so she set up Frankie's Coffee Shops.

Long before Starbucks, Mum took the 1950s coffee bar and reinvented it. At a time when Britain was desperate for decent coffee, she provided it, and a great place to drink it too. Her cafés had armchairs and newspapers. Bigger branches had rooms with TV screens and table football and a jukebox and opened until late at night. They served soup, snacks, sandwiches and cakes but never, ever, alcohol. Still don't. But, despite that, Frankie's coffee shops are cool. She found the knack of appealing to all ages and all types. In the daytime it was the sort of place you could meet your granny, while at night you didn't have to apologise for suggesting a Frankie's Coffee Shop on the way home from a movie.

What started as a little, hippyish establishment soon grew. She set up franchises – very strictly controlled – until there were Frankie's Coffee Shops in most big towns. My mother had always been the business brain when she and Theo and Bill had their restaurant, and now she went into overdrive. She often said, 'Work is the best medicine, as Granny Allen used to say.'

Don't get me wrong. Frankie wasn't a bad mother. Not at all. It was almost as though she was trying so hard not to smother me that she left me almost too much alone. She didn't want to get too close to anyone any more, not even me. And certainly not Bill.

In any case, her business took huge amounts of time and

energy. And because it was such a novelty – ahead of its time, fairly traded and organic – she was always in the newspapers, on radio and television, commentating on this, that and the other. She was the absolute model of the perfect business, the perfect employer, the perfect ethical entrepreneur. What's more, she talked well and passionately, looked stunning and stylish and even made a profit – most of which, needless to say, was ploughed back into good causes. She was a one-woman retail phenomenon.

But all that didn't always make her easy to live with. Hard-working, high-minded, high-achieving, successful mothers with high moral standards and an insatiable work ethic aren't always the best flatmates for day-dreaming, chaotic teenage girls with a serious shoe habit and a pathological desire to sleep till lunchtime.

Frankie's New Road branch is aimed at ladies who lunch. It has huge squashy sofas, piles of glossy magazines and walls decorated with fashion ads. It is light and stylish and welcoming. And, as always, very busy. The place buzzes with chatter and is a glow of colours and good smells.

There, tucked in the corner in her trademark black, is my mother. She has a phone to her ear and a pile of papers in front of her. She likes to take her work round to the various coffee shops and work in the middle of it all, so she can see what's going on and her staff and customers can talk to her. It's another reason the media love her.

I bend over to give her a quick hug and kiss. As always, she makes me feel large and awkward. My mother apparently takes after her father's family and is small-boned and neat. She says I have inherited characteristics from her mother's family and that's why I'm so tall with enormous feet. Still on the phone, she gives me a quick acknowledgment as I sit down and order a smoothie – apple, pear, ginger and beetroot. Beetroot? I have to try it. When it comes, I sip it tentatively, then with more enthusiasm. Mmm, yes, it works. As I lean back, untangling the different flavours on my tongue, I watch my mother as she discusses a problem at one of the branches. The lines round her eyes I am used to. They've been there from the time my father and brother died. Maybe it's the light, but today they seem deeper. The black, stylish as it is, does little to flatter. Sorrow had aged my mother when she was young, but now she's fifty and age is beginning to do its bit as well. She is as smart as ever but there is, I realise sadly, a hardness about her.

She finishes her call. 'Sorry about that, darling, but you know what it's like.' And I do, I do. 'Do you mind eating here? They have some wonderful fish soup today. And the new bread is delicious.'

So we sit there and have the fish soup, thick and creamy with lots of mussels. I dig each one out with the shell of another and lick the creamy, lemony sauce from my fingers. It's all very good. But my mother's eyes are constantly darting hither and yon, watching the staff, watching the customers, thinking, considering.

'Oh I forgot,' I say suddenly, producing the little bag of tomatoes, 'Bill sent you these.'

She looks into the bag and closes it up again without taking any of the tomatoes. 'And how is Bill?' she asks politely.

'Pining for you,' I say. 'I gather you haven't seen him for some time.'

'I've been busy,' she says. 'But I hear the bistro's going well. It's madness him having to start all over again. Why he sold his last restaurant before he went travelling, I've no idea, especially as he only stayed away for a few months. So much for his midlife gap year. I told him it was a daft idea.'

'You know he hoped you'd go with him,' I say, picking

up a crumb of bread on my fingertip. *Waste not, want not* – another Granny Allen saying. When Bill went on his travels, I knew he had texted or emailed or sent silly postcards from every stop, hoping to tempt her out to join him. He only came home again because she wouldn't.

My mother snorts. 'He might have time to abandon everything and jaunt round the world like an overgrown adolescent, but the rest of us have work to do, businesses to run.'

'Bill would maintain,' I say, 'that you have lives to live too.'

She gives me a withering look. And I see Bill still doesn't stand a chance.

The waiter brings our coffees and my mother turns the tables on me.

'So, how's your love life? Everything OK with Jake?'

'Mmmm.' My mother and I don't really do girlie chats, but I need to talk to someone. 'I think so. But, to be honest, he's been a bit odd lately.'

'In what way?' She looks at me sharply. 'Is he working?'

'Oh yes, doing something on the new breed of football managers. He seems quite involved in it. Thinks it could really make his name.'

My mother looks approving. 'Sounds interesting,' she says. 'So what's the problem?'

'Oh, probably nothing,' I say. 'Anyway,' I continue, trying to be more positive in the light of my mother's sharp gaze. 'We're off up north for a week or two. He wants to do something about the millionaires buying up grouse moors and turning themselves into English gentlemen.'

'You mean like, what's the name, Simeon Maynard? Slimy Simeon?'

'The very one.'

'Now I'd really like to know where *his* money came from.

14

Nowhere respectable, I'll bet. If Jake can get to the bottom of that, I think it would be a real can of worms,' says my mother. 'Anyway, where are you going?'

'Somewhere in the back of beyond called High Hartstone Edge,' I say. 'It's literally in the middle of nowhere, it's—'

'I know exactly where it is,' says my mother, surprised and almost smiling. 'It's where Granny Allen came from.'

'Really? *The* Granny Allen?' We had this picture of Granny Allen at home, a faded photo of an oldish woman with thick hair tied back and a determined expression, sitting bolt upright outside her cottage, gripping her Bible firmly. She might have been dead for well over a hundred years or more, but her influence still lingered on. If I tried to throw anything away – from an old dress to a chicken carcass – then Mum always said Granny Allen would come and haunt me. She'd been told that by her mum, who'd been told it by hers, and so on and so on, right back to Granny Allen, who ruled the family back in the nineteenth century. You told the truth, kept your word, helped people when you could and, above all, you worked hard and stood on your own two feet. Lounging round, doing nothing, was condemned as a very un-Granny-Allen-like activity. Anyway, she was always there in the photograph, with her Bible and that stern expression, watching my every move.

And as for drink . . . Well, you could see Mum was just programmed to set up Frankie's Coffee Shops really. Apparently, Granny Allen had brought up her younger brothers and sisters, then her own family, and then her grandchildren too, all from a tiny farm high up on some bleak northern fellside. She must have been very tough, very determined, but not, I guess, a barrel of laughs.

'She was actually your great-grandmother, or even great-great, I'm not sure,' Mum was saying. 'I went to Hartstone

Edge with my mother when I was very small. We went somewhere by train, which seemed to take forever, and then it was a very long drive after that, up high and winding roads. My great-aunt lived there then. To be honest, I can't remember much about it, I was very young. Lots of hills and sky, I remember. And sheep. And a stream with a ford and a little packhorse bridge. I remember playing on it with some cousins. It's probably all changed now, of course. It was always a hard place to make a living.'

For a moment she looks miles away. 'I've always meant to go back there. But the time was never right. But now you can go instead and tell me what it's like. Anyway, it will be good for you to have a little break, even if it's a working holiday. How long are you away for?'

'We've booked the cottage for two weeks, but we can probably extend it if we want to.'

'Take plenty of warm clothes. You'll need an extra layer up there, especially at this time of year. High Hartstone Edge! What a coincidence.' We look at each other and this time my mother really does smile as we say in unison, 'What would Granny Allen say?'

Chapter Three

It had rained all the way up the A1. Grey roads, grey traffic, the constant spray from lorries. The further north we headed, the worse it seemed to get. I had long since lapsed into silence. Jake was concentrating hard on the road ahead as he peered past the windscreen wipers into the gloom ahead.

'Shall I drive for a while?' I offered.

'Might be an idea,' he said, 'I could do with a break. Look, there're some services soon. We'll stop and get a coffee. Give the rain a chance to stop.'

The service station didn't look promising. The only free space was at the far end of the car park and we had to run through the rain, dodging the puddles and then into a world of flashing video games and the smell of chips. We bought some papers and some coffees and sat down at the only table that wasn't piled high with heaps of dirty, greasy plates.

The coffee was only just drinkable, but at least it was good to be away from the constant whoosh of the windscreen wipers. I leant back, stretched my legs and flipped vaguely though the heap of papers. Suddenly, I sat bolt upright.

'That's her!' I said. 'The girl from the club!'

'What girl?' asked Jake, puzzled, as I twisted the paper round to show him.

'"Supermodel sensation, Foxy, has hunted herself down a very tasty new contract", Jake read. '"The stunning redhead, who has taken the fashion world by storm since her first appearance on the catwalks at London Fashion Week two years ago, has signed up to be the new face of Virgo cosmetics in one of the company's biggest ever deals. No chicken feed for fabulous Foxy!" Was she at the club? I don't remember seeing here. And' – he looked back at the page – 'I'm sure I would have . . .'

'No. She left in rather a hurry,' I said. And told him the story of how she had jumped out of the window and down into the street.

I expected Jake to laugh. Instead he was furious. 'Why didn't you tell me this?' he asked so fiercely that the family at the next table paused in the middle of chomping through giant burgers, nudged each other and stared at us.

'Because the princes arrived, and everyone was buzzing round them,' I said, astonished at his reaction. 'It just put it out of my mind. Sorry. I didn't think you'd be so interested.'

'*Of course* I'm interested.' He looked at me as though he couldn't believe what he was hearing. 'A top model jumps from a toilet window in a club full of Premiership foot-ballers and royal princes. Don't you think that's just a little bit interesting?'

'Well, yes, of course it is. But so was everything else that was going on. I just didn't think . . . I mean, I just don't understand why you care so much. What are you doing? It's not the sort of story you normally do. I thought you were writing about dodgy millionaires. Or are you selling celebrity stories now? What's happened to your famous principles?'

That was, I know, a bitchy thing to say. And I regretted it immediately. But too late.

Jake stood up. Very quietly, deliberately, he gathered all the papers, left his half-drunk coffee and walked out. I picked up my bag and ran after him. 'Shall I drive now?' I asked when we got to the car. But he just glared at me and got in the driving seat. We drove on in the rain and silence.

He was frowning, but I don't know whether that was because of the weather or because of me. I never seemed to measure up to Jake's standards. Even back at journalism college, where he was the star of the course. I always thought he would team up with one of the very bright, scary girls, like the Staveley twins, Felicity and Arabella, who were heading straight into television or national newspapers. But they all went their own ways and somehow it was just Jake and me and it seemed fine, even if I went into food writing, which for Jake didn't count as proper journalism.

Jake practically lives at my place, but he still keeps his old bedsit, a few miles away, where the cupboards are full of his neatly labelled files and a few basic clothes hang on a hook at the back of the door.

As we headed north, I could feel the silence between us, and wondered why he was suddenly so concerned about models and footballers. But somehow I didn't think he was going to tell me. He didn't tell me much any more.

We left the motorway and turned onto a road that led through small towns, then large villages, then small villages, then just about nothing at all. The rain had finally stopped, which was just as well, as we seemed to be climbing higher and the road was little more than a single lane as we kept tucking into hedges to let cars and tractors pass. Soon there weren't even hedges, or many trees, just a few scrubby bushes, bent from the wind, and dry-stone walls. And no more villages, just occasional houses spread out over a vast, empty moorland, dotted with sheep.

'Where now?' asked Jake. It was the first thing he'd said for an hour.

I scrabbled in my bag for directions. 'We come to a place called Hartstone and, just past the pub – that's good, it's got a pub – and the old chapel, there's a track marked "High Hartstone only". We turn up there and in about a mile there's a farmhouse and that's where we go to collect the key.'

The narrow road suddenly rose so steeply that it was almost perpendicular. Then, as Jake steered carefully past a large jutting boulder and rounded another bend, I gasped. 'We're on top of the world!'

After all that climbing, we were now on a plateau. To left and right the moors stretched out for miles. Ahead was a small group of buildings and beyond that the road tumbled down and we could see another valley, a stony blur of blues and greens and greys stretching out into a hazy purple distance.

Never before had I had such a feeling of space and distance. I don't think I'd ever been in such an empty space. Bit of a shock for a city girl. Even Jake in his foul mood looked momentarily impressed, and slowed the car to take in the vastness of the view. Then we drove past the pub, grey and solid and hunched against the weather, saw the old chapel, which now seemed to be an outdoor pursuits centre. Or had been. It was boarded up and looked sad. Apart from that there was only a handful of houses. Where were the people who came to the pub? Where were the people who had come to the chapel? Were there even any people up here?

I spotted the 'High Hartstone only' sign and we turned and bumped off up the track, which twisted across the vast open space of the moor. It seemed a long mile.

Suddenly we could see a small collection of buildings,

dropped down at the base of another high hill that seemed to soar right up to the sky. The road led straight into a farmyard and stopped. That was the end of it. Literally the end of the road.

'Is this it?' asked Jake.

'I suppose so,' I said, having no idea. With that a woman emerged from one of the barns across the yard. She was tall, striking, with a heavy plait of greying auburn hair and, although dressed in jeans, wellies and an ancient battered waterproof, moved with a casual sort of elegance. I'd never seen anyone quite like her before.

Jake sat in the car, arms folded and a deliberately blank expression on his face as if to say that this was nothing to do with him. So I got out of the car, stiff from the journey, and walked towards her. She would have been intimidating, if she hadn't been smiling in welcome. 'Mrs Alderson?' I asked tentatively.

'Hello there!' she said cheerfully. 'You must be Miss Flint and' she glanced towards the car, 'Mr Shaw?'

'That's us,' I said, relieved, thinking how nice it was to hear a friendly voice after the hours of silence in the car. She had deep dark blue eyes and the most amazing skin, and her wrinkles were definitely laughter lines. Tucked into the neck of her jumper was a vivid jade scarf that lit up her face and contrasted sharply with the dingy mud of her jacket.

'Good journey? Found us all right?'

'Yes, fine, thank you. Excellent directions,' I said, extra brightly to make up for Jake's silence. She gave us both a quick look and I swear she knew that we'd had a row en route. But she just smiled again. 'That's the cottage up there,' she said, pointing up the hillside behind the farm.

In the middle of its vast steep expanse of fellside, I could see a solitary grey stone house built into a hollow. It must have been half a mile from the farm and the only building for miles, apart from a few tumbledown cottages and some abandoned stone barns, with high, dark doorways. It was a weird, empty landscape. What's more, there seemed to be no road up to it. I began to wonder just what I'd booked.

'You'll have to back out of the yard and follow the track through the stream. Don't try and get over the bridge. It's built for horses and pedestrians, not cars. The key's in the door. I've put the heating on and I think everything's self-explanatory. But if not, just pop down and we'll put you right. Anything you need, just ask. If I'm not here, I'm not far.'

I thanked her and we got back into the car and Jake manoeuvred it out and along the track.

'A bloody ford!' he muttered. 'Let's hope it doesn't rain much more or we'll be washed away. You couldn't have chosen anything further away if you'd tried.'

'But Simeon Maynard's grouse moor is just over there,' I waved vaguely, 'That's why I chose it. Only a mile or so as the crow flies.'

'I am not a bloody crow,' said Jake through gritted teeth as we splashed and bumped through the ford, past the narrow packhorse bridge.

The stream . . . the ford . . . the packhorse bridge . . .

My mother's voice echoed in my ears. This must have been where she came with her mother, my grandmother. This must be where part of her family – my family – had come from. So I wasn't coming somewhere new and strange. I was coming home. What a thought. My ancestors had lived and worked in this strange, empty landscape. I tried to get my head round it and felt quite ridiculously excited.

Unlike Jake. 'This track is going to do nothing for the

suspension of the car. We'll be lucky if the exhaust doesn't drop off before the end of the week,' he grumbled as he pulled up alongside the cottage.

We sat in the car and stared at it. It wasn't a pretty house. No roses round the door. No cottage garden. Grey and solid, it was a no-nonsense, take-me-as-you-find-me sort of house, looking down the hill and across the moors. The road was so steep I felt I could drop a stone down the chimney of the farmhouse far below us. We got out of the car into a gust of wind so sudden and strong I thought it would blow us away as we ran indoors, heads down and jackets flapping. I wondered where on earth we'd come to.

But inside the cottage was warm and welcoming. As well as the central heating, there was a wood-burning stove in the small living room, which was cheerful with brightly coloured curtains and rugs and a big squashy sofa. The kitchen was modern farmhouse, lots of terracotta and pine and a stunning view from the window above the sink. On the table was a tray with mugs, a teapot, a fruit cake and a wedge of cheese and a note saying there was milk and a bottle of wine in the fridge.

Relieved that there were at least some elements of civilisation in this wild and windblown place, I dumped my bag on the floor, switched on the kettle and looked at the huge folder of information.

Jake, meanwhile, was stamping round, clutching his mobile and muttering angrily.

'No signal! No bloody signal!'

'Try outside,' I said, calmly, 'it might work better there.'

But two minutes later he was back. 'Not even one rotten bar. Absolutely nothing.'

I'd made some tea and was looking through the notes Mrs Alderson had left. 'It says here that there's Internet access from the pub.'

Jake looked horrified. 'From the pub! The pub all that way across the moors? You mean we haven't got it here?'

'Nope,' I said, still reading. 'Problem with phone lines, or lack of them. Too isolated apparently.'

And that's when Jake lost it. 'You mean I've got to drive down the track and through that bloody stream to the pub every time I want to check my emails?' he shouted. 'That you've brought us to a place in the back of bloody beyond, that has no mobile phone signal, no phone and no Internet access and is halfway up a mountain in the middle of a bloody moor in the middle of nowhere? Tilly, I'm meant to be working here. This isn't a bloody holiday! How can I work without the tools of my trade?'

'Well, it's not far to the pub,' I said soothingly. 'You can get a mobile signal there too, it says here. Come on,' I continued, trying to coax him into a better mood. I seemed to have been doing a lot of that lately. 'Have a cup of tea and some of this fruit cake. It's really good.'

'Don't you understand?' he yelled in a fury, 'I can *not* work here. It is utterly impractical. Out of the question. We can't stay here. End of. Put your bag back in the car. We'll have to find somewhere else. Maybe the pub for tonight until we find something else. Come on.' And he walked out of the warm, welcoming kitchen and back to the car.

I started to follow him and stopped. As he stood by the car waiting for me, his jacket billowing out in the wind, I thought about how tricky things had been with Jake. I thought how he seemed to have changed lately. I thought about how I seemed to spend so much of my time trying to please him, keep him happy – and failing. I thought about how we hardly spoke about his work and never ever spoke about mine. I thought about the way we just didn't seem to fit together any more. I thought about the long silence all the way up the Great North Road. And I wondered if what we had was really worth another row, another few days of tiptoeing round him trying to keep him happy. I thought about that stream and the ford and the packhorse bridge. And without really meaning to, I made a decision.

'I'm not coming with you,' I said, my voice shaking only a bit.

Jake looked at me as if I were mad.

'Come on, Tilly, don't be stupid. It's no time to play games. It's been a long day. I'm tired. We need to find somewhere else to stay.'

'I've got somewhere. I'm staying here,' I said, very calmly, though I knew as I said it that it was about much more than where we stayed tonight. Or where we stayed for the next two weeks. I knew that – as far as Jake and I were concerned – after two years together, this was a point of no return.

Jake was quieter now, but impatient, exasperated. 'Look, be realistic. I can't stay here with no phone reception and no Internet. And you can't stay here by yourself.' He looked at me as though I were terminally stupid. Come to think of it, he often did that. And suddenly I'd had enough.

'Why not?' I thought of the little packhorse bridge and the stream. My family had lived here. It might be strange, but I had roots here. Already I could almost feel them tugging at me. I wasn't going to turn round and go before I'd had even a day to explore.

'Because you'd be on your own and—'

'Maybe I want to be on my own.'

My words hung in silence. Jake stood and looked at me for a few, long seconds. I stared back. Coolly. Calmly. I hoped he couldn't hear my heart thudding.

'Right,' he said, 'I've got no time to play games with you. If that's the way you want it, suit yourself.' And he got into the car, slammed the door and drove angrily down the track.

I watched him go, watched the car twist down the hill, sploosh through the ford, past the farmhouse and the bridge, and then disappear, like a little Dinky Toy along the winding track over the moor, getting ever smaller until he was out of sight, and I was alone. In a little house on the top of a moor, miles from anywhere.

For a moment I wanted to run down the hillside after Jake, saying sorry, sorry, all a mistake. For another moment, I felt desperately sad and abandoned – even though I was the one who had done the abandoning. For yet another moment I was panicking, terrified of being alone miles from anywhere.

But then, while all that was going on, I felt the small stirrings of a strange new feeling. I was so surprised that it took me a moment to work out what it was. Then I realised. It was relief – relief at not having to put up with Jake's increasingly sour moods, of always having to do things his way, of living with the feeling that I didn't quite measure up somehow. And there was something else too – a sort of excitement at a sudden sense of freedom.

This was my decision. My choice. I'd taken control. That's it. Deep breath. I had taken charge of my life. So now what do I do? There was only me to ask, only me to answer and only me to worry about. This took some getting used to. Wonderful but frightening. I tried to think, be practical.

It was late afternoon and already getting dark. I quickly explored the rest of the house. Up a steep narrow staircase was a double bedroom where you could lie in bed and look straight out at the miles of hills. There was a smaller bedroom and a tiny bathroom that looked reassuringly new. I unpacked my bags, which didn't take long. My few things looked a bit lonely all by themselves in the wardrobe. I drew the bedroom curtains and put all the lights on.

Then I went downstairs, sat on the sofa and wondered what to do next. I looked at the stove. The house was warm enough, but a stove would be cheery, wouldn't it? A house like this needed a real fire. It should be fairly easy to light. There were even instructions. I'd never been a girl guide, but I reckoned I could light a fire. Of course I could. Buoyed up by new optimism, I had no doubts. Well, not many. I knelt down in front of the stove as if I were praying to it, found matches and a couple of firelighters, handily left on a shelf, followed the instructions carefully. Ow! The first time I let the match burn down and scorched my fingers. But at the second go it was suddenly blazing, flames licking round the sticks. Result! I left the doors open and sat back in the glow to feel the heat. Lighting a fire was very satisfying in a deeply primitive sort of way. I felt quite proud. Already in my new independent life I had achieved something I had never done before.

For the first time I noticed the samplers hanging on the wall above the stove. Framed pieces of needlework, probably done by a child and, by the look of it, many years ago. Age had faded the bright colours of the embroidery, but the tiny, careful stitches were as sharp as ever, the message clear.

'*Tell the truth and shame the Devil*,' it said, firmly. Right. No messing there.

The other sampler was more difficult to read, the reflection of the glass blanking out the message. I looked at it from different angles until in the end I stood with my nose almost on the edge of the frame and suddenly the letters snapped into focus.

'*Carpe diem*,' it said. '*Seize the day.*'

Well, that's what I'd done, hadn't I? I had seized the day,

well, the moment anyway. To be honest, I wasn't usually very good at spur-of-the-moment. I always wanted to know whether the day was going to be worth seizing first. And by the time I'd done that, it was often too late. Letting Jake drive off without me was the boldest thing I'd done.

Had I been right to let Jake go? My new-found confidence after the fire-lighting success was beginning to ebb away. Never mind just now, this evening, tonight – what about next week, next month? What was going to happen?

As I drew the sitting-room curtains I could see that outside everywhere was grey and misty. Seriously creepy. My heart thudded in panic. Where were the lights? There were no lights! All my life I have lived with streetlights, advertising lights, car lights, lights from shop windows, petrol stations, tube stations. I don't do darkness. Don't think I've ever really seen it. There was a glow of murky yellow light from the farmhouse below and, apart from that, nothing. Just a thick, misty, grey silence, smothering the house and miles of moors in all directions, swallowing everything up. Despite the heating and the fire, I shivered. What was I doing?

There was a sudden noise outside. I leapt back from the window, my heart racing. Then laughed at myself, a little shakily. A sheep. Of course it was a sheep – there were hundreds of them outside. I listened carefully and I could hear the sound they made as they tugged the grass up with their teeth and chomped away. Amazing what you can hear in the country. I closed the curtains again carefully, shutting out the mist and the moors, pretending they weren't even there.

On the deep stone windowsill was a curious collection of objects. A clay pipe, some small ridged blue bottles, a larger green one, two doughnut-shaped circles made of clay, I think, with holes in the middle, a brooch with no pin, a bone comb with no teeth, a Victorian penny . . .

They were, I supposed, all things that had been found round and about. Small objects lost or thrown away hundreds, maybe even a thousand or more years ago, by people who had lived here. I thought of that huge grey misty emptiness. Hard to imagine that anyone had ever lived here, so remote from anywhere.

Gently picking up the brooch, I wondered who'd worn it and when, who'd bought it for her and why? Who had used the comb or the liquids from the little bottles? They'd lived here, probably surrounded by mist and sheep too. And they'd been my ancestors. Down the years, I felt a small connection with them, whoever they had been. This had been their home. For now, at least, it was mine.

My tummy rumbled. And I remembered that the little box of emergency supplies I'd packed for our supper – cold chicken, cheese, bread, butter, a bottle of wine, was still in the boot of Jake's car. This definitely wasn't the place where you could dial up a pizza. Even if the phone worked. I wondered idly where the nearest takeaway was and I remembered something from Mrs Alderson's notes.

'Ready meals in freezer. Price list on lid. Settle up at end of stay. Emergency cupboard in back porch. Anything used from this MUST be replaced as soon as possible. Very important. Thank you!'

I looked in the freezer at a neat stack of obviously home-made dishes. Lamb casserole. Lamb stew. Lamb and capers. Lamb curry. I thought of the sheep whose bleat had made me jump. 'Aha,' I thought, 'I know where you'll end up.'

There were also some pork, beef and chicken meals too. It seemed rude to eat lamb while the creatures were roaming round outside. So I opted for a chicken and herb casserole and bunged it in the microwave. While I was waiting for it to ping, I went to look at the Emergency cupboard in the back porch. Candles, Primus stove and gas cylinders, torches, a couple of lanterns, a tin marked 'matches', tins of beans, sardines, corned beef, tuna, soup, a selection of vacuum-packed ready meals, two pairs of wellies, a spade and a snow shovel. Thank goodness it was still only October.

I found the wine in the fridge – thank you, Mrs Alderson – and what with that and the casserole – very good, proper chicken, with parsley and lemon and a touch of thyme, followed by some of the light, crumbly Wensleydale cheese – I had a very nice supper in front of the fire. Being independent, I found, makes you quite hungry. Yes, of course, I still felt a bit nervous, but I was warm and cosy and had already got used to the sound of the sheep.

I thought about Jake. Had I been a bit too hasty? It would be much nicer if he were here with me, beside me on the squashy sofa, watching the flames in the fire . . . Except we probably wouldn't be, would we? He'd be working or watching what he wanted on television. I cradled the phone in my hand and looked at Jake's picture on the screen. Did I really love him? Did I miss him? Had I ever loved him?

The last few weeks had been tricky. Jake had been moody, distracted. When I was talking to him he had hardly been listening to me. His mind was elsewhere. I wondered if he'd found someone else. He had plenty of opportunity with his work.

Maybe he was just fed up with me. I sometimes wondered if we'd only got together because we were the two left behind when everyone else had paired off. Yes it was good, but . . . We still had separate lives. Or rather he still had a separate life. I gazed into the flames and tried to find answers. There weren't any there. Not tonight at least. I was suddenly very tired.

After locking the doors and windows – and going round them all again to make sure I had – I went up the stairs, singing loudly as I went. I needed a noise. I didn't like the silence. I wasn't used to it. Another thing I'd never known. At home there was always a buzz from the street and from the other flats. You'd hear people going up and down the stairs, the distant murmurings from a television, music or bathroom. I regularly went to sleep with the noise of the drunks rolling home and woke to the sound of traffic. But here there was nothing. Apart from the sheep, all I could hear was my own heartbeat, pounding away more loudly than usual.

I sang louder, wondering what people would think if they saw me. The double bed seemed very big and cold without Jake alongside me. I shivered slightly. 'Good night', I said to his photo on the phone, preparing myself for a night of worrying, as outside the mist swirled, the sheep bleated. I was miles from anywhere, with no man, no car, no phone signal, no Internet. Utterly alone.

Chapter Four

I slept like a log. It was gone eight o'clock when I opened the bedroom curtains and peeped out on a sunny autumn morning. I could see for miles to some distant smoky blue hills. In the farmyard below me the day had clearly begun hours before. Cows were wandering back to a field, followed by a young lad with a big stick, a couple of dogs were barking and someone was loading bales of hay onto the back of a quad bike.

I showered quickly, made some coffee and wondered what to do that day. I had only myself to think about. Odd. And only I could decide what to do. Odder still. There was no one else to dictate to me or to discuss it with. I had work to do but not for a few days. I was completely free. Which was wonderful but unnerving too. I tried to think, to make a mental list.

If I was going to stay here on my own then I needed to get in touch with the outside world. I needed to be able to use my phone and the Internet. I needed to do some shopping, buy some food. Where were the nearest shops? And how would I get there? Admiring the view was all very well, but I needed to be out and about. Above all, I desperately needed a car. I was well and truly stuck. I had already arranged a couple of *Foodie* interviews for the week and how was I to get there? Totally impractical. What an idiot

I was to think I could. Jake was right, after all. But I didn't want him to be. Maybe, after all, I should get in touch with him . . .

I thought about all this while I drank the coffee and then made some more, lingering at the window to drink in the view. But I had to do something. I couldn't just sit here all day.

I had just decided that I would walk down to the farm and consult Mrs Alderson, maybe ask if I could use her phone – quite simple really – when I heard a car struggling up the hill and then pull up outside the house. Jake! I unlocked the door and stood there, suddenly somehow shy, wondering what was going to happen.

Had last night just been a tiff – the latest of many that could just be forgotten, smoothed over? I'd proved my point, stayed the night by myself. Maybe we could just get back to where we were. But was that what I really wanted?

Jake smiled at me, a polite smile, not unfriendly, but he didn't rush and kiss me. 'You OK?' he asked.

'Fine,' I said. I didn't rush and kiss him either. Part of me was relieved to see him. But another part wasn't quite so sure. It looked as though I could get things back to normal, but already I was wondering if I wanted to. Coffee?' I offered, at ease in my new home.

'No thanks. Just had some.'

I looked, questioningly.

'Found a bed and breakfast, back down the dale. Bit old fashioned but pretty decent. Internet access and a reasonable mobile phone signal. Enormous breakfast. It's a double room. I said you might be joining me. I thought . . .'

It would have been so easy. I could have just packed my little bag, given the key back to Mrs Alderson, and gone to the B & B with Jake. No problem. If he'd come back the night before, when those sheep had started bleating and made me jump, I probably would have done. But as it was, I had done a night on my own, surrounded by mist and sheep. I had not only coped, I had also envisaged a future without Jake.

'I don't think so. But thank you,' I said.

He looked aghast. 'You're not staying here? You can't!'

'I can,' I said, feeling more determined.

'But you can't use your phone! And there's no Internet.'

'There is at the pub.' I was surprised at how calm I was. How easy everything suddenly seemed. 'What I need is a car.'

'Take mine,' said Jake instantly. He was, after all, a decent bloke. 'And I'll hire one. We probably need two anyway, if we're both working. We should have thought of that. Come on.' He reached out and put his arm around my shoulders. 'This is silly, Tilly. You don't really want to be here by yourself, do you?'

It was good to feel his arm around me. But I also knew it wasn't right. Not any more. And I was also suddenly irritated by the way he called me Silly Tilly. People always thought that was *so* original . . . I hadn't minded so much before, but lately he'd been doing it more often and suddenly I'd had enough. I thought of the samplers on the sitting-room wall. '*Carpe diem*'. '*Tell the truth and shame the Devil*.' So I took a deep breath and I did.

'I don't think there's much point in being with you, Jake,' I said, carefully. 'I don't think things are the same any more. Something's changed. These days you don't seem to be with me really.'

'I know. I'm sorry. But I'm working on this project . . .'

'. . . about football club owners. Yes, I know.'

'Well, not entirely. There's more to it than that and the more I looked into it, the more I found. There's a lot of very dodgy stuff going on.'

34

'What sort of dodgy?' Despite myself, my curiosity was sparked.

'There are some very unpleasant characters involved, not least Simeon Maynard. Everyone knows there's something going on, but nobody's talking and it's impossible to prove. I've been trying for weeks.'

'But why didn't you tell me? You're working on this really big story and yet you say hardly a word about it to me. Doesn't say much about sharing, does it?'

'No, well, sorry, but I have talked it over with Flick.'

'Flick?'

'You know, Felicity Staveley, from college. Well, she's now working on that investigative programme on Channel Nine, and she said—'

Flick. Felicity Staveley with her perfect hair and gallons of confidence. She was meant to be a lowly TV researcher, but had already appeared on screen looking stunning and knowledgeable.

'So are you and . . . Felicity, well, are you . . . ?'

'No, of course not,' said Jake quickly. Too quickly. 'It's just that she has lots of contacts and we're old friends and it seems logical.'

'Of course,' I said coldly. 'Absolutely logical.'

Only Jake could fancy another woman for her contacts book. But Felicity's ambition was a match for his and I knew then that I had well and truly lost Jake. And I didn't even mind. Well, not much. I felt oddly distant from him. This was all so unreal anyway – this place was another world. 'Look, if you don't want to be without the phone and the Internet, keep in touch with . . . Felicity, why don't you stay at your bed and breakfast? But I want to stay here.'

'You can't stay on your own.'

'Jake, will you please stop telling me what I can or cannot do. Of course I can!' And hey, I *so* enjoyed saying that – especially when I saw the stunned expression on Jake's face. 'But I need a car.' I flipped through Mrs Alderson's folder. There was a leaflet about taxi and car hire from a garage about ten miles away. 'If you take me to the garage so I can hire a car, that would be helpful. Thank you.' My tone was brisk and businesslike.

'But . . .' Jake looked as if he wanted to carry on arguing, persuading, talking. But he also looked baffled. He wasn't used to my taking decisions so calmly. He suddenly shrugged. 'OK, Tilly,' he said. 'If that's what you want.'

'It is.'

Maybe it was my imagination. But I thought he looked relieved.

When the man at the Dales Garage had heard where I was staying, he'd led me smartly away from the neat little rows of shiny Ford Focuses and instead taken me round the back and shown me a rusty Escort van. 'Engine's fine and there's nowt left on bodywork to hurt much more,' he said. I wasn't that sure, it looked a heap of trouble for me, but as he was asking just a tiddly sum for it, the deal was done. Jake tried to intervene, but I waved him away. A rusty Escort van was suddenly my vehicle of choice.

'Anyway, I like the registration number, PIP,' I said to Jake, who looked at me oddly.

'I think the northern air has done something to your brain,' he muttered. 'Ring me if you want anything,' he said. 'And here's the address of the B & B.' He gave me a card. Our hands touched for a moment. 'There's always half a double bed there for you.'

'I don't think so. But thank you.'

He gave me a hug, suddenly awkward. I gave him the briefest of kisses and then climbed into PIP and drove off with barely a backward glance. I'd checked my phone – I discovered this morning that you could get a signal just at the top of the track from the farm to the main road by the old chapel. But now I needed to check my email.

I bounced along in my little rusting van, crunching the gears every now and then as I got used to it on the steep narrow roads. The previous owner must have weighed about twenty stone because the driver's seat was in a state of collapse. The carpet was full of holes and there were odd gaps in the dashboard. But there was a radio. I pushed a button and Madonna came belting out and I sang out loud along with her at full volume. I was on my own in a strange place, in a strange van and suddenly it wasn't scary, it was exciting, exhilarating. 'Who's That Girl?' Me!

The Miners' Arms, like the farm and the cottage, was grey stone and solid at the top of the moor. Just three or four houses and the old chapel were its only neighbours. As I pulled up in the car park, my new-found confidence faltered a little. Walking into strange pubs and bars alone could always be a bit dodgy. But the sign was newly painted and the windows sparkled. I could do this. Of course I could. I carefully locked PIP – though I didn't believe that anyone could possibly want to steal it – and walked into the pub.

Inside there were rough stone walls and flagged floors and it smelt warmly of wood smoke and polish and further in of tantalising food smells – proper food. My stomach rumbled. Two fires burnt brightly in huge fireplaces at either end of the bar. At a table near one of the fires, two middle-aged couples in walking gear were enjoying coffee and cake. Near the other fire sat an old man reading *The Northern Echo*, a pint in front of him. Another couple of men were tucking into pies, steam escaping from the golden pastry and the meat tumbling out in a thick, rich gravy.

The walls were covered with old photographs. And more

of those samplers. '*If at first you don't succeed, try, try and try again*', said one, around a picture of a very fierce-looking spider, while the other said it was '*Never too late to make amends*'. Very virtuous.

A young girl with gleaming blonde hair was sitting knitting behind the bar. As soon as she saw me, she put down her knitting and smiled. 'What would you like?' she asked.

'I've really come in to use the Internet,' I said, 'but I've just realised I haven't had any breakfast.'

She laughed. 'Coffee? Orange juice? Bacon and mushroom muffin? Scr—'

'Stop there,' I said. 'Coffee, juice and bacon muffin, please.'

'The computers are round the side there, I'll bring the coffee over for you.'

I smiled happily and followed her directions. This must have been the best Internet café ever.

In a tiny little snug alongside the bar were two computers, a printer and a huge old farmhouse settle, covered in rugs and cushions. There were shelves full of books and leaflets on local history and on another table was a pile of today's newspapers and a selection of magazines, everything from *Farmers' Weekly* to *Celebrity Gossip*. Bliss. The girl brought my coffee, which was good too – strong and rich, without a hint of bitterness. I checked my email – in twenty-four hours my inbox was already overflowing with rubbish – and confirmed my interview with a cheese-maker the next day. And then, quickly, I emailed Jake. Just to say that the little van was fine. I knew it was over between us, even without Felicity – sorry, I just couldn't bring myself to call her Flick – but it was somehow important to keep on good terms. I was just emailing my friends Polly and Susannah and wondering what to tell them about Jake – they'd never really liked him, not really – when a tall man with wild, curly hair and a scruffy sweater sat down next to me at the other computer. 'Morning,' he nodded. 'Your muffin's ready. It's on the table near the fire.'

I signed off the email and sent it quickly to Polly and returned to the cosy bar. As I ate the muffin – brilliant bacon – I looked at the photographs on the wall. They were a mixture of old and new. And it took a while for it to dawn on me that they were of the same places taken years apart, or rather, more like a century apart.

In front of a low archway that seemed to lead directly into the side of a hill, workmen in waistcoats and stout trousers, caps and long moustaches carried hammers and picks and gazed solemnly at the camera. Next to it was the modern scene – the same archway, but this time surrounded by walkers in brightly coloured cagoules, peering and pointing. A picture of the chapel dated 1900 had a hundred or more serious-faced worshippers in their Sunday best – very uncomfortable those clothes looked – lined up on the steps. The modern version showed half a dozen lads in jeans and T-shirts laughing as they unloaded canoes off the roof of a minibus.

A long view across the moors was full of industrial buildings, tall chimneys, a huge water wheel and clusters of activity. The modern version was bleak, empty, just a few ruins and a lot of sheep. The photograph was stunning. The photographer had caught the shadow of a cloud scudding across the hill. Very atmospheric.

Who were all those old people? What had happened to them? How had a place so busy become so empty?

'Lead mining,' said the blonde girl behind the bar as she followed my gaze. 'A century ago and more, there used to be hundreds of men working up here. They used to be packed into lodging houses during the week and then walk back to their families at the weekend. They say the lead for the roof of the Houses of Parliament came from up here.

It must have been like the Klondike. Hard to believe now, when it's just sheep.'

'I'm amazed the pub survived.'

'It didn't. It was closed for fifty years and was just a house. Dexter –' she nodded her head in the direction of the Internet snug, so I assumed she meant the guy with the wild hair and scruffy sweater – 'inherited it last year and decided to reopen as a pub this summer.'

'Brave move.'

'S'pose so. But it's going OK. Really well in fact. He does some of the cooking too. He's not a bad cook either. For a photographer. He took all the pictures – well, not the old ones obviously, but the others.'

'These are really good. Does he work for anyone in particular?'

'No, just for himself. He does a lot of books and colour supplement stuff. He hasn't done much lately though because he's been working all hours getting the pub right. But he's hired a chef now, so I expect he'll get back into it.'

Some more customers came in and she put her knitting down again to serve them. She seemed to be knitting a lacy sort of scarf.

I remembered that I hadn't looked up the directions to the cheese-maker. I looked across. Dexter had finished on the computer. Presumably he was in the kitchen preparing food for the people who'd just come in, but some walkers were busy online now. Never mind. I was very comfortable in this cosy bar. I thought about a glass of wine but, being my mother's daughter, and having the van outside, I opted for another coffee and flipped through one of the papers. That model was all over it again. '*Foxy's gone to ground!*' said the headlines. After signing her huge contract, the model had gone missing. Probably drugged up somewhere, I thought. No, not drugged. When she leapt up and through that window she hadn't seemed a bit like a hunted animal. She seemed the one in charge, well ahead of the pack, as if she were playing a game. I wondered, idly, what had become of her, where she was.

By the time the walkers had finished on the computers and I'd gone online and found the directions I needed, the bar was empty. I was just picking up my coat ready to leave when Dexter came through to the bar, looking serious and carrying two plates of sausages. 'Right, Becca,' he said to the barmaid, 'earn your keep and tell me which of these you prefer. You too,' he said to me, offering me a plate. 'Unless you're in a hurry . . .' His sudden smile completely transformed his face. He was, I realised, quite good looking and probably not as old as I thought, maybe just ten years older than me. And I decided I wasn't in a hurry at all as he went on, 'I try and use everything as local as possible, but it's got to be good, so all opinions welcome.'

I sat myself back at the bar and tried two bits of sausage. 'Definitely the second one,' I said.

'Why?' asked Dexter.

'The first one was good, but highly spiced, so all you could really taste was the chilli. Good, but overwhelming. The second one was quite simple, but proper meat, proper flavour. Didn't need the spices to tart it up.'

Dexter nodded approvingly and I felt as though I'd won a prize. 'Couldn't have put it better myself,' he said. 'That's the one we'll go for. Have another bite to be sure.'

So there I was, perched at the bar of a stone-flagged, wood-smoky pub on top of a moor in the middle of nowhere, eating sausages, with grease on my chin, when we heard outside the sort of roar made only by a very expensive, show-off car. It stopped right outside. A moment later the pub door opened and in strode two men. Young, fit and extremely good-looking men, radiating testosterone and confidence and that sort of glow that belongs to the very rich and very successful.

Becca gave a small, breathless yelp. I gawped. It was the last thing I'd expected in the middle of nowhere. I blinked and stared to make sure. There was no mistake. Footballers. Clayton Silver and one of his team-mates, the young Italian Alessandro Santini.

The last time I'd seen Clayton Silver was in Club Balaika back in London. What on earth was he doing here?

Suddenly the bar, which had seemed so warm and cosy earlier, now looked faded and dusty, dimmed by the dazzle of these celebrities. I'd felt so comfortable perched at the bar, and now that cosiness was spoilt. Only Dexter remained completely unfazed.

'Good afternoon, gentlemen,' he said. 'And what can I get you?'

'A decent sat-nav would be a start,' said Clayton Silver, removing his dark glasses. (Dark glasses. In England. In October. What a poser.) 'The money I paid for that motor and it dumped us in the middle of a stream. A fucking stream, man! Don't you have roads up here?'

'Depends where you're trying to get to,' replied Dexter.

'Some big house, Sim Maynard's place.'

'Ravensike Lodge. Well, you're very close,' said Dexter, 'but there hasn't been a road across there for fifty years or more. It's just a track now. You'll have to go back down the dale for about ten miles and then turn off and come back up the other side of the moor. Shouldn't take you long in that car. Just watch out for sheep.'

'Sheep! All we've seen is sheep!' said Silver. 'There's sheep all over the roads. Why don't they stay on the grass? Why do they want to eat roads? Why did we decide to drive? We should've flown up. We'd be there now. Relaxing, not getting stuck in streams on mountains. God, I need a drink.'

'Stuck in streams?' asked Dexter, clearly trying not to smile.

'Yeah. The road just stopped. Bang. Middle of nowhere. In a farmyard or somewhere. There was a bridge, but that didn't go anywhere. Just the stream. The sat-nav lady kept telling us to go straight on, but there was no straight on to go to. Nothing. It's the end of the world up here.'

He looked baffled and angry. But suddenly, instantly, his mood changed and he smiled – a beautiful wide, handsome smile, as if he realised it was all a bit silly really. He shook his head, 'All that money on that car, and we were just sitting in a stream. Could have opened the window and done some fishing.' He laughed. 'It took us ages to get out of there. Thought we'd have to get out and push. I think we need a drink before I trust that thing again.'

Alessandro ordered a Peroni but Clayton Silver was looking at the wine selection chalked on the board above the bar. He smiled and picked out the most expensive one there. 'Let's try some of that.'

Dexter opened the bottle. 'It's a shame it won't have time to breathe.'

In one smooth, silky movement, Silver sat on one of the bar stools, waved his hand – beautiful long fingers, immaculate nails – to dismiss such quibbles. Then he looked at Becca and me. He smiled that amazing 100-megawatt smile straight at us. 'You ladies care to join me?' he asked.

I wanted to say no, if only because I didn't like the way he just assumed I would say yes. He was clearly used to women swooning at his feet. Not me. I began to slither off the high stool, ready to make my escape.

On the other hand . . . Maybe in my world of new-found freedom, I should just go with the flow. *Carpe diem*, the sampler had said. Seize the day. Why not?

Becca had no doubts at all and gathered her wits before

I did. 'Thank you,' she said with great aplomb, putting down her knitting. 'That would be very nice.'

'OK, thank you,' I said, trying to find a balance between being polite and unimpressed, and slithering, not very elegantly, back onto the stool.

And that was how I got to know Clayton Silver . . .

Chapter Five

I couldn't deny it. Clayton Silver had the most gorgeous eyes that lit up when he smiled. The trouble was that he knew it all too well. I remembered him arriving at Club Balaika, with the cameras flashing and the security men clearing the way for him. Well, there were no VIP booths in The Miners' Arms. We were all equals here. He passed me the glass with the wine glowing in the bottom, reflecting the firelight.

'Breathe it in first,' he said, 'the smell's almost enough to get drunk on by itself.' As his eyes looked into mine, I looked away quickly and breathed in the rich smell of the wine. 'Now take a small sip.' I looked over the glass at him. I wanted to say, 'Look, sunshine, I've drunk plenty of decent wine before you walked in here. My godfather's restaurant has one of the best cellars in the country and I'm a respected food writer.' But I dutifully sipped.

The wine slid down, soft and velvety. I closed my eyes for a moment, relishing the flavour. It was delicious. 'Oh wow!' said Becca. 'That really is good.'

'Glad you like it,' said Clayton, still gazing at me. His hair was cropped close, revealing the shape of his skull. His skin was the colour of pale coffee. He had a Jamaican grandfather, I remembered I'd read somewhere.

But I refused to be impressed by his glamour and

confidence. Just because he was good at football, and got paid ridiculous amounts of money for it, didn't make him a god, I thought crossly.

'Not bad,' I said about the wine. 'Though I've had better.'

He looked at me and smiled again, as though he knew exactly why I'd said what I had. 'Lucky girl. But this is still pretty good to find in a pub surrounded by grass and sheep.'

Condescending or what? I'd only just discovered this was my ancestral homeland, but I was already indignant on its behalf. 'Just because people live in the back of beyond doesn't mean they don't appreciate good wine,' I said, while Becca blinked at me, surprised.

Then Clayton spotted the plate. 'Sausages!' he said and helped himself.

Then suddenly he was laughing again about the stream and the sat-nav. 'That car's a city car. It needs streets and signposts and lots of nice tall buildings to make it feel safe. That sat-nav lady ain't a country girl at all.' And Dexter drew him a little map showing how to get to the shooting lodge and asked him if he was going to be doing any shooting. Clayton grinned and said yes, he knew a bit about shooting, but not those sort of guns, and we smiled because we knew Clayton Silver had grown up on the sort of estate where guns were commonplace.

Just then the door opened again and a tall figure in working clothes – boots, jeans, shabby waterproof and a woolly hat – came in and went up to the side of the bar. Dexter's eyes seemed to light up for a moment. 'You're back!' he said, sounding pleased. 'I'd heard.' But the other person muttered something, looked in our direction and walked out again. Dexter's expression was weird. He looked pleased and almost disappointed at the same time and watched as the figure walked back to the car park and jumped into an old four-by-four. Then he smiled to himself and went back to drawing his map. Funny. I didn't have him down as gay.

But his face had definitely lit up.

Becca suddenly remembered the knitting she'd just put down on the bar and carefully picked it up and put it away in a big hessian bag.

Alessandro, who'd only been in this country since the start of the season, watched her and then smiled shyly and said that his mother and his sisters liked to knit, to make things. So Becca reached into her bag again and unwrapped some tissue paper to show him a finished scarf. The scarf was brilliant – the lacy knitting interspersed with big appliquéd flowers in bright sunshiney colours of yellow and orange – and looked wonderful.

'Is beautiful,' said Alessandro. He placed it gently round Becca's neck. 'Is more beautiful on you.' He grinned while Becca blushed. The charmer.

I was still holding my coat, ready to go, but Clayton asked me if I was local and I said no, just staying up here writing for a food magazine, but I knew the stream where he'd got stuck. Despite myself I was soon chatting to him like an old friend – about London and restaurants, about roads and sheep. Apparently the footballers were only up here for two days because they had to get back to training, and suddenly the wine bottle was empty and they were leaving. Clayton picked up his car keys and walked out, just assuming Alessandro would follow him, which he did. Alessandro blew Becca a kiss while Clayton said, 'Goodbye, Miss Tilly,' very formally but grinning as he did so. Then they were gone to the sound of the expensive car roaring off back down the dale.

'Well!' said Becca, giggling. 'That certainly brightened up the afternoon.'

'Bit full of himself though, isn't he, that Clayton Silver?'

I said, cross with myself for getting drawn in by his easy charm and trying not to recall his smiling eyes, his tight black T-shirt, his broad shoulders and his grin. I remembered the actresses who'd arrived at Club Balaika with him. Well, they were welcome to him. How upset the new celebrity-conscious Jake would be to have missed them.

With that, a group of spindly, mud-covered cyclists, clad in very unflattering bright yellow Lycra, parked their bikes outside and came in demanding soup and sandwiches. The magic had definitely gone. Becca sighed and went to serve them. I quickly sent a text to Susannah, saying, 'Country life MUCH more interesting than I thought,' and tucked my phone in my bag. Then I got it out again and sent a text to Jake, telling him who'd been in the pub. Seemed only fair. Then I went off to the loo.

There was a sampler in the passage, the twin of the one in the bar. '*Wine is a mocker*', it said in neat, tiny stitches. '*Strong drink is raging.*' Which was a bit daft to have in a pub. No wonder Dexter had hidden it away out of sight.

But then in the Ladies there was yet another of the things on the wall next to the Tampax machine. '*Vanity of vanities. All is vanity.*' I could see it reflected in the mirror when I was brushing my hair. Probably Dexter's idea of a joke. I thought of some small girl having to spend hours stitching it. It seemed a very stern lesson to learn so young.

'Probably see you tomorrow,' I said to Becca back in the bar.

'You never know, we might have some more interesting customers,' she grinned as I went out to find PIP in the car park.

Chapter Six

I took a deep breath. I'd only had two small glasses of wine. I was driving just over a mile. I'd be all right. I got into the little van and off I went up the high moor road.

In the farmyard I could see Mrs Alderson doing something with a hose. Torrents of water were pouring over the yard as she waded along in wellies. She waved and I turned in. I'd better explain to her about Jake, I suppose. I stopped the engine and stepped out onto the damp concrete and was hit with a very agricultural smell. Cows, I guessed, wrinkling my nose and looking down at the small rivulets washing against my shoes.

'Oh, it's you!' said Mrs Alderson, surprised, and directing the jet of water into the furthest corner away from me. 'I thought it was Reuben Stephen. This is his van.'

'Not any more,' I said, and explained as she laughed. 'I hope old Wes isn't charging you full rent for this heap!'

'No, just a token gesture.'

'Good. Well, this car knows its way round these tracks, so you'll be all right. And Wes will always come out and rescue you if it breaks down. Are you sure you're OK up there on your own? I noticed your young man . . .' She stopped, tactfully. 'I mean, it's perfectly safe, but if you're not used to it, it can be a bit spooky.'

'It was fine, thank you,' I said firmly. 'I lit the fire and had one of your ready meals for supper. It was great, thanks.'

We both looked up the fellside to the cottage. Above it I could see a quad bike parked and a tall figure striding over the moor with a bale of hay. I couldn't be sure, but it looked very like the person who'd opened the door of the pub and left so quickly.

'Matt, my eldest,' said Mrs Alderson quickly. 'Home for a while and helping out. If there's anything you want, just ask.'

I thanked her and wanted to ask about the house and the stream, tell her about my mother, but with that I was suddenly deafened by a vastly magnified telephone bell echoing round the yard. 'Sorry. Telephone. Waiting for a call. Got to go,' said Mrs Alderson, throwing the hose down, lunging for the tap and striding into the house.

I backed out of the yard and through the stream. I thought of Clayton Silver and his glamorous car. I laughed, and for a split second, I felt the car slip as the water seemed to want to take it downstream over the slimy stones. My insides lurched. Concentrate, girl! I got control again, revved the little van and roared up the track, my heart thumping a little. I hadn't liked the way the van had almost gone. Could have been nasty. Maybe I shouldn't have had that second glass of wine. Could one handsome footballer so easily make me forget a lifetime of indoctrination?

Strong drink is a mocker. I should have paid more attention to that sampler. I got out of the van and shook my head clear in the sharp clean air.

As I did so, I spotted the track – well, a path really, certainly not wide enough for a car – that wound enticingly round the back of the house. A walk would do me good. I set off up the path, which went on a steep slant up to the top of the moor. A solid path, bumpy but clear enough, flattened grass scattered with cobbles and stones that were shiny from being trodden on by countless feet. I could feel the muscles pulling at the backs of my legs and was glad the stunning views gave me the excuse to stop and get my breath. Although it was late afternoon, it was a much clearer day than yesterday.

After the muggy crowdedness of London streets, there was something unnerving about these moors. So much space; so much emptiness. How did you know where you were or find your way? Or even who you were?

But the fresh air was just what I needed after the encounter with Clayton Silver.

He clearly thought he was so important just because he could kick a ball around a bit. Expecting everyone to be so impressed. Just because he had a nice smile and knew his way round a wine list. But, I had to admit, there was something about him. He was just so . . . alive. Even when he was just sitting on a bar stool with a glass of wine in his hand, you could feel the energy in the man. 'Quicksilver,' they always called him in the headlines. The trouble was that he made headlines not only on the sports pages but elsewhere in the newspapers and celebrity magazines – when he wasn't scoring goals, Clayton Silver liked to party, usually accompanied by the latest in a long line of gorgeous-looking women. Typical footballer. Overpaid and full of himself. Odd that I should have been in his company twice in the space of a few days – and in such different places – but Clayton Silver was not part of my world and never would be. I put him firmly out of my head.

By now I was nearly at the top of the path. Down below me I could see Matt Alderson buzzing along on the quad bike. Suddenly, I was on the ridge and could see down into the next valley. I recognised it. The derelict buildings, abandoned cottages, that great sweep of landscape – it was a scene from one of Dexter's photos. An abandoned industrial scene. At first glance you'd think no one had ever lived up here, ever, but what had Becca said? Like the Klondike. I wanted to go down and explore it, but it would soon be dark. In any case, I didn't want to roam too far. I was scared of getting lost. I turned back, over the ridge, and slithered back down to the cottage.

Going down such a steep slope was just as much effort as going up. I stopped for a moment, fearing I would go headfirst if I wasn't careful. My foot had caught in something. I bent down and picked up a small piece of leather with a buckle attached. I turned it over in my hand, wondering what it could be. Too big to be off a shoe or jacket. Maybe it was part of a bag, or maybe even a harness for a horse or pony. I thought of a pony picking its way down this steep and narrow path, a packhorse, maybe, that had come over the bridge. Caught in the buckle was a knot of some material. As I tried to see what it was, it came unfolded and proved to be a short length of cherry-red velvet ribbon. Goodness knows how long it had been scrunched up with the leather. Yet, as it unrolled, it was still cheerily bright and as luxuriously soft as it must have been when it first got caught on the buckle, however many years ago. Odd. I stroked it as I made my way back to the cottage.

Even close up, under the lights, I could tell no more about the bit of leather, the buckle and the ribbon. It was a worthless bit of stuff, I imagined, but I couldn't throw it away. Instead, I put it carefully on the windowsill with the other finds, my contribution to the house and its history.

I lit the fire again – easy-peasy now I knew what I was doing – but as I curled up on the sofa and gazed into the flames, all I could see was a laughing footballer with a gorgeous grin. I got up and switched on the television. How dare he invade my head?

The photographer carefully placed the last box of photographic plates into the corner of the cart, sandwiched it in with his battered carpetbag and deftly tied down the tarpaulin that covered it all. Once again he checked the buckles and straps on the harness of the sturdy little pony and climbed into the narrow seat.

He longed to be away from the town with its dark narrow streets and the people who plagued him. He yearned for fresh air, open spaces, and subjects for his camera more interesting than the parade of the town's traders, their fat wives and their spoilt children. Every day the families would come in, sit in the chair, just so, standing behind the pile of books, or the globe or the potted plant or the painted rustic scene which he supplied to furnish the photograph. He should be grateful to them that they enabled him to live well enough to buy the latest new equipment, which fascinated him. But he wanted to use his camera for more interesting things to record for posterity.

He picked up the reins. 'Walk on, girl, walk on. We're off adventuring again.'

Chapter Seven

The cheese-maker took some finding. There was no sat-nav in the van, of course, so I was following the map. Trouble was that some of the roads were so small that either they weren't on the map or they just didn't look like roads. And they don't do an *A–Z* of bits of moors and hills. Finally I crawled up a steep and narrow road with a dry-stone wall on one side and a high hedge on the other. I just prayed I didn't meet anyone coming towards me because I wasn't sure if I could back up to one of the passing places.

But it was worth it: the lady was terrific. She and her husband had inherited an old family recipe – the last in existence – for High Dales cheese and had started off making it in a bucket in the kitchen of their city-centre semi. They finally got it right, moved to a farm, made tons of cheese, won awards and made it famous. It was a great story, perfect for *The Foodie*. Even worth putting on the white overall, hat and hairnet I needed to go into the dairy with its rows of cheeses stacked on the shelves. Back in their office, they put a generous plateful of samples of their cheeses out for me to try. I asked questions and scribbled the answers while nibbling at a chunk of light, salty, crumbly cheese. Wonderful. They gave me some samples to take home with me too. Cheese on toast for supper.

When I told the cheese-maker where I was staying and

that I had to call in to The Miners' Arms to use the Internet, she promptly went back into the dairy and brought me out a huge chunk of cheese, which she wrapped in tinfoil and stuck in the bag with the others she'd given me.

'Dexter Metcalfe is a good customer of ours and that's a new cheese we've been trying – made with nettles. Give this to him and tell him to let me know what he thinks. He knows his food, does Dexter.'

'They're shooting today,' said Becca as soon as I walked in. She was pulling pints for a group of walkers. 'Dennis the gamekeeper went past in his smart shooting suit and Len went past with the beaters in the game cart. Do you think they'll call in afterwards?'

'Who? The beaters?' I asked, baffled, not even totally sure what beaters did.

'No, silly, Clayton and Alessandro.' I loved the way their names slipped so casually off her tongue, as if she'd known them for ever.

'Shouldn't think so. They've probably got food and drink enough where they are,' I replied, cross that she assumed I was just as interested in the two footballers as she was. As if I'd even thought of them at all.

'Mmmm . . . It would be good, though, wouldn't it?' Becca was going dreamy over the pumps.

'Becca, they're only footballers,' I said. 'They're good at running round in shorts kicking a ball. Like small boys, only paid more. They're not finding a cure for cancer.'

Yikes! I sounded just like my mother. Now that was a scary thought.

While I waited to use the computer, I sat with a coffee – definitely a coffee this time – and flicked through the papers. Despite what I'd been saying to Becca, for the first time in my life, I started with the sports pages. But there were no pictures of Clayton Silver, nor Alessandro. It was full of pictures of other footballers from other teams who had been playing the night before. I turned back quickly to the main pages, as if I hadn't actually *meant* to look at the sports pages, skipped over the serious stuff and studied the gossip columns. But there were more pictures of the girl from the nightclub.

'That Foxy model seems to have well and truly vanished,' I said vaguely to Becca as I turned the pages.

'Don't worry, she'll turn up,' said Dexter, grinning as he came up from the cellar with a box of mixers. 'Just gone to ground temporarily, no doubt. Give the pack a bit of fun.' He was laughing, as if it were some huge joke. Then he stopped, as though he'd just remembered something. 'How did you get on with the cheese-maker?'

'Excellent. Really good. I've got something for you. Some High Dales nettle cheese for you to try.' I took the carefully wrapped package from the bag. Dexter brought some savoury biscuits and a knife from the kitchen and we sat either side of the bar eating slivers of the cheese, which, we decided, was excellent. I felt as if we were already old friends. I watched him as he ate the cheese. He was about ten years older than me, I guessed. Despite his easy smile, his face was lined and lived-in. His jumper might be shapeless but it had once been good, like the shirt he wore underneath it. At one time he'd clearly had an eye for good clothes. It was a big leap to go from being a successful photographer to a publican in the middle of nowhere. I wondered what had brought him back.

I asked him about his photographs, especially the one of the valley I'd seen the evening before.

'I sometimes feel as if the place is full of ghosts,' he said. 'As if all the people who've ever lived up here are still here; as if they've never left the dale. I waited hours for the light to be right for that picture and when I printed it up I almost expected to see ghosts in the pictures – the old lead miners, farmers, the Vikings. Even the Romans. As if they couldn't get away. Like me,' he laughed.

'Did you not get away?'

'Oh, yes. Not much choice really. After college, I went to Leeds to work for an agency, then I had a few years in London, doing more and more work for myself, my own projects. Then I got married and moved up to Manchester . . .'

Married? Oh, maybe he wasn't gay after all then.

'. . . but then my marriage fell apart.' Oh. Maybe he was . . .

'. . . and then my dad died and I inherited this place. It had been let out for years. I didn't really know what to do with it. But my wife – ex-wife – wanted her share of the Manchester house – like, immediately. She is one scary woman. So we sold that. And I was just wondering what to do, where to go, and then the tenants moved out of here so I thought I could spend the money doing this up. Have a sabbatical. Otherwise known as coming back to lick my wounds. Finding yourself orphaned and divorced in a matter of months concentrates the mind a bit. I needed time to think. And this seemed the best place to do it.'

He looked suddenly embarrassed, as if he'd said too much. I tried to think of something cheerful and positive to say.

'You seem to have made a good job of it. The pub, that is.'

'You think so? Thanks. I'm really pleased with the way it's going. It's just . . . well, it's hard to get out taking pictures when you're supervising builders, and talking to brewers and sourcing food and hiring staff. I want to make a go of this, but I want to get back to the day job too.'

'But you've only been going a few months. In a few

months more, you'll really be established, then you can take up the day job again as well.'

'Yeah, well, I hope so. Still, this always used to be a pub. Had a terrible reputation years ago, but then it closed and there're no pubs in this end of the dale. One or two cafés, but not much for tourists and visitors. We want to bring money into the dale and this seemed one way to do it. Of course, it's cost a lot more money, time and effort than I ever thought possible. But yes, I'm back.'

'For ever?'

'Who knows? For now at least.'

'Back where you started.'

'No, not really. Not even that.' He looked sad for a moment. 'Because while I've been messing up my life, other people have been moving on with theirs. Out of reach. And now it's too late.'

'It's never too late,' I said encouragingly, if rather fatuously, nodding at the sampler on the wall.

'Sometimes it might be,' he said, and shrugged and went into the back, returning with an armful of logs.

Oh dear. There was obviously a lost love in his past, but I didn't know him well enough to enquire further. Sitting there at the bar, trying bits of food, just as I had yesterday, I noticed that Becca looked up hopefully every time the door opened, but it was just the usual groups of walkers, cyclists and people out for afternoon drives. I sent some texts, checked my emails, treated myself to a bowl of soup and a baguette. It was comfortable and cosy in the pub, but I had to go. I had the cheese-maker interview to write up. And it was getting dark.

'If you get lonely up there, you can always come down in the evening, for a bit of company,' said Dexter as he threw another log on the fire. The wood crackled and the sparks shot up. 'Not so many visitors in the evening. More locals.'

'Nice thought, but I've got work to do. Anyway, I'm not sure I would like to go through the ford or up that track in the dark.'

'There's always someone who'd give you a lift back up – if you don't mind the back of a pick-up or a quad bike.' He cleared my plates away and, with a wave to Becca, I went out into the gloom.

This time, drunk on neither wine nor exotic footballers, I managed the ford without any problem and PIP roared up the track. Already the house felt like home. I switched on all the lights, made myself a strong coffee and settled down to work. First of all I looked through my notes, marking good quotes, underlining parts, linking passages. Usually I worked in the office or at home with Jake to distract me. It's amazing how much more work you can get done when there are no distractions.

Soon I opened up my laptop and started writing. The words flowed and the piece almost wrote itself. I finished the rough draft. That would do for tonight. I'd read it again and polish it in the morning. Like soup, a piece was always better when you'd left it to cook for a bit. I switched off the laptop, yawned and stretched. It was ten o'clock and I was suddenly hit with a wave of loneliness as well as fatigue.

If I'd been at home now, working at the table by the window in my little sitting room, Jake would probably have been there, working on his own laptop or sprawled on the sofa, flicking through the news or sports channels. He'd have brought me a glass of wine, maybe a little plate of cheese and biscuits or some hot buttered toast. And when I'd finished working, I would have cuddled up against him on the sofa.

I missed him. But was that because he was Jake, or just because he was someone, anyone, to be there? I was beginning to see that we'd just drifted into our relationship. Bits of it had been good. And I realised – almost for the first time, that yes, he brought me toast and cheese and things – but only when he fancied them for himself. And while I worked, Jake would lie there with the TV blaring, constantly flicking between channels. But if *he* was working and I wanted to watch something, he'd get cross, because how could he concentrate with all that noise? So I would read a book or listen to my iPod so he could work in peace. I'd been pretty dumb, hadn't I? Not quite a doormat, but heading that way. Silly Tilly indeed.

I thought about it as I flexed my stiff shoulders, made my way upstairs and ran a hot, deep bath. And as I lay there, listening to the sheep – not scared at all now – I realised that yes, I was a little bit miffed that he could talk to Felicity, work with her and not me. So maybe my pride was a little bit dented. But my heart? I probed the idea and my heart like worrying a bad tooth. A twinge, maybe. But agony? No. I didn't think so. I twiddled the tap with my toes and added a great gush of hot water and settled back comfortably. I could live without Jake.

The track was steep, the rain like icicles. The photographer dismounted and walked alongside the pony as they plodded up the bleak fellside and thought about the photographs he had taken that morning, an old man and a boy cutting peat. He thought he'd possibly caught an expression. He hoped so. He longed to get back to his studio, the darkroom, to find out. It was a lucky chance to find someone like that. The overseer at the small mine there hadn't been too sure about photographs, nothing that would stop the men working. He would call back. But first he had to get into the next dale, get pictures of mines, machinery and the men who worked them.

The path was slippery now, partly from the driving

rain and partly from the mud that flowed down from a ramshackle row of cottages that seemed to have grown up from the fellside and seemed ready to collapse back into it. One or two showed signs that the inhabitants had made an effort, with makeshift curtains made from sacking, but most were indistinguishable from the midden heaps behind them. Above him he could see another house. Even through the driving rain he could see it was in a better state than the others, with clean windows, a proper path and a tidy wall providing some slight shelter for a sparse vegetable plot. A bedraggled hen squawked as a tall woman emerged from the house carrying a bucket, which she filled from the water butt with one hand, the other holding a shawl over her head. She must have sensed the photographer looking at her, for she stopped and turned.

For a moment, despite the rain, she stood perfectly still, gazing down at him. She was straight-backed and strong-jawed, unflustered and unbothered. Her long skirt and shawl were the colours of the fellside behind her. She seemed made of the very soil and rock.

'Good afternoon!' said the photographer cheerily through the rain, touching his hand to his dripping hat.

'Never so good for taking pictures,' said the woman.

'Ah, you already know my business in the dale.'

'Word travels.'

She would, he knew, make an admirable subject for his camera. Just so, with the steep and narrow track beside her and the towering expanse of hill behind. He touched his hat again. 'Would you be interested in a photographic portrait?' he asked.

She looked down at him and for a brief second seemed almost amused at the thought. Then her mouth hardened again. '"Vanity of vanities, all is vanity," says the preacher,' *she said. 'But you are in need of shelter. If you wish, you can rest out of the rain a while.'*

'Gladly. Thank you.'

He tied the pony to the gate, checked that the tarpaulin was keeping his precious camera dry, and then followed the woman into the house.

Chapter Eight

The next morning was wonderful, one of those autumn days that are almost still summer. Even up there, at the top of the world, I could feel the warmth through the window. It was only my third morning here but already it felt right. I felt at home. I burbled happily to myself as I sat at the kitchen table, with my laptop and a mug of coffee, and kept glancing out at the glorious views while I tidied up my piece on the cheese-maker. Finally, satisfied with what I'd done, I saved it on to a memory stick, ready to go down to the pub and send it off. But I didn't have to go yet, did I? The sun was shining. That track at the back of the house was too enticing. Work done, I had no one to answer to but myself. Not even Granny Allen could argue with that.

I tugged on my walking boots, bought last year for a holiday in Wales with Jake. The fleece too. At least I looked the part.

It didn't take me too long to get up to the ridge again. Pausing at the top to get my breath, I looked down the dale. I thought about what Dexter had said. It was like looking at ghosts – those abandoned buildings, the ruined houses. A whole industry had thrived here and then vanished. The path plunged down past abandoned heaps of stones that must once have been buildings for the mines. Tall chimneys towered over empty spaces where hundreds of men once worked but now were left to sheep, which sheltered among the soaring pillars and cropped the grass, as if nothing had ever disturbed the peace.

I felt a little uneasy, like an intruder. Was it sensible to be up here on my own? Jake had thought it wasn't sensible for me to stay the night in the cottage on my own, but I'd done that, hadn't I?

Some new railings and a warning sign surrounded an arched entrance opening straight into the hillside. 'Danger. Old mine workings. Keep out,' it said. I peered into the entrance, could see the skilfully arranged pattern of bricks in its ceiling, still supporting the moor above it. At my feet were rusty railway lines. Even though they were much grown over with grass and turf, I could follow them into another vast arched building, open now to the elements, with birds fluttering among the high bricks. I sneezed and the sound echoed and bounced round the huge empty and deserted space. It was an eerie place. What must it have been like here, I wondered, with all those men and machinery, the noise, the activity? The buildings could have been in-habited by a race of giants. Now they had all gone. Now it was just me, the sheep and the birds and silence. Weird. Seriously weird.

Walking alone in this strange landscape felt like the start of an adventure but just a little creepy. It was reassuring to see a Public Footpath sign. Very twenty-first century. It was a good firm track, too, easy walking on the springy turf. I had no map, no idea of where I was or where I was heading, but I couldn't get lost. I would just walk on for another twenty minutes or so, then turn round and come back. The track curved round a low hill. I would just see what was on the other side . . .

I strode out briskly. The air smelt clean and fresh and was nicely cold on my face. It really woke me up. Bouncing along a turf path is a lot more fun than pounding away on a treadmill in the gym, and certainly better without the posers and preeners and designer Lycra. Above me I could hear the cries of birds. Didn't know what they were. Maybe I'd get a bird book and find out, I thought. This country air was definitely getting to me.

I suddenly realised that nobody knew I was here. No one. I was completely free. I didn't have to get back at a particular time or for a particular person. Or fit in with anyone else's plans. My heart thudded a little at the thought. It was frightening, but it was also wonderful and exciting. Total freedom, to please myself. I did a little skip to celebrate and then strode out along the path.

I could hear another noise now, a strange sound that I sort of recognised but couldn't quite place. Some farm machinery, I supposed, though I didn't think there was much actual farming going on up here, not the sort that used combine harvesters or things like that. Apart from hearing *The Archers,* when Mum was listening to it, I was a bit hazy on all things agricultural. But I was pretty sure that this wasn't the sort of land where you grew things, apart from grass and sheep. Whatever was making the noise, though, it had to be big. I'd soon find out, as I rounded the bend at the foot of the hill. And then I saw it.

A helicopter. Right in front of me. So close it seemed enormous. Like a huge buzzing dragonfly perched on a flat, white-painted piece of moorland. I could feel the force from the blades, and see it sending ripples across the grass. What a strange place to find a helipad. But then I looked further and understood. Just a few hundred yards away was a vast house, all Victorian turrets and chimneys, surrounded by a high stone wall and large gates. 'Ravensike Lodge', said a sign. 'Private'.

Of course. Ravensike was originally a Victorian shooting

lodge, that's why it was plonked down in the middle of nowhere surrounded by moors and grouse and partridges and all those things that people liked to shoot at. And now it was owned by a billionaire who owned a glitzy football club and a helipad. I wondered what the grouse made of that. Don't suppose it made much difference to them who took a pot shot at them.

Intrigued, despite the noise and the blast from the blades, I walked slowly towards it. A man was sprinting down the drive. Presumably he was the passenger the pilot was waiting for. He ran effortlessly, fluidly. He was clearly pretty fit. He wore black jeans and a black leather jacket. His hair was closely cropped, almost shaved. He had a beautifully shaped head.

Oh my God, it was Clayton Silver. Was there no getting away from the man?

I wanted to turn and run back to the cottage, but instead I just stood there staring at him; he must have felt my look because he stopped on the edge of the helipad and glanced over in my direction. He looked away and then back again.

'Miss Tilly!' he shouted above the roar. 'Is that you?' He ducked under the rotor blades of the helicopter and then strolled towards me.

'You skipping work?' he shouted, the draught from the helicopter blades whipping his words away. 'Shouldn't you be writing about sausages?'

'Cheese-makers!' I yelled. 'And I've done it. I'm just getting some fresh air before I go back and do some more. I didn't know where this path led. I'm just—'

'Come for lunch.'

'Sorry?' I couldn't have heard properly.

'I said come for lunch. I've got to see someone in Newcastle. Come along.'

'But I can't. I mean . . .' Did I even want to go to lunch

with him? Why did this man keep popping up in my life? First the club, then the pub and now, just when I thought I'd found one of the most isolated parts of England, he turns up there too. I shrugged my arms to show I was in jeans and a fleece and boots and, in any case, wasn't too impressed by celebrity footballers.

'That don't matter.' He laughed. 'The pilot's getting a bit antsy. You've got ten seconds to make up your mind, Miss Tilly. Lunch or no lunch. Deal or no deal. Ten . . . nine . . . eight . . .' He was grinning as he turned to go back to the helicopter.

The nerve of the guy! He was so in love with himself that he expected everyone else to be as well. Just turning away like that, as if I would meekly follow him. Who did he think he was?

'. . . four . . . three . . . two . . .' He turned back, grinning and stretching out his hand towards me.

Despite myself, I was smiling now too. Why not? What was the point of this sudden feeling of freedom if I didn't do things I'd never done before?

I'd done most of my work for the day. A helicopter ride was always going to be fun, whoever it was with. My mum always told me never to get into strange cars. She never said anything about strange helicopters. *Seize the day . . .* I grinned.

Clayton grabbed my hand and we ran under the blades and jumped up into the helicopter. As we soared upwards, the ground dropped away, glorious views stretched out for miles. Clayton was still holding my hand. I eased out of his grip and, rather primly, sat on my hands as I looked out of the windows.

Inside the helicopter it was still noisy, not ideal for intimate conversation, even if I'd had a clue what to say, so I contented myself with working out where we were. We flew over miles of moorland then above the motorway. 'Durham Cathedral!' I said, pointing into the distance. Then, a few minutes later a huge metal giant loomed up on a small hill at the side of a motorway, families looking like dolls playing at its feet. 'It's the Angel of the North!' I exclaimed and then, 'All those bridges! It must be Newcastle.'

We followed the Tyne for a while – I hadn't realised it was a country river too – until we hovered over a golf course and then landed gently in the grounds of a huge country house hotel, where the helipad sat in the middle of perfectly tended lawns. Clayton helped me out of the helicopter and then yelled to the pilot, 'I'll give you a call, mate.' As if it was just a normal minicab. We walked across a path and into the hotel. It was one of those seriously stylish places, where they were so cool they didn't bat an eyelid at my walking boots. I wanted to giggle. This was turning into a ridiculous adventure.

'Good morning, Mr Silver,' said the receptionist. 'Your guests are waiting for you in the Brown Room. Would you like coffee or drinks brought through?'

'No thanks. But I'd like a table for lunch, in about half an hour. For two.'

'Certainly.'

'This won't take long, Tilly,' said Clayton. 'Get yourself a drink or whatever you want and I'll be back soon.' And he vanished, leaving me in my jeans, boots and fleece in one of England's poshest hotels. I had no bag, no money, not even a lippy or a hairbrush. The receptionist was hovering.

'Can I get you anything, madam?' he asked.

'Some coffee, please,' I said. 'And I don't suppose you could conjure up a hairbrush? A comb? Anything?'

'Of course, madam,' he replied, as if it was the most normal request in the world.

He rematerialised about two minutes later, with a dinky little bag containing brush, comb, toothbrush, toothpaste, soap, face cloth, and razor. How many guests must arrive here as ill prepared as I was? I dashed to the Ladies, cleaned my teeth, brushed my hair, helped myself to some of their richly scented hand creams and cologne and felt a little better. Back in the reception area, the coffee was waiting for me. I sat back in the leather armchair thinking that I might as well enjoy all of this.

Then Clayton was standing in front of me, smiling down. 'Time to eat,' he said, 'and to drink something a bit more interesting than that.'

'What about the people you were meeting?'

'Gone,' he said dismissively. I didn't ask more. But I wondered who they were, why he would be meeting them all the way up here. I wondered if it was the sort of thing that Jake would want to know about.

We sat in the big bay window of the dining room, with a view across lawns down to the river. The menu was full of delicious things. I dithered over Thai-scented salmon salad with lemon potatoes, or maybe quails' eggs and capers, pigeon and celeriac, pumpkin gnocchi or sea trout . . . I would have liked to ask for a copy to show to Bill. Clayton hardly seemed interested. 'Just bring me some grilled chicken with lots of vegetables,' he said to the waiter, but then spent ages poring over the wine list.

'I know, Miss Foodie, who cares about every mouthful,' he said in a laughing, mocking tone, 'but food is just fuel to me. Yeah, I can see what the club dietician means about not too many pies and pizzas and all that, but food is just there to keep you going. But wine . . . well, wine is something else. Do you know,' he asked as he finally made his choice, 'I was seventeen before I first tasted wine? I thought it was for poofs and posers. Then Denny Sharpe, the manager at my first club – he was a bit of a wine buff – he gave me a glass of Château Lafite. "Just shut up and drink that slowly," he said, and I was like, wow, why didn't anyone ever tell me about this before?! I was hooked. It is just *so-o* good.'

'Clever Denny.'

'Yeah, he was. Not just about the wine. I was a bit of a smart-arse street kid, I guess, thought I knew it all. I knew nothing. Absolutely rock-all. But Denny was good. He was good with all us young lads. Tried to keep us in order – I say tried, because we were a wild bunch all right. He and his missus took us out to places like this, proper places, you know what I mean, taught us our table manners and stuff. He even had us doing exams.'

I looked at him, enquiringly.

'Bunked off school too much to do exams, didn't I? Too busy playing football. Reckoned I didn't need exams. But the club – well, Denny really – said there was an awful lot of life once our football days were over, so they got this tutor guy in. And me and a couple of others got some exams. I've got English, maths, PE and geography,' he said proudly. 'I'd have done some more but then I moved into the Premiership and it was all different then. And I was nineteen by then, so they reckoned I was all grown up, couldn't tell me what to do.'

'Must have been hard studying after you left school.'

'No, it was all right really. Sort of interesting. There was just four or five of us and the teacher was pretty good. Didn't treat us like kids. Couldn't really. Even then we were earning shed-loads more than he was. But it was pretty cool. Never done anything like that before. My mum didn't do books. Too busy trying to survive. She was only a kid herself when she had me.'

I was trying to remember what I knew about Clayton

Silver. A tough childhood, on a council estate where gangs and guns were commonplace. He was always being held up as an example of how sport could make a difference, provide a way out for a lad with talent and determination.

'No dad?'

'He skipped off when I was still in nappies. Turned up again when I signed for the Premiership and said he wanted to make up for lost time. Yeah, right. Just wanted a slice of my money, more like. Told him where to go.'

For a moment his lively face looked bleak, far away. So I told him about my father and the drunk driver.

'So we're both half-orphans then,' he said. 'Not easy, eh? But I had lots of dads. Different one every few months. Mum would get lonely. Not surprising, she was only young. Then some bloke would move in, start throwing his weight around and then there'd be a row and in the morning he'd be gone too. There was a lot like that. Losers, most of them, absolute losers. Except for Travis. Travis was all right.'

'What made Travis special?'

'Well, for a start he stuck around longer than most. He could cope with my mum's moods and tempers – which took some coping with, trust me. She had a mean temper on her. And he used to take me to the park, so we could both get out of her way. He'd kick a ball about with me. He was sound. It was Travis who took me to the Lions Boys' club. Knew the guy who ran it. Told him I had talent. That was my big break, all thanks to Travis. He used to come and watch me, cheer for me. I told everyone he was my dad. Wished he was.'

'What happened?'

'Oh, in the end even he had enough of my mum. I looked for him, you know, when I signed for my first club. I wanted him to know. I wanted him to be proud of me. But I couldn't find him. Then a few years later I heard

71

he'd died, been killed, knifed. Got into an argument with the wrong guy. '

He took a fierce forkful of the vegetables piled high on his plate.

'What's your mum doing now?'

'Selling overpriced clothes in a little shop in Spain. She went out there a few years ago with some guy she met on holiday. Actually, he seems all right. Don't see much of him. But he makes Mum happy. Him and the sun. She's really nice when she's happy, you know? If it had worked out with my dad, she might have been happy all the time and been a different person. Who knows? Anyway, I bought her this shop and a villa, so if it all goes pear-shaped – which it usually does with my mum – then she's got somewhere to live and a job to keep her occupied. But this guy seems to have lasted longer than most. He's a lot older than her but they do a lot of travelling together and a lot of partying. She's having fun and deserves that. Like I say, she was only a kid herself when she was left with me. Can't have been easy.

'Was it the same for your mum?' he asked. 'Was there always a new dad in the morning?'

I shook my head. 'The complete opposite. She didn't want anyone else. All she cared about was me and work. Too much so, sometimes. I wished she had let another man into her life. It might have taken the pressure off . . .' I went back to my meal – wonderful juicy scallops with lemon and ginger and the finest angel-hair spaghetti I'd ever tasted. My childhood hadn't always been easy, but hearing about Clayton's I had no right to complain.

'Which just goes to show,' Clayton went on, 'that in the end you're on your own and you've just got to look out for number one, because no one else is going to do it for you.'

There was a moment's silence as we both backed off from the conversation that had quickly got so heavy.

72

But soon Clayton was relaxed again. He leant back in his seat, took a sip of wine and grinned at me over the glass.

'You look nice, Miss Freshface,' he said, 'All clean and outdoorsy.'

'Well, I feel a mess,' I said, and told him about the goodie-bag of brush and comb, which made him laugh.

'I guess they're well used to providing such things for unexpected female visitors,' he said.

There was a sudden frisson in the air, a little ripple of something that suddenly made me feel not so safe. What had I got myself into – getting into a helicopter with a complete stranger, about whom I knew so little? If I had to make a run for it, I was done for. No money. No credit cards. I'd have to hitch back to High Hartstone Edge. It would take me some time. Especially as I wasn't even sure exactly where I was. As I began to panic, some spaghetti unrolled from my fork and fell messily onto my chin. Clayton leant over and gently wiped it away with his napkin. He held the napkin close to my face for a little while longer than necessary. 'What big eyes you've got,' he said, gazing into them. 'Beautiful big eyes,' he said slowly, dreamily, seductively . . .

Then he suddenly crowed with delight.

'And you blush! Oh Miss Freshface, you blushed.' This had him chuckling to himself. 'You know, I spend a lot of time with a lot of lovely ladies. Seriously hot ladies. They have all the clothes, the hair, the look, you know. But not once have I seen one of them blush. But you, girl, are the brightest, prettiest pink. I can't really believe you're a city girl. Really, you're a little country miss at heart, like that girl in the book, Tess, that's it – Tess of the D'Urbervilles.'

Oh God, why did I blush so easily? Now he probably had me down as a little girlie completely overcome by the big famous footballer. As if.

So to change the subject, I told him about my great-great-grandmother and how my family was from round here. He looked almost wistful for a moment and said it must be nice to have roots somewhere, to belong.

'Oh, I'm as much a stranger as you are, but it's interesting seeing where some of the family comes from, tracing any connections. And yes, I think it already feels special somehow.'

The waiter cleared our plates away and offered desserts. Clayton shook his head but said, 'The lady will have one.'

'No, it's all right. I'm fine, thanks.'

'Have a pudding. I bet you'd like to really.'

'Well, yes,' I grinned. He'd clearly read my mind. 'Go with the flow,' I'd said, hadn't I? 'I suppose I would.' So I ordered the lemon tart, so deliciously sharp and lemony that it almost made my eyes water. Clayton watched me eat it, rather as though he were an indulgent uncle. As I took the final forkful, he smiled, 'It's good to see a lady enjoying her food.'

Which, of course, immediately made me feel huge and greedy. I bet the women he normally took out for lunch did nothing more than nibble a lettuce leaf with no dressing. Maybe an olive if they were going really mad. I went pinker.

'Aren't you shooting today?' I asked hurriedly before he could comment on it again. 'I thought that was the point of coming up here.'

'Nah, it's pretty boring really. You stand where you're told, wait for some guys to shoo all the birds in front of you and you go bang! bang! and that's it. And it's all rules and etiquette and, "If you don't mind, sir," and a game-keeper with a seriously bad attitude. I wanted to go off and shoot in another direction. I could see plenty of birds there, but he just says, "I'm sorry, sir, we're not shooting those drives today." Well why not, eh? And you should see the clothes. He was wearing a suit right out of a picture book, like that boy in the film about the trains, you know, the one with wotsername in.'

'Jenny Agutter? *The Railway Children*?'

'Yeah that's the one. All tweedy with trousers to the knee and bright red socks. What a prat.'

By now Clayton was well into his stride. I could just imagine how he stood out on an expensive shoot, even amongst new-money millionaire businessmen and a bunch of footballers.

'I asked him how many birds we'd shot and he said, "About thirty brace, sir." Thirty brace? What's that mean? It means sixty, yeah. So why couldn't he just say sixty?'

As I laughed he glanced at his very expensive watch and sighed. 'Well, Miss Tilly, we'd better go. I have to be there when they come back and then we're back in training tomorrow.'

I sipped my last drop of wine as he paid the bill. For a nanosecond, the waiter's eyes lit up as he checked the amount and his impassive mask almost slipped, so I reckoned Clayton must have left a generous tip. Show-off. He made a couple of calls and when we went out, the helicopter was waiting for us. And we were heading home.

As the helicopter came down by Ravensike Lodge, I looked out anxiously for the shooting parties, but they were out of sight, thank goodness. I didn't think that the game-keeper would take too kindly to a helicopter buzzing through his carefully driven birds. We got out, the rotor blades slowed down gradually to silence. The pilot walked off with a wave and Clayton and I were still standing there, with only the sound of the sheep.

'Thank you for lunch,' I said. 'And the helicopter ride.'

'It was a pleasure,' replied Clayton. 'Are you OK to get home from here? If not, I can get someone to drive you.' He nodded his head towards the house.

'No, I'm fine, thanks. It's been good.' And it had. I was surprised at how much I'd enjoyed myself. When he wasn't showing off, Clayton Silver could be OK, really. I supposed.

'Hey, I guess I'd better have your number, yeah?'

'Well, yes. If you think . . . I mean . . . Well, why not?'

He took out his desperately stylish phone, keyed something in and then handed it to me.

I saw that he'd typed 'Miss Tilly'. I tapped in my number and I resisted the urge to scroll down through his other numbers. I didn't want to seem too keen, so I just smiled and handed it back to him, as if it were neither here nor there.

He put his phone in his pocket, then put his arms round me and kissed me, first on the cheek and then on the mouth, just lightly but very nicely indeed. I didn't want to enjoy it. But I did. Quite a lot. I tried to look indignant but I failed.

'I'm glad you could join me,' he said. 'I enjoyed the conversation and I just loved making you go pink!' And, of course, I immediately went bright pink again. I was cross with myself. Cross with him. He laughed and added insult to injury by kissing my cheek once more before turning and loping back up the drive and in through the gates of Ravensike Lodge, which opened magically as he approached. I expect famous footballers get used to that sort of fairy-tale thing.

The house was sparse, but clean. It had a flagged floor scattered with pegged rugs and a fire burned cheerfully in the range. As the photographer's eyes adjusted to the gloom, he noticed with surprise a small selection of books on a shelf by the window, and, in a chair by the fire, a boy of about eight or nine, his leg wrapped in makeshift bandages round a wooden splint, resting on a stool.

The boy seemed to be knitting. He turned to look at the stranger.

'My youngest,' said the woman. 'He hurt his leg in a fall and cannot yet get back to work.' She dipped her head and shrugged off her shawl. He almost gasped at the sight of her hair – a rich red auburn. As she shook her shawl, one thick lock of her hair came loose and fell gently down around her throat. Impatiently, she pinned it back and he marvelled at the elegance of her movement. He could, he thought, have been looking at one of the society women who came to his studio to be photographed, not someone scraping a living in this wild dale. She nodded in the direction of the boy. 'Until he's back at work he can knit and make himself useful that way.'

She went to the fire, stirred something in the pot, tasted it and looked at the boy. 'You can have your broth now.' The boy's face lit up.

The woman looked at the photographer. 'You're welcome to a drop.'

'That would be very kind.' He was cold and wet and some broth would indeed be wonderful, but he knew there wasn't much food to spare in this household. 'But only a drop, please, Mrs . . .'

'Allen. Matilda Allen.'

Chapter Nine

'A helicopter? Up to Newcastle? With Clayton Silver? For *lunch*?' Becca was seriously impressed. 'And he asked for your phone number? Oh Tilly, that is just so amazing.'

'Not really,' I said, trying to be cool about it. 'The helicopter was quite fun,' I admitted grudgingly, but I didn't mention the kiss. 'No, the best bit was that we sat and talked and had a proper conversation about what it was like when he was a kid. He had a rotten childhood and he has just done so well.'

After Clayton had kissed me, I had wandered back along the path to the cottage, slightly stunned. I hadn't noticed the ruins, the birds, the sheep, I no longer thought of all the men who had worked here a century or more ago, I was too busy replaying the previous four hours in my head. You go out for a walk in the middle of nowhere and the next thing you know you're whisked to one of the country's most exclusive hotels by one of the country's most eligible bachelors. In a helicopter. I laughed to myself because it was so ridiculous, I could hardly believe it. But there, in the pocket of my fleece, was the goodie-bag with the hotel's crest on. It really had happened.

But who were those men he had met? And why wouldn't he tell me about them? I thought of Jake's suspicions and was glad that I was in no danger of getting involved with Clayton.

Back at the house, I tried to bring myself back down to earth. I made a pot of coffee, but while I was waiting for it to brew, I went over the conversation in the hotel so much that by the time I came back to the present, the coffee had gone cold and I had to make some more. Finally, I got myself sorted, drank the coffee, had one more check through the cheese-maker piece and set off down to the pub to email it. The battered blue four-by-four was in the car park and I could see the tall figure in the shabby Barbour was at the back of the bar talking to Dexter. There was something familiar . . . and I guessed it was probably Matt Alderson, whom I'd seen striding across the fellside. With that, Becca came through with a mug of coffee. 'Here you are, Matt,' she said, and then asked, 'Where's Matt?'

For Matt Alderson seemed to have melted away from the bar, leaving Dexter busily wiping down work surfaces with a determined air and Becca with a baffled expression.

'Would you like this coffee?' Becca had asked me. 'Shame to waste it.'

'Thanks,' I'd said, which was when, in return, I had told her about my helicopter trip with Clayton Silver.

'Oh wow!' she said, enthusiastic, amazed and begging for all the details; I was more than happy to oblige. 'And he asked for your phone number? Now that really *is* a good sign,' she said.

I shrugged. Did I really care? He so clearly thought he'd impressed me with his helicopter and posh hotel and fancy wine. All very nice, but only stuff, really, just *stuff*.

On the other hand, I remembered the way he'd talked about his dad and Travis, his sort of stepdad, and his pride at getting his GCSEs. Now that had been a surprise.

Maybe there was more to Clayton Silver than a tight T-shirt and decent ball control.

Finally Dexter came through with some spicy soup for customers and said, a little grumpily, 'The computer's free now, if you want it.'

'Better had, I suppose.'

I disappeared into the little corner and dutifully emailed my article over, plus notes and details for photographers. Then I emailed my mum because I thought she'd probably made a better fist of things than Clayton's mum had. I couldn't tell her that in so many words. And certainly not in an email, but it was sort of important to make contact, get in touch, so I just said that all was well but I still hadn't had time to track down our family roots. And, of course, I had to tell Polly about my amazing lunch date . . . As I was writing to her, an email pinged in from Jake. Short and to the point, he asked, 'Everything OK?' Which I guess was him thinking he'd done enough to discharge any duty of care he might feel he owed me.

'Brilliant!' I typed back. 'Clayton Silver flew me up to Newcastle for lunch.'

'Ha ha,' came the reply.

'No, really.'

'If really, then tell me more,' typed Jake.

So I told him the story – much more briefly and down-beat than I had told it to Becca. But I did mention the meeting with the strange men. I was curious.

'Any idea who they were?' he typed back immediately.

'No. He went into another room to talk to them so couldn't hear anything. Looked perfectly anonymous men in suits.'

'Be careful, Tilly,' Jake wrote back. 'Footballers live in a different world. Clayton Silver moves in some very dodgy circles. You don't want to get close to him.'

'You're right. I don't,' I replied, but just to wind him up and to show him that yes, I did have a life of my own, thank you, I added, 'But who knows?' though I did really. Clayton Silver wasn't my type and I certainly wasn't his. I'd read the gossip columns and the celebrity mags. I'd seen the pictures. I guessed I knew what footballers were like. And so I got on with arranging my next interview.

When I'd done that, I did have a sort of thought about Googling Clayton Silver, to find out more about him, but one of the family history mob was making noises about how he'd booked the computer to start at least ten minutes ago ... Anyway, what would be the point? Inspired by the sampler about '*Wine is a mocker*', I was drinking an elderflower and ginger cordial and watching Becca knit.

'I don't understand how you can just pick it up and knit a few stitches, put it down and then pick it up and know exactly where you are,' I said, remembering my few hopeless attempts at knitting as a child.

'Practice,' she said. 'My mother's the same, knits every spare minute. Not that she has many. So did my grandmother. And my grandfather. Couldn't stand to be idle. Once upon a time, everyone in the dale used to knit – men and women and children. That was a hundred years or so ago, of course, but it still carried on.'

Whenever I could, I would clear any tables, to give her a bit more knitting time. I'd only been coming here a few days, yet already I felt part of the pub, part of the family. How could my life change so much in just a matter of days? I stacked up the plates left behind by a family with two very messy children and, as I was coming back with a cloth to wipe the table, the door opened and a small Asian guy came in. He went up to the bar and said politely, 'I come to buy scarf please.'

Dexter looked baffled, both by the man and by his request. 'Scarf?' he said, rather helplessly.

'Scarf made by Becca,' said the man firmly.

Becca leapt in. 'Right, well, I only have one here with me now. I have more at home, or you can buy them at shops in Hawes, Alston, Allendale, Richmond, Durham—'

'Must have one now please. Mr Santini asked specially.'

'Alessandro?' Becca's face lit up. 'He wants one of my scarves?' Then her face fell a fraction. 'He's not coming to get it himself?'

'No. He must be back in London, to play football.'

'Never mind, next best thing,' said Becca happily, and found the scarf she had shown Alessandro two days earlier. It was still carefully wrapped in tissue paper. Becca rummaged down below the bar and into her hessian bag, from which she produced a card. 'High Dales Designs. A twist on tradition by Becca Guy.' It had her email address on. She quickly added her phone number too.

'Nothing to lose, is there?' she grinned as she saw me watching.

'Anything can happen.'

She handed over the parcel and the man took it carefully and then produced a bundle of notes.

'No, no!' said Becca, before peeling off two and pushing the rest back. 'Forty pounds is plenty, really.'

'You're missing a trick there, girl,' said one of the cyclists in the bar who'd been watching with some amusement. 'If he wants to give you hundreds, just you take it.'

'No. Forty pounds is the price and that's it.'

Alessandro's messenger shrugged, pushed the rest of the notes back in his pocket, thanked Becca again, made a small bow and left.

Becca and I stood either side of the bar and grinned at each other. All in all it had been a pretty good day.

*   *   *

The next day I had to tend to my life. I snaked back down the dale to a small town. After the track up High Hartstone Edge, the road that had seemed so perilously narrow when Jake and I drove up a few days ago now seemed like the M1. When I got to the small town it took me a moment to realise what was odd about it: there was no supermarket; in fact not a single chain store or national name at all. Every shop was independent and individual. Wonderful. I joined the queue at the baker's, relishing that bread smell as I dithered between a crusty cottage loaf and an enticing small square loaf full of seeds and nuts. In the end I chose them both. 'Best way. Spoil yourself,' smiled the assistant as she deftly wrapped the loaves in sheets of tissue paper and popped them in a paper carrier bag with string handles. The bread was still warm and it took all my willpower not to start nibbling away at it as I walked along to the proper old-fashioned grocer's where they had a wonderful coffee grinder and the smell filled the air.

It was market day, so I spent a happy hour wandering round the stalls, buying crisp local apples, greengages, knobbly carrots and huge creamy parsnips. 'Try some,' said the man selling chutneys, offering me a plate of crackers and a spoon to dip into the jars, and I finally settled on Hot Plum Relish and a jar of Malay vegetable pickle, both so good that they hardly needed meat or cheese. I bought homemade savoury wafers and some oat biscuits from a stall called 'Aunty Annie's' and I heard someone actually say, 'How do, Annie?' And I was sure she was an aunty, too. We must do another market feature on *The Foodie*, I decided, it was such a brilliant way to shop.

Standing back from the cobbled marketplace there was a small but very stylish department store; one window was filled almost entirely with scarves I instantly recognised as Becca's. They were really very good – bright pinks and purples, scarlets and blues, full of style and fun – and she should be charging a lot more than forty quid for them. If she sold them in London, she could make a fortune.

But the best thing of all was that I could get a phone signal here too. I sat squashed into a seat at a crowded café, my shopping bags at my feet, and scrolled happily through my messages. There was a number I didn't recognise. Probably a misdialled one. I clicked on it just to be sure.

'Hello miss freshface. how r u? lunch was good. c u soon.'

I clutched my phone, stared at it hard and scrolled quickly on to the next message. I didn't want Clayton Silver in my life. Didn't want him sending me texts. Then I scrolled back . . . and read Clayton's message again. Not exactly a love letter, was it? Not quite up there with great romantic missives of our time. Part of me was irritated by this attention. My finger went straight to 'Delete' but then I stopped. Because another part of me was ridiculously pleased that Clayton had bothered to send a text. Maybe the lunch, our conversation, had meant something to him too.

'For goodness' sake, girl, you have nothing in common. Stop acting like an impressionable teenager.' I gave myself a good talking-to, but I'm not sure how much notice I took of myself. I was still staring at the phone and chewing a delicious chunk of parkin when there was a knock on the window. I looked up. Jake was standing outside.

'It's all right, pet, he can sit here. I'm just going.' An elderly lady with half a dozen bulging shopping bags manoeuvred her way out of her seat with some difficulty and Jake slid in next to me.

'How did you know I was here?'

'Well I saw that rust-heap of a van parked up the road so knew you'd be here somewhere. I just kept my eyes open. How are you?'

'Fine.'

'Are you all right on your own in that house?'

'Yes, thank you.'

'And you're managing with work?'

'Yes, thank you.'

'Oh for goodness' sake, Tilly. I'm trying to be nice here. At least meet me halfway.'

The phone with the text message from Clayton burned in my hand. I didn't want to get into this with Jake. But Jake was right; he *was* trying to be kind. And maybe we needed to talk. And here was as good a place as any. Surrounded by people, we couldn't shout and yell.

'Could we have another pot of tea and some more parkin, please?' I asked the waitress.

'I don't want any parkin,' said Jake crossly.

'Yes, you do – it's delicious, all gingery and treacly and chewy.'

'Why are you always trying to push food onto me?'

I put my cup back in the saucer. 'Am I? Do I? I mean, did I?'

'Yes. All the time.'

I thought about it. 'Maybe, ' I said slowly, 'because food has always been important in our family. Even when my mother found it difficult to talk about things, especially anything to do with my dad, she would cook, try new recipes. A new recipe was a sort of offering, a gift, a way of bridging a gap. And, of course, it's one of the greatest gifts you can give. I mean, you're actually sharing the very stuff of life, aren't you? I mean . . .'

'Tilly,' said Jake wearily, 'it was just an observation. I didn't want a psychological treatise.'

'Oh.' Yet again, Jake had somehow put me in the wrong, made me feel silly. And I realised I didn't have to put up with it any more. 'I wasn't expecting to see you again,'

I said. 'I thought you'd be far too busy researching with . . . Flick.'

'Did you really go off in a helicopter with Clayton Silver yesterday?'

'Ah. So *that's* why you've searched me out. For information. For work. Not out of concern at all.' Which was, in a funny way, a relief. I was getting used to the idea that the ties between me and Jake were now well and truly cut. 'Actually, yes, I did. Some posh hotel near Newcastle.'

'So who did he meet?'

'Dunno. Just two men. I told you in my email. Why?'

'Well, I knew he wasn't at the shoot yesterday. But when Clayton Silver didn't turn up yesterday, nobody seemed surprised or cared much. And when you think how much it costs to have a gun at a shoot – we're talking thousands – it just seemed odd that no one minded.'

I pushed the parkin towards him and poured him a cup of tea. 'Do you think something's going on? Something dodgy?'

'Well, there are rumours, but nothing I can get to grips with. Maynard's spending a fortune trying to turn himself into a respectable English gentleman – the country house in Surrey, the shooting lodge up here. The trouble is that no one quite knows where his fortune came from.'

'Something crooked?'

'Possibly. Undoubtedly. But it's impossible to prove. He calls himself a property developer and certainly he made a lot in the boom years, but no one can get to the bottom of it. There are too many companies, not enough information. I have spent days trawling through records, reading annual reports, company accounts, trying to make sense of it all. It's bloody difficult. In any case, half the stuff's offshore or is just untraceable. A football club is a wonderful cover-up.'

'Doesn't that make money?'

'You'd think so, wouldn't you? But then think about the stupid money footballers get paid. It can't all come from Sky TV or selling replica shirts to little boys. There's a lot of dodgy dealing going on somewhere and it's hard to pin down. Interesting that many of the usual hangers-on – minor royalty and all those impoverished aristos – don't want much to do with him, not even his grouse moors. He's left with jumped-up City boys, soap stars and footballers.'

I felt uneasy. 'Would that have been Maynard's helicopter I had a lift in?'

'Oh yes. A couple of footballers have their own, but not Clayton Silver as far as I know. That would have been Maynard's all right.'

'Do you think the footballers are involved in this dodgy stuff?'

'Probably not in the really big league. But there again, there's an awful lot of corruption that's hard to prove. There were all those scandals in the Eighties and Nineties and they've just shown that Italian football is rotten to the core. So it's hard to say. But if I were you, I would definitely steer clear of footballers, especially any that have any connection with Simeon Maynard.'

I was quiet for a bit, thinking about what he'd said and wondering if the helicopter jaunt hadn't been so much fun after all, when Jake took an absent-minded bite of parkin. 'Mmm, you're right, this is good.'

'Told you.'

We looked at each other and smiled.

'It seems weird to be sitting in a café at the top of England with you,' I said.

'You could always move in to the B & B where I am.'

'I don't think that would work, would it?' I had tasted a

few days of freedom and realised how much easier it was making life on my own.

'But you can't really like being by yourself in that isolated dump,' said Jake. 'It's not safe for a woman on her own.'

'Oh, don't be daft. It's quite safe. And it's not a dump. And anyway, I like it there.' I could feel my confidence rising with every sentence. I didn't mind arguing with Jake because I didn't really care what he thought any more. I could say what I liked. It was a glorious feeling. Even more exhilarating than taking off in a helicopter.

'Anyway, won't you be going back to . . . Flick soon? She must be longing to know how you're getting on.'

'We've been in touch.'

'I bet you have.'

'Look, it's work. Anyway, she's in London. You and I came up here together and I feel responsible for you.'

'Please don't. I can take full responsibility for myself, thank you.'

He shrugged. It was over. Really over.

I wondered if this is the way a love affair ends. Not with a huge row and high drama, but over a cup of tea and a slice of cake in the middle of a market-day teashop, while elderly women around us rested their feet and checked their shopping lists and dithered between a cream slice or a scone.

Very civilised. Very soulless. And very sad – not because it was ending, but because maybe it had never really begun. Already I was looking back and wondering what had kept us together so long.

'Anyway,' said Jake, 'time to go. I've got an interview lined up in half an hour.'

We slithered our way out of the seats. A young woman pounced on our place with a triumphant shout of, 'Over here, Mum!'

I paid the bill while Jake waited outside for me. 'You know

where I am,' he said, as I came out pushing my purse back in my bag. 'Keep in touch. And just be careful, Tilly.'

'You're worrying about nothing,' I said, gathering all my bags in one hand, the other already in my pocket clutching my phone. He kissed me quickly on the cheek. And then we walked off in opposite directions.

Chapter Ten

For the next three days I threw myself into work. Granny Allen would have been proud. I'd visited a wonderful smokery by the sea – the most delicious smoked salmon and trout, and strings of kippers hung over piles of oak shavings that would make amazing pictures for *The Foodie*. Bill had told me about a family who made all sorts of things out of sloes – chocolates and cakes as well as sloe and damson gin. The daughter of the family took me out and showed me the hedgerows all around the farm, which were full of sloes they hadn't picked yet, waiting for a good frost. I peered into the black twigs, not really sure what I was looking for, until I gradually spotted the lovely, purplish fruit, like tiny plums. I would never even have known there were sloes in there, but once you knew where to look there were masses. They were too bitter to eat alone but they tasted great in gin. I had just one mouthful and I could feel the warmth hit my system like the magic cordials from fairy stories. The family insisted I tasted everything – especially the chocolates – and then loaded me up with samples.

But it was a long drive to their farm in PIP and my head was rattling and my back aching when I got back. I went straight to the pub but the place was heaving. Even Becca was too busy to knit a stitch of her scarf, and Dexter was busy dashing between the kitchen and the bar. I couldn't check my email as both computers were hogged by people working on their family history. Judging by the number of books, papers and printouts they had scattered around them, they were going to be a long time. Wearily, I got back into the van and headed for the cottage. I'd have to come back later. In the meantime, what I needed was some fresh air, so as soon as I'd dumped my bag, I changed into jeans and boots and set out.

To prove I wasn't subconsciously looking for helicopters and Clayton Silver, I took a slightly different path, one that followed the line of the valley. Down in the distance, near the farm, I could see one of the Aldersons backing a trailer up through a gate. By the look of it – though it was difficult to tell from this distance and in all the layers of clothes they were wearing – it was Mrs Alderson on the tractor and a man who was at the gate, yelling instructions. Ahead of me, up the hillside of grass so pale it was almost grey, I could see the quad bike and Matt Alderson carrying a huge bale of hay as if it were as light as a feather, and throwing it down for the sheep, while a sheepdog ran round in little bursts, supervising everything, stopping every now and then to look at Matt as if to say, 'Is this all you want? I can do lots more complicated things than this, you know.' Then when Matt got back on the bike and bounced off down the fellside to get another bale, the dog leapt on the back and sat there, ears pinned back by the breeze, looking like a superior footman on an old-fashioned coach.

It took me a while to realise that the heaps of grey stones scattered on the hillside weren't just natural outcrops of rock but had once been houses and barns, built with stone hacked out of the hill and now doing their very best to return to it. This little valley was less industrial than that on the other side of the hill. The ruins looked more domestic. This might always have been farmland, right back to when the Vikings worked their way up here. Though what sort of farms could they have been? They could barely have made a living, that's for sure. Grass grew through the stones and sheep nibbled in what had once been someone's kitchen or bedroom. Occasionally, the remains of low walls marked out what had once been a garden. Long ago, someone had tried to grow things here – with how much success, I wondered? Certainly now the only difference between the garden and the fellside was that the former gardens had a few more nettles.

The houses could never have been much more than two rooms and a single storey. The cottage where I was staying had clearly been extended and was a comparative palace. They seemed to have put more effort into their barns rather than their homes; the barns were higher, firmer, more solid and seemed to have lasted better. There was another building that even had a proper door, albeit one that appeared propped up rather than secured. It had a window, too, though no glass in it of course, and a small surrounding wall. I wondered what it could have been.

Growing up through what was left of a wall was a small twisted tree, branches covered with fruit. Apples, I saw, when I got closer, very small apples. I picked one and tentatively bit into it. Arrgghh! Nearly as bad as the sloes. So sour that I could feel my mouth drying up. I flung the apple along the fellside and startled sheep lumbered in all directions, protesting loudly. 'Sorry, sheep!' I shouted.

There was something else on the crab-apple tree, some unexpected splashes of colour fluttering from some of the furthest branches. Intrigued, I balanced on one of the stones that had rolled out from the wall and, with one hand hanging on to a spindly little branch, I leaned into the tree. With one final stretch, as small sharp branches dug into my shoulder, I managed to grab one. It was a ribbon, a velvet ribbon, deep and luxurious. Just like the scrap I'd found before and taken back to the cottage. I let the spindly branch whip back, jumped down off the stone and examined the ribbon carefully. Apart from the deep crease at one end where it must once have been tied and folded, it was as bright cherry red as when it was made. Was it new? Old? Hard to tell. But it certainly wasn't nylon velvet. I rubbed it gently with my thumb; it was much too luxurious for that. Where had it come from? I couldn't see many walkers going in for gaudy cherry velvet. I thought of tying it back on the tree again, like a Christmas decoration or a flag. But instead I put it carefully in my pocket. It was somehow too pretty and unexpected just to scatter to the wind again. But the other one stayed there, caught on twigs, reminding me of Tibetan prayer flags, snapping in the breeze.

The breeze was getting up. Colder, stronger, more of a wind than a breeze now. I pulled the collar up on my fleece. Looking up along the valley I could see thick dark clouds ahead. They were black and low and seemed to race up the narrow dale like a menacing incoming tide. Time to turn back. Would I get back before the storm broke?

No chance. I had barely turned round when the sting of hailstones bit into me, pounding my face, my head, my back. The icy pellets were like gunshot, freezing cold and incredibly painful. I yelled and put my hands up to protect my face from their sting. Whichever way I turned, there was no escape. I could hardly lift my head up. Could hardly open my eyes to see where I was going. I was barely twenty minutes from the cottage but there was no way I could go back in this. With that the black sky was lit up with a sheet of lightning. The thunder crash followed seconds after. I was frightened. No houses, shops or precincts to pop into for shelter. On that empty fellside, I felt horribly exposed and vulnerable.

I thought of that odd little building with the drunken, propped-up door. Maybe I could get into there and shelter for a while. Anything was better than this. Head down and into the wind, I made my way towards it, my feet slithering on the damp grass, which was already heaped up with hailstones. As I took my hands from my face and glanced up quickly, I could see that Matt Alderson had had the same idea and was heading down the hillside on the bike towards shelter. The sheepdog now wasn't sitting up so jauntily, but lying as flat as it could make itself on the back of the bike.

Matt got to the building a moment before I did, jumped off the bike, balanced on top of the stone wall, grabbed the edge of the window above and with one swift supple movement, was through it.

There was something familiar about that movement. I had seen something like it very recently. I kept my hands away from my face and risked the pounding of hailstones to keep looking. The jump through the window had knocked off the cap Matt was wearing. Before I covered my face with my hands again against the driving hail, I just caught a glimpse through the empty window of copper-coloured hair, gleaming and dazzling through the darkness of the storm.

Baffled, but with no time to think, as the hail sent icy rivulets down my neck and my hair was plastered to my forehead, I made for the drunken door while another roll of thunder crashed above me. As I came near, it juddered open awkwardly as if on only one hinge. Behind it, beckoning me in to shelter, was Matt Alderson. But this was no young man. Matt Alderson was a girl and – despite the bundled layers of clothes – one I recognised immediately. Last time I'd seen her was in a glamorous nightclub in London, but this time her copper hair tumbled round the drenched shoulders of an ancient bulky waterproof, her feet were encased in solid green wellies, and a collie dog was twisting round her feet.

'Foxy?' I said, stunned. 'What on earth are you doing here?'

Chapter Eleven

'Actually,' said the tall girl politely, if rather frostily, 'I hate that name. I prefer to be known as Matty, short for Matilda, after my great-great-grandmother.'

'And I,' I said, equally politely and also just a bit frostily, 'am known as Tilly, short for Matilda, after *my* great-great-grandmother.'

This formality would have been more impressive if both of us hadn't been dripping wet and squelching through the puddle in the muddy doorway.

Matty frowned. 'Your great-great-granny wasn't Granny Allen too, was she?'

'She was, yes.'

'Granny Allen who lived in this valley? In our farm and the cottage above it?'

'The very same.'

We looked at each other for a while in the gloom of the building while the hail rattled the roof. Then Matty laughed and said, 'Then we must be sort of cousins, mustn't we?'

'I guess so.'

'Well then. Hello, cousin!'

I grinned back. 'Hello, cousin Matty. How very nice to meet you.'

We shook hands and now my eyes were getting used to

the light, I studied my new-found relative. I'm tall, but she towered over me. Even without make-up and in her battered work clothes she looked stunning, dazzling in the gloom. She was, I thought glumly, exactly the sort of woman that lived in Clayton Silver's world. This long-lost cousin was already making me feel like the poor relation.

But I had to be sure. 'You *are* the model. I mean it is you, isn't it? The one they call Foxy?'

She sighed. 'Yes I am. That's me. But look, it's only a job, OK? I mean it's a great job, but that's all it is.'

'But . . .' I still couldn't get my head round this. 'Why are you here? What are you doing?'

'Well, today,' she said in a slightly impatient way, 'I've been ruddling the tups. Do you know what that means?'

I shook my head. Hadn't a clue.

'It means I get a big bucket of sort of paint and I get the tup – that's the ram – and daub the paint all over his chest, so that when he serves – i.e. has it off with – the ewe, she is left with a bloody great daub of paint on her back. So we know which ewes have been served. OK?'

'OK,' I said, a little grumpily, 'thanks for the lecture.'

Matt relented, looked suddenly young and vulnerable, and added in a kinder tone. 'Look, this is my home. My parents, my brothers and sister are here. It's where I belong. It's where I come back to. Where I escape to. Where I get things into perspective and realise what really matters. I come back whenever I can.'

'Don't you like being a model then? The jet-set life and all that?'

'Of course I do, most of the time. It's a great job as long as you don't take it too seriously. But it's like being on a ride at the fair, you know? It's different and it's fun and it's all very exciting, but it's not real. Whereas this –' she waved her arm round the little building, the sheep trying to get

97

shelter under the grey rocks, the hail slashing down on the fellside – 'this is real.'

A bit too real for me, right now, I thought, shivering.

Matty stood for a moment at the empty window, gazing out at the hail as the wind whipped her hair around her face. She scrabbled in her pockets and found an elastic band. Underneath her thick woollen gloves she was wearing another pair, skin-tight thin cotton that she didn't take off.

'So are you one of the people staying up at the cottage?' she was asking, as she tugged her hair through the band. 'Are you researching your family roots? Just about everyone else seems to be these days.'

'Well, yes. Only it's just me. My boyfriend and I, well, my ex-boyfriend and I seem to be going our separate ways.'

'Oh dear. Sorry. That's a shame when you're on holiday.'

'Sad really, very sad, but not, actually the end of the world,' I said. 'Quite the opposite, even. Anyway, it's a working holiday and he couldn't work without the Internet and phone reception.'

'What does he do?'

'Journalist.'

'Ah.'

I could feel her tensing slightly and she moved away from that subject quickly. 'So how's the family research going?' she asked. 'Have you found out quite how we're related? Are you descended from the ones who went to America or Australia?'

'I don't quite know exactly. I'm not doing my family history, never really thought about it much, to tell the truth. But since I've been here . . . well, I'm sort of intrigued. I'd heard of Granny Allen, of course, but I didn't even realise until I told my mum where we were going that this is where she came from. My mum can remember coming here when she was a little girl, playing in the stream by the packhorse bridge with her cousins.'

'Well, in that case, it was probably with my mum. She was born here and bred up here. You'll have to talk to her about it. Come back down with me once this storm has stopped.' Matty's smile was genuine and welcoming. 'Mum would love it.'

We listened for moment. If anything, the storm had got worse. I looked around the building in which we were sheltering. It had an earth floor, smelt not entirely pleasantly of soil and stale grass and was clearly used as a storeroom, stacked high as it was with blue and yellow plastic sacks, and huge drums of different chemicals and bales of hay.

'Make yourself comfortable,' said Matty. 'We might have a long wait.' We settled down on a couple of bales. They always look quite comfortable, but they were itchy scratchy even through my jeans. 'Lie down, Tess,' she said to the dog who curled up between us and I was glad of her warmth against my leg. The wind and the hail blew through the empty window and down the back of my neck, the plastic bags fluttered and the door rattled. But it was still a lot better than being outside.

'It used to be a chapel,' said Matty. 'One of those strange sects that flourished for a while in the eighteenth century. I don't think they had many worshippers, even then.'

I wanted to ask her about it, all sorts of questions about the people who had lived up here where there was hardly even a hint of a road any more. But there was something else I wanted to know even more.

'Why did you jump out of the window at Club Balaika?' I blurted out. 'Why have you gone into hiding? Why—'

'Ah, it was *you* in the Ladies at Balaika!' She gave me a quick look and her expression – just for that moment – was very much top model rather than northern farm girl. 'I knew

I'd seen you somewhere before. Strange.' She looked at me, studying me. 'When I saw you then, at the club, I thought I knew you. Must be the family likeness. But, as you noticed, I wasn't in the mood to stop and find out. Anyway,' she went on, reaching to stroke Tess's ears, 'if you have or had a journalist boyfriend, you should know better than to believe everything you read in the newspapers. I have *not* gone into hiding. I have *not* reneged on my contract. I have *not* run away. Honestly, reports like that make me so *angry!* The simple truth is that I was booked to do the *Virgo* shoot in Egypt this month and it's been put back a few weeks so everything's on hold. Suddenly I had a free diary, so I thought I'd come home. Pretty normal sort of thing to do, wouldn't you say? And as you might have noticed, home is not a place where you sit round on your bum all day. There's always plenty of work to do, so I do it.'

'But I still don't understand why you jumped out of the window.'

'Oh that.' She grinned. 'Simple. I was bored.'

'Bored?'

'Oh God yes! I was there with this group of lads who run one of the indie music channels. I don't even know why I went, really. Nice enough lads, but so . . . *young* and totally up themselves. It was bad enough when they were talking about work but then they started on cars . . . Honestly, it was worse than being in The Miners' Arms on darts night. I just couldn't be doing with it. And there was also . . .' she hesitated for a moment. 'I don't know, there was a funny atmosphere there that night. That Maynard who's got the shooting rights in the next dale was there. I just felt . . . well, that it somehow didn't feel right. I didn't want to be there any more.'

I remembered how I'd queued with Jake, desperate to get in. I couldn't be that blasé.

'I was going to leave, perfectly tidily and respectably through the front door,' Matt continued, 'but then I saw the security people getting jumpy and I recognised one of the bodyguards so I guessed the princes were probably arriving and I knew all the paps would be there. And I couldn't face it. I just thought there must be a better way out, and there was.' She grinned again. 'Good, wasn't it?'

'Fantastic,' I said. 'I was well impressed.' And if I thought about her uneasiness about Clayton Silver and his friends, I pushed it to the back of my mind.

Now I knew we were cousins, the atmosphere was easier between us.

'I didn't know we had a supermodel in the family,' I said. 'How come you got to do that? I don't suppose there are many girls from here who do something so exciting.'

'Well, my mum did,' she said. 'So you can forget about us all being little country bumpkins as soon as you like.'

I blushed. 'Sorry.'

'You're all right. Don't worry. Mum won a competition when she was a student – her flatmate entered her for it.'

Suddenly it all made sense. There was definitely something about Kate Alderson, a natural poise that marked her out. I thought of that perfect skin, the little scarf that was eminently practical but also had an undeniable dash of style. Once you knew, it was easy to believe that she had once been a model.

'Mum had all sorts of modelling jobs down in London, some of the big names too. She did a lot of magazine covers and some catwalk. And she could have done a lot more. But she'd already met my dad by then, known him forever, really. He farmed over in Cumbria with his brother. So when my grandad – Mum's dad – was too ill to run this place, Dad came over here. Modelling and farming don't mix really. Especially when we're all the way up here.

But Mum did a bit for a while. Brought in some very useful money. There's not much money in hill farming. Great life, but no money. She used some of her modelling money to buy a bit more land and a tractor. Said she brought it as her dowry and Dad only married her for the tractor. Don't laugh – that can be too near the truth in this part of the world.'

'So did you always want to be a model too?'

'Never really thought about it, though I always liked looking at the pictures of mum in her modelling days. Most I'd done was a couple of charity shows in the village hall. I didn't mind it. But I always wanted to be a photographer.'

'A photographer?'

'Yeah, I was always impressed . . . Dexter. You know Dexter, who runs the pub now?' Did I imagine it or did her voice go odd when she mentioned him? No, it must have been the effect of hailstones down the neck of her jacket. 'Well, when I was a kid, well, early teens, he was working for an agency and doing a lot of work for himself. He had a studio in an old workshop down the dale and I thought he was wonderful, used to follow him around asking about cameras and pictures. I must have been a real pain in the arse, but he was really kind, answered my questions, even gave me my first camera and then, when he saw I was serious, helped me choose the next one. I was only a kid, but he really listened to me. I had the photography bug and he taught me a lot. He was so lovely, so patient . . .' She paused and looked thoughtful, then shook her head as if to clear it. 'When I thought of studying photography at college, he helped me look at courses, told me what to look for . . .

'But he went down to London and got married and I ended up on the other side of the camera. Long story, but to do with an old friend of Mum's. And yes –' she grinned – 'it was exciting for a farm girl like me. I thought it would be a good gap-year thing, but that was five years ago and I still haven't taken up my uni place yet.'

'Will you?'

'Don't know at the moment. I'm not going to do modelling forever. Well, you can't anyway, can you? It's not really a job for a grown-up. But it's good money and I have some plans, some ideas – but we shall see.'

I remembered my suspicions. 'So Dexter isn't secretly gay then?' I asked.

'Dexter? Gay?' Matt hooted with laughter. 'Far from it. Whatever gave you that idea?'

'Well, I thought you were a bloke when you were in the pub. Dexter's eyes lit up when he looked at you, so—'

'Did they?' she asked eagerly, 'Did they really?'

She smiled to herself as she looked out through the open window and then said, 'Anyway. I think that storm has moved away, the hail seems to have turned to rain. I think that counts as an improvement. Do you want to give it a go?'

'Yes please.'

This time, Matty left through the door, but it was such a fiddle to open it, and then try and close it so it didn't blow down, that I could quite understand why she'd gone in through the window. I climbed on the back of the quad bike and felt the rain soak straight through my jeans as we shot off back down to the farm, this time with Tess loping alongside us.

I squelched into the farm's back kitchen, a huge stone-flagged square room, with a stone sink, two big freezers, a rack of ancient-looking coats and a row of industrial-strength wellies with waterproofs abandoned on top of them. In one movement, Matty stepped out of her boots and over-trousers, hung up her waterproof and shook out

103

her hair. I'd taken my jacket off but was still struggling to undo the wet and knotted laces of my walking boots. When I did and saw that my soaked socks left wet, muddy footprints, I took those off too and padded barefoot into the warmth of the main kitchen.

It was just as I had always imagined a farmhouse kitchen to look. In the centre was a long table, with a high settle on one side and solid-looking chairs on the other. Behind was a vast dresser, its shelves full of interesting plates and jugs and mugs, as well as bits of paper, keys and notebooks, photographs.

One wall was taken up by an Aga, the alcoves alongside it full of pots and pans. From a huge steaming casserole, Mrs Alderson was ladling something that smelt delicious into a row of foil containers, lined up on a big tray. She worked quickly, methodically.

'Hello, Mum,' said Matty, passing me a warm towel with which to dry my hair. 'I found a long-lost cousin up on the fellside. I thought I'd better bring her home to meet the family.'

Mrs Alderson looked up. 'Ah,' she said, 'I did wonder . . .' She filled the last of the foil trays. 'Matt, take these through to the back to cool down, please.'

As Matty manoeuvred the huge tray, Mrs Alderson piled the empty casserole into the sink, along with the ladle, wiped the Aga and the table and then looked at me kindly.

'Tilly Flint,' I said, 'short for Matilda. My mum's Frankie, formerly Thwaite. She came to stay here when she was little.'

Mrs Alderson laughed. 'Ah, yes, I remember Frankie. We have some photos somewhere. She came to stay one summer when I was a child and insisted on keeping up with us, balancing on the bridge, wading across the beck, even though she could only have been four or five and the rest of us were about ten.'

'Sounds like my mum.'

'And is she – I'm sorry, we lost touch many years ago when our mothers died – isn't she the one they call Fairtrade Frankie?'

'That's her,' I said.

'I thought it must be. I didn't know her married name but when I see her on television I always think, 'There's an Allen. Same with you, though you have a lot more of the look and the build too. I'm Kate by the way.'

I felt unduly pleased to think I had a real family. For so long it had just been me and my mum and I always envied other people their brothers and sisters, uncles, aunts, grand-parents and cousins. The nearest I had to family was Bill and, lovely though he was, that still left quite a gap.

A big four-by-four pulled up in the yard with a toot, and out tumbled a boy and a girl aged about twelve, clearly brother and sister, though the boy had the same fair skin and copper hair of his mother and older sister, while the girl had a mop of dark curly hair and bright pink cheeks.

'School taxi,' said Matty. 'The twins. Ruth and Isaac, known as Zak.'

The twins shouted as they came in through the back kitchen, dumping coats and bags as they headed straight for the cake tin.

'This is our cousin Tilly,' said Matt.

Zak and Ruth stopped for a second, looked, smiled, said 'Hello' and carried on raiding the cake tin.

'It's stopped raining so I'm just going up to see Snowball,' said Ruth.

'Well, don't go far. It's very wet. Keep to the tracks,' said her mum.

'OK,' and she was gone.

'I'm going to help Tom on the van,' said Zak.

'But he's not home yet. Hasn't he got football or something? That's why he took the motorbike.'

'Football, yes, but he's not staying long so I'll go up and get started. Don't worry –' he said as his mother shot him a fierce look – 'I won't do anything that Tom hasn't said I can do. And yes I'll be careful and yes I'll put everything back and yes, I'll put my overalls on. And yes—'

'Go!' said his mother laughing, and turned to me. 'Will you stay for your tea and meet the rest of this family?'

'Yes, please, I would like that, very much indeed.' I had been standing near the Aga and realised there was steam coming gently from my jeans.

A small motorbike buzzed into the yard. The boy riding it raised an arm in triumph as he nosed in just ahead of a Land Rover. He took off his helmet and shouted something to the driver getting out of the Land Rover and I thought I was seeing double. As they walked, laughing, into the house together it was clear they were father and son – two tall men, one broad-shouldered and solid, the younger still slim as a reed, yet both with dark curly hair, pink cheeks and open, cheerful expressions.

'Hello. So who have we here?' asked the older man, padding into the kitchen in thick socks and rootling with his feet under the Aga for a pair of bright red slippers.

'This is Tilly Flint, a long-lost cousin that Matty brought in from the rain. And this,' she turned to me, 'is my husband Guy and out there is our son Tom.'

Tom was still in the back kitchen struggling into a pair of overalls, his bag abandoned in the corner. He came and shook hands. 'Hello, Tilly Flint,' he said pleasantly, but clearly anxious to be gone as he glanced at his mother. 'I'm going up to the workshop to do a bit on the van while it's still light. I'll do homework after tea.'

His mother nodded. He smiled at me again and vanished.

'He wants it ready in time for his seventeenth birthday,' explained Kate. 'And it will be.'

Guy was beaming at me. 'Now then,' he said, in an accent a lot stronger than his wife's, 'another long-lost cousin, eh? We've had a fair few of those coming through here over t'years. Another Allen, are you?'

'My great-grandmother was.'

'Ah well, there's plenty of 'em around, especially in America. For every one we sent over there, I reckon there must be thirty coming back. You're definitely one of the bonnier ones. Well, I'll catch up with you a bit later, if you don't mind. Will you give me a hand with the beasts, Matt?'

Matt went back into the outer kitchen, climbed back into her boots, over-trousers and waterproof and followed her dad out across the yard.

'Yes, there must be Allens in every corner of the world,' said Kate, as she started tackling a pile of potatoes. 'And most of them doing well for themselves. Granny Allen made sure of that. She might have been a tough old bird but she did her best by all the children.'

'Why did they all go away?'

'No work here. The lead mines were a huge industry, had been since Roman times, but they dwindled and died. And there was nothing else.'

'But what about farming?'

'Ha! Once there were more than twenty families living in this valley. Now, apart from a few holiday cottages, there's only us. We use all the land that the twenty families had between them – two and a half thousand acres, a lot of land – and it barely keeps us going. Oh, it's a great life, a marvellous life, I can't imagine any other. But it's not an easy one. And Granny Allen all those years ago saw the way it was going and she encouraged her children and grand-children to seek work wherever they could find it – coal mines, iron works, America, Australia.'

'My grandmother was in service in London before the war.'

'That's right. Two sisters want into service. One was in Durham, but the other went to Newcastle and then down to London. It's what lots of the girls had to do. Their only chance of work.'

'But not everyone went. Otherwise you wouldn't be here.'

'No. One or two of the lads stayed locally and some of the girls came back to marry. My grandfather kept the farm going, and then my father. I left, of course, for college. And stayed in London for a while afterwards. Could have stayed forever really, and that would have been the end of the farm. But I'd already met Guy and it seemed right that we should stay here. The house was dreadful! Practically falling down because my parents had had no money to do anything with it. So every modelling job I did, I thought, 'Well, that's a new bath,' or, 'That's the windows fixed,' or, 'That's the Aga.

'I suppose I was just one of those like my grandfather, who just couldn't leave this place, however hard it was. A lot of the lead miners had come here from other parts of the country, but I think we must always have been here. Even though the estate owns most of the land hereabouts, we own our house and a hundred acres – we rent the rest – so I think we must have been here way, way back, at least to the fifteen hundreds and possibly before. Like the sheep, we're hefted to this dale.'

'*Hefted?*'

'Sheep roam but they always come back to their own territory, their own patch of land where they know where they belong. That's why there are no fences on the moors.

Sheep are free to go where they like, because they'll always come back.'

Hefted. It was a good word, a good thought.

'But then it makes life tricky,' Mrs Alderson went on. 'People like our Matt who go away to work but still want to be in the dale. Always a hard one, that.'

Tea was a great family affair. Kate produced another dish of the same casserole. It was lamb slowly cooked with root vegetables: rich, sticky and full of flavour. Everyone ate huge amounts, even Matty. Not many models would dare eat that much. There again, I didn't suppose many models would spend their spare time doing ten-hour shifts on a farm.

At first I found it easiest to concentrate on the food. I was a bit overwhelmed by the sheer noise, the chat and teasing, the banter and bickering of family life. The cheerful chaos was so different from the meals of my childhood and adolescence – just my mother and me: congenial enough but a lot quieter than life with the Aldersons.

Ruth was trying to convince Matty to take her back to London with her. 'I could be the latest modelling sensation,' said Ruth persuasively, leaning her elbows on the table with her knife and fork clutched firmly in her hands. 'You could take me with you on shoots and photographers would say, "Who is that beautiful child? She has such an *amazing* face it positively sings to the camera. We must use her." And then I would earn megabucks and could buy Snowball a smart new saddle. What do you say, Matt?'

'I say that you should wait a few years and make the most of having Snowball and space and time to ride him,' said Matt.

'And if you're not going to eat that, I shall,' said Zak, his fork poised over Ruth's plate. She snatched it and tucked in quickly, thoughts of stardom temporarily forgotten.

Kate dished out second helpings and, in the lull, tried to bring me into the conversation. 'So you work for a food magazine do you, Tilly?' she asked. I explained a bit about what I was doing, which seemed to meet with general approval. 'We need people to take more interest in where their food comes from, to realise the work that goes in to doing it properly,' said Guy. And Ruth was wonderfully impressed when she heard who my mum was.

'You mean I'm related to Fairtrade Frankie? That is *so-o* cool,' she said. 'Why are you working on a magazine? Don't you want to work with your mum?'

'No, not really,' I said, 'and it would be tricky. It's not a question of just helping out in the coffee shops any more – I've done plenty of that. It's big business now and very much Mum's baby.'

Faced with their cheerful confidence, I couldn't quite explain that, lovely though my mum was, she always made me feel so *inadequate* somehow. She wouldn't trust me near her company. Fine when I was a student waiting or washing up, but actually involved? Making decisions? No, I couldn't do that.

'Anyway,' said Guy comfortingly, 'you need to make your own way in the world. You might come to it one day. Like one of these might come to the farm.'

'There are far easier ways to make a living,' said Kate.

'Aye, there are,' said Guy, sighing for a moment, but then he grinned at his wife. 'But you wouldn't change it, love, would you? Not the twelve-hour days, seven days a week, fifty-two weeks a year. Why, you could prance around all day in fancy frocks having your photo taken like our Matt does now. All champagne cocktails and parties and what-ever other nonsense she gets up to. But why would you want that when you could be up at dawn sorting out the mole traps in the dark, or on the fellside, foddering, with a nice easterly wind blowing round your back? No contest, is there?'

Kate laughed. 'No contest.'

'Well, I shall be a model too,' said Ruth confidently. 'Or I might be an actress. I haven't quite decided yet.' I loved her confidence, and envied it too.

We finished the meal with a thick creamy rice pudding with a swirl of sharp, tangy sauce. I couldn't place the flavour.

'There's apple in there, but something else. Not blackberries? I asked.

'Crab apples and elderberries,' smiled Kate. 'We don't have many trees round here, but at least those we have produce something useful.'

'And delicious,' I said, already thinking of a 'Food for free' feature, with lovely pictures of elderberries and those small crab apples on the tree with the red ribbon.

After we'd cleared the table, loaded the dishwasher and had a cup of tea, the twins disappeared to do their homework, still arguing as they thundered up the stairs. Tom and Guy went to do a last round of the animals. Kate offered me the computer to check my email. 'We've got broadband down here, but it took a call from our MP before we got it.' There on the wall in the hall was yet another sampler. *Waste not, want not.*

'Where *did* all those samplers come from?' I asked. 'Everywhere I go I'm faced with improving texts. Here, up in the cottage, and there's at least three in the pub.'

Kate laughed. 'You'll find them in just about every house in the dale. That's Granny Allen for you. She was apparently horrified at the shiftlessness of some of the families up here, especially when times were hard. If the girls could stitch and sew neatly, then they stood a better chance of getting a decent job in service. So, as if she didn't already

111

have more than enough to do, she started sewing lessons, first of all as part of the Sunday school, and then for some of the older girls too. God knows where she found the time. But the samplers were a sort of instant reference that the girls could show to potential employers. And, being Granny Allen, of course the mottoes had to be of a strictly improving nature.'

'So they must have been, well, I don't know, the equivalent of showing someone a diploma or something.'

'Exactly. For the girls seeking jobs, a neatly stitched sampler would have been as good as a couple of A-levels. Brilliant idea really. Stitch your own reference.'

'Granny Allen was pretty special.'

'Very special – even if she did look a bit of a battleaxe.'

I quickly checked my mail. Damn.

'Something wrong?' asked Kate, who was sorting out some papers on the other side of the desk.

'Just two people that I've been trying to get hold of. They've come back to me at last, but they've both suggested the end of next week. And I should be back in London by then. One of them's a monk – he runs the orchards at the abbey – and says he's running a retreat so it's a bit difficult to take time out for the media. Fair enough, I suppose. It's hard to argue with a monk.'

I stared at the screen helplessly. I wanted to see both these people as I thought they would make good features. 'I suppose I could go down and come back up again for one night.'

'Do you have to go back yet?'

'Well, yes, though I suppose . . .' I realised that I wasn't ready to go back yet. I liked this place, felt sort of at home here, even though it was totally different from anything I'd ever known. Besides, I'd just discovered this amazing family I didn't know I had and I longed for a greater chance of family life – now I'd almost got used to the noise. 'I suppose I could stay for a little while longer. The magazine wouldn't mind because I'd only be out doing features in any case. Ah, but I've only booked your cottage till Saturday morning . . .'

'That doesn't matter. Look, we've got no one booked in until New Year. Why don't you stay on for a week or two? Until you've got your interviews done? After all, you're family. If I can't put up a cousin for a week or two, then it's a bad job.'

'That's wonderful,' I said, and felt happy to be made welcome here; to be taken into this new family.

'If you could get your mother up here as well, that would be great. Though I expect she's a bit too old now to be balancing on the bridge.'

I thought of my mother as I'd seen her last, tense and lined. Hard to imagine her carefree and balancing on bridges, even as a child.

'It would do her good. But I doubt if I could drag her out of London.'

'Well, have a try. It would be good to see her again.'

With that, Matty came into the study, yawning. 'Right, I'm going to collapse in the bath now,' she said. 'Would you like a lift up to the cottage before I do?' she asked me.

'Brilliant. Thank you,' I said, although to be honest I didn't want to leave this nice warm kitchen, but I said my thank-yous and goodbyes, stuffed my soaking socks into the pockets of my soaking jacket, pushed my feet into my boots and hopped up into the Land Rover, which smelt of hay and diesel and animals.

'Would you like to come in, have a glass of wine?' I asked Matty. There were so many questions I wanted to ask that I hadn't had the chance to in the middle of all the family chat.

'Nice thought, but no thanks,' she said. 'I'm shattered.' And then grinned and said quickly, 'Oh, go on, why not?'

She tugged off her boots and wandered into the sitting room while I opened a bottle of Cabernet Sauvignon I'd bought at the upmarket grocer the day I'd seen Jake. She was looking at the items on the windowsill.

'That's a lovely ribbon,' she said, looking at the cherry-coloured velvet. 'I wonder how it got here.'

'I found it on the track at the back of the cottage.'

'It's so bright it could be almost new, but I don't suppose it is.' She stroked it thoughtfully and then took the glass of wine I was offering her.

'Mmm, nice,' said Matty appreciatively, sipping it with a sigh and looking round. 'It's still strange to see this house so clean and cosy now,' she said. 'For years it was virtually derelict. Tom and I used it as a den. Then Mum and Dad decided to rebuild it and let it out. Dexter did a lot of work on it, you know.'

'Dexter?' Photographer, chef, landlord and now builder: was there no end to his talents?

'Yes, just as a holiday job when he was at college. Apart from the specialised bits – electricity and plumbing – it was just Dad and Dexter who rebuilt this place. He can turn his hand to anything. That's how he started me on photography.'

'Really? How?'

'Well, Dexter took lots of pictures of the cottage before work started and then took pictures every day as it progressed. When he went back to college, he left me one of his old cameras and told me I had to carry on the work. I was only about ten, but it really gave me the bug. So I dutifully took lots of pictures – they're all in an album down at the farm. And that was it. I loved the way you could photograph change. Fascinating. It was weird how in every picture you could see what there had been and what was going to be. Dexter was my hero. He is the only person outside my family who thinks about this place the way I do.

'You have a choice in the dale,' she went on. 'Half the lads never go anywhere or do anything, and live the exact same lives as their parents and their parents before them. Fine, if that's what they want. But it wouldn't suit me. Then the other half leave the dale as soon as they can and never come back – apart from Christmases and funerals. What I liked about Dexter was the way he managed to do both, especially when he had a studio here. He brought the buzz of a bigger world with him – new ideas, new ways of looking at things; literally, in his case. His pictures were always in the colour supplements and magazines. But he never changed; he was still rooted here. Then he got married, of course, and left.'

'But he's back again now.'

'Yes. But it's too late.'

I didn't ask for what. Instead I said, 'But he's opened the pub. That's a good thing, isn't it?'

'Yes, of course it is. But he should still be out there taking fantastic pictures.'

She said it so fiercely that I had to spring to Dexter's defence. 'But he's had a bad year – with his dad and the divorce and stuff. He needs time to recover from all that.'

'But it's such a waste. And if he's not careful, he'll get himself into a rut.'

She sounded sad, and partly to lift her mood and partly because I really wanted to know, I asked, as casually as I could, 'So d'you come across many of the footballers when you're in London, then?'

'Oh God yes. Though I could do without most of them.'

'Oh.' I must have looked disappointed because Matty

115

laughed. 'They're not that bad. There are some really nice lads. And lots of them I never see, because when they're not playing football or training, they're at home with their wives and families like normal human beings. It's just . . . well, some of them, a few of them, are so stupid. They can play football brilliantly and we turn them into gods. They have more money than they know what to do with and yet not the sense they're born with.

'Girls fall over themselves to be with them. Go into any club where footballers go and there's always a little posse of girls out to grab one. They don't care which one. They just want the money and the lifestyle. So the lads see the girls just lining up for them and they just work their way through them.'

'So is Clayton Silver typical?'

'Well, he's always got a string of girls, of course, but there's been no real scandal attached to him. But his team don't have the best reputation. Plenty of partying and some of it gets out of hand. I mean, there was that rape allegation last season. It never came to court because I think the girl was probably paid off. But there was the fight in the dressing room where two teammates nearly killed each other – and they were meant to be on the same side. And lots of stories of drink and drugs – plenty of coke around. And the gambling, of course.'

'Is Clayton Silver involved in all this?'

'Hard not to be, I would have thought. Why should he be any different?'

'Anyway, it must be the same for you,' I countered.

'In what way? How do you mean?' asked Matty, looking over the rim of her wine glass.

'Well, just like girls want to go out with footballers, there must be plenty of men who want to go out with models. I bet you're chasing them off.'

'Half the men I meet are gay – that's the fashion industry for you. Of the rest, well there are some – footballers, singers in second-rate bands who are so far up themselves that they believe their own publicity. Then there are all those who are so drunk or stoned that they can barely stand up, let alone hold a conversation. Oh yes, you also get the City types who seem to think that model also means tart. Some of those throw their money around nearly as much as footballers and are just as obnoxious. More so, really, because they're meant to be bright while no one expects a footballer to have brains. Anyone who wants to go out with a model just because she's a model is a sad bastard I can do without.'

'There must be *some* nice men out there. Gosh, if a rich, successful model can't get a decent man, what hope for the rest of us?'

'Plenty,' said Matty. Then she laughed. 'Well, yes, of course there *are* some quite decent men out there – not many, but one or two. But I look at them and wonder how they would get on dealing with a calving or mending a wall.'

'But you can't expect City types to know that!'

'No. But I want them to look as though they could if they really had to. I need someone who would fit in up here as well as London. Otherwise it just wouldn't work. Anyway, all I'm saying is that it's not a real world down there; it's built on air and spirits and silly amounts of money, so you can't expect people to be normal.'

Soon she was telling me stories of prima-donna designers, of fearsome fashion editors and the outrageous behaviour of some of the other models. I was still smiling at her story of the model whose poor assistant had to supply lunch each day of precisely six grapes, two sticks of celery and a red jelly baby, when Matty stifled a yawn.

'Sorry. That bath really is calling me.' She emptied her

glass in one gulp and made for the door. She was just wriggling into her boots when she said, 'Tilly, I know your boyfriend, or ex-boyfriend or semi-detached boyfriend is a journalist, but you won't tell him I'm here, will you? Amazingly, the red-tops have never found their way up here, and I'd like it to stay that way for as long as possible.'

'Of course,' I said. It hadn't even occurred to me. 'Anyway, we're family now, aren't we?'

Matty laughed. 'I guess we are.' She turned to go and then turned back. 'Does Dexter's face really light up when he sees me?'

'It does. Yes.'

She was still smiling as she climbed back into the Land Rover.

Matilda ladled some broth into two small basins and gave one each to the boy and the photographer. The steam rose up, hot from the bowl. It smelt surprisingly good. He seized his spoon.

'For this good food and all thy mercies, we thank you, Lord.' Mrs Allen's voice was low but firm. The photographer felt rebuked. 'Amen.'

'Amen,' he muttered, and tucked into his soup. He drank it gratefully. He wasn't offered, nor did he expect, a second helping.

'So you tramp the countryside taking photographs for a living, do you?'

While the boy drank his broth, Matilda Allen had picked up his knitting and carried on with it, deftly and swiftly slipping the stitches from one needle to the other as she spoke.

'Yes, my card.' Reaching into the pocket of his damp jacket, he took out a slim card-case. He wondered if the

books on the shelf were Mrs Allen's, if she could read. She could.

'Well, William Peart, do many folk want to be pictured in your photographs?'

'Yes, thankfully, or I should earn no living. I send my photographs to London and they arouse much interest in those who would know more about our country and its people but are unable to travel and see it in person.'

The boy spoke up suddenly. 'We have photographs, sir. Of my brothers in America. Can you make pictures like that? How is it done?'

'Shush, James,' said his mother reprovingly. But the photographer smiled. 'I will be happy to explain and to demonstrate. If your mother were willing . . .'

She nodded. 'Yes, I have photographs of two of my sons. For the other I have no need of pictures, as I see him every day. He farms with his uncle, my brother, at the farm below. My brother has no sons of his own to help him. My daughters are in service, one down in London. We have to send our children away to make a living. My other sons worked in the lead mines, but since the Spanish lead has come to be sold so cheap in this country, they have sought better lives in America.' She looked bleak for a moment. 'They went with their cousins and it was a long voyage and William only sixteen.' But her face brightened. 'And now they have been building a new mine near a river as big as the sea, the Mississippi, they call it. Miles has charge of a new smelter and they sent me pictures to show that they have arrived and are making something of themselves. It is reassuring, as I doubt I will see them again in this world.'

'It would be reassuring for them perhaps to have a photograph of their mother looking well. If you were to

119

*let me photograph you, I would give you a print or two
that you could send to the Mississippi . . .'*

'Perhaps, Mr Peart, perhaps,' said Matilda Allen as
she carried on knitting.

Chapter Twelve

I was at The Miners' Arms so early the next morning that Dexter was still on his knees doing the fires, his trademark baggy jumper even grubbier than usual. He looked up from his labours and gave me a sudden, wonderful smile. I smiled back, laughing at myself about how I thought he had been gay and Matt had been a bloke.

'Hey Dexter,' I said, 'why didn't you let on when I was rabbiting on about Foxy being missing? You might have said something!'

'Ah well, that's our little local secret, only revealed to a privileged few. Mainly those who have known her since she was a cheeky little tomboy, running so fast that the lads couldn't catch her. All long legs and ponytail, that one. Then she grew up. Beauty, brains and determination. It's a helluva combination.' He looked miles away for a moment. 'So you've met our famous supermodel now, have you?'

'More than that. We're cousins.'

'*Everyone*'s cousins round here,' said Dexter, screwing up pages of the *Hexham Courant* and piling sticks on top ready for a new fire. 'But she's done well, has Matty. At one time you know she wanted to be a photographer herself.'

'Mmm, I know, she told me. Still does.'

'Told you that, did she?'

'Yes. And how you gave her her first camera and how she used to follow you around.'

'Yes, well,' said Dexter, standing up with the bucket of ash in his hand, the smile gone from his face. 'That was a few years ago now. A lot's happened since then. And she's got better things to do than follow *me* around.'

'She was saying you'd taught her everything she knows.'

'Did she indeed? I wish! No. Matty Alderson has moved a long way from our world now. Out of our league. Out of mine anyway. Lives in the stratosphere now, does Matt. I've seen it. I know what goes on.' He sounded unexpectedly sad, bitter even.

'But she still wants to come back,' I said. 'Still puts her work clothes on and helps out on the farm.'

'Oh aye, playing at it a bit. Like Marie Antoinette dressing up as a shepherdess and just as real. It's all right doing it when you know you can go back to London and earn thousands a day. That's just playing.'

I thought of Matty striding across the fellside with a bale of hay for the sheep, bouncing down on the quad bike in the hailstorm, or doing whatever unspeakable things she said she'd been doing with the rams. Didn't seem much like playing to me.

'I think she belongs here. Like you do. You both had to go away for work, but you came back. You've come back for the pub and Matty comes back because she's happy here . . .'

'But she won't come back here for long,' said Dexter. 'Nothing could bring her back here. She'll find some rich man and that'll be it. We've lost her.' He fell into a gloomy silence. He had, I noticed, tiny flecks of grey in his mad curls.

But, more immediately, I was still wondering how on earth I'd managed to confuse the stunning Foxy with a bloke. I mean, she was one of the most photographed women in the country, and just because she wore old jeans and a tatty Barbour, I decided she was a man. I wondered, quite seriously, if I needed specs. I hadn't dared tell Polly yet. She'd think I'd totally lost it.

Becca was meant to be polishing the tables but she had the papers spread out on the bar and was studying them intently. She lifted her eyes up for a moment. 'Did you really not know you were related to Matty Alderson?' she asked, astonished.

'No. Our families lost touch ages ago. Mum would never have realised that Foxy's real name was Matty Alderson. If she had, then she'd have probably made the connection.'

'No. Matt likes to keep that quiet. It gives her some sort of privacy, I suppose.'

'But how has she managed to keep it secret? I'd have thought it would have been great PR for her – shepherd as model and all that. The papers would love it. They'd be up here like a shot to get pics of her up on the fellside, with the sheep, striding off with bales of hay . . .'

'Then it wouldn't be somewhere she could escape to, would it? If people started coming up here to gawp?' Becca shuddered. 'That would be terrible.'

'But how come no one's told the papers?'

'Because the people who know her, know she'd hate it,' said Becca simply. 'Anyway, if you're related to Matt, then it probably means you're related to me too. I think the Aldersons are some sort of cousins of my mum's. Or is it my dad's? No matter.' She had lost interest in genealogy and was looking again at the newspapers. 'Look at these. Here're pictures of Alessandro and Clayton at last night's match. Don't they look gorgeous?' She pushed the paper towards me.

Both men were caught mid-air, Alessandro's long hair

whipping round his head and his normally rounded baby face looking fierce instead. Clayton was at full stretch, his face a grimace of determination and his legs a knot of muscles.

'Look a bit different from when they were in here, don't they?' I said, as noncommittally as I could. 'Do you know if Alessandro liked the scarf? Did he get it all right?'

'I expect so. I haven't heard anything,' said Becca, and went reluctantly back to polishing tables.

'I meant to ask you,' I said, 'could you make a scarf for my mum? She'd love one – especially if she knew it was made up here.'

'Yes, of course, no problem,' said Becca. 'Any particular colours?'

'Well, she wears a lot of black – lots and lots of black, so I guess that would have to be the base, or it would just be a waste of time, she wouldn't wear it. But if you could make all the embroidery and embellishments as bright and cheerful as possible? That would be good. And tell you what . . .' I dug deep down into the pocket of my jacket. 'Could you manage to work this bit of ribbon into it somewhere for me?'

I handed Becca the piece of cherry-red velvet I'd found on the tree. She turned it over in her hand and, just like I had done, stroked it. 'Lovely colour,' she said. 'Wonderful texture. Is that all you've got?'

'Yes, I just found it up on the moor and it seems too pretty to waste.'

Becca put the ribbon carefully into her big knitting bag under the counter and went back to looking at pictures of footballers.

I couldn't say anything about that because I went straight to the computer and, before I did anything else, I Googled Clayton Silver. It was all there, the story of his life in different interviews, the single mother, the rough estate, the bunking off school. There was a nice piece about when he got his GCSE results. He looked so proud and so young. It was when he was at his first club and he still had a terrible haircut, before he'd got that gloss that being rich and famous gives you. There was an approving comment piece by one of those smug middle-class lady columnists, saying what a great example it was when people like Clayton Silver made education cool. Far better than any government initiative. But she was right. I felt sort of proud of him too.

Dimly, I heard the beep of a mobile phone in the bar and could hear Becca talking. Her voice sounded surprised and then breathy with excitement, until finally I heard her say, 'Well, yes, fine, seven then. See you there,' as if she were restraining a whoop of delight.

She came rushing round the corner to me and gabbled, 'That was Alessandro. There's a big football charity dinner in Newcastle tonight. He and some other players are flying up. He wants me to go with him! Tonight! Newcastle! He's just rung. He's sending a car! Oh, I can't believe it.'

She was standing there, her eyes shining with excitement, still clutching her phone and the cloth with which she'd been wiping the tables. With that, my phone rang too.

'Hello, Miss Freshface. What you doing this evening . . . ?'

The bright lights of the hotel reflected on the Tyne and the massive single arch of the Millennium Bridge gleamed silver as Becca and I peered out from the huge four-by-four with its tinted windows as it edged its way through the crowds of revellers on the quayside. If it was like that midweek, what must it be like on a Friday night? Our driver – a taciturn Cockney called Tony who'd barely said a word since he'd picked us up – stopped the car right in front of the entrance and leapt out to open the door for us. Some of the waiting crowd stared in our direction.

'They must think we're someone important,' giggled Becca, as she sashayed into the hotel entrance with great aplomb.

I had not wanted to go to this dinner. Not at all. Mainly because Clayton Silver was so damn sure that I would. Yes, I know that I'd had a very pleasant lunch with him, but that was different, a one-off. He couldn't think that I would come running every time he snapped his fingers or dangled the chance of a free meal in front of me.

I did not need free meals. I did not need famous footballers. Most of all, I did not need Clayton Silver and his ridiculous self-assurance. I wasn't some silly little groupie or wannabe-WAG, dazzled by him. I had my own life, thank you. And I told him all that. Quite firmly. He just laughed.

'Miss Tilly, this is for charity. You'd be keeping me company and helping me support a really good cause. And I know you're just too nice not to do that. So I'll send a car. It will be at the pub at seven. You want to help a charity, don't you?' And he was still laughing as he ended the call, not giving me time to refuse.

So here I was, arriving at a glitzy Newcastle hotel to join him for an evening. What could I be thinking of?

As soon as I told Becca that Clayton had invited me, she took it as a done deal that we were going together.

'But I don't want to go!' I said. 'I don't want to be one of Clayton Silver's groupies!'

'But it might be fun,' said Becca, 'and if you don't go, I don't want to go by myself. And—'

'Oh, all right,' I said, finally, with bad grace, feeling as if I were back in primary school and being pressurised by my best friend. 'But I haven't got anything to wear. I've only got work clothes and jeans. I wasn't expecting to be going to fancy dinners.'

'We can sort that. Easy! I'll help you.'

I couldn't let her down. I was only going to keep her company, right?

I nearly changed my mind again. We had spent most of the afternoon getting ready. I'd abandoned work. Becca had rung one of the other barmaids to cover her shift, though as Becca was gabbling hopelessly on the phone, I'm sure Jan had no idea why. Probably thought Becca had finally flipped. I'd had to dash down to the little shop that sold Becca's scarves to buy myself a dress and shoes. Amazingly, the dress was easy to find – a very simple silk shift in a deep, dark green that looked quite ordinary on the hanger but surprisingly good on me. I couldn't believe my luck. That ran out with the shoes: in the tiny shop I had been given the choice of precisely two pairs in my size – and I thought longingly of all the shoes I had back in London – but they would have to do, I thought as I keyed in my credit card PIN. No time for anything better. Clayton might call me Miss Freshface, but I don't think he'd be too impressed if I'd landed here in my hiking boots.

So here we were. One of the doormen had already moved very politely to greet us and block our path. We gave our names, both of us suddenly panicking that we might be turned away, that it was all a joke. I hoped not, because Becca was so excited. At least this time, I'd brought phone, money and a credit card with me. I might get stood up but I wasn't going to be stranded.

The bouncer glanced at his clipboard, bowed slightly and waved us in. The doors opened and another flunkey ushered us up a grand curved staircase. As we made our way care-fully – especially me in my new shoes – up the stairs, I wondered what we would do when we got to the top. Along the balcony I could see a gathering of men in dinner jackets and lots of glamorous-looking women. They gazed down at us for a second then, clearly deciding we were of no interest, looked away again.

Suddenly, there, at the top of the stairs, grinning, were Clayton and Alessandro, both of them looking elegant in dinner jackets and startlingly white shirts. 'Good evening, ladies,' said Clayton, bowing elaborately, kissing me, then Becca. Alessandro bowed and kissed us both too. 'Tony called to say he'd delivered you.'

Yeah, like a parcel.

Clayton stepped back for a moment and looked me up and down. 'Wow, you scrub up well,' he grinned. I glared at him.

'I'm only here to keep Becca company,' I said, stiffly.

'Well,' replied Clayton with a very serious face, 'that's extremely kind of you. I hope you won't suffer too much. I'll do my best to try and make it bearable.' With that, he passed me a glass of champagne from the tray of a hovering waiter and led me to the banqueting room.

The evening was in aid of a cancer charity. The wife of Ted Blake, a local footballer, had died when only thirty years old, leaving him a widower with three young children. After a year out of the game he had returned as a successful player, then manager, brought up his children and raised millions for research into the illness that had killed his wife. Now, ten years on, he was on the verge of marrying again and this was possibly his final grand fundraising event. He was mingling with the guests, working the crowd, shaking hands, greeting people, laughing. 'I'm warning you all, I hope you've got your wallets and chequebooks handy because tonight you're going to need them!'

The crowd was full of footballers' faces that I vaguely knew, and a lot of older faces that I recognised from television, though it was harder to recognise them in real life and posh clothes, and they all looked smaller than they did on television. There was a scattering of stunning girls too. Tanned and toned in designer dresses and shoes so high I'm amazed they could walk in them. I felt suddenly very drab in my hurriedly bought outfit. Clayton caught me looking enviously as one girl with a sheet of long blonde hair and a tiny sequinned dress sashayed past in heels at least five inches high. He grinned. 'Can't see her walking along no moors in those,' he whispered.

But I had nothing to prove. Whether Clayton really wanted me there or not didn't matter a fig. I might not have my favourite outfit on, but I looked perfectly respectable. It was another new experience, another small adventure. I could sit back and enjoy it.

I even managed to smile at one of the cameramen, several of whom were wandering round the room. The pictures they took immediately appeared on a huge screen above the stage. I appeared briefly, smiling, and not looking too bad. It made me smile even more. Clayton leant towards me and pointed at the camera and I could see it at the same time on the vast screen. It made it strangely unreal. Then the cameras cut to some of the glamorous girls who flashed enormous smiles and impressive cleavages.

We were being ushered to our table. My place card said merely, 'Guest of Clayton Silver,' and I wondered why he had asked me and not brought along one of his many London girlfriends. Still, I was here now, and I might as well make the most of it. On my other side I had Bert, a retired football manager, whom I also recognised from television. He was famous as being a bluff, no-nonsense northerner. His wife Joan was kind and motherly. She decided that Becca looked just like her granddaughter. 'Eeh, you're just like our Kim,' she kept saying, and treated her with kindly interest, and kept asking Alessandro if he was homesick.

Ted Blake stood up and welcomed us all, said that everyone there tonight had given their services for free. 'There'll be many opportunities for you to give money tonight,' he said, 'I hope you make the most of them.'

It was an amazing evening. Even before the first course we had a short set from a top girl band, the members of which then went round selling raffle tickets at a tenner each. The MC was a top-rated comedian who kept popping up with more jokes and cajoling us to spend, spend, spend. I went to buy a raffle ticket from one of the girls, but Clayton put his hand on mine as I reached for my bag. 'No you don't, girl, this is my treat,' he said, and peeled off £100 from the bundle of notes in his wallet and then put the raffle tickets on the table in front of me. I glared at him, picked up the tickets and plonked them right back in front of him. Then I waved the girl back, got out my purse and bought some tickets myself.

'I can do my own charity-giving, thank you,' I said to Clayton, who looked surprised but laughed.

Most of the time the conversation ranged across the table and centred on football, on players, league rankings, contentious refereeing decisions. But all the time, in between, almost protected by the surrounding noise, Clayton and I were having our own private conversation too.

'I'm glad you could come,' he said, as he took a sip of his Merlot. 'I know phones don't work where you're staying: it's like a Bermuda triangle up there, isn't it? I thought I wouldn't find you. But I'm glad I did.'

'I thought you'd have plenty of people you could ask,' I said, swallowing the suggestion that he might have given me a little more warning.

'Yeah, well, London girls don't travel too well. They need at least three days to get ready.'

I thought for a moment. It clearly meant I was not in the same class as the girls I'd seen him with in the club. I didn't need it to be underlined.

'Well, you're wrong. I'm a London girl, born and bred.'

'No you're not,' he smiled. 'You belong on those moors, all clean and outdoorsy. Or in the pub eating sausages with grease on your chin.'

Instinctively I put my hand up to my chin and then laughed at myself and he kissed the top of my head. Patronizing smoothie.

But Joan, my grandmotherly neighbour, smiled approvingly. 'Nice to see the young ones at an event like this. Not many of them can be bothered. And it's such a good cause. Have you two been courting long, pet?' she asked as we set about our trio of salmon starter.

'Oh, we're not courting,' I laughed, loving the old-fashioned phrase. 'I only met him a week ago. Before this we've only had lunch together once. I hardly know him,' I said, keen to put some distance between us.

'Eeh, well, you look just right with each other,' she said, and I took the remark and turned it over and over in my mind, examining it like a present waiting to be opened. Or a bomb waiting to explode.

Between the first and the second course, a very distinguished doctor stood up and spoke briefly of how desperately they needed more money for research. Then the comedian came back and told us that the envelopes in front of us contained forms on which we could make donations. It was a new scheme, he said, to encourage people just to give an hour of their time, or an hour of their wages.

'If I had a Premiership player's salary for an hour, I could live for a month,' he said. 'Instead we could help find a cure for cancer. So what are you waiting for? One hour, lads, come on. If you can't work it out, we're happy to do the sums for you!'

Clayton looked up at the picture of the young mother and her children. He pulled the envelope towards him. 'Guess I'd better put some money in the pot,' he said.

'Good for you!' I said.

'Yeah, I suspect you always do the right thing, Miss Tilly.'

'I wish!' I said. 'But you've got to try, haven't you?'

'Have you? Why?'

'Because, well,' I floundered, and thought of my mum and her endless talks about helping others . . . redressing inequalities . . . the privilege of generosity, etc, etc, etc. 'Well, it makes the world a nicer place, doesn't it?'

Clayton nodded and smiled. 'Yeah. It makes the world a nicer place. That's cool. I like that.'

He took his credit card from his wallet and filled in the form in the envelope. Before he replaced it and sealed the envelope, I leaned over to see how much. The figure filled in said £10,000.

'That's more than an hour's wage, even for you,' I said slowly. Even if he were showing off, he was certainly paying for the privilege. 'That will make the world quite a bit nicer, I think. And maybe let a few more children have their mothers around for longer.'

'I hope so,' said Clayton. He gazed at me for a moment, straight into my eyes, and it was as if the whole room vanished, the noise and the people, the comedian and his prattle, the waiters and waitresses, all faded out. For a moment I felt giddy, struggling, desperately trying to get my feet back on the ground. Then 'Hey Pete!' Clayton said to the footballer sitting opposite him. 'What d'you reckon to that young lad United played last night?' and the conversation returned, inevitably, to football.

On the other side of the table I could see that Alessandro and Becca were getting on very well, their heads, one so blonde, one so dark, bent together talking. Alessandro was busy with one of the heavy paper napkins, folding it this way and that until he had turned it into a rose, which he presented, with an extravagant bow, to Becca.

'That's beautiful!' she said, her face pink and happy as she took it. 'How do you know how to do that?'

'I worked with my uncle in his restaurant. I learnt to do this there,' he said, looking very pleased with himself and not at all like his fierce, determined image in the paper that morning.

'I shall give you real flowers,' he said, 'but for now, this is the only flower I have.'

Bert and Joan beamed approvingly. Not to be outdone, Clayton stretched out and picked one of the freesias from the table decoration and presented it to me.

'For you, Miss Tilly.'

'Oh, don't be daft,' I said, putting the dripping flower back in the vase. 'It'll only die. Let it stay in the vase where we can all enjoy it.'

As the meal went on, everything became more relaxed. People were wandering about the room. Many people stopped at our table to talk to Clayton. Other footballers came whooping up, giving high fives. A couple of people asked for his autograph, for their children. Clayton obliged cheerfully. It was getting warm. We seemed to have eaten and drunk so much already. The comedian announced that the auction would start in twenty minutes. A gay group, famous for singing outrageous lyrics, were doing a set in the foyer outside. A brigade of waiters and waitresses swept in to clear the tables.

Clayton took my hand. 'Let's get some fresh air,' he said, and led me out into the foyer, past the band and towards

133

a glass-covered balcony that seemed to hang over the river. It was cooler there and blissfully quiet. Just us and the lights on the water.

'You were very generous with your donation in there,' I said.

'Yeah, well. Bad enough to grow up without a dad, even worse without a mum, even a mum like mine,' he said. 'And we all know I ain't earning the minimum wage,' he laughed.

'What will you do,' I blurted out, 'when you don't play football any more?'

'Hey, that's a big question, a very big question,' he said, gazing out at the water. 'Maybe do my coaching badges. Maybe television. Maybe just enjoy being rich. There's this man does my money for me. Tells me what do with it. 'Cept I keep buying wine with it. And pictures.'

'Pictures?'

'You know I didn't think I knew anything about art, but there's this Celia, she works with the man who looks after my money, she took me to a gallery and said I didn't have to *know* anything about art, just see if I liked anything.'

'And did you?'

'Yeah,' he said dreamily, 'yeah I did. I bought an Iolo John painting. Huge it is, just blue and white and green, but it sort of looks a bit like the sea, a bit like the sky. I don't know. Just a lot of clean space. Like being in the air.'

I nodded. 'I saw some of his paintings at the Royal Academy last year. After all the installation-type pieces of blood and bottles and dead cows, you can actually get what he's on about. They're beautiful.'

'The money-man reckons it's a good investment. But I just like it on my wall.'

'I'm sure it's fantastic.'

'You can see it when you come round.'

I stayed very calm. 'Oh. I'm coming round, am I?'

'I hope so, Miss Tilly. It would be nice if you did.' And he leant forwards, took my face in his hands and kissed me. He smelt of wine and coffee and a wonderfully citrus cologne. I surfaced, blinking.

'Gosh,' I said. Clayton hooted with laughter.

'You are *so* not like any other woman I know,' he said. And kissed me again. Then took my hand and led me back into the banqueting suite where we were the last to return to our table. As we wriggled our way back into our seats, Becca grinned at me, and my grandmotherly neighbour smiled indulgently. The auction was about to start.

This was a serious event. The auctioneer – a sports presenter – could really do his stuff. He started with auto-graphed football shirts which local businessmen paid up to £500 for, and was moving on through such delights as a hot-air balloon ride, a spa weekend, a week in a Tuscan farmhouse, the last going for £10,000.

'Lot Fifteen, a silver and amber necklace, specially designed and donated by top jeweller Theodore Bukala. "*Rectangular silver links interspersed with polished amber in an unusual modern setting,*" it says here. "*Striking and elegant with an intriguing contemporary simplicity.*" Who's going to start me off? A thousand pounds anyone. Yes, to you sir . . . Fifteen hundred, anyone giving fifteen hundred?'

Becca and I looked on amazed as the bidding rose quickly to £10,000, then more slowly to £15,000. 'Any more?' asked the auctioneer. 'It really is a lovely piece, absolutely unique – and all for such a good cause. Any more?'

With that, Clayton casually lifted his menu card and the bidding was on again. It was between him and a player from Man United and Becca and I could barely dare to look as the bidding rose over £15,000, then £20,000, and finally up to £25,000. Then the other player's girlfriend must have decided that £25,000 was enough because I could see her put her hand on the man's arm and he shook his head at the auctioneer.

'Twenty-five thousand one hundred,' said the auctioneer. 'I think that's our final bid. Any more? Any more?' He looked round the room in the silence. 'Going, going . . .' And then brought the gavel down with a short sharp rap. 'Twenty-five thousand one hundred to Mr Clayton Silver.' And he moved on quickly to the hire of a small yacht currently moored in the Mediterranean.

Just as the bidding finished, a waiter appeared with a tray of brandies.

'I think we need those,' said Bert. 'Here, lad,' he said to Clayton, 'you'd better have a couple of these, the amount you've spent tonight.'

Clayton looked relaxed as he downed the brandy and a man appeared with a portable card payment machine. Clayton paid up and the man produced the box. The necklace was beautiful. As the man said, it was simple and elegant, the amber small, smooth and polished. It was absolutely beautiful.

'So that's twenty-five grand's worth, is it?' said Clayton. He lifted the necklace out of its presentation box.

He stood up, came behind me, and carefully fastened the necklace round my neck.

Joan clapped her hands in glee and excitement. 'And you've only known him a week, pet! Not bad going for a week!' she laughed.

I blushed bright red and looked round at Clayton. 'Oh no. I'm only trying it on,' I explained. 'It's not for me.'

'Yes it is,' said Clayton. 'Who else am I going to buy it for? Begging your pardon . . .' as he grinned at Joan.

'But surely . . . there must be . . .' I was stunned. I had never in my life even tried on anything costing £25,000, let alone been given something.

'I bought it for you,' said Clayton, quietly, looking at me. 'I wasn't thinking of anyone else. And very good it looks too.' Then he laughed. 'And worth it just to see you going pink again.'

I don't really remember much after that. There were a few more speeches. A lot more drink. A lot of cheering. By now I was leaning right back against Clayton, comfortable, at ease. Becca and Alessandro had disappeared, I noticed.

'Well, that's me done, my dear,' said Joan, getting up from her seat. 'I'm off to my bed.'

'Are you staying here?'

'Yes, aren't you?'

'I'm not sure.'

In fact I had no idea what was happening later. The elderly lady patted my shoulder as Clayton talked to her husband.

'Good luck, pet,' she said. 'But just remember, footballers aren't like other people. They're a funny breed. They don't live in the same world as the rest of us. And I should know, I've been married to one for more than forty years. And they're a lot stranger now than they were when our Bert started out.'

With that she took her husband's arm and walked out of the room.

A red-faced man came bustling importantly up to Clayton. 'We leave for the airport in five minutes. Where's Sandro?'

'Around somewhere,' said Clayton vaguely. 'Can't be far.'

He pulled me gently to my feet. 'Come on,' he said. He got out his mobile, sent a text and then rang Alessandro.

'Time to go,' he said. 'See you downstairs in five minutes.'

Then he put his arms round me, brushed a wisp of hair from my eyes and said, 'Sorry we've got to go, sweetheart, I've got training tomorrow and the plane's waiting. Tony'll be downstairs to take you home when you're ready. It's been really good to see you. I'll see you again soon?'

'But . . .' It didn't seem right that the evening should end like this; that we were going home separately. Especially as I was wearing the amazing necklace.

The red-faced man came stomping back. 'Clayton, it's time to go!'

Clayton whispered to me. 'He reports right back to our boss man. Any problems and – wow, do we hear about it. So I've got to go, gorgeous. See you soon, yeah?' He kissed me again and went off with the red-faced man.

I was left on my own, wearing a necklace that had cost £25,000. I stroked it as I walked down that huge staircase.

Downstairs, Becca was already waiting. Outside, the black four-by-four swept up and Tony leapt out to open the door. Becca and I climbed in.

'Did this really happen?' she asked, still clutching the rose Alessandro had made for her as we slumped in the back of the car and it raced down the A1. 'Did all that really happen?'

'I think so,' I replied, though actually I too found it tricky to believe. But as the car sped down the motorway, and Becca chatted breathlessly about Sandro, I could feel the weight of the necklace on my throat and I could remember the way Clayton had looked into my eyes.

The rain had stopped and a clear watery light filled the dale. Perfect for photographs. Matilda Allen had insisted first on being photographed seated with her Bible. That was the reminder she wanted to send to her children. But then Peart persuaded her to stand as he had first seen her, in her garden with her shawl round her head, a background of fellside and stone. A fine, strong woman.

'Your husband . . . ?' he asked tentatively.

'Killed in the mine eight year ago.'

'I'm sorry . . .' But he wondered how such a woman had never married again. Not for want of asking, he suspected.

'My wife too,' he said, 'ten years now. And our baby daughter with her.'

She flashed him a look.

'Then we've both known loss, Mr Peart. And learnt to endure it.'

Chapter Thirteen

As soon as I woke up, I put the necklace on again, scarcely able to believe that Clayton Silver had given it to me and fastened it round my neck. It looked particularly fetching with my pyjamas as I made my first pot of coffee of the day, my hair like a scarecrow's and my mascara giving me panda eyes.

But, even through the slightly fuzzy thinking after too much wine the night before, one thing was clear. I couldn't keep it. I just couldn't. Twenty-five thousand pounds' worth of necklace? What would Granny Allen say? What would my mother say, come to that? It was beautiful, but definitely not for me. Suddenly it seemed to be burning my skin. What could I have been thinking of? What did he expect in return? How much had I had to drink? Quickly, I took it off and tucked it carefully into its velvet-lined box.

I would ring him, thank him and sort it all out. But first. I had to get to a phone. Living up here didn't exactly make for spontaneous action. Tony had brought me back right to the cottage, splashing disdainfully through the ford. So the van was still at the pub. I tucked the box into my bag in the wardrobe. And, after a quick shower, and dressed in jeans and boots, I set off down the track.

Matty was in the farmyard talking to the driver of a milk tanker. When they saw me, the driver waved genially as he pulled out of the yard and Matty walked over to me. With her hair in a single long plait over her shoulder and no make-up it just emphasised the natural flawlessness of her skin.

'No van?' she asked. 'Has it packed up already?'

'No,' I said, 'but last night . . .' and I told her the whole story, about Clayton and the dinner and the auction and the necklace.

'Twenty-five thousand pounds! Just like that. And then he gave it to me – just as if it was the paper flowers from the napkin.'

'Flash bastard,' said Matt, seriously unimpressed. Her reaction was just what I needed to bring me down to earth. 'Let's face it, twenty-five thousand isn't much more than a day's wages for someone like Clayton Silver. Still, very clever. Makes him look good. I bet his generosity "accidentally" gets leaked to the press. But at least it made some money for a good cause.'

I nodded miserably.

She looked at me sharply. 'You're not keeping the necklace, are you?'

'No!' I said. 'That's why I'm going to the pub now. I want to ring him, tell him so.'

'Good,' said Matt. 'Bad enough that he can act big without you going all girly and grateful on him. Just remember, those footballers like to show off, throw their money around. They lose that much on a game of cards on an average evening. More money than brains, that's for sure. Anyway, do you want a lift to the pub? I've got to go down to the village.'

'Great, thanks. I don't mind walking but I have a lot to do and the sooner I talk to Clayton the better.'

As we rattled down the road to the pub, Matt said, 'I'm flying out to Egypt tomorrow.' She looked almost hungrily out as shadows of clouds scudded over the short grey grass. 'I guess the weather will be a bit different from here.'

'Very glamorous,' I said.

Matt snorted. 'You're joking! The hotel will be fine – when we're there, which won't be much. But out on the shoot it will be hot, dusty, everything covered in flies. Like the time we were shooting in Marrakech and I was trying to look cool and mysterious while mosquitoes were biting my ankles.'

'Is it really that awful?'

'No, of course not. And I get paid silly money. It's a whole lot easier than Mum and Dad's life, where they have to get up at dawn, day in, day out. When you have animals to look after you can't get sick or take a day off or just snuggle back under the duvet when you want to. I can just wear a few clothes and a daft expression. If I ever feel hard done by I remember the winter we all had flu and it snowed. Getting out of bed in the dark and the icy cold when your legs are like cotton wool and you can hardly lift your head and you have to go outside and see to the animals and there's a gale-force wind and the sleet is driving into your face – now *that*'s what I call hard work.'

I tried to imagine it. I couldn't.

'But what would you *really* like to do?'

'I don't know. I love the buzz of London and there's so many opportunities . . . but the more I'm away from this place, the more I miss it, the more I feel I belong here.'

'Like Dexter, I suppose,' I said. 'I mean, he could have sold the house, and not bothered to turn it back into a pub. But something brought him back.'

'Yes, it did, didn't it?' said Matt thoughtfully. She was silent for a moment then continued, 'I'd really like to share my time between both places I guess – not farming, I'll leave that to the rest of them. But I'd like to find a way of living and working up here. Of keeping the farm going so it will be here for always – well, for as long as any of the family want to farm it. Anyway,' she shrugged, 'I might not be flavour of the month for much longer, so I'll make the most of it till then. What about you?'

'Oh well, once I've finished all the interviews I've got lined up I'll have to go back to London too. Sort out my life.' I wasn't sure myself if I was pleased or not to be going back. This was turning out to be a nice little holiday, a small escape from reality. 'It seems a shame to leave all this. I know I'm a townie really, but I'll definitely be back.'

Now I'd found this place I wanted to keep a bit of it for me. It was, after all, the place that had given me that wonderful sense of freedom.

As Matty pulled the Land Rover into the pub car park we could see Dexter in the yard at the back splitting logs. He swung the huge axe effortlessly and added to the pile of neatly quartered logs piled up in the basket beside him. He looked up.

'Well hello! I wasn't expecting you back today. Thought you'd still be gallivanting with the rich and famous. And talking of the rich and famous, hello, Matt.' He smiled at her. She leaned out of the Land Rover window and smiled back, surprisingly shyly. The two of them stared at each other so awkwardly that I couldn't work out what was wrong.

'Coming in?' asked Dexter.

'Why not?' said Matty, and jumped neatly down from the vehicle.

Jan was on today. 'So Becca not back from your Newcastle adventures yet?' asked Matty.

'Yes, she's just on a day off. We came back last night.'

'You mean your famous footballers didn't expect you to stay the night with them? I'd have thought Silver would

143

have expected something for his twenty-five thousand,' Matt was saying wryly as Jan bustled off to clean some tables.

'No. No, he didn't. It was a bit odd really. They weren't staying; they all had to fly back to London.'

'You got away lightly, then.'

There was a rumble as Dexter unloaded the logs into the basket by the fire. 'So you two are long-lost cousins, are you?' he asked, gazing at Matt.

'Yes, thanks to Granny Allen, of course,' said Matt, glancing up at him and then looking quickly away.

'Ah, talking of which,' said Dexter, suddenly sounding nervous. 'I have an idea for a new project. Come and look at these for a moment. See what you think.' He hurried us over to the high-backed wooden settle at the far side of the bar. The seat was covered with photographs, many very old. Stern portraits, serious wedding groups, many looking very Granny Allen-ish, as well as some of miners, farmers, a wonderful postman with extravagant whiskers. 'These are all people from the dale, mainly in Victorian times.'

'Where did you get all these from?' I asked, intrigued.

'Oh, there were a few photographers working in the dales in the nineteenth century. The Victorians were very big on finding out how strange savages lived – and they thought the frozen north was pretty much the edge of the known world. So there's quite a lot of old pictures about. Some of these are mine already. Others are from neighbours. But some – and this is what gave me the idea – some I've copied from the people who come here doing their family history. These are their great-great-great-grandparents. They've brought the photos with them when they come to see where Granddad lived.

'When you look at the old pictures and then at the modern people, it's very interesting.' Dexter was getting really enthusiastic. 'It's amazing how often there's still a family resemblance. Sometimes the interest is in the sheer contrast – one of these weather-lined faces compared with her pretty, pampered descendant. But see that one . . .' He picked up a faded photo of an old farmer in heavy tweed suit and waistcoat with a proud expression standing by a pair of plough horses. 'Well, his grandson came back here. He came with *his* grandson who'd driven him. The lad was only about twenty but he stood outside by his car, one of those posh Minis, and the expression on his face was exactly the same as this chap in the photo with his horses.

'So I thought, wouldn't it be interesting to do photos of the modern people in the same places or the same poses as their ancestors? It would really show up the contrasts and the similarities. And it would sort of finish the story, too, wouldn't it? – all those people who left the dale. We'd know what became of them. Well, some of them. What do you think?' He looked anxiously at us both, but especially at Matty.

'I think it's a *brilliant* idea!' said Matt, as she looked at the pictures and then beamed at Dexter. 'It's pictures, people, history, a sense of place; it's stories, it's everything!' She was laughing with enthusiasm and approval. 'Can I be in it? With Mum and Granny Allen?'

'Yes please,' said Dexter, smiling happily now that we – or rather Matt – had given such approval. 'I hoped you would be.' Soon the two of them were busy sorting through the photographs, talking excitedly. 'That's Pete Metcalfe's granddad – I've seen the picture in their house . . . What a wonderful head. Oh, she's lovely, who's she? Now that *must* be an Allen . . .'

It wasn't that they were ignoring me; it was just that they had completely forgotten I was there. I left them to it and disappeared into the snug with my phone to send a text to Clayton. 'Thank you for a fantastic evening . . .' No,

145

'fantastic' sounded a bit extravagant. 'Thank you for an excellent evening.' Still a bit grovelling. 'Thank you for a good evening.' That was the right tone – polite but not carried away, 'and for organizing a lift home.'

So what do I say about the necklace? 'Thanks but no thanks'? Er, no. I stared at the screen so long it went black, so I clicked it back on and texted quickly. 'Necklace amazing but need to talk to you about it.' And sent the message straightaway, before I had time to think about it further.

Immediately, the phone rang and my insides lurched nervously. Could Clayton reply so immediately?

'Hi, Jake,' I said, carefully keeping my voice neutral.

'Sorry, battery's going so I'll be quick,' he said. 'I'm going back down to London tomorrow. I thought I'd ask if you want to come with me?'

'No, thank you,' I said without a moment's hesitation. 'I'm not ready to go back yet. I'm staying on for a week or so. I have a few more interviews lined up.'

'Fine.' His tone was chilly but I was just happy that it wasn't my problem now.

'So, thank you for the offer, Jake, I appreciate it, but I shall make my own way back to London, thank you.'

'You're sure?'

'Positive.'

'Right, I'll see you back down there then.'

'Possibly. Goodbye, Jake.

'Oh and Tilly,' he said, just as my finger was about to press End call. Reluctantly I lifted the phone back to my ear.

'Remember that model you somehow "forgot" to tell me about? The one who jumped through the loo window at the club?'

'What about her?' I asked, already beginning to panic at what he was going to say.

'Well, a couple of the red-tops have tracked her down. Her real name's apparently Matilda and she's from this part of the world. Some farm near here somewhere. So thank you very much, Tilly. If you'd told me sooner, I might have found her first, which could have been very useful to my career. But too late now. Anyway, goodbye, Tilly.'

The phone went dead and I sat staring at it, horrified. The paparazzi knew Matty's name and roughly where she lived. Hartstone Edge was her bolthole, her escape from the world. How could it ever be that again if the press knew where she was? I looked across the bar, where she and Dexter were still enthusing over the pictures. I had to tell her . . .

'Matty . . .' She looked up, her eyes still sparkling over something Dexter had said. Then she noticed my expression. 'What is it?'

'The press know where you are. They know your name and that you live somewhere near Hartstone. Jake, my boyfriend – ex-boyfriend – just told me.'

'You mean *you* told *him!*' snapped Dexter, his expression suddenly terrifying. 'All the time you've been on the computer here or on your mobile, that's what you've been up to.'

'No, no. Absolutely not,' I said, frightened of this furious Dexter.

Matty looked at me, her expression frozen. 'How else did they find out?'

'I don't know. Jake just said that they knew. He was angry that he hadn't found out first. I didn't tell him. Honestly. I wouldn't. Ever.'

'You didn't? Not even a hint? You're sure?' Matty was glaring at me.

'Absolutely. Not even the faintest whisper. Anyway, I've hardly even spoken to him since I found out.'

'Well, it doesn't matter how they found out, what's

147

important is that they have.' She slumped down on one of the benches, her hands stuck into her jacket pockets and her long legs tucked under her, looking utterly miserable. 'It was only a matter of time, I suppose. I was lucky to have got away with it for so long. I don't mind it in London, but not here . . . Oh God, they'll be all over the place, getting in the way of Mum and Dad. Trying to get secrets out of folk. It'll be good for business, Dexter, but hopeless for everyone else. Awful. And I'm off to Egypt tomorrow. So they won't even get any pictures of me anyway.'

With that my phone rang again. I turned my attention to it, glad to get away from Matty's misery. Not Jake this time. Not Clayton Silver. Instead it was Penny, my mother's PA.

'Hi, Tilly. Penny here. Nothing to worry about, but I know your ma won't tell you, and she's had a bit of an accident. Courier came off his bike and crashed right into her. She fell awkwardly and has a broken ankle and a twisted knee, and is a bit bashed and bruised.'

'Oh God, Penny. Is she all right?'

'Nothing too serious, but she'll be out of action for a time. She's been to Casualty and I've taken her back to the flat. Inez, her cleaning lady, is with her and has volunteered to stay with her for the rest of the day. I'll sort her out with shopping and things and see that she's OK. She told me not to tell you, but sometimes not even your mother can be right all the time and I thought you'd want to know.'

'Of course. Thank you for telling me. Thank you for what you've done for her,' I said, trying to think straight, concern for my mother completely driving out what Dexter was saying to Matty.

'She was a bit shaken up by it all, as you can understand,' continued Penny. 'But now she's back into overdrive mode, insisting that she can carry on working and we're not to fuss. You know what she's like.' I did. Only too well.

148

'Penny, I'll be back in London as soon as I can, late tonight probably. If needs be, I can cancel interviews for next week.'

'She'll probably be fine by tomorrow – apart from the broken bones, of course – but I think it would be good if you could pop round.'

'I will.'

I rang Mum immediately.

'So are you finished up north? Aren't you due home this weekend?'

'Yes and no,' I said. 'There's lots to tell you and I'm actually staying on for a few more weeks.'

'Oh.' There was a pause and then, 'Well, that's very good. I'm glad it's going so well.'

'But I have to come back for a few days, to sort things out, so I'll be round late tonight, depending on when I can get a train. I'll ring you en route,' I said. And my mother – fierce, independent Frankie Flint – actually sounded relieved.

'That's wonderful, darling,' she said, and really seemed to mean it. For once my mother seemed to need me. It was an odd feeling.

I ended the call and told Matty and Dexter what had happened. They went through the motions of being concerned. They said all the right things. And I *think* they believed I had nothing to do with Matty being tracked down. But they were preoccupied. As I went on the computer to check train times, I could hear them still talking about it.

And then, just as I went out to get PIP to get back to the cottage and pack, I heard Dexter ask Matty, 'What time do you leave for Egypt tomorrow?'

'Early afternoon. Why?'

'Just enough time. I've got an idea.'

149

'You're back, then,' said Matilda Allen. The sun was shining and for once there was no wind blowing through the dale. The photographer fanned his face with his hat. Mrs Allen was in her garden hoeing cabbages. He was amazed that anything grew in such thin soil, and understood the complicated arrangements of bushes and boarding that protected the vegetable beds from the usual blasts.

Mrs Allen's weathered face looked rosy in the sun. It had also turned some strands of her hair to silver and gold, so she seemed surrounded by a halo of light. She didn't pause in her work as she talked, making her way efficiently along the rows of young plants. William Peart thought briefly of his late wife. In truth, he could scarcely remember her. She had been as pretty and delicate as a doll when he first knew her. Then the prettiness faded. Disappointments had left her frail and fractious. If he stayed at home she complained that there was not enough money in the studio work for them to live as she would like. When he had taken the decision to go out and about and find suitable studies for his camera that he could subsequently sell, naturally she complained of his absence. He had been on a final trip, hoping to get some extra money for their new responsibility, when she had gone into labour long before her time. A daughter, they told him, when he came back from his travels to learn he was a widower with two funerals to arrange.

That done, he had carried on taking photographs, travelling ever further afield, making longer, more difficult journeys, because he didn't know what else to do. And a man had to live. Gradually he found he enjoyed the travelling, the challenge of setting up his camera in ever more remote places, where many people did not even know what a camera was.

He had not been tempted to marry again. There had been a number of elderly spinsters or widows. Women who fussed and prattled and cooed like so many pigeons. He had felt no need of a wife who would demand his time, his protection and chatter constantly at him and keep him from his renewed interest in his work.

But sometimes, just sometimes, as he grew into middle age and his hair began to fleck with grey, he thought with a pang, of comfort, companionship and then dismissed it as an impossible idea.

'I've brought you the photographs I promised,' he said, looping the pony's reins round the gatepost.

'You'd better sit down in the shade. I'll bring you some nettle beer.'

She looked at the pictures carefully and accepted the copies he gave her of her sitting at the door, with her Bible. 'Thank you. I will send these to my sons as a reminder of their home and upbringing.'

That time he took pictures of her in the garden, and standing at the cottage door, with the jug of nettle beer. They were still talking – of America, of the dangers of the crossing, of the wool trade, the new chapel; of the dangers of importing raw materials and exporting the country's young men and skills – as the day cooled. He was surprised at her interest and knowledge of such subjects.

'We live isolated in this dale, but I like to know about the world, just as those people who look at your photographs want to know about us. The Miners' Institute has a library and periodicals and when my brother borrows them, I read them too.' She looked down the valley and he could see her son, his leg now well mended, trudging wearily up the path from work. She took down a muslin parcel of fatty bacon hanging in the smoke-blackened

151

rafters, deftly cut a few slices and put it on a plate with chunks of bread and some cheese. She went to stand on the stool to put the ham back but, before she did so, cut a few more slices, wrapped them in another chunk of bread and handed it to the photographer.

'For your journey,' she said. 'It's a long way if you're heading back down the dale tonight.'

He took the offered food gratefully. 'Thank you,' he said. 'I shall think of you as I eat this.'

She almost smiled.

Chapter Fourteen

'Mum! You look dreadful!'

'Well, thank you, dear,' said my mother. 'You really know how to make a girl feel good.' She tried to smile but it was clearly painful. I was shocked to see how badly she was hurt. One side of her face was bruised and swollen and she had a terrific black eye where apparently she had landed on the bike handlebars. One wrist was strapped up; one ankle was in a cast. She moved carefully, obviously in pain, as I bent down to kiss her, carefully finding a place on the not-quite-so-bashed side of her face.

It's frightening to see your mother like that, suddenly vulnerable. Especially my mother, who had always been so strong and determined, never needing anyone. I tried to remember if she'd ever been ill when I was a child. Vague memories of a bout of flu, the occasional bug, but all of them treated as irritating inconveniences, nothing that had actually stopped her and made her, literally, put her feet up.

However, being Mum, of course, she now had her laptop and phone on the table beside her and had clearly been trying to work.

'I told your mum she must rest. But she pays me no attention. Not at all!' Inez was fluttering round. 'Work will wait. Cafés can still work without Frankie Flint, but she will not believe.'

'Inez and Penny have been marvellous,' said Mum, indicating the sofa on which she lay, with her feet up, cushions and rugs stacked within reach. 'Penny's dealing with all the office stuff and Inez has looked after me here. She even stayed the night.'

'Oh, Inez! Thank you.' I remembered that she helped look after her grandchildren. 'If you want to go . . .'

'I must go and help my daughter. But I will call you.' She went to get her jacket and bag and, as I walked out into the hall with her, she told me, 'You look after your mum. She will try and do everything and she mustn't. It is hard for her to walk, to get about. She needs someone to carry her, a nice strong man! All women need a nice strong man!'

'Right, Inez, I'll see what I can do.'

Inez had stocked up the fridge with basics, so I was able to make Mum and me some buttery scrambled eggs and added generous slices of the smoked salmon I'd brought back with me from the smokery by the sea. As we ate it off trays, I told her all about my adventures, and especially about meeting cousin Kate and her family.

'You know I saw a picture of that girl – they call her Foxy, don't they? – in the paper and I thought she just had a look of the family. In fact, she reminded me a bit of you,' said my mother.

'Of me? I wish!' I said. 'Matt is well over six inches taller, two dress sizes smaller, with stunning hair and cheeks you could cut paper with.'

And, I added to myself, is probably right now trying to outwit Wapping's finest. If only she could leap away from them as easily as she'd leapt out of that window. But surely they couldn't find her on her home turf? There of all places she'd know how to avoid them. But it wasn't that simple, I thought glumly. Not to mention the fact that she still probably thought it was all my fault.

154

'But tell me more about Kate,' Mum was saying. 'No, tell me first about Jake. How are things between you? Did the working holiday work out?'

'Not quite,' I said and started the story. By the time I'd finished it was getting dark and Mum was nodding off. She must really have been bashed up a bit. She normally coped on about five hours a night. I drew the curtains, put some lamps on. And while Mum dozed, I nipped into the next room and, as I always did in emergencies, I rang Bill.

He arrived within the hour, just as I was trying to help Mum to the loo. Tricky – with a bad wrist she really couldn't manage the crutches she needed because of her ankle – so we were progressing slowly as she sort of hopped while hanging onto my shoulder and I had an arm around her waist. When the doorbell rang I had to leave her propped up against the table in the hall while I went to answer it.

'Bill!' She glared at me. 'You rang him!' she accused.

'Yes, and what a good thing she did,' said Bill, not even blinking at Mum's battered face. 'Are you trying to get to the bathroom or back from it?'

'To.'

'In that case . . .' He put down the bunch of flowers and basket of food he was carrying and simply picked up Mum, carried her to the bathroom, came out, closed the door saying, 'Yell when you want a lift back,' and came back into the kitchen where I was hunting for a vase for the flowers.

'She looks terrible. How is she?' he asked.

'Stubborn,' I said.

'Well, we know that. But we'll look after her,' he said, like a man with a mission.

And he did. He helped her back into the sitting room, then sat talking to her, telling her stories about the restaurant and the staff there, the suppliers he had found and some of the customers. He built a colourful picture of a little world.

'You'll have to come round and see it for yourself.'

'Hardly at the moment,' said Mum, wincing as she tried to move.

'No. But soon. I'd like you to see it.'

'Maybe,' said Mum, noncommittally.

At least she seemed almost pleased to see him.

Meanwhile, I was back in my teenage bedroom. I had long since taken down the pictures of the Gallaghers and Hugh Grant. (I know, I know, but I had been very young then.) But it still took me back to a time when life seemed to be just beginning and I had no idea how it would all turn out. I couldn't help thinking that maybe I hadn't got very far, really, as I absentmindedly reached out to touch Jake that first night back and found myself instead almost falling out of the single bed.

Not that I got much sleep. I was on night duty – in bed, but ever wakeful for Mum if she needed anything – painkillers, a drink, help to the loo. 'Good practice for when you have babies,' said Mum as I brought her extra cushions to make her foot comfortable. I smiled grimly. The way it was going, I was clearly doomed to be one of those perpetual bridesmaids and godmothers to my friends' children. But Bill would normally turn up mid-morning and immediately the atmosphere lightened. Mum even stopped protesting when he carried her round the flat, though she occasionally scolded him about the restaurant. 'How can you leave it to come and look after me?' she asked.

'Because I have good staff. They can cope for a few days. And you know, *your* staff can cope too, if you let them,' he said. 'Think about it. No one's indispensable. Not even Frankie Flint.'

On my second day back, I'd popped out for milk and

156

papers, bread and coffee. Just two weeks in the far north had made me really excited about being able to go round the corner and find a newsagent's and deli. I even beamed happily at Tesco Express – anything that didn't involve putting on boots or driving down a bumpy track every time you needed a pint of milk. In the newsagent's I picked up a whole pile of papers and magazines, hoping to distract Mum and keep her from fretting too much about work.

As I waited to pay, I looked idly at one of the front pages and nearly dropped the lot.

'*Foxy tracked to ground!*' glared the headline. '*Foxy's mountain hideaway!*'

'*The model and the muck heap!*' '*Our sexy shepherdess!*'

Oh God, I was almost scared to look. They'd found her. Bang goes her peace and privacy. And the peace and privacy of her family. I thought of Kate and Guy and wondered how they would cope with photographers trudging through the farmyard. I thought of the photographers swarming over the area looking for her. Going into the pub and asking questions. It was horrid, invasive. It spoilt everything. I ran home, praying that Matty had really believed me when I said I'd had nothing to do with it.

I got back to the flat and thwacked the papers down on the coffee table alongside the sofa where Mum lay propped up. 'Disaster!' I said, starting to scrabble through them while explaining what it was all about.

'Oh, God this is awful! They've all got something about Matty! Every single one!' I wailed. 'Even the posh ones!

Mum had picked up one of the tabloids that I had hurled across the table and was thumbing through it slowly. 'But these pictures are fantastic!' she said. 'Is this really Kate's daughter? What a stunning-looking girl.'

I took the paper back from her. The pictures *were* fantastic. Matty in jeans and jumper on the quad bike, her hair streaming out behind her . . . Matty striding up the fellside, looking slim as a wand with Tess beside her . . . Matt lugging a hay bale, with the horses, backing up the tractor and trailer . . .

'These don't look snatched photos,' said my mother, studying them carefully. 'Matty certainly isn't avoiding the camera. She seems to be positively playing up to it. I mean, look at that one,' she said, pushing the paper towards me. 'She's practically lapping up the lens.'

It was a close-up of Matty on the quad bike. She was leaning over the handlebars, laughing straight into the camera, looking full of life and energy, happy and – I tried to think of the expression – *mischievous*. That's right, she looked mischievous, almost triumphant, as if this was all some great joke.

'There's something else odd,' I said. 'Normally when she's working on the farm, she has her hair in a plait or tied back, or bundled under a cap. But in nearly all these pictures her hair is loose. And' – I looked closely at the pictures in front of me – 'those aren't her work jeans. Those look a much better fit. And where's her battered old Barbour? And her five layers of clothes?'

I flipped quickly through the rest of the papers. There were similar images in each one. They were amazing pictures. Every one seemed to capture Matty at her most relaxed and consequently even more stunning than usual and there were also masses of the scenery, showing the fellside in all its glory. Intrigued, I turned the page to see the picture by-line, to see which agency had got there first.

Suddenly it all became crystal clear.

The photographer who had taken every single picture in every single paper was Dexter Metcalfe. That must have been the idea he'd had just as I was leaving the pub.

'Instead of waiting for the paparazzi to find Foxy, they've beaten them to it,' I said to Mum. 'It's a brilliant idea – Dexter took all these pics. And now he's flooded all the papers with them, he's killed the market. These photos are fantastic. No paper's going to pay good money for snatched pictures not as good. There wouldn't be any point. Dexter's beaten them all to it and now Matty's safe in Egypt. Ho ho.

'They must have done the pictures before Matty flew out. They must have worked like crazy. Then Dexter got every single paper to use them.'

'He must have influence. Or good contacts,' said Mum. 'Very impressive bit of work on all accounts. He must be a very clever man, that Dexter, as well as a talented photographer. If he's as good as this, I'm surprised he's happy running a pub.'

She lay there for a while, looking at the different photos, until gradually she dozed off again, one of the papers slipping from her hand onto the floor. I eased it gently from her grasp and was folding it to put it on the coffee table when I saw the picture. I'd been so busy looking at pictures of Matty that I hadn't noticed this one.

It was Clayton with a very blonde blonde – long hair, glowing tan, glossy pout and the sort of cleavage that costs a fortune. The designer seemed to have run out of material when they made her dress, and what there was didn't cover much. She and Clayton had their arms round each other. Judging by the expressions on their faces, they had had a good evening and there were no guesses about how they would finish it off.

'Footballer Clayton "Quicksilver" and actress Kim Scarlett seen leaving exclusive West End restaurant Mario's in the early hours of Sunday. Last week Clayton paid over £50,000 for a necklace at a charity event but doesn't seem to have given it to girlfriend Kim yet. Maybe he's saving that for extra time . . .'

Fifty thousand pounds? So much for accurate reporting. But if that's Clayton's girlfriend and she's expecting him to come up with a necklace, there's even more reason for me to get it back to him. Though I suppose he could buy £25,000 necklaces the way I bought bangles for a fiver off the stall by the tube station. I looked again at the photo. I'm sure that wasn't one of the girls he was with when I saw him in Club Balaika. But he clearly wasn't a one-woman guy.

I shut the paper on the picture, folded it up and banged it on the coffee table, making Mum stir in her sleep. Now I was keener than ever to cut these few small links that had so strangely connected us. An odd set of circumstances had brought him into my life, but the sooner he got out of it the better.

Mum was on the mend. The damage to her wrist hadn't been that bad and, after a few days, she was able to manage the crutches well enough to hop around the flat. But her ankle was going to take weeks, if not months, to heal properly. Bill still popped round with food from the restaurant and I'd done all the shopping she needed. Penny came round every morning and gave a detailed report of all that had been going on in Mum's empire and took instructions back. Emails pinged back and forth all day to Mum's laptop. The world was beginning to return to some sort of normality.

One morning, when Penny was with Mum, I'd been round to my own flat and collected some more clothes. It seemed curiously soulless and empty. As I picked up the post, a key slithered out from between some envelopes. Jake's key. He'd been round to take his things and just posted the key back through the door. I looked through the mail. No note. Well, thanks very much, Jake.

He'd taken all his books from the bedroom shelf and his clothes from my wardrobe, though one of his jumpers was still on the floor behind a chair where it must have fallen before we went north. I picked it up and held it against my face and felt a strange sort of emptiness. I felt nothing for Jake now. Well, no more than a mild affection born of a few years shared. If we could manage to keep that I would be very happy. As for love . . . I hoped he'd be happy with Flick. Well, maybe I wouldn't go quite *that* far.

Mum's bruises had faded to an interesting green and yellow shade. Obviously getting better, but actually looking worse, making her look like a horror movie extra.

'Are you sure you're going to be all right if I go back north this afternoon?' I said.

'Of course. Now I can hobble round I'll be fine. Inez and Penny are here and I don't seem to be able to get rid of Bill. We have a system and even if I can't get into his car, I can get into taxis fairly easily. Once my face doesn't scare the punters I can get back to proper work, so yes, you go and get back on with your life. And catch up with your sleep too.'

It was true. I'd hardly slept since I'd been at Mum's. A decent night's sleep would be such a treat. But with her wrist recovering, she was a lot more mobile now. I could get back to work with a clear conscience.

'Give my love to Kate and the long-lost family,' Mum said.

'You'd really like them. Can I tell them you'll be going up to see them?'

'Oh yes, one day. But not yet. Once I'm back at work I'll have far too much catching up to do.' Her accident hadn't mellowed her that much, it seemed.

I'd booked myself on an evening train so that I would be back in time for an interview with some apple-growing monks on Thursday. But there was something I had to do first. That necklace was still burning a hole at the bottom of my bag. I had to get it back to Clayton but I could hardly just stick it an envelope and post it, even if I knew his address. I got out my phone, took a deep breath, but I couldn't ring him. What if he was with Kim? Or his team-mates? Or didn't remember which one I was out of all the females hanging round him? That would be awful, having to explain myself. No. So I texted. 'Need to talk to you. Are you around this afternoon?'

A reply pinged back almost immediately. 'Back from training 4.' And giving the address.

Hey. That had been easy.

Then of course I worried about what to wear. Of course I didn't want to impress him. On the other hand, you can't turn up on the doorstep of one of the fittest men in Britain in your scruffs, can you? Even if you're just returning an unwanted gift. I know I couldn't compete with the Kims of this world, but I could scrub up with a bit of effort. I was wearing black trousers, but didn't have a suitable top with me. I rummaged through my mother's wardrobe and found one of her numerous black tops – this one had a low boat neck and batwing sleeves with deep embroidered cuffs. She normally wore a silk shirt underneath it. Boring. I did my hair and make-up with extra care and reckoned that after an hour's effort I'd got the right casual-hardly-bothered effect I was after.

Bill arrived just as I was leaving and whistled in approval. 'Very fancy just for a train,' he said. 'I hope the other passengers appreciate it.' He looked at me quizzically, but no way was I going to tell him what I was up to.

'Look after yourselves. And each other,' I said, hugging them both.

'We shall,' they replied as they stood in the doorway,

Mum leaning determinedly on her crutches, despite her obvious discomfort, and refusing all help from Bill.

I ran down the stairs and into the taxi and set off for Clayton Silver's house.

Chapter Fifteen

The houses were big, solid, expensive and discreet. Not the sort of street I expected to find Clayton Silver living in. But, as the taxi slowed down and the driver was asking, 'What number did you say, love?' I spotted it.

'Twenty-two, I think it must be that one. It's got to be,' I said, peering out of the window.

'If it's the footballer you want, then that's the one,' said the taxi driver. 'That's got to be a footballer's house, hasn't it?'

Behind the high, gated wall, I could see the top of a tall modern house soaring to the sky. It had been squeezed into a narrow plot, but what it lacked in width it made up for in height and balconies. Each of the four floors was wrapped around by huge curving decking, the architectural equivalent of Ray-Bans, breaking up what seemed to be towering walls made entirely of glass. In this street of quiet, old-fashioned wealth, it looked totally out of place – no doubt a bit like Clayton – but it was sunny and frivolous and strangely beautiful, like a ship about to break free of its moorings.

I had my luggage with me ready for my trip north and, as I put the bags on the pavement and paid the driver, I wondered how I would get in through these gates. There must be an intercom somewhere, a tradesman's entrance.

With that, a huge black Hummer came up the road. Blacked-out windows and personalised numberplate. It looked more like something from an invading army than a car. It slowed down by the gates, which automatically opened for it. I couldn't see who was behind the windows. The car stopped, a window purred down and Clayton leaned out of the window, smiling. 'Well, hello, Miss Tilly. How nice of you to drop by. Come in.'

Dutifully, I followed the car through the gates. Clayton switched off the engine, left the Hummer where it was and came back and picked up my bags, then ran up the stairs where the front door also opened apparently magically, but actually by a tiny Filipina woman.

'Cheers, Maria,' he said, dumping my bags in the vast entrance hall and then leading the way up the wide curved stairs into a room full of light. With the floor-to-ceiling windows and curved balcony stretching round the entire length of the room, it seemed as if we were hovering above the treetops.

'Wow!' I said.

'Good, yeah?' asked Clayton as I walked to the balcony to admire the view over the street, the park and down across London.

'Fantastic. And just not what you'd expect in a road like this.'

'That's why I had to have it. Things that aren't what you expect are always more interesting, aren't they?' he grinned. 'So, would you like a drink? Wine? Champagne?' he gestured at a bar in the corner.

'No, thanks, what I'd really like is a cup of – oh gosh!'

One wall of this amazing room was taken up by a huge plasma TV set, but on another was a painting, even bigger, twice the size of the TV screen. It was just dashes of colours really – blues and greens and a splash of white – yet you knew it was a boat on a wide bright sea. As I looked, the huge voile curtain, tucked back to the side of the curving window, billowed out with the breeze and added to the impression of sails and waves.

'It's the one you told me about. It does make you feel you're out on the sea, doesn't it?' I said, and Clayton whooped triumphantly.

'That's why I had to have it. Sometimes I lie on that sofa and look at that painting and I'm not here in London but I'm floating above the sea, free as a bird, just letting the winds take me. Some people just don't get it. But you do. I thought you would. No, I *knew* you would.'

He was standing there, still in his tracksuit and training top, smiling at the painting. 'That picture cost me shed-loads of money, but every time I look at it, it makes me happy. Got be worth it, yeah? Keeps the money-man happy and keeps me happy too. He puts money away in stocks and shares and things for me, but that ain't much fun, is it? You can't *look* at them. That's why I keep buying pictures. Want to see more?'

'Yes, please. I do.' And I did, but in any case Clayton's enthusiasm was appealing. When he'd said he'd liked pictures I'd thought that he just bought them to be flash, but as he showed me round I realised I'd got him wrong. He might not be an expert, but he was an enthusiast and, as the man said, he knew what he liked.

'Look, this is one I bought when we were playing a European cup match in Italy. We had a day free and I went off by myself for a bit, found a little gallery and saw this painting and I had to have it.'

It was a classical style painting, a view through an ancient arched window, ivy growing alongside. Through it you could see the glorious remains of a Roman building, but also a high Renaissance palace with huge door and crumbling paintwork and, just in the corner, a glimpse of a modern, gleaming, high-rise office block. In the shadows of them all were two people. You couldn't tell if they were a couple or not, or whether they were turning towards each other or walking away.

'It's like the more you look at it, the less you know – and it could be any time, couldn't it?'

I was intrigued not just by the painting, but the thought of Clayton in a foreign city, leaving his team-mates and wandering off by himself round backstreets and art galleries. I looked at him, thinking of all the different bits of Clayton Silver I knew from what he'd told me and what I read, and trying to put them together. It was a tricky jigsaw. I wonder if Kim Scarlett understood him.

Other paintings were starker, simpler, bolder – huge splashes of colour or intriguing subtle patterns of swirling colours. We went downstairs – the wood of the stairs was so expensive, so smooth, so beautiful, that it was a work of art in itself – where an inner hall was hung with some laddish paintings – Lewis Hamilton winning a grand prix, a horse race, a boxing match and, inevitably, one of Clayton scoring a goal, light gleaming on the taut muscles of his thigh as he was captured, leaping up about to kick the ball. 'That's meant to be the winning goal, but if I'd kicked that at the angle he painted it, it would have missed by miles,' he said.

The hall led into a games room with a full-size pool table, table football, yet another huge plasma TV and another well-stocked bar. And a cupboard full of trophies and medals.

'My playroom,' he smiled. 'Gym through there,' he said, pointing. 'I didn't have space for a full-size swimming pool, but there's an infinity pool. And also a wine cellar, of course.

'Oh and I guess you'd better see this one . . .'

We were going back upstairs now, up another equally beautiful staircase, with windows along its length. It was, I realised, built into a sort of tower at the side of the house and I could see down the street and the row of houses with their high fences and designer gardens. We'd come out into what was obviously Clayton's dressing room – walk-in wardrobes, rows of very expensive shoes, leather boxes containing cufflinks. Through one door I could see a huge wet room, through another a glimpse of his bedroom – black and white patterned duvet, lots of mirrors . . . And on the wall a picture of a nude, long blonde hair tumbling down onto her breasts, flirtatious eyes, pouting mouth. Poor girl. She probably meant it as a great present, but really it made her look needy, desperate. I realised I recognised the girl.

'That's Sapphire O'Mara!' I said. A few years ago, Sapphire had won a reality TV show and now made a living being a celebrity, doing chat shows, quizzes, opening super-markets and going out with footballers – famous on account of being well known.

'Yeah. We had a thing going for a while and she had that done for my birthday. Knowing Sapphire, she was prob-ably having it off with the artist. Can't get rid of it: Seb Tarn's work's going for a fortune now. Sapphire always could pick rising talent. But it's not too tactful when I'm entertaining . . .'

He spread his hands wide and shrugged as if he were totally puzzled by the world and its ways.

Suddenly I realised I was standing virtually in his bedroom. Definitely not a good idea. Especially when he was looking at a painting like that. How daft could I be? Come upstairs to look at his paintings. Oh my God. Dim or what? I turned and almost ran back down the stairs and into the huge living room. Clayton laughed and loped slowly after me.

On the low table in front of one of the huge orange leather sofas was a tray with tea things, including a plate of small and delicious-looking pastries. Afternoon tea? Another surprise. But there was also a pitcher of disgusting-looking liquid.

Clayton smiled. 'Maria thought you looked like an afternoon tea lady. Must mean she likes you.' He poured some of the foul-looking liquid into a high glass and drank it down.

'Full of goodness. Nutritionist's orders.' He smiled at me over the top of the glass.

'You're quite safe, you know, Miss Tilly,' he said. 'I don't bite.'

'This is all very nice,' I said, flustered, 'but I just came to talk to you about the necklace. I—'

'Why don't you just have your tea that Maria's made for you, while I go and have a shower and change. Then I'll come down and we'll talk. Unless you want to come up and shower with me . . . ?'

'No!' I said, shocked, and tried not to imagine Clayton's naked body with water cascading over it.

'Back in a minute.'

By the time I thought of something calm and sensible to say, he'd gone. I thought of leaving the necklace on the sofa and just going. No. I had to wait. I had no option really. So I poured some tea and looked around.

Remembering Jake's research and my own misgivings, I wondered if this could be the home of a corrupt footballer. What did I expect to find – boxes of used tenners stuffed in the corner? Brown envelopes bulging with cash? But I made a quick study of the room to see what it could tell me.

There was a huge reclining armchair opposite the wall with the TV set. I could just imagine Clayton lounging back there with the remote in one hand and a glass of wine in the other. There were a couple of games consoles, a stack of DVDs. But there was a bookcase too – a quick glance showed that Clayton Silver liked thrillers, sports books and travel guides and also had a collection of books on modern art. Which didn't surprise me as much as it would have done a while ago.

The shelf full of photographs mainly featured football teams and triumphs. Lots of medals, cups and champagne. There was one in bright foreign sun of a shop front with a big ribbon across it and Clayton and an older woman about to cut it. His mum, I guessed. Very tanned, very blonde, looking very pleased with herself. And why not? Another photo showed a pleasant middle-aged couple pictured sitting in a garden. The man looked vaguely familiar and I realised I'd seen him on television occasionally. It was Denny Sharpe, the manager of Clayton's first team, the one who'd been like a father to him. It was nice to see his picture there. I looked quickly along the rest of the pictures – but there weren't any of women. Every week Clayton Silver was pictured with some new model or actress, but none of them had got as far as his picture shelf. *Interesting.*

Suddenly cheerful, I decided it seemed a shame not to try those pastries that Maria had brought, and they were only small. I nibbled one. It tasted deliciously of almonds.

I rummaged in my bag and took out the box with the necklace in it and placed it on the coffee table. I opened the box for a last look. I wondered if Kim Scarlett would wear it. I'm not sure if it was her sort of thing. But how was I to know? I was just running it through my hands, feeling the weight and smoothness of the silver, the gloss of the amber, admiring the deceptive simplicity of the design, when Clayton came back into the room. He leant over my shoulder, so close that I could smell the very expensive scent of whatever he'd used in the shower. He wore a dazzling white T-shirt and beautifully cut jeans. Gulp. It was hard to ignore the sheer physical power of the man. But I was determined to try.

'So this is what a twenty-five-thousand-pound necklace looks like, is it?' he said. 'I didn't get to study it the night I bought it. Too busy looking at the lady wearing it.' He turned his head – his beautifully shaped head – and smiled at me.

He was so close to me I was actually having difficulty breathing. I moved away from him, took a deep breath and said firmly. 'It's a beautiful necklace but I can't keep it, so I'm giving it back to you.'

His smile faded. He looked puzzled as he stood up and moved around to face me.

'And why can't you keep it?' he asked, with a hint of coldness in his tone, that was just a bit scary. Too bad. I knew what I had to say and ploughed on with it. *'Tell the truth,'* as the sampler in the cottage said.

'Because it was so expensive. And you don't really know me. And it's not . . .' I groped for the word I wanted and suddenly found it. 'It's not . . . *appropriate.'*

The scary coldness instantly left Clayton's eyes and he hooted with laughter. 'You're telling me that it's not . . . appropriate . . . to give you this necklace. Appropriate?' The world almost gurgled in his throat.

'Yes,' I said, beginning to feel like something out of a Jane Austen novel. 'I mean, you don't know me. It was very nice of you to take me to the dinner – and to lunch before that in the helicopter. I don't mean lunch in the helicopter,' I was gabbling, 'but you know what I mean. Anyway, that was very kind of you and thank you very much. I had a very nice time. But the necklace – well, that's just too much.

I mean, that's the sort of present you only give to someone when they're very . . . and I'm not. Am I? I mean, I don't know you. Do I? So I can't. I really can't. But thank you.'

I put the necklace back in its box and pushed it across the coffee table to him.

Clayton was still towering over me, his hands in his pockets.

'You are certainly a one-off,' he said. 'That is the first time, the very first time, anyone has ever returned a present to me. And definitely the first time anyone has said that something had to be "appropriate".' He rocked on his heels.

'But it's like this,' he went on. 'I bought the necklace as a way of helping Ted Blake's charity. He's a nice guy. It was sad about his wife and he's trying to make sure the same thing doesn't happen to other mums. That's good. I gave him twenty-five thousand pounds. I could have given him twenty-five thousand pounds anyway, and not got anything back at all. But this time, I got this nice necklace. Now I can't wear it. Might get the guys talking. So what am I going to do with it? Why, give it to a nice lady, of course, and hope she wears it. Otherwise it would just sit in its box and no one would ever see it. And that would be a shame because I think it's quite a nice necklace.'

'It is. A very nice necklace. But . . .'

'Now what buts?'

'Well, surely, there must be . . . you must have . . . I mean, you must have plenty of other women you could give this to, women you know better than me.'

He looked thoughtful for a moment. 'Well, there are lots of ladies, yes. Always lots of ladies. And do you know what, Tilly? Every one of them would have snatched that necklace so fast they would nearly have taken my hand with it. But not you. And that just makes me even more sure that you should have it.

'After all, it's just a necklace. I bought it to help a mate's charity. And now I've got it, I have to give it to someone, and I think it would look nice on you. So . . .'

He picked up the box with the necklace in it, bowed in a jokey way and handed me the box. 'This necklace is for you. For being different. For keeping me company at that dinner and because it looks great on you and I shall think of you wearing it.'

I was still sitting on the sofa. He leant down towards me, took the necklace out of its box and, once again, slipped it over my head. There was that wonderful closeness of him again, that difficulty in breathing. The infuriating part was that he knew damn well the effect he was having on me. And I was determined that he wouldn't.

Why does life have to be so complicated?

'Tell you what,' Clayton was saying. 'There's a viewing tonight that I've been invited to. You could come too. Then maybe we could have dinner. Would you like that?'

He moved away and was looking out of the window, as if my reply didn't really matter that much at all. Which made it easier for me to say. 'No. Thank you for the offer, but I can't. I'm booked on a train this evening. In fact,' I glanced at my watch, 'it's time I was leaving.'

Clayton turned back and looked at me. 'Don't go,' he said. 'You can catch a later train.'

'No. I have to get back. I have an appointment with a monk tomorrow. You can't let monks down. Probably a sin.' I started to ease the necklace off over my head. I still wasn't sure what I was going to do with it.

But Clayton took hold of both my hands in his, so I had to let the necklace fall back round my throat, and looked into my eyes. 'What time are you seeing your monk?'

'Lunchtime.' Damn! Why didn't I say ten o'clock? That

would have made life more straightforward. Why did I always have to tell the truth?

'Then that's easy,' said Clayton triumphantly. 'We can go to the gallery. We can have dinner. You can catch the last train. If you're not seeing your monk till lunchtime, you've got time for a nice lie-in. No probs.'

'No, I can't. I have to . . .'

'Yes you can. Unless you really, really don't want to be with me. And I thought we were OK. I thought we liked each other. Aren't we friends? Can't friends spend an evening together?' He smiled. 'Please?'

I was lost. I was torn. I was tempted. I knew exactly what I *should* do, what would be the sensible plan. But there again, in the last few weeks, in this strange freedom since Jake and I had split, I had got used to adventures, most of them involving Clayton. And so far, it had been fun. I laughed.

'OK. You win. But I must get the last train. I really must get it.'

And if I'd known what would happen, would I have done things any differently?

Chapter Sixteen

Despite its easily missed entrance, the gallery was long, thin, light and airy. A waitress offered us a glass of wine. I took one, but Clayton waved his away and took water, which he sipped while studying the catalogue.

A seriously smart woman in a severe suit was bearing down on us purposefully. The gallery owner, I guessed. 'Clayton!' she gushed with one of those very bright smiles that go nowhere near the eyes, '*so* glad you could come.' She looked at me questioningly.

'Marcia. Hi!' said Clayton. 'This is my friend Tilly Flint. Tilly – Marcia Longwood. It's her gallery.'

Marcia extended a chilly hand. 'How do you do, Tilly?' she said, but this time her unsmiling eyes never left my necklace.

Because, yes, I was wearing it. Because in any case it turned my black clothes into an outfit and if you're going to go out with a footballer, even to a fairly low-key viewing, you've got to up your game, haven't you?

Marcia was gushing about the paintings, the artist, a hot raw talent. She was sure Clayton would . . . *identify* . . . with the young man.

'Well, it's sure to be interesting,' said Clayton, gently walking away from her and towards the pictures. One or two of the other guests looked up and nodded at him politely. They clearly knew him or recognised him, but they weren't going all silly on him. They certainly weren't papping him on their mobiles the way people had done outside Club Balaika.

The paintings themselves were powerful, dramatic and bleak. If the paintings made a statement, it was an unequivocally depressing one. Cityscapes full of dereliction and no hope. Boarded-up houses and burnt-out cars. Industrial wastelands of abandoned factories. Children playing outside dock gates overgrown with weeds. L. S. Lowry meets Leonard Cohen. On a bad day. The pictures had a lot to say but I wasn't sure whether I would actually want them saying it on my living-room wall.

Clayton looked at me and raised his eyebrows. I guessed he was thinking the same as me. We whispered conspiratorially.

'I grew up in places like that,' said Clayton. 'It's what I got away from. I'm not paying good money to be reminded of it all the time.'

Nevertheless, he made a few notes on the catalogue and went back to take another look at two or three of the paintings. Then he put his water glass back on a tray, nodded briefly at some of the other visitors, said goodbye to a disappointed-looking Marcia, took my hand and we fled.

Out in the street, a taxi immediately screeched to a stop in front of us. Impressive.

'So, Miss Foodie, where do you fancy?' Clayton asked as the taxi driver waited for instructions.

My mind flipped through all the great London restaurants that I longed to visit. Clayton was reeling off a list of suggestions – all the sort of places where you would normally have to book weeks – if not months – ahead. And also the sort of places where there were always photographers outside.

'It's up to you,' I said. 'You know the places where you can get in, where you're most comfortable.'

'OK, right,' said Clayton, 'good thought.' Turning to the driver, he said, 'Number Thirty-eight, please.'

Number 38 was so discreet that the taxi driver could barely find it. But as soon as we walked in, there was no question that we would get a table. Inside it were small, intimate, high-backed benches keeping each table private from its neighbours. The sort of place where you come for privacy rather than to be seen. Such a relief. As I slipped along one of the benches, I giggled. Clayton looked at me questioningly.

'Thank goodness we've come somewhere like this. I had visions of photographers and my picture in the papers and people asking, "Who's that scruff with Clayton Silver?"'

'You're certainly no scruff. But would you really not like to have your picture in the paper?'

'Oh, no. I'd hate it. Especially just for being with you.'

'Am I so bad to be seen with?' He looked surprised.

'No, no.' How did I get myself into this mess? 'No. I meant that I wouldn't like to have my picture in the paper just because I was with you. No one would take my picture otherwise, would they? I wouldn't mind if I'd actually *done* something on my own account – like my mum. My mum's often in the papers, but that's because she's actually doing something, not just because she's gone out for a meal.'

'Lots of girls would love to have their picture in the paper with me.'

'Yes I know, I'm sure they would. But I wouldn't. Well, not because . . . I mean not just because . . .'

Clayton was laughing now. 'Don't worry, Tilly, I know just what you mean. Well, I think I do. And if you mean what I think you mean, then I think I like you for it.'

We looked at each other and burst out laughing. The waiter, offering us menus, didn't blink.

'Do you think that artist bloke ever has a laugh?' asked Clayton. 'Judging by his pictures, he could certainly do with one.'

'Yes, but I could see what he was getting at. He did make you think of how bleak some parts of our cities are.'

'Yeah. I was lucky to get out.' He looked thoughtful for a moment. 'My old manager, you know, Denny Sharpe? I told you about him?' I nodded. 'Well, he's working to set up a football academy at the club.'

'To spot new talent?'

'Yeah, I guess so. But he wants other kids there too, who might not make it as professional but who just enjoy playing football. Beats playing with knives on the streets. Like I played for a boys' club that Travis took me to, but Denny would get it all under the club umbrella. That would get even more kids involved.'

The waiter was back for our order. I settled quickly for sea bass and truffles. Clayton, predictably, went for steak and chips, but had taken a lot longer over choosing two bottles of French wine – Pouilly-Fuissé for me and a red Burgundy for him.

'But we can share, of course,' he said. And we did.

'You know Denny gets his footballers to go into school, help kids with their reading and such,' said Clayton.

'That's a brilliant idea,' I said. 'Footballers will make reading cool. Denny Sharpe sounds quite a man.'

'He is,' said Clayton. 'I owe the guy a lot.'

'Couldn't your club do that sort of thing?'

'Nah,' said Clayton, nodding appreciatively to the sommelier as he tasted the wine, 'our manager's not the community type. The guy's Italian. He'll be here for a year or so and then move on. He's OK, but all he cares about is football and winning. Anything else just gets in the way. I guess he doesn't even notice the streets outside the ground. But we're winning and that's all that matters.'

'And what about Simeon Maynard?' I asked, interested to see Clayton's reaction.

'Well, he's the money-man, isn't he?' said Clayton. 'He's the one who's bankrolling us. We're his club, his little toy.'

'So where does his money come from?'

Clayton shrugged. 'Who knows? Who cares? As long as he buys in good players, we're not bothered.'

'Maybe you should be.'

'Maybe we should, Miss Tilly, but sometimes you know it's better not to ask too many questions, especially with someone like Maynard. Look, he rescued the club. He's bought in some great players. We're racing up the table.'

His face lit up. 'Do you know what it's like to play with the best? All my life I was always the best player in any team I was in. Always. Like I was God, you know? And now there're ten others on the field just as good as I am and another ten waiting for a place. Some of them can work magic. And you know what? Every match, I have to work out of my skin to be the best. Because I'm playing with these guys, I'm working harder, training harder. Every moment of the match I can't stop thinking, can't stop concentrating. It's like driving at a hundred miles an hour, you can't let up.

'There are kids in the team just eighteen, nineteen: they call me the Old Man. Old Man? I show them. They are geniuses on the ball. But you know what? I can still outplay them, still score when they don't even know where the ball is. They're just standing there looking, saying, "How did he do that?" And it's fan-fucking-tastic.

'I'm playing better than ever because I have to show these kids how it's done. And that's all thanks to Sim

Maynard and his money. OK, the man's a slimeball. We don't have to like him, do we? And I can see why people hate him. I don't rate him either. In fact, he's a right pain in the arse. But he loves football, likes to hang out round footballers. He's the little boy who's got his real live Subbuteo team. And if that means he's spending his money on our club instead of building an island off Dubai, well, I'm not going to moan about it, am I? It's his money. He can spend it how he likes.' He grinned. 'Especially if he's paying my wages. Especially if we're winning.' He sat back triumphantly.

With that, our food arrived, and Clayton and I forgot about Maynard. Instead we ate and talked and drank and talked. About football, about Denny Sharpe, about paintings, about our childhoods, about the people Clayton had met, about some of the other footballers and their girlfriends. About one footballer who'd come back from his honeymoon alone.

'Alone?'

'Yeah. They'd been together for a few years, had a kid. But she was just on the make, just one of those who was determined to bag a footballer – any footballer, as long as he was earning a hundred thousand a week. She got her teeth into him when she had the kid. Then, once they were married and it was all legal; once she had her bit of paper – well, that was it. Didn't have to be nice to him any more. It will cost him an absolute mint.'

'Oh dear,' I said, in mock sympathy, 'it must be *so* difficult for you, having women throw themselves at you.'

He grinned. 'I struggle with it. But it's not fair, is it, taking a kid away from its dad? She's making it difficult for him to get access. Not right, is it? Kids need their dads, don't they? Especially lads. I mean, who's going to teach them football, otherwise?'

180

'There are other things to being a good father than teaching your son how to kick a ball,' I laughed.

'Yeah, I know, but it's still high up on the list, isn't it? Still part of it all.' He looked wistful. He was a grown man, still pining for the dad he'd hardly known and never forgiving him for walking out. 'I don't know how a dad can do that.' He looked fierce and sad at the same time. 'I could never do that. If I had a lad, I'd never leave him.'

'I know. I know,' I said.

Somewhere along the line, in that mellow glow that comes from good wine, good food and good company, I realised – without a hint of panic – that I had missed that last train . . . But it didn't matter. There would be one very early in the morning. I could catch that. I'd still make it for my monk.

We were the last to leave the restaurant. The other high-backed booths were empty and the waiters were clearing up, discreetly, but still making it clear they were ready to go home, as Clayton paid the bill and we went out arm in arm into the night.

'I'll have to go via your place to fetch my bags,' I said as we got into the cab.

'Of course,' he said.

When we got to his gates, he didn't ask the cab to wait. Neither did I. I felt emboldened.

'A nightcap?' he asked, as I perched on the huge sofa and looked out at the lights of London.

I nodded dreamily. He poured me a glass of grappa. 'Bottled sunshine,' he said. I sipped it happily. On top of all the food and wine I'd had that evening, it slid down wonderfully . . .

Clayton had disappeared. Gone to the loo, I supposed. Never mind. He'd be back in a minute, and then I'd call a taxi and go home, back to my own flat, just for a few hours, because I had to be up early. Very early. I tucked my legs up under me. The sofa was very comfortable. Soft and squashy. I snuggled down into it. I rested my head on one of the arms. I was so tired, so sleepy. I would just close my eyes for a moment, just for a moment, until Clayton came back from the loo . . .

What? Where? Why? As I blearily opened my eyes, I struggled to work out where I was. Not in a bed, on a sofa. Ouch, that explained the cramp in my leg and the crick in my neck. Yet I had a duvet over me. But all my clothes on. Why was I on a sofa with a duvet over me? And whose sofa was it anyway? Outside the window, I could see the first grey light of dawn breaking across London.

Ohmigod! I sat bolt upright. I was still at Clayton's flat. I looked at my watch. Seven a.m.! I'd been there all night. Oh no . . . I had a train to catch. I had to go quickly. But how? I leapt up from the sofa, cramp and crick forgotten, and went off in search of a bathroom. I caught sight of myself in the mirror. Not a pretty sight. I had to find Clayton, or the way out. There were staff, weren't there? The lady who'd let me in. Maria. Where was she? How did I get out of this place? Help! Where were my bags? I didn't even know how to open the fancy gates. I couldn't just sneak out – I'd have to find someone. And quickly.

Why had I been here all night? I'd meant to go back to my own flat. It was the grappa – I shouldn't have had it. I must have gone to sleep. Dimly, I had a very vague, half-memory of a faint chuckle, of someone putting the duvet over me, of the lights being switched off.

Downstairs, after going through endless rooms, I finally found the kitchen, a huge palace with every gadget ever seen. I would have loved to explore further, but not now. There was no one around. At least I had found my bags,

182

which were just inside the hall. I looked at the front door. Tentatively, I tried to open it.

C L A N G G G G G G G G G G G G G G G G ! ! CLANNNGGGGGGGGGGGGGG!

An alarm shattered the silence and made me jump in the air, my heart pounding. Had I done that? I looked at the control panel at the wall and had no idea how to turn it off. It would wake the whole house, the whole street.

CLANGGGGGGGGG! CLANGGGGGGGGGGGGG-GG!!!!!!!!!!!!

Oh help.

'Is that you, Tilly?'

I looked up the wonderful winding staircase to see Clayton standing at the top. Actually, he was hopping on one foot while tugging on a pair of grey training shorts. Even half asleep, even in a panic, even still not quite knowing what was going on, I could see that he looked seriously fit.

CLANNNGGGGGGGGG! CLANNGGGGGGGGG!

'What's the matter, Tilly? Why's the alarm gone off?' He loped down the stairs in about three strides and clicked the buttons to stop the alarm. The silence was wonderful.

'Sorry about that, but I've got to go,' I said. '*Now*. I must catch that first train. If I don't . . . I've got no chance of catching it now. And the photographer will be coming and I won't be there and it will all have to be be . . .' Oh why had I been so *stupid* as to go back to Clayton's? And then to go to sleep?

'I'll take you,' said Clayton.

'No, it's all right,' I said automatically and then thought again. 'Actually, no it isn't. Yes please. If you don't mind.' There was no time to be polite and fanny on.

'No problem. Got your bags? Well, come on then.' He raced up the stairs, came back still in his shorts, but with a pair of leather flip-flops on his feet and his car keys, his phone and a fleece in his hand.

He was tugging the fleece over his head and we were dashing out of the door just as Maria was appearing, tiny and bleary-eyed, anxious.

'It's OK, Maria. Just a false alarm. Go back to bed.'

She stood there in the doorway, shrugging helplessly as the car beeped open.

'We'll never make it!' I said as I clambered up into the front of the Hummer.

'Now that sounds like a challenge!' grinned Clayton, and we roared off, barely giving the automatic gates time to open as we raced through them.

The first junction we came to was blocked by solid traffic. Clayton flung the Hummer into reverse, backed up the road at sixty m.p.h., swung into another road and barrelled it between two rows of parked cars.

And that was just the start . . .

Never have I experienced a drive like that. Clayton steered in and out of the traffic, bore down on drivers in front, raced through side streets, nipped in and out of bus lanes.

'You're all right, Tilly. This car's too big to argue with.'

'That's meant to reassure me?' I yelped, clutching at the door handle.

At one point – when we were moving back out of a bus lane and Clayton was forcing our way back into a line of traffic so he could overtake the bus, I had my hands over my eyes, scared to look. From one chink between my fingers I could see the side of the bus about a finger's width away from my window. Instinctively I swerved away from it and fell right against Clayton as he was pushing his way in front of a little Fiesta. He avoided the Fiesta, but then I could see a row of bollards looming up on the driver's side. I shut my eyes again.

Clayton was laughing.

'How can you *laugh*?' I squeaked. 'Look, please stop. It doesn't matter if I miss the train. I'll ring them, I'll cancel. I'll arrange another day. I'll . . . Help!'

He'd slammed the brakes on because of a speed camera. Then immediately revved up again. Now he was hammering along with two wheels on the road and the other two on the central reservation.

'Clayton! Will you stop! I'm sure there was another camera. There was a flash!' I looked round to see if I could spot a camera, but we were already gone.

'You wanted to catch a train. You're going to catch a train.'

'You're *enjoying* this!'

'Miss Tilly, I *love* it! Haven't driven like this since I was sixteen.'

I wondered if it was too late to start praying . . .

Suddenly, amazingly, he was slamming the brakes on and jumping out. 'King's Cross, madam, you've got one minute to catch your train.'

'I don't believe it!' I slumped back into the seat, as shattered as if I'd run the distance. 'We've made it!'

'Only if you're quick. Come on!'

The car was straddled across double yellow lines right next to the station entrance. Clayton grabbed my bags out of the boot. As he did so, his phone rang. He took it out of his pocket and flung it onto the dashboard. He still had his keys in the same hand, so when the phone flew, they did too. The button on the fob must have hit the dashboard.

There was one of those soft clicks. You know, the soft click made by a large expensive car that has just automatically locked all its doors – with the driver on the outside and the keys on the inside . . .

'Shit!' said Clayton, staring at the car helplessly.

'Oh God, what will you do? Have you a spare set? Can you phone home? Oh no, your phone's in there.' I felt hopelessly responsible for what had happened.

'Don't worry. I'll sort it,' said Clayton. 'Now which platform?' And he was racing off with me panting behind him. We'd found the platform and were running down it, past the engine just as the guard was shutting the door. Clayton snatched it open again, bundled me in, pushed my bags in after me. The guard glared at us, shut the door again and the train started to pull slowly out. I looked out of the window and could see Clayton standing on the platform, waving, triumphantly.

Under the disapproving glares of the other passengers, I collapsed, panting, onto the nearest seat as the train headed north.

Chapter Seventeen

I fell hopelessly in love with the monks. Brother Ambrose and Brother Patrick were like Little and Large – one huge, one tiny, but both smiling, jolly, welcoming and, at the same time, so wonderfully calm.

It had been a fraught journey. No shower, no wash; I hadn't even cleaned my teeth. I was glad I wasn't sitting next to me. Once on the train I'd tried to get myself washed and changed. I don't know if you've ever tried that in the loo of an Intercity express racing north at 123 m.p.h., but I wouldn't recommend it. But I'd managed as best I could and, after a coffee and a BLT, felt a bit more human.

As for the necklace, I had carefully put that back in its box and wrapped it in one of the thick jumpers I was taking back north. It looked as though that necklace was now mine whether I liked it or not. There was no way that Clayton was going to accept it back.

While I was dancing on one foot trying to put clean knickers on, wearing my trousers round my neck because there was nowhere else to put them, I kept thinking of Clayton and last night. Honestly, the fittest footballer in England and I went to sleep! To sleep? Why had I accepted the grappa? Why hadn't I gone straight home? Had I hoped to end up in the big bed with the black and white duvet? No. Well, probably no. No, definitely no. Maybe . . .

But I'd enjoyed the evening. Of that I was sure. And Clayton seemed to enjoy it too. Time had flown. But to go to sleep . . .

My head was still churning with all that had happened when I got off the train and found PIP. Amazingly, she started first time. But then I had to drive over the moors to find the monastery, with a few wrong turns here and there, constantly looking at my watch. For once, the gods were on my side and I managed to arrive at the monastery almost on time but, as I pulled up in the courtyard, I was hot and bothered, with my mind still all over the place.

But Brother Ambrose and Brother Patrick were delightful. They took me and the photographer – a guy called Clive whom I'd never worked with before – to the apple orchards, which spread down the side of a valley with a view for miles. And as I breathed in the crisp autumn air and gazed over the lines of trees and the distant hills beyond them, I gradually realised that all I could hear was the swish of their robes and the distant baa-ing of sheep. Just the huge stone walls of the abbey and silence. I took a huge breath and sighed as I followed them along the grassy path.

Brother Patrick led us round the edge of the orchard, unlatched a little wooden gate and took us into an old barn, stacked high with wooden trays and baskets, arranged in higgledy-piggledy heaps on the earth floor. It all smelled wonderfully of sweet apple juice, with undertones of wood and soil and a slight, tantalizing whiff of alcohol. Somewhere a wasp buzzed dozily. Most of the apples had been juiced, but there were still a few trays of the late fruit – apples of all shapes and sizes, often with stalk and leaf attached – waiting to go into the simple old-fashioned wooden machine. It all looked like one of those arty illustrations for chichi rustic cookery books that don't tell you how to cook anything sensible. But this was real, a working operation. Clive's eyes lit up as he started arranging pictures. This was such a gift for him. Brother Ambrose and Brother Patrick took turns to explain all about the apples – many of them from ancient stock – and about the juicing and the cider press. They made sloe gin too and were waiting for the first frosts before they picked the sloes.

'And that will be soon, I think,' said Brother Ambrose. 'The weather is about to turn. You can smell the cold in the air.'

As they stood there talking to me, explaining so kindly and carefully what they did, their hands tucked into the wide sleeves of their habits, they radiated an air of such calmness and certainty that I just wished they could bottle that along with the cider. I tried to say something along those lines, but Brother Ambrose just laughed.

'We are monks, but we have to live in the world too,' he said. 'We have to pay our bills, repair our roof. Our cider is an advert for us. Your article, which I'm sure will be wonderful, and the pictures so artistic' – he looked up at Clive, who by now was perched on top of the cider press, trying to get pictures at clever angles – 'will remind people we are here. That monks don't just exist in history books or cartoons. That while the world goes on in its mad way, we are here in the hills, picking our apples, making our cider and praying for them.'

The two of them beamed at me. 'And we shall pray for you too,' said Brother Patrick.

Apart from weddings, I've hardly been inside a church for years, but when Brother Patrick said he would pray for me, he made it sound like a gift. Mind you, by then I was feeling very light-headed. But we drank some apple juice together and they gave me and Clive a bottle of cider each to take home. As I revved up PIP and drove out of the monastery grounds and down the winding track back to the main road, I did feel – not exactly blessed – but calmer. Less fraught.

Until I switched on the car radio.

'. . . Premiership footballer . . . *crackle, crackle* . . . Silver . . . *hiss* . . . questioned by police . . . *whoosh whoosh* . . . Prevention of Terrorism Act . . . police spokesman . . .'

What? I pulled over and tried to tune the radio, but it just crackled even more. The wonderful moors played hell with radio reception, especially when the radio was as ancient as PIP's. Had the newsreader said Silver? It sounded like it, but I couldn't be sure. And a terrorist? Never. The wonderful feeling of calm immediately vanished as I stabbed the buttons and tried all channels. But by the time I finally got clear reception, the news bulletins were over, and all I could get was a phone-in on incontinence. I tried my mobile. No reception. Of course. How did people live up here? It was like going back to the Dark Ages. Oh dear. So much for the calming influence of the monks. I sounded like Jake. I glared at the phone, at the radio, at the moors, and headed the rattling van back to Hartstone Edge and The Miners' Arms.

'Hi, Tilly, welcome back,' said Becca, while pulling a pint for a thirsty walker. 'How's your mum?'

'Mum? Oh, fine. Well, OK. Thanks,' I gabbled as I rushed through to the snug, where a bewildered-looking visitor glared at me as I hastily moved his papers off the seat by the second computer and clicked on the news sites.

There were blurry pictures of Clayton, still wearing what I last saw him in – shorts, flip-flops and a fleece. What was going on? He was being led away by two policemen. Why?

Then there were pictures of his car, surrounded by policemen. Someone putting cordons in place.

Then I read the story . . .

Premiership footballer Clayton Silver was detained by Metropolitan police this morning and questioned for two hours under the Prevention of Terrorism Act. Silver – one of the highest-earning English footballers – was taken in after a black Hummer, believed to be registered to him, was found abandoned, blocking the entrance to King's Cross station at the start of the morning rush hour. A man, thought to be Silver, accompanied by a woman, had been reported fleeing the scene.

Police cordoned off the station entrance and specially trained sniffer dogs were brought in to search for explosives. The station was closed and all trains cancelled while police pursued their inquiries. The station is now open again and trains are running normally.

A police spokesman later said that Silver had been released without charge but that in such sensitive times anything suspicious had to be fully investigated. 'We would like to remind the public of its duty to behave responsibly, as careless actions can involve huge amounts of police time and resources which could be better spent elsewhere.'

Silver's agent apologised on behalf of the footballer and said it had all been a simple misunderstanding. Silver deeply regretted any inconvenience both to the police and to the travelling public. A spokesman for his club said there were no plans to take the matter further and that Silver would be resuming training as normal tomorrow.

Silver has played for Shadwell for six years and has been part of the Premiership winning team that has been built up since the club was bought by businessman Simeon Maynard.

Another grainy CCTV picture showed Clayton racing across the concourse at King's Cross. He did, I admit, look decidedly dodgy. I was so far behind him, I wasn't in the picture.

King's Cross closed? Clayton questioned by police? London brought to a standstill? – well, a bit of it – all because of me? Oh God. I found myself going bright red, then pale as I put my head down on the keyboard and almost wept. The person using the other computer shifted his chair slightly, further away.

Becca came into the snug, fizzing with excitement. 'Guess what, Sandro rang and . . . Oh, are you all right?'

By this time I had my head in my hands and was peeping through my fingers at the computer screen, trying to make the story go away. Becca leaned over my shoulder and looked at the screen. 'What's that all about?' she asked, baffled, 'Clayton a terrorist?'

I groaned. 'We brought London to a halt,' I said. 'And I really need a shower.'

'I think,' said Becca, perching on the edge of the computer table, 'you'd better tell me the whole story.'

I did. She looked concerned. Then she started smiling. Until, in the end – when I got to the bit about Clayton flinging the car keys against the dashboard – she was whooping with laughter. She peered at the pictures on the screen. 'What *does* he look like? Have you spoken to him?'

'Oh God no. I mean, what do I say? "I'm sorry I've subjected you to public humiliation and ridicule and made you a laughing stock?" Come on – his team-mates will be giving him hell. I bet those pictures will be all over YouTube by now and –' I suddenly panicked –'I bet there are idiots out there who really think that he's some sort of terrorist.'

'On the other hand – it wasn't you who threw the keys and locked the car, was it? That was all his own work. That wasn't your fault.'

'Yes, but he was only driving me because I'd overslept. He was doing me a favour. I knew I should have come back last night. I *knew* it.'

'So what are you going to do now?'

'I'm going to have to ring him. Though goodness knows what I'm going to say.'

I quickly pulled out my phone before I could change my mind. It went straight to voicemail, which was a relief. 'Hello, Clayton, it's me, Tilly. I've just been reading about what happened. Look, I'm really, *really* sorry. I hope it hasn't been too awful for you and that it's all over now. Sorry. Hope everything's OK.' I paused. I felt I should say something else but didn't know what. 'Sorry,' I added again and ended the call. I looked up at Becca, who was losing the battle to be sympathetic because obviously there was something exciting she wanted to tell me.

'Sandro has called twice. He's so sweet. He really wants to see me again soon. He wants me to go down to London!'

'That's brilliant, Becca!' I said. And it was, because she looked so happy. 'Great news. I'm really pleased.'

'But he's up here again soon. Oh Tilly! He is just so lovely, isn't he? He's not just a typical footballer, is he? Just gorgeous, and kind, and gentle, and—'

'You're right,' I said, 'he's just a lovely Italian boy who happens to be brilliant at football.'

Despite his bravura, huge price tag and mammoth wage, Alessandro seemed a little lost in his new world, and wary of the many predatory girls who fluttered round him so eagerly. Maybe down-to-earth Becca was just what he needed.

I left the computer and walked back into the bar where Dexter was serving. I waited till he'd finished and then spoke, uncertain of what his response would be. Did he still think I'd tipped off Jake? My conscience was clear, but while I'd been in London I had kept thinking about it, and hoping there would be no misunderstanding between us. 'Brilliant move with the pics, Dexter,' I said, sounding more confident than I felt. 'Took the wind from their sails a bit.'

There was a long pause while he sorted out the change in the till drawer and I waited nervously for his reaction. Then he looked up at me and grinned. 'Yeah, good, wasn't it? Helluva rush, though. And not exactly ideal conditions, but Matty is a real professional. As is Kate.'

'Kate?'

'Oh God, yes. She was wardrobe mistress and make-up consultant as well as assistant director. She had a great time. The whole family was involved. Tom and Guy were the techies and lighting men and the twins were running round as gofers. It was fun really. And the picture desks really came through for us.'

'They must rate you highly.'

'Yeah, well. Still got a few contacts. And when you're offering pics of Foxy, well . . . So well done, Tilly. If it hadn't been for your boyfriend telling us what was going on, we'd never have beaten them to it.'

'Sorry?' I didn't understand at first. I'd still been thinking they were blaming me for blowing Matty's cover, but in fact I was now a heroine for saving the day. What a turn-around. And definitely a load off my mind.

Now all I had to worry about was Clayton. And getting some sleep. Dexter was offering me a drink, but I shook my head.

'Right now,' I yawned, 'I really must get a shower and get to bed.'

I wanted to wait at the pub as long as possible in case Clayton rang, but I couldn't. I tottered out to PIP and back through the ford and up the track to my second home.

Chapter Eighteen

He hadn't rung. I had gone back to the cottage, fallen straight into bed and slept till nearly midnight. When I'd woken to go to the loo, I'd slipped my jeans and fleece on and driven PIP up to the road to check my phone. Nothing. I was surprised at how disappointed I was as I bumped back down the track, slipped off my clothes and back into the still-warm bed.

At first light, I was back up at the chapel again to try my mobile, but there was no message. Definitely a signal. But definitely no message. I sat there in the van for a while, gazing at the boarded-up chapel and the fading sign saying 'Local Education Authority Outdoor Centre', but however much I stared at that and the stunning view and then back at the phone, there was still no word from Clayton.

I realised I cared. I had spent about ten hours in the company of Clayton Silver but I was beginning to admit to myself that I wanted to spend more. True, he was a bit full of himself. But I guess if you were one of the country's top footballers, you were entitled. True, he cared about winning more than anything else. But I guess that was part of the game too.

On the other hand, there was the man who had started out with precious little and achieved an awful lot, who could laugh at himself when he got stranded in a stream, who liked books and pictures and fine wine, who was generous to his friends and to waiters, who could be gentle and funny and kind and who cared about his mum and who one day wanted to be a good dad.

Should I text him again? I sat shivering in PIP – the monks were right, the weather *had* changed, it was distinctly sharp – and weighed up the pros and cons. Oh, what had I got to lose? Slowly – because my fingers were freezing – I tapped out, 'Hope embarrassment has faded and all is OK.' Then I reversed PIP on the frosty grass and went back along the track.

I could see a tall figure working in the corner of the farmyard. Even in the dim light, and even though she was bundled up in layers of clothes, I recognised Kate. I gave a little toot and she straightened up and waved me over. I edged into the yard and called out, 'Good morning! I bet you've been up for hours.'

'Of course,' said Kate, her long hair bundled up under the sort of flap-eared cap worn by American hunters in cartoons, 'I don't think I could lie in bed even if I wanted to.'

I couldn't make out what she was carrying, dangling from her hands.

'Moles,' she said. 'Just been seeing to the traps.'

'Oh.'

'Just let me get rid of these and I'll be ready for a coffee. Want some?'

'Er, yes please,' I said, trying not to look at the limp velvet bodies.

I went into the kitchen, and while Kate removed her top layers of clothing and scrubbed her hands at the stone sink in the scullery, I filled the kettle and put it on the Aga so it was boiling by the time she came in. As she made the coffee and we waited for it to brew I had to ask her. 'Why do you kill moles? They're so pretty.'

'Ha!' she snorted, 'pretty damaging too. They burrow into the soil and then into the barn and that lets moisture into the hay, which then rots. So yes, they might be pretty, but they're also lethal. Looking pretty doesn't get you very far up here.'

'Did all right for you and Matty,' I smiled. 'I gather you have a new career as assistant director for Dexter Metcalfe.'

Kate laughed. 'What a day that was! And I gather we have you to thank for the tip-off. You gave us just enough time. When Matty came back and said what had happened and what Dexter had suggested, I didn't think it would stand a chance. But it had to be worth a go. Dexter was brilliant. Made me quite nostalgic for my modelling days. The twins thought it was great. Ruth was in her element.'

'What about Tom and Guy?'

'Oh, they muttered a bit about seeing to the stock but they worked wonders rigging up lights in the yard.'

She looked thoughtful for a moment. 'It's still a great shame now that they know who she is and where she's from. But I'm pretty sure it will be a nine-day wonder. Thanks to Dexter. And you. We can all get back to normal now.'

'How's she getting on in Egypt?'

'Oh, fine. Though she says it's far too hot.' She glanced out through the windows at the chilly grey morning. 'Not like here.'

I sat at the table, my back to the Aga, my hands round the big mug of coffee. But Kate was busy going to cupboards, setting out scales and a mixing bowl and lining up ingredients, pausing only in passing to take a glug of coffee. Her hair was piled up into a loose knot on the top of her head. She wore twinkling silver studs in her ears and as she moved elegantly round the big kitchen she could have been posing for one of our swish photo shoots of celebrity kitchens. She certainly didn't look as though she'd just been killing moles a few minutes before.

She must have noticed me staring at her earrings.

'One of my vanities,' she said. 'The others are using bucket-loads of moisturiser and always wearing gloves, a thin pair for protection and a thick pair for warmth. As does Matt. When you've been dealing with the sheep you're liable to end up with indelible blue dye all over your hands. And I'm still vain enough for that not to be a good look.' She smiled. 'We're not all Hannah Hauxwell, you know.'

I dimly remember that television series about an old lady in a man's raggedy coat and boots, struggling to keep her tiny farm, high in the Pennines, going. Absolutely nothing like Kate, who was now briskly measuring out ingredients into a bowl.

'Chapel anniversary tea,' she explained. 'Next village down the dale. Special service, brass band, tea afterwards. Social event of the year.'

'Chapel?' I said wonderingly, chapels not exactly figuring prominently in my world.

'I know. We don't go very often, but it's a link with the past, and people come back for it – so it's a sort of reunion of those who've left the dale long since. So many chapels have closed, including ours, so we try and support those few that are left. Anyway, how's your mum? Have you persuaded her to come up and see us?'

'I hope so. But not until she's a bit more mobile.' I told her about Bill trying to help and how she refused all offers.

'That's an Allen family trait, I'm afraid, ' she laughed.

'That line where independence becomes bloody-mindedness. The Allen women are known for that. I sometimes think it's not always a good thing. We must miss out on things because we're too stiff-necked to compromise. Or even to listen. Granny Allen has a lot to answer for.'

'I'll remember that,' I said as I put my mug on the draining board, thanked Kate for the coffee and went back out into the cold.

But I didn't remember, of course.

Although I kept checking my phone, there was still no message from Clayton. Back in The Miners' Arms at lunchtime, I checked through all the papers. Those pictures again. And yes, he did not look his best. He'd hate that, I thought. Really hate it. Most of the comments were good humoured. There were a couple of good cartoons too. But in one or two there was just that underlying niggle of the 'no-smoke-without-fire' school of journalism that would make you think that maybe Clayton Silver was involved in something dodgy. They linked him with Sim Maynard's questionable dealings too. I thought back to the men he'd met the day of the helicopter trip. And all that Jake had warned me about. Maybe they were right. Maybe I *was* being ridiculously naive. Maybe I'd been just like everyone else and fallen under the spell of a rich football star. I almost threw the papers across the room, just as Becca came in for her shift.

'I've finished the scarf for your mum,' she said, handing me a carrier bag.

I opened it and pulled out the most wonderful scarf. It was black, as I'd asked, but tucked into the lacy pattern was a riot of brightly coloured flowers – vivid pinks, scarlets and purples, almost but not quite clashing and looking gloriously vibrant. And at the centre of each one was a piece of cherry-red velvet, so bright that it seemed almost to glow.

'Is that all right?' asked Becca anxiously. 'It was the best way I could think of using the velvet.'

'It's brilliant, Becca, absolutely brilliant!' I said. Despite the black background it was wonderfully cheerful, the sort of scarf that made you smile just to look at.

'Mum will love it,' I said. How could she not? 'I can't wait to give it to her. In fact . . .' I had to go down to the next village to the little shop and post office for bread and milk. 'I'll send it to her today. It'll cheer her up.' I looked at it happily as I carefully put it back in its carrier bag and then got out my purse to pay Becca.

'And tell me all about Sandro.'

'Oh, he is just so nice,' said Becca, blushing. 'He's rung twice and he just likes to talk. I think he gets a bit lonely. He lives in this block of flats where there was another Italian footballer, but he's moved away. He's learning to play golf because a lot of players do that and he's never played before, so he's hoping he can join in. Clayton took him to a driving range for practice last week. Did he tell you?'

'No. He didn't mention that.'

'Sandro said it was good fun. He likes Clayton.'

I felt unaccountably pleased. Though why should it matter to me, especially as he hadn't called?

'Look, I don't seem to be able to get hold of Clayton. If Sandro rings again, will you ask him how Clayton is, for me, please?'

'Of course. But I don't think he'll ring today. They've got a big match tomorrow, so they'll be travelling. But if he does, yes, of course I will.'

I went off to the post office. There was a sampler there

too. *God helps those who help themselves*, it said. Only underneath someone had added: '*. . . but not from the stock, please*,' which made me smile. I posted the packet to my mum, stocked up on bread and milk and ham and some locally made chutney, went back to the cottage and started writing up the piece about the monks and their orchard, while I munched on ham sandwiches. I took a break and listened to *The News Quiz*. It was full of jokes about Clayton. Somehow, I didn't think he'd find them funny . . .

This time he wanted to take her a present. But had no idea what. His wife had always been easy to buy pres- ents for – brooches and ornaments, frivolous things for show. But Matilda Allen was different. He thought about it as he printed up the last of the photographs before he set out on his journey again. He would like to buy her a shawl, not the practical one she wore as she went about her work, but a splendid shawl in extravagant reds to pick up and chime with her hair.

But she wouldn't like that. Too personal, too pre- mature. In the meantime, perhaps there was some small thing, neither too personal nor too practical, that would be a suitable gift. He went back into the shop area at the front of the studio and then stopped. Of course. She had photographs of her sons but they were tucked away in her Bible. He would take her some frames. Then she could be surrounded by pictures of them. Just the thing. He picked out a selection from the stock in the large cabinet in the shop.

Next morning as he walked round to the stable to harness up the pony and load up the cart, he had to tuck in to the narrow pavement to let the brewery dray and its heavy shire horses pass. As he squeezed into the haberdasher's doorway, his eye fell towards the window and its crowded display. One small section caught his attention. Quickly, before he had time to think about it and change his mind, he ducked in through the tiny door.

Chapter Nineteen

The wind whipped around the cottage and icy rain slashed against the windows. I felt sorry for the sheep. And even more sorry for Kate Alderson, buzzing around on the quad bike, taking feed up to them. I snuggled back down under my duvet, knowing that down at the farm they had been out in the weather for hours. I had one more interview to do – a farmer's wife who made proper puddings, sticky toffee, lemon and ginger, and gooey chocolate, all in a converted barn – and then I could go home again. I was tempted to nip down to London and just come back up, but that seemed a bit feeble just to escape from the weather. While I was here I could do more research for other pieces that I could come back up and do another time – in the summer, perhaps. Did they have summer up here? It seemed hard to believe right now. I pushed the duvet back and plodded off to the shower. If I wanted communication with the world, I was going to have to drive to find it.

No word from Clayton, though the papers were full of him again. Apparently he'd played brilliantly the night before. 'He may not be a terrorist, but he certainly terrified the opposition,' was the general theme. Simeon Maynard was in the news too. A couple of his deputies had left his companies with no warning. 'Are these rats deserting the sinking ship while the vultures begin to circle?' asked one paper with a wonderful rag-bag of mixed metaphors. The more serious newspapers were talking of investigations by the Serious Fraud Office and the Department of Trade and Industry. I wondered how Jake was getting on with his own investigations.

I had plenty of time to read the papers. The foul weather meant that the pub was practically deserted. Dexter was trying to do some paperwork.

'Aren't you tempted to go back to full-time photography?' I asked idly, looking at some of the colour supplement pages, and thinking what a cracking job he'd made of the Matty pictures.

'Yes and no. Yes because I enjoy it. It's what I do. What I am. But no, not the same as I was doing before. I've been there, done that, and buggered up a marriage partly because of it. Or married the wrong woman in the first place. I want to take pictures but I don't want my old life.' He shrugged. 'Something will work out.' Again he pushed his hair out of his eyes. 'Bloody hair,' he muttered. 'Must get it cut.'

'I'll cut it for you,' said Becca brightly, coming in from the kitchen with mugs of tea for us. 'I'll do it now, if you like. After all,' she looked round the empty bar, 'we're not exactly rushed off our feet.'

'Are you safe with scissors?' Dexter asked warily.

'Had a Saturday job at *Through the Looking Glass*. I've cut hair loads of times. And let's face it,' she looked witheringly at his tangled curls, 'I can't make it much worse, can I? When did you last have it cut?'

'Um, for my dad's funeral, I suppose.'

'Dexter, that was a year ago! Get in the back now! Tilly – shout if we have a customer.'

While the back room was turned into a salon, I settled at the computer. There was a nice email from my mother thanking me for the scarf. 'Wonderful to think that there is still such talent in a place like Hartstone Edge,' she said. 'It is so bright and cheerful I am looking forward to wearing it.'

Bright and cheerful? Mum sounded positively chirpy. Maybe the accident and the enforced rest had done her some good.

After about twenty minutes, Becca appeared in the bar. 'Are you ready for the transformation?' she asked. Dexter followed her, looking a bit embarrassed but totally different. Becca had done a great job. Dexter's hair now lay in crisp flat curls close to his head. The new cut emphasised his strong features and made him somehow look more purposeful. I'd always thought he was quite good looking, but now I could actually see his face and his wide grey eyes I realised he was handsome – in a rugged, lived-in sort of way. Becca raised her eyebrows and gave me a quick conspiratorial grin as we admired him.

'Thanks, Becca. I can see where I'm going now,' said Dexter as he came and sat next to me at the other computer. 'The paperwork can wait. I'm going to get on with this.' And he gestured towards a huge pile of old photos, part of the project that he'd been raving about with Matty.

'How many have you got there?' I asked. 'You must have hundreds!'

'Word's got round that I'm interested,' he said. 'People keep turning up with them. There were two sisters in yesterday brought me this lot . . .' He held up a bulging carrier bag. '. . . They've been clearing out their mother's house and found all these. They've kept a few, but didn't know what to do with the rest so gave them to me. They heard I was collecting.'

'Are you?'

'Well, yes, although I never thought it would take off like

206

this. Some of these are brilliant. Lots of old family snaps, of course, but others that go back a hundred years or more, portraits and pictures of people at work. Obviously a professional photographer was going round capturing "picturesque" scenes. Fascinating. Some of them are a bit fragile, so that's why I'm scanning them in, so at least we'll have permanent records of them.'

'Pity there's nowhere to display them.'

'Exactly. Oh, there are a few in a couple of the local museums, and you can buy prints of some of them, the most famous ones. Everyone has that Granny Allen and her Bible picture. But it would be great to have a proper display.'

'How are you doing matching up people and their ancestors?'

'That's really taken off as well. I took a picture of those sisters on the steps of the old chapel. Their parents were married there, so we have the wedding photo. That's good because, not only does it show the family, but it shows how the chapel's changed too. It looks very sad now compared with its glory days.'

I tried to imagine what it must have been like when the chapel had been full of people belting out hymns.

With nothing better to do – and perhaps because I was still hoping Clayton might ring – I stayed in the pub for the rest of the morning, helping Dexter with the pictures as he tried to sort them into groups. The faces were fascinating –a man and a boy cutting peat, a boy lying back with his leg in a sort of splint. He was knitting and staring, fascinated, at the camera.

'It must be odd to have so many professional pictures of a place like Hartstone,' I said, as I put some more into the 'Farm workers' folder. 'He must have made a few trips up here, because these are taken at different times of year.' The boy and the horse were taken against a light covering of snow. Some of the others looked as though they were taken in high summer. Others could be any time.

'Something must have kept the photographer coming back.'

'Something – or someone.'

We got on with the sorting and scanning. Dexter seemed to have set himself a pretty enormous task. An email pinged in for me. 'From Matty,' I said, surprised.

'Oh, what does she say?' asked Dexter eagerly.

I skimmed the message quickly. It was mainly about the triumph of beating the paparazzi at their own game. And thanking me for the tip-off. But there was more.

'She's sent me some pictures.'

I downloaded them, about a dozen or so, and clicked open on each thumbnail image and laughed. They were clearly photos she'd taken during the fashion shoot in Egypt. But while she'd been waiting her turn, she'd taken pictures of the other models – but showing all the tricks that you never normally know about. You could see an assistant flapping a fan to create the windswept look, another holding a piece of cotton attached to the hem of a skirt so it flared at just the right angle. A dog apparently looking eagerly at the model's face was actually looking at another assistant who was holding a piece of meat, just out of shot.

Then there was a shot of the model standing on a camera case, and the photographer kneeling on the sand at her feet. Then a better one of the model toppling over and landing in a heap laughing. And all the stylists and assistants rushing to get her right again and someone triumphantly holding up a false eyelash that had fallen in the sand.

Dexter was looking at the pictures, smiling but appraising. 'I always knew she had a good eye,' he said approvingly. 'Could you forward these to my email? Do you think Matt would mind?'

'I'm sure she wouldn't,' I said, and pushed the keyboard over to him so he could type in his address. I wouldn't be surprised if that was *precisely* what Matt had hoped for.

A little while later he came over with a bottle of very good wine and poured me a glass. 'A thank you,' he said, 'for help in sorting this lot out.'

I put my hand over the glass when he offered more. I wasn't going to go slithering down the beck again.

'It's all right. I'll give you a lift and if you tell me when tomorrow I'll come and get you. Least I can do.'

As it was raining and the wine was good, I said, 'Yes please. Thank you.'

True to his word, he took me back to the cottage and came in for a moment. 'I know every stone of this house and still have some of the scars to prove it,' he laughed. 'It's good to see it lived in.'

He bent down to look out of the small window and immediately picked up the tiny bit of buckle with the scrap of velvet ribbon. 'There's a story there, I expect,' he said, turning it over in his hand. Then his eye fell on Granny Allen's sampler. '"*Carpe diem. Seize the day.*" What's that meant to mean?' he said.

'I think it means making the most of the moment – don't wait for things to happen but do something about it.'

'*Carpe diem,*' said Dexter, running his hand over his newly cropped hair, while the other still held the buckle and its scrap of ribbon. 'Why not? Got to be worth a go, hasn't it?'

Kate invited me to lunch on Sunday. Proper roast pork with all the trimmings. As Guy carved and Kate passed the plates round, Tom bowed his head and I thought for a moment he was going to say grace. Instead he intoned in tones of deep solemnity, 'Let us remember Pinky, poor pig of this parish, who died that the rest of us might stuff our faces this lunchtime.' And he crossed himself very piously while the twins giggled.

'Oh dear,' I said, remembering the happy snuffling pigs I'd watched rootling round their patch of ground. 'Was this one of yours?'

'Yes,' said Tom, still solemn, 'I am happy to say that I knew my dinner well. It's fair to say we were on speaking terms – well, grunting on her part, but we communicated on a deeper level. But her living has not been in vain. It is a far far better thing. Oh sod this,' he said back in his normal voice. 'Pass the gravy please.'

We ate large chunks of poor Pinky, with crispy roast potatoes, honeyed parsnips and mounds of crunchy carrots and red cabbage with apple, followed by a deliciously sharp blackberry pie and creamy homemade custard. 'We'll have you know,' said Zak, 'that we picked all these blackberries and we've got the scratches to prove it.'

All the time the chat was of the farm and friends and Tom teased the twins and Zak teased Ruth and Guy teased Zak. They were still full of Dexter and Matty's impromptu photo shoot.

'I'm definitely going to be a model,' said Ruth. 'Everyone else runs round and does the work and Matty just stands there looking beautiful. Easy.'

'Eew,' said Zak, affecting a model-like demeanour, 'Ay'm just driving my tractor through the yard. Oh, please don't get pig shit on my thousand-pound trousers.'

And so it went on, with a great deal of laughter, and I thought a little sadly of the perfectly pleasant but quiet Sunday lunches my mother and I had always had together when I was a child. Suddenly I felt sorry for myself that I'd missed out on this cheerful chaos of family life, and just as sorry for my mum. And I wondered how life would have been if my father and brother had just been a minute or so later setting out that day . . .

In the middle of it all, Matty rang; she was at the airport waiting for a delayed flight to London, longing to catch up on her sleep and her washing.

'We're eating Pinky!' bellowed Zak down the phone. 'She was lovely.' And the phone was passed around and I too had a brief chat with Matty.

'What's all this about Clayton Silver being a terrorist?' she asked. 'I've just heard about it.'

'Trust me. He's not. And it was actually all my fault. Well, partly.'

'What? How?'

'Too complicated to tell you now, but let's just say he was rescuing a damsel in distress. And though he drove like a maniac and parked in a daft place, he's no more a terrorist than you are. Or Pinky.'

'OK, I believe you,' laughed Matt. 'Did you get my email?'

'Yes. I thought the pictures were brilliant. So did Dexter. I hope you don't mind, but he was sitting next to me when they came, so I had to show him.'

'Sure. What did he think?'

'He loved them. He said you had a natural eye.'

'Did he really?' She sounded excited.

'He did. Didn't you show them to the photographers you were working with?'

'You're joking, aren't you? They wouldn't even bother to look. But Dexter thought they were good?'

'Yes, he did. Really.'

Even on a mobile from an Egyptian airport, I thought I could hear a small sigh of satisfaction.

'Anyway, I'm intrigued by how you turned Clayton Silver into a terrorist. After I'm back, when you have time, ring me and tell me the whole sorry story.'

'I will. I will,' I said, passing the phone back to Kate.

Afterwards, while the twins and Tom cleared the table and loaded the dishwasher, Guy, Kate and I sat down in front of the fire with cups of tea and the papers. The heat from the fire was glorious compared to the grim day outside, and it made my toes curl up with happiness. Guy was soon snoring gently, *The Sunday Times* fluttering up and down on his chest. Kate went into the kitchen to see that all the clearing up had been done properly. Then, just as I was dozing off myself, she started going out to the car with tins and trays of cakes.

'Let me give you a hand,' I said, shuffling my feet back into their shoes.

'Thanks, that would be good.' She was struggling to hold the car door open in the wind. We soon had things loaded up.

'Would you like me to come with you and help at the other end?' I asked.

'No, don't worry. There'll be plenty of people there. Unless you'd like to?'

'Why not?'

Exclusive nightclubs, helicopter trips or chapel teas. I'm all for new experiences these days.

The chapel was three miles down the dale, in the same little village that had the shop and post office. Already the brass band were there, unloading their instruments and tuning up. I was surprised at how young so many of them were. Some looked doddery and ancient, but quite a few were only kids – thirteen, fourteen, fifteen, maybe. The tea was being laid out in the schoolroom next door to the chapel. It smelt slightly of damp, polish, and egg sandwiches. Here, too, were more samplers.

'Judge not, that ye be not judged,' said one sternly, in neat little stitches. though the message was a bit blurred behind

the mottled, fly-specked glass. '*Pride goeth before a fall*' and, '*Love thyself last*' demanded others. I looked away to the tables below them.

'My God, what a feast!'

The tables were spread with endless plates piled high with sandwiches, fruit loaves, scones, cream cakes, fruit tarts, jam tarts, dishes of trifle, sausage rolls, plates of cheese, gingerbread, Victoria sponges, pies, quiches, fairy cakes, Swiss rolls. I had never seen so much food.

'Well, it's a celebration, lass, isn't it?' said an old lady, clearly in her best coat, hat and pinny. 'You've got to make an effort.'

Celebration. And suddenly a thought for a whole new series for *The Foodie* magazine popped into my head. 'Celebration' – weddings, birthdays, chapel teas, Bar Mitzvahs, street parties, stag nights . . . My head filled with images of all sorts of food, from five-tiered wedding cakes with handmade decorations, to chocolate fountains, whole salmon, tapas, profiterole bombes or pork pies. Yes. What a wonderful last-page piece that would make. I would suggest it to Pete as soon as I got back. I was so busy treasuring the possibilities of this wonderful new idea that I didn't for a moment notice the slight ripple of anxiety around me.

'Where's the extra cups? And all the paper plates?'

'Gwen was going to get them, but she had to go to Kirby Stephen, their Emma's baby's on its way.'

'Has anyone else got them?'

'Eeh, I don't think so.'

With that an elderly man in a dog collar popped his head round the door. 'My goodness, what a spread,' he said. 'I always say that this chapel has the best anniversary tea in the dale.' And he clearly meant it. 'Right, the band's ready, so if you'd like to come through next door.'

'But what about the plates?' hissed one of the ladies. 'And all the extra cups?'

'I'll get them,' said Kate, doing her jacket up again.

'Where are they?' I asked.

'Just at The Miners'. Dexter said we could borrow extra from him. He got the plates for us too.'

'I'll go,' I said, 'if you don't mind me driving your car. Then you can go in to the service.'

Kate hesitated. But she wasn't one for shilly-shallying. 'Smashing,' she said, handing over the keys. 'Dexter should have them all ready. And you can just sneak in the back later, if you like.'

With that the band struck up a rousing tune. The school-room emptied and I scampered out through the rain to Kate's car.

Dexter had all the cups, saucers and plates waiting on a table by the door. 'I was just about to bring them down myself,' he said. 'I was wondering what was happening.'

He helped me load them up and I drove carefully back down to the chapel. Once I'd staggered into the school-room with the box, I thought I might as well unpack them and set them out. Cup and saucer, cup and saucer, on the trestle tables covered with white sheets. The huge urn was hissing gently away. A line of teapots stood waiting, ready to be filled. A ramshackle collection of varied milk jugs and a big tin of Nescafé, a paper cup full of spoons. There was something so homely and timeless about it. It would make a lovely picture for the magazine.

From the chapel next door I could hear the brass band doing their stuff and the voices singing alongside. It was cheering. I wandered round the schoolroom, looking at the fly-specked samplers and faded photos – a Sunday school anniversary picnic from years ago, solemn little girls in pinafores, a presentation to somebody for something – lots of men in black suits and whiskers; an anniversary service from the 1950s – people overflowing down the steps and onto the road outside. The chapel was full today, but still nowhere near that full.

I was thinking of all the people who had lived in this dale and of how it was now emptying, with deserted houses, abandoned barns, when even above the triumphant playing in the chapel next door I could hear a strange noise. There it was again.

Oh God, it was my mobile. I was so rarely anywhere where there was reception these days that I just wasn't used to hearing its sound. How bizarre. I fumbled it out of my pocket.

'So is that the lady who got me into so much trouble?' His voice was deep and throaty with the hint of a laugh.

'Clayton! Oh God, I am just *so* sorry. Was it dreadful? Have you had a lot of stick about it? I felt so awful, if I hadn't fallen asleep—'

'You try and give me back my present. You fall asleep on me. You get me arrested.'

'I know, I know, I'm sorry.' The band and congregation next door were now belting out *'Rejoice, in the name of the Lord!'* at full volume. It was a bizarre accompaniment.

'So what happened? I mean, you were only a minute, weren't you?'

'Nah. I got a cab right back to the house, yeah? But when we got to the gates, I didn't have the remote control – that's in the cars.'

'But there's a keypad at the side, isn't there?'

'Yeah. But I couldn't remember the number. It's in my phone. And my phone was in the car, and the car was at King's Cross, wasn't it? And the taxi driver guy was getting really antsy by now.'

Luckily Maria, dear little Maria, had come out to feed

the birds and seen him and let him in so he could get his wallet.

'So I just let the cab take me straight back, but we must have been gone – oh, I don't know, maybe an hour by then. And when I went to my car, there were all these bollards and barriers round it and a load of police. That's when they took me in.'

'But surely if you really were a terrorist, you wouldn't come back to get your car?'

'Right. I told them that, but would they listen? Would they shite. So we had to go through the whole thing: what was I doing, why had I left my car, why had I gone off and abandoned it. Why why why.'

'Oh gosh. Were they horrible?' For a moment I imagined police brutality and torture tactics.

'Nah,' Clayton laughed. 'Not really. One was a bit of a little Hitler but the other two were OK. They knew it was just a cock-up. At the end I had to fill in a form to say if I thought I'd been unfairly questioned or discriminated against.'

'So what did you say?'

'I said yes – because the guys were all Spurs supporters. They thought that was pretty cool really and asked for my autograph . . . and not just on the form. The worst part was all the guys at training taking the piss out of me. And some of the supporters at the game on Friday.'

'But you played brilliantly. I read the match reports.'

'Did you? Yeah, well, I thought I'd show them what they could do with their jokes: stuff 'em right where the sun don't shine.'

'You seem so relaxed about it! I was getting worried when you weren't answering your phone. I thought you must be really angry about what had happened.'

'Well, yeah, it wasn't good. And those pictures in the

papers! How can I be the king of cool looking like that?' he laughed. 'It'll be a nice story for the autobiography, though, won't it?'

I could feel a great weight lifting from my shoulders. If Clayton could laugh about it, I needn't feel guilty. It had taken him a few days to sort it out in his head, but now he was laughing at himself. I was, I realised, grinning myself.

'So where are you now, Miss Tilly the Terrorist?'

'I'm up north. Actually in chapel at the moment. There's a service going on the other side of the wall.'

'You're in chapel?' He sounded surprised. 'Are you a church lady too?'

'Not at all. Just helping out.'

'But you're up north, yeah? With all the sheep?'

'Yes that's right.'

'How long for?'

'End of the week. I've got an interview with a pudding-maker arranged on Friday, so I'll probably come back Saturday or Sunday.'

'Make it Sunday.'

'Why?'

'Because then you can do something to make up for getting me arrested.'

'Anything.'

'*Anything?*'

'Well, *almost* anything.'

He chuckled. 'We're playing up north on Saturday. And Sim Maynard has got a big Halloween party at his lodge. He wants us all to go. Should be a good party and we have to keep him happy. Will you come with me?'

Right at the back of my mind there was the tiniest niggling doubt about Maynard and Ravensike Lodge. I buried it quickly. 'You want me to come to a party with you? On Saturday? A Halloween party?

'Yeah. Not fancy dress, but you'd better dress fancy. OK?'

'OK. Yes. Why not? Well, what I mean is, yes, I'd like to.'

'Great. I'll ring you later, sort out details.' And the phone went dead.

I clutched the phone and looked round the musty schoolroom with its pictures and samplers, the egg sandwiches and chicken legs, the hissing urn and the brass band and singing coming from next door. Suddenly this felt like the best place on earth.

He'd asked me to a party! Despite the trail of chaos I seemed to have left in his life, despite the fact that he had the pick of all the eligible ladies in the country, he had asked *me*. I was so happy I couldn't stand still. I used my phone – which I was still clutching – to take pictures of the room and the table, to remind me of my 'Celebration' idea. I danced up and down the trestle tables, setting out the last of the cups and saucers. I sang as I set up the stacks of paper plates. I even sang along to the hymns. Clayton Silver was a decent guy and I was going to a party with him. Well, wouldn't *you* sing?

When the ladies of the chapel committee – all best coats and sensible shoes – came out before the last hymn to make sure the tea was under control, they beamed at me approvingly.

'Why, lass, you've done a grand job,' smiled one elderly lady as she removed her coat and tied an apron over her smart tweed skirt and matching cardigan. I beamed back at her, full of love for the world, for life, for her and especially – suddenly and blissfully – for Clayton Silver.

He could see her in the distance as she walked over the packhorse bridge and up the path to the cottage. She walked easily, carrying something carefully, the steepness of the track not troubling her. As she neared the cottage, she must have heard him or sensed his presence because she turned and looked. She did not wave or acknowledge him.

But when he too reached the top of the path, the cottage door was open. On the table he could see the pitcher she had been carrying up from the farm.

'Well, Mr Peart,' she said, her mouth set in a firm line, yet her eyes seemed to be smiling, amused, 'you seem to be quite a regular visitor. I hadn't realised the dale held so many suitable subjects for your photography. The people down in London will be very knowledgeable about us.'

'There are always a variety of subjects,' he said, uncertain for a moment. 'And I find this dale interesting.' He thought of the premises he had seen to let in the village on the main road down the dale. The spacious house had a big garden and an orchard and, more importantly, a workshop that could very conveniently be adapted to a studio and darkroom, should a man wish to uproot from a town and move to the quieter confines of the countryside, especially a man with the right sort of wife.

True, there was the boy to consider. But he seemed bright enough, and he would need a new apprentice.

'Will you take some buttermilk?' Mrs Allen asked. 'It is straight from my son's cows. I have charge of them as my daughter-in-law is not well and is in any case no dairywoman.'

'Thank you, yes.'

It was years since he had drunk buttermilk, rich and creamy. Having poured him some, she took the pitcher and put it in the cold stone storeroom at the back of the house.

He unwrapped the frames he had brought with him.

219

At first she refused to accept them. But when he placed a picture of one of her sons in one and propped it on the mantelpiece, she agreed it was pleasant to look up and see him there, still part of the house where he grew up. She allowed him to put the other photograph in its frame and the two young men gazed proudly down at their mother. This time Matilda Allen allowed herself to smile as she gazed at them.

'There is another small thing,' he said, pulling the haberdasher's packet from his pocket.

Chapter Twenty

Clayton and Alessandro strode into The Miners' Arms. But it was very different from that first time, weeks ago. True, they still had that gloss and glow of money and success and yes, they were still swaggering – I think it was the only way they knew to walk – but this time they were smiling and Sandro's face lit up when he saw Becca. He went towards her and took her in his arms, to a chorus of cheers from the locals in the bar.

I stood still, waiting to see what Clayton would do. He grinned at me, looked me up and down in approval and then kissed me on the cheek. 'Wow, you look good, Miss Tilly,' he said, stepping back to get a better view, then kissing me again. 'Really good,' he murmured, as I breathed in the scent of him.

'Well, you're not so bad yourself,' I said, nervous of this new relationship, not quite knowing how to behave.

'You're wearing the necklace,' he said, approvingly, running his fingers gently along it, making the skin of my throat tingle.

'I couldn't not, could I?' I said.

He gave me one of his huge, slow smiles. 'Good.' Then one of the oiks at the bar shouted, 'Blown up any railway stations lately?' and guffawed loudly at his own wit. One of his mates kicked him and he muttered a sort of apology and Clayton just raised his eyebrows in tolerant exasperation, which gave me a short stab of pride. Another chap said, 'Good win today. Great goal. Bloody brilliant goal in fact.'

Clayton grinned, 'Yeah it was, wasn't it? Thanks,' he said, as a chorus of football pundits chimed in over their pints. As they started discussing the match, I took the opportunity to nip to the loo. I might like him, but I'd never be content discussing the offside rule. As I checked my reflection and happily admired myself in the silver and amber necklace and Matty's dress, I spotted that sampler again. *Vanity of vanities; all is vanity.*

I paused for a split second and then shook my head and grinned. Tonight was going to be a great night. I went back to the bar and Clayton.

'Have a good evening!' yelled Dexter as we went out to the car.

'Watch out for witches!' shouted Jan, who was standing in for Becca behind the bar.

Clayton and Sandro were in great humour. They'd picked up a car to fetch us and done some shopping on the way too.

'Oh what's that!' yelped Becca as she slithered into the back with Sandro.

'Pumpkins!' laughed Clayton. 'We got some Halloween stuff when we called in for petrol.'

They must have bought everything in the shop. Witches' hats, pumpkin lanterns, devil horns that flashed red, even glow-in-the-dark teeth and a broomstick. Sandro popped a witch's hat on Becca's head. 'But you are too lovely to be a witch,' I heard him murmur.

Clayton drove confidently down the narrow roads but not, thank goodness, as fast as he had that morning in London. Wisps of mist would suddenly surround us, the car lights just emphasising the denseness of it. Even in the warmth of the car, I shivered.

'Perfect for Halloween,' said Clayton cheerfully. 'Ghoulies and ghosties everywhere,' and he walked his fingers along my leg.

'Stop it!' I said, slapping his hand. 'No talk of ghosts please.'

'Why, you don't believe in ghosts, do you?' he asked, surprised.

'No, of course not. On the other hand, if there were ever a time and a place for them it would be here.'

We could soon spot Ravensike Lodge, even from a few miles away. The lights spread out in the mist and there were more lights of cars arriving, a procession up the long drive, so constant a stream that the magic gates barely had time to shut. As we crunched from the car park through the chilly damp air to the house, I pulled my little black silk jacket closer to me. Actually, it was Matt's black silk jacket. When I'd told Kate where I was going, she'd suggested I borrowed something of her daughter's.

'There are acres of clothes up there. Take what you like. She won't mind, I assure you.'

I'd had a wonderful time looking through the heaps of clothes, many of them just stuffed at the back of the wardrobe that had been built across the corners of the long, sloping bedroom with magnificent views across the moors. Such an incongruous place to find so many designer labels, many of them one-offs. The dresses were all hopeless on me – much too tight. I definitely didn't have my cousin's supermodel figure. The only possibility was a glorified vest of a dress – strappy and cleverly cut in a beautifully soft material. On Matt it would look stunning. On me it would look just like an overgrown T-shirt. But then Kate pulled out the jacket – beautiful black silk in tiny Fortuny-style pleats, shot through with silver.

'Try those together,' she said.

'Gosh!' I said as I looked in the mirror. The dress was a little snug but OK, and with the jacket it somehow made me look a foot taller and inches thinner.

'There!' said Kate approvingly. 'You could almost be Matty's twin.'

Which was definitely an exaggeration, but a very confidence-boosting one.

So I stepped into the entrance hall of Ravensike Lodge feeling on top of the world. I looked as good as I ever had and I was on the arm of one of the most eligible men in England. More importantly, one I was getting to know and like. It was all a bit ridiculous and I wanted to laugh out loud as we made our entrance. Especially as Clayton had pulled out a witch's hat as we got out of the car and popped it on my head. 'The nicest witch I'll know tonight,' he said. 'Just wait until midnight.'

Ravensike Lodge was perfect for Halloween. It was a huge Victorian building, all carved oak and antlers. Very gothic. The Halloween decorations were terrific. The party planners had definitely earned their fee. The entrance hall was hung with proper pumpkins carved into lanterns. Just as well we'd left our plastic versions in the car, I thought. They'd look pretty feeble compared to this lot. Bats hung from chandeliers, silver cobwebs from every picture. Witches whizzed on broomsticks up to the ceiling. There were flickering flame effects. Huge cauldrons of drink that bubbled wonderfully.

Waiting to greet us was a tall woman with piled-up black hair and the tightest scarlet dress I'd ever seen. Lynette was Simeon Maynard's third or maybe fourth wife and at least twenty-five years younger than him. 'Clayton! Alessandro! Wonderful!' she said, shimmering up to us.

224

'Lynette!' said Clayton, and brushed cheeks with her.

'Do have a drink,' said Lynette, barely glancing at Becca and me. 'Simeon will be out in a minute. He's just dealing with a few things. You know what he's like . . .' She laughed. I think she meant it to be a light tinkling laugh but it sounded more like a cackle. Appropriate. Luckily, some more people were arriving behind us, so she moved on to swoop on them instead.

A skeleton pranced up to me, bearing a tray of bright red and green drinks. 'A potion?' he cackled. 'Devil's Delight or Witch's Brew?' then whispered in a very camp way, 'It's all right, sweetie, they taste nicer than they look. But there's plenty of champagne around too.' More skeletons whirled past with trays of drink and exotic canapés.

Clayton looked around. 'No Maynard,' he said, 'what a shame,' in a tone that showed he didn't mean that at all. 'He normally likes to do the gracious host bit.'

I remembered what he'd said about Maynard thinking of Shadwell as his very own Subbuteo set, and was in no great hurry to meet him.

Dry-ice clouds billowed into the hall, almost meeting the real-life mist from outside. Up on a small stage, a DJ wearing a mask like a Venetian plague doctor was pumping out some great music. A few people danced in an absent-minded fashion. The light and the dry ice made for a weird effect. Not helped when devils with tridents poked and prodded the guests into different rooms. One was like a cave, hung around with spiders and giant cut-out toads with glittering eyes. In another, set out as a casino, people were already putting money on the roulette wheel, the glamorous croupiers managing that perfect blend of professionalism and bored indifference.

Clayton nodded at a group of men in the far corner. 'Poker school's started early,' he said. 'Don't suppose they'll move from there all night now.'

225

'Do you play?' I asked.

He grinned. 'It has been known,' he answered. 'It has been known . . .'

One of the men, spotting Clayton, called across. 'You up for it later? Let me get some money back?'

'No thanks,' said Clayton. 'Got better things to do this evening,' and he turned and kissed me. 'No trains to catch. Or miss,' he grinned. 'And maybe this time you won't go to sleep on me.'

I loved it all. I loved the way he could joke about things that I had found so embarrassing. The panic of that morning when I'd woken up on his sofa all cramped and dribbly, and then the awfulness of that car journey and the police questioning and all the stick he got for it on TV and radio and in the papers.

True, he needed a bit of time to deal with things. But once the first fury or embarrassment had worn off, he could laugh about it. And here he was, with his arm round my waist, gazing into my eyes. I remembered that night in Club Balaika, struggling to get Jake's attention, and I smiled back at Clayton.

'What's so funny, Miss Tilly?'

'Nothing, nothing at all. I'm just . . . well . . . happy.'

His eyes smiled and he said, 'Do you know what? I think I am too.'

Back in the hall, we danced for a while. It was just an excuse to be close to him, to feel his arms around me and mine round him. For that moment, in that time and place, everything just felt right. Well, almost. I just wished it had been someone else's party, a party we'd gone to because we wanted to, not just because Clayton was paid to be here.

When the DJ pushed his plague mask up onto his head to sort his music out more easily, we wandered head in hand into a room that had very lifelike flame effects licking at the walls. A doll-like girl – size zero, blonde hair extensions, no light behind her huge vacant eyes – screamed in horror at the fake spiders and clutched at her partner, one of Clayton's team-mates. Her vertiginous heels scrabbled on the wooden floor as she made the tricky manoeuvre to turn round and leave the room. I wondered how she would have coped with Kate's early-morning mole traps.

The music was fainter here, just a pulsating background so you could hear yourself speak. The men were, inevitably, talking football. 'Excuse us,' said Sandro apologetically to Becca, 'it is good to win and we are still so . . .' He groped for a word. '. . . excited about it.'

I didn't mind. It was just good to stand there with Clayton's arm around me, listening to him replaying the match, watching him move in his world. And watching the other women too. One looked like a real-life Barbie doll. Very tall, huge boobs, long legs; she was made of so much silicone that I hoped she'd keep away from the fire, or she'd melt. She was already drunk and clinging desperately to a footballer I didn't recognise. He looked pretty out of it too.

Some of the other women were stunning. Frighteningly so. Definitely high maintenance. One or two others were very attractive but almost ordinary. No, not ordinary, *real*. That was the word. While they were dressed to kill and out to enjoy themselves, you had a feeling that they had lives of their own elsewhere – jobs, kids, hobbies. This was only a part of it. And not the most important part either. One was looking dubiously at her bright green drink.

'Do you think it's safe?' she grinned at me.

'It tastes better than it looks,' I said. 'Not that that's hard.'

She sipped it tentatively. 'Mmm, still pretty disgusting . . . My name's Nell, by the way.'

'Tilly,' I said, realising I recognised Nell, wife of Clayton's team-mate, Jojo François. She was a regular on a daytime TV show I'd seen when I was looking after Mum.

'Weird do, isn't it?' she said. 'We only came because the lads were playing up here and my gran lives on Wearside, so I could kill two birds with one stone.'

'Yes,' I said, 'I'm working up here at the moment. I guess that's why Clayton rang me.'

She studied me for a moment, trying to place me in the pattern of footballers' girlfriends. Just as I was doing with her, I suppose. Then she put her glass down. 'It's no good. I can't drink that. The boys are going to be replaying that match for ages yet. Shall we go and see if we can find a proper drink?'

I glanced at Clayton who smiled at me and let go of my hand and kissed it quickly. 'Won't be long, Tilly,' he said, laughing. 'We're almost at my goal now.'

Becca was entwined round Sandro and, as she had a blissful smile on her face, I guessed she was perfectly happy where she was. I smiled as I followed Nell into the next room, Clayton's kiss lingering on my fingers. 'Have you known Clayton long?' she asked as we made our way through the throng.

'Just a few weeks,' I said.

'I thought I hadn't seen you before,' she said. 'So how did you meet Clayton?'

'Oh, I'm just working up here for a magazine. He came into the pub where I go to use the computer.'

'Ah,' she said, 'I thought you seemed to have a few more brain cells than his usual girlfriends . . . Oh, I'm sorry,' she added hastily, 'that wasn't meant to sound . . . well, you know . . .'

She looked so crestfallen that I smiled. 'No, it's all right. He does seem to have a record of a different blonde every week.'

'Goes with the territory,' said Nell cheerfully. 'The girls throw themselves at the footballers. They'd have to be made of stern stuff to turn down such opportunities. Many of them have the brain cells of a cabbage and the sex drive of a rabbit, so that doesn't matter. But with some of the others – Clayton, for instance – it stops them meeting people they might really connect with.'

'So how did you meet Jojo?'

'I interviewed him for daytime TV – one of the first interviews I was allowed to do, and that was only because I spoke French, in case he went to pieces and couldn't remember his English. I realised that, as well as a footballer, he was actually a really interesting person. So I didn't let him get away! I appointed myself his interpreter – cunning move. And,' she grinned, 'I've been giving him English lessons ever since. Anyway,' she added, 'Clayton certainly seems smitten.'

I went bright red and beamed. Clayton smitten? With me?

'Oh no,' I said, firmly, 'we hardly know each other.'

The place was filling up now but, apart from the staff, there seemed to be no sign of our so-called host. Yet another waiter offered us a tray of brightly coloured liquid.

'There are champagne cocktails and there is a bar, madam, in the library,' said the waiter, noticing our lack of enthusiasm. Nell and I went off in search of the bar. We came to a huge oak door, barely open.

'This looks like a library,' said Nell confidently, pushing at the door. But immediately it was pushed shut again, though not before we'd had a glimpse inside. There was a man I recognised as Simeon Maynard and a couple of others. They seemed to be arguing. Maynard was shouting at one of the men, while he scrabbled through a pile of papers on a desk. The desk drawers were open and another man was on his haunches, taking out piles of files and pushing them into a holdall.

It was an odd scene, but we had only a split second to make sense of it before the door was shut. Nell shrugged.

'So *that*'s where our host is. He doesn't seem to be enjoying his party very much. Not very hospitable of him to hide away, is it? Not like him at all,' said Nell and then, triumphantly, 'Ah here we are.'

The library was, in fact, a huge wide corridor leading to a massive conservatory, where staff were bringing out trays full of food – proper food, not eyeball-type canapés. Looked promising. In front of the shelves of books – which looked suspiciously unreal – were two long bars. From one, waiters scuttled back and forth with the luminous drinks. From the other, barmen were pouring more conventional drinks.

'Vodka?' asked Nell, and I nodded. The barman poured two huge shots and passed them over to us. Another offered a range of mixers and, when I nodded, added a glug of raspberry juice. I took a sip.

'Now that's what I call a drink,' said Nell, approvingly.

It was strong stuff. I realised I hadn't eaten since breakfast and was glad to see a waiter with a tray of canapés.

'Eyeballs or dead men's fingers?' he asked, offering tiny stuffed quails' eggs and long narrow pastry cases filled with what turned out to be mushroom but which looked distinctly odd in the strange pale light of the library.

'This is one of the oddest parties I've ever been to,' I said to Nell. 'The food so far is straight from a children's party, the casino's like something out of a Round Table fundraising effort, only with proper money, and as for the rest . . .'

I meant to sip the vodka slowly but the glass was empty very quickly. As was Nell's. She'd asked me about the magazine and we talked about food, for which she clearly had a passion, strangely enough for a footballer's wife. She also mentioned her children.

'My mum's with them tonight. So I should be having a

wonderful time and forgetting about them, but I can't really,' she said. 'I miss them. Still, I'll be home tomorrow. Let's have another drink and work our way back round to the boys.'

We took our drinks, picked up a few more canapés and tried to make our way back to the room with the pretend flames where we'd left Clayton and Jojo. Maybe we could bring them back some proper food. I certainly needed some. I felt oddly light-headed. Light-headedly odd. As we passed through the hallway, a group of women were arriving. There were maybe six or seven of them, falling over each other and giggling. They'd clearly had a few already. They looked round boldly. They were a striking group, wearing a lot of make-up and clothes that were just a bit too short, too tight, too low. Like any group of girls out for a good time on a Friday night.

Two of them were reaching out for drinks from the tray, the others busy gawping around them. One of Maynard's men was already moving towards them, surprisingly smoothly considering his bulk. But one of the women pre-empted him.

'It's all right, pet,' she said, 'Ramon invited us. Aye, all of us. We met down the Quayside and he told us about it. Look,' she shoved a piece of paper beneath the muscleman's nose, 'he even wrote it down for us. Ravensike Lodge. That's where we are, isn't it? By, it's a bloody long way. Cost us a fortune to get here. Are you not going to give us a drink, like?'

'Wait here,' said the muscleman. 'Don't move.'

'OK, pet,' said the woman, undaunted, 'but we can have a drink while we're waiting, can't we?' and she helped herself to a glass off the tray. 'Come on, girls, don't be shy.'

'Oh no. I was afraid of that,' muttered Nell.

'Afraid of what?' I asked, beginning to feel uncomfortable.

'The local tarts have arrived. Daft things. They just want a footballer, any footballer, and this is the way they do it. In which case,' she put her drink down, 'I don't think this is my sort of party.'

With that Ramon and another young footballer whom I didn't recognise, appeared on the stairs. They looked at the girls, then at each other, and laughed. It didn't seem a particularly nice laugh.

'So, ladies, you made it!' Ramon said.

'Why, of course. You invited us, didn't you?'

'We did. Yes, we did.'

He nodded at the muscleman who shrugged his massive shoulders and went off. One or two of the other young men who had been drinking and talking football came over to the girls, who giggled delightedly.

Now I felt very uncomfortable. I looked for Nell but she had already disappeared. I tried to follow her but couldn't and instead stood, staring, fascinated at the women, as they knocked back the drinks with terrifying speed. Soon they were surrounded by a group of young men. The noise level ratcheted up.

I realised I had to go to the loo. The Barbie doll girl was there, head down, leaning on the washbasin. For a moment, I thought she was being sick and then, when she stood up, I could see her reflection in the mirror and the telltale trail of white powder around her nostrils.

'What are you staring at?' she asked challengingly.

'Nothing. Nothing at all,' and I nipped quickly into the loo and bolted the door. What would Granny Allen say?

I waited in there until I heard her go out and the door slam. I washed my hands carefully and looked at myself in the mirror. I looked OK but I felt distinctly odd. Not quite drunk, but not quite sober either. Sort of dizzy and blurred round the edges. Partly the vodka on top of champagne and whatever that green drink was. Partly the encounter with Barbie girl. Partly the strangeness of the evening. Suddenly, what had seemed fun now seemed frightening. Unpleasant. I realised, that, like Nell, I didn't want to stay. I would find Clayton. Maybe we could go back to my cottage.

A horrible thought struck me. Had Clayton invited me because I was nearby and available, one of the local tarts? I didn't want any footballer. I wanted Clayton Silver. And I wanted him not because he was a footballer, but despite the fact that he was. But that didn't explain why Clayton wanted me. Maybe he didn't see it like that. He probably had girls in every part of the country. Why had I kidded myself I was different?

By the time I left the loo, the noise level seemed to have soared. The music was louder, people were shouting. Lights were dimmer. Couples were entwined. As I tried to find Clayton, I found myself pushing past people. There was a man whose face I recognised from television, a footballer turned commentator. He leered at me.

'So who are you?' he asked, putting his arm between me and the wall so I couldn't get past. I noticed the cut of his expensive suit but I could also smell the whisky on his breath, see the acne scars on his face, the spittle on his lips. As he bent down towards me, I ducked sharply underneath his arm and escaped, nearly bumping into Becca.

'We've had enough,' she said, 'I think we're going to go. Sandro's just trying to sort out a car and a driver to come back to mine. Do you want to come too?'

'I'm going back to find Clayton,' I said. 'See what he says.'

Now it was very important to find Clayton. How could I have wandered off from him? The memory of his kiss had long since faded. I wanted to be back with him, his arms round me. I so much did not want to be at this party any more.

I finally made it back to the room with the flames apparently flickering up the walls. In the menacing red glow, I could see Clayton standing there. I thought he might have been looking for me, but instead he was staring at Barbie girl, who was standing in front of him. Swaying slightly on her huge high heels, shouting strangely at Clayton, one of her long, scarlet-nailed fingers was jabbing at him as she tried to make a point.

'What sort of a man . . . what sort of a so-called man runs out on his own son, eh?' she was shouting, spitting almost. 'This cheating bastard,' she announced to the room in general, 'this cheating, lying shit-face walked out on my sister and his kid. Never gave them a penny. Never bought the boy a present. Never even sent him a fucking birthday card! Clayton Mister Quicksilver footballer is as bad as all the rest. He's earning thousands and thousands a week and my sister, my little sister and my nephew, his son, are living on benefits in a grotty flat. What does he care? Sod all! That's what the great Clayton Quicksilver is really like. Just like all the rest.'

I looked at Clayton. I expected his furious denial. But it didn't come.

'For God's sake, Chrissie, we've been through this,' he was trying to say. If anything, he sounded bored. He certainly wasn't denying it. It was almost as though he didn't care.

And I felt a chill inside me. Could it be true? Could Clayton Silver turn out to be just the sort of irresponsible bloke I'd once feared he was? Please not. That bubble of excitement I'd felt when we'd arrived and danced together had gone flat and stale and was making me feel sick. Out of the corner of my eye, I could see a young girl in the hallway, one of those who'd arrived in a group, giggling as two young men led her up the stairs.

Back in the flames room, people were standing in a circle, watching Clayton and Barbie girl.

'Is this true?' I asked the man standing next to me, who I realised was Jojo.

He shrugged. 'I 'ave 'eard stories. But there are always such stories. It is part of being a footballer, no?'

Barbie girl was still shouting at Clayton, still jabbing at him. Then, as she swayed back and forth, she slipped, staggered and fell to the floor. Her skirt, already short, rode up to her hips. A few men laughed bawdily, mockingly. A couple of others reached down, helped her up, led her away out of the room. As she went, her arms draped round a man who could barely walk straight himself, she was still shouting over her shoulder. 'You're a bastard, Clayton Silver! A cheating, deserting bastard who can't even acknowledge his own flesh and blood!'

I tried to get closer to Clayton. 'Is this right?' I asked. 'Is this right what that . . . woman . . . says?'

'You don't understand,' he said wearily. 'It was a long time ago.'

And I lost it. Right there, in the middle of the flickering fake flames, the entwined couples, the gawping drinkers. Surrounded by skeletons and witches, and prancing devils, the eerie glow of the lights and the dizziness of the drink, I couldn't tell any more what was real or not. It was all a nightmare, an absolute nightmare.

'A long time ago! When it happened doesn't make any difference. All the things you've said about your own father. How you missed him. How he let you down. How you would never do that to your son! And you did! You did!' I remembered his sad eyes across the table, still hurt at the way his father had deserted him. He had sworn he would never do that and I had believed him, trusted him.

235

'Tilly,' he said, putting his hand up to stop me. But I was unstoppable.

'I thought you were different, Clayton Silver. I thought, I really thought . . .' I almost sobbed at what I had let myself think. But I'd been wrong, hadn't I? I should have stuck to my original opinion of Clayton Silver – as a self-obsessed show-off. Just like so many of them, with more money than sense and certainly no sense of responsibility, not even self-respect. Why had I let myself be misled? Just because he had a nice smile and liked to invest in paintings, I'd built up a picture of the sort of man I wanted him to be, a picture I'd painted myself and wanted to believe.

'She's right,' I said. 'You're a cheating bastard and a pathetic specimen of a man.' I was angry with him, and angry with myself, furious and disappointed and hurting so much that it had turned out this way. A small thought at the back of my brain reminded me that Jake had been right after all. That was the final straw.

I turned and fled.

There was a chorus of whistles and catcalls and I could hear Clayton somewhere shouting, 'Tilly! For God's sake.' But it was too late. I was running out of the hell-like room, out of the oak and antlered hall, past the drunk and laughing footballers, past the high-class tarts, past the waiters with their foaming cups of bright green liquid and their dead men's eyeballs and dead men's fingers and the awful awfulness of it all, out into the night where the cold air hit me like a slap.

I stood there in the light from the entrance hall, wondering what to do next when I heard Becca's voice, 'Tilly? Is that you? Do you want to come with us?' I could just see her, standing in the mist by the open door of a waiting car.

'Oh yes, yes please!' I said, almost crying as I ran towards the car. Desperate to get away from Clayton Silver, and even more desperate to escape from the seedy, squalid, sordid world he'd lured me into.

Chapter Twenty-One

I huddled in the back of the car, wrapping Matty's tiny jacket round me.

'What happened in there?' asked Becca, concerned. 'Are you all right?'

'Fine. Fine,' I lied.

'Where's Clayton? Aren't you . . . ?'

'No.'

I knew I was being rude but I just couldn't begin to explain. Not yet.

'Ah,' said Becca and, to cover my silence, started prattling on about the party, the tarts, the people, the drugs. She was worrying about the girls that she'd seen disappearing with some of the footballers. 'I hope they're all right,' she said. 'They seemed so drunk. They could hardly get up the stairs. Maybe I should have— Hey, Sandro! What are you doing?'

The car had lurched heavily. Sandro was peering through the windscreen and I realised he could hardly see where we were going as the thick fog swirled round the car. It muffled us, like a huge damp blanket pressing down. I pushed further into my corner and tried to get Clayton out of my head. But my head was full of him and the strange menacing scenes from the party. Halloween parties are meant to be scary. But this had been different. A very real unpleasantness.

The car bumped again and seemed to slither across the road. Sandro swore and rubbed the windscreen in front of him, trying to see where he was going. It made no difference.

'Where are we?' I asked.

'I'm not sure,' said Becca, her voice anxious. 'We shouldn't be far off from the main road and the turning back up to Hartstone by now.' The car bumped and lurched. There was a sickening scraping sound. 'But it doesn't even seem as if we're on the road. Careful, Sandro! You must be going into the ditch. Get back on the road! We'll stop, see exactly where we are. Unless you've taken the wrong turning.' She peered through the thick fog that seemed to be pressing down on us ever more. 'I can't see where we are. There doesn't seem to be an edge . . . I don't think we're on the road. You've gone the wrong way.' Her voice was getting increasingly anxious. 'We're not even on the road, we're on a track. Stop so we can see. Sandro! Stop! Sandro!'

It was the last thing I heard. Becca's voice soaring, screaming, as the car left the track and plunged into nothingness. For a brief moment there was a feeling of exhilaration as we lost contact with the ground. 'We're flying!' I thought ridiculously as Becca screamed.

I was thrown forward and snatched back by the seat belt. But I seemed to be upside down, swirling into the fog. Then there was a huge bang and a crash of metal as the car hit a rock and bounced, knocking my head against the window and rattling my teeth together. Then it lurched up into the air again, wavered for a second and then crashed on to its side and slid round with a terrifying grating noise. There was the sudden awful sound of smashing glass and a rush of cold damp air into the car. It rocked for a moment, then shuddered to a stop.

Silence. Darkness. No screams. No shouts. Just grey,

damp, suffocating silence. And the fog filling the car, bringing the Halloween night in with it.

I don't know how long I lay there, unable to move, unable to think. It could have been seconds, minutes, even an hour. But the silence went on.

I was lying on the side of the car, almost upside down. I could feel the door handle pressing into my hipbone. The car was on its side, the door on the ground. I moved myself slowly, experimentally. I could feel my toes. I wiggled them. My fingers too. My head hurt and, when I tried to lift it, I yelped as my neck hurt too. But I could move it. That had to be a good sign, didn't it? The seat belt was tight round my throat, almost choking me. I couldn't work out where it was fastened so that I could undo it. I had no sense of the right way up, or round, or anything. I put my hand round the belt at my throat and followed it down. Or up. I found the fastener but couldn't remember what to do. Did you press it or what? I prodded around ineffectually for a while, and then suddenly it slipped free. The pain in my neck eased a little as the belt loosened, but I found myself falling further into a crumpled heap behind the driver's seat. But if I tried gently, ignoring all the pains in different bits of me, I could get a grip somewhere and heave myself up.

There! Done it. I was sitting on the door, leaning against the seat.

The others! What about the others? I pulled myself up and I could just make out Sandro in the darkness. His head was resting on the smashed glass of the driver's window, his face jammed up against a piece of rock. I reached my fingers out, delicately, gingerly, frightened, to see if I could feel him moving, breathing. I felt something wet and sticky on his face, on my fingers. Blood.

Oh God. Becca was slumped on top of him, her body hanging from its seat belt, her head lolling.

Please don't let them be dead. Please don't let that have happened.

What should I do? I couldn't think. I knew I had to be calm and sensible but I seemed unable to think where to begin.

I moved carefully, frightened that the car would shift, but though it groaned spectacularly it hardly moved. It was jammed on the rocks and stuck in the side of the hillside. The engine was off, the lights out. Before I could do anything I would have to get out. I tried to move in the cramped space. Various bits of me screamed in agony, but it didn't matter. What mattered was getting out.

I had to get help. That's it. That's what I had to do. But how? I moved around carefully so I could reach towards the other door. As I groped my way along the back seat, I realised I was groping through piles of plastic that had fallen on top of me. The pumpkins!

Suddenly, in a moment of clarity that later I could never understand, I remembered that the pumpkins were lanterns. I picked one up, embraced it in my arms and felt gently round it. There! A tiny switch. I pushed it and the car filled with a horrifying orange glow from the grinning jaw and empty eye sockets.

And I giggled. God forgive me. With Sandro and Becca lying there I giggled at the sight of the pumpkin. And I started shaking. I always wondered what people meant when they said their teeth chattered, and now I knew. My teeth were off on a dance of their own and my body was shaking so much that I was almost in convulsions.

But with the glow of the lantern I could find the door handle above me. I reached up. It clicked open and I managed to push the door up and open. I wriggled round and freed my feet. I had no idea how far it was to the ground. I inched myself out and then dropped. The car hardly rocked at all. My legs buckled underneath me and I found myself kneeling on the wet grass. I stretched back into the car and got the pumpkin and stepped carefully round to see Sandro.

He was breathing. Thank you, God. But his head and his throat were surrounded by ragged shards of glass and metal. Just the slightest movement ... I needed to smash them off, if I could do it without disturbing Sandro. I tried pushing it with my hand but the glass and the pain just sliced into my fingers. I battered it with my elbow and that worked for a moment, but Matty's silk jacket was no protection. I needed something to bash with. The broomstick! There'd been a broomstick, hadn't there? I groped around the floor of the car, located it, and used it to smash as much of the glass away as I could and then wrapped a plastic witch's cloak into a cushion and gently slid it between Sandro's neck and the window. Just in case. He made no noise but he was still breathing.

Where there's life, there's hope.

I couldn't work out how to get to Becca. I couldn't get through the driver's door, obviously, because Sandro was there. But with the car up on its side, I couldn't reach her from the passenger door either. With that I heard her moan and mutter something.

'Becca! Becca!'

She groaned and, in the light of the pumpkin, I could see her eyes flutter open. 'The car's crashed,' I said urgently. 'I don't know where we are.'

Becca moved her head. 'Eerrggh,' she said. 'My shoulder ... my arm ...'

I looked more closely in the light of the pumpkin. Her shoulder seemed to be sticking out at a strange angle and her arm was dangling down oddly towards the gear stick. I'm sure it wasn't meant to be that short of shape.

242

'Don't move, Becca,' I said. 'Don't worry, I'll sort something out.'

I scrabbled round in the back of the car. I didn't think my phone would work, but it had to be worth a try. I thought I'd felt something warm and woolly in there too. A blanket maybe. I hauled it out. It was a stylish coat. Sandro's, I guess. I flung it over Becca so it also draped over Sandro as well. I piled some witches' cloaks on top of them. The thin plastic might keep out some of the damp.

'There. That will help keep you warm.' I thought of undoing the seat belt, but then Becca, her crazy shoulder and arm would collapse right onto Sandro. No, I would have to leave her as she was.

Back in the car I had felt something leather. Clayton's jacket. I suddenly remembered what had happened. How he'd proved to be a cheat after all. But I couldn't afford to have principles right now. I shrugged into the jacket, noticed almost automatically, even in my strange state, the luxurious softness of the leather, and relished its warmth around me. There were witches' hats, but I couldn't think of anything to do with them. Devils' horns. I switched them on too. Only a little flickering glow of red, but it might help someone find us. More pumpkins. I found the switches and lit them. Maybe someone would see us. Find us.

At last I found the thin strap of the tiny bag I'd brought out with me. I felt for my phone and switched it on. Its screen lit up but there was no signal. 'No network coverage,' it said. And I sobbed.

Then it dawned on me, horribly, crawlingly, like the fog creeping into the car, that no one would look for us because no one knew we were missing.

The party people – if they had even noticed, let alone cared – would just assume we'd gone home. People at home would think we were at the party. If we didn't come home, they would presume we had stayed there, that we were having a riotous time. It could be hours, maybe even days before they raised the alarm.

How would Sandro and Becca last that long? How would I?

One of those blessed samplers flashed into my brain again. *God helps those who help themselves.*

I would have to go for help. But where? Which way? I had no idea where I was. I could be trailing the moors for hours. There were rocks, cliffs, bogs and mine workings. Even in daylight I could get hopelessly lost. But in the dark and the fog, I stood no chance at all. But what else could I do? There were still seven hours until daylight. Becca and Sandro needed help. Sitting here panicking would help no one. Maybe somehow I could get back to Ravensike.

I picked up the pumpkin and limped slowly round the car. Even a yard or so away, the shape of the car was almost swallowed up by the fog; all I could see was the stupid orange glow of the pumpkins. But even in that eerie light I could see the steep hillside above me. We had come over the sheer drop of a small cliff. I could make out the scars where the car had sliced off the grass at the bottom, but above were just rocks. There was no way I could get back up there. Dejected, I turned down, the other way.

I was wearing party shoes that scribbled and scrabbled and sank into the moorland. I stopped and wanted to cry. Really, it seemed to be the most productive thing I could do right then. But holding the pumpkin, as I inched past the car wheels in the air, I peered down. Maybe there was something a bit firmer there . . . Tricky to see, but maybe there was a sort of path. It could, of course, just be a trail left by the sheep, but no. There were stones and cobbles, worn smooth. It *was* a path.

Well, that was a start. But where did it go? I hobbled a

244

few tentative steps and thought I could make out a shape in the fog. A wall, perhaps? Right up close, I could see the outlines of a ruined building. That was something. But which one? There were scores of them round here. But there was a path. Ow! I'd walked into a tree, a narrow branch had whipped sharply across my cheek. Like a razor-cut in the cold. There were virtually no trees up on the moors and yet I'd managed to walk right into one. Brilliant. I held the pumpkin lantern up so I could see more clearly to avoid it. Crab apples. There were tiny wizened crab apples hanging from the branches. As I looked at them I remembered that sharp, sour taste when I had bit into one. And there, just out of reach, hanging from a twig, was a piece of something fluttering in the fog.

I couldn't reach it. I tried to stand on a stone, hold on to the tree, but it was out of my reach. But I'd bet my life that it was a piece of cherry-red velvet ribbon and that this was the ruined house at the bottom of the valley I had passed on the day I had met Matt. It had to be!

Well no, actually, it didn't. It was probably a chocolate wrapper abandoned weeks ago by a walker. But there was a chance. My only chance. I hung the pumpkin from one of the twigs of the tree, which was so weedy that it bent right down under its weight and took most of the light with it. I took off one of my shoes and slithered on the stones as I reached up, right up and . . . yes! I hooked the heel over the thin branch and brought it back just within reach. As I grasped the fluttering piece of material, the branch whipped back out from under the shoe and up out of the eerie orange circle of the pumpkin light. The material in my hand ripped away and I was left holding just the tiniest scrap of it. But it was enough. As I rubbed it in my fingers, I didn't need the light to know that this wasn't a chocolate wrapper but velvet ribbon.

It was the same tree I saw that day I met Matt. It had to be. The building seemed right. The broken wall, the crab-apple tree. I had to believe it. I rammed the ribbon into the pocket of the leather jacket. My brain, which had previously been numb, suddenly went into overdrive. I tried to remember which way I had approached the house that day. Think. Think. I had come this way . . . and reached that way . . . and seen the house . . . here, and the tree there . . . So if I faced that way, I should follow the path along the valley bottom and eventually get back to Kate's house.

Could it be that easy? It would mean that Sandro had tried to drive along the path I'd walked when I bumped into Clayton on the day of the helicopter ride. That did make a sort of sense. That he'd veered right instead of left when he'd gone through the gates in the fog.

I groped my way back to the car. Becca's eyes were open now. 'Are you OK?' I asked.

'No,' she said, which sort of proved she was really.

'I think I know where we are,' I said. 'I'm going to get help. I've left you the pumpkin lanterns.'

'Don't be silly,' said Becca, her voice slurred. 'Too dangerous. You'll get lost . . . Arggh!' She had tried to move and was now gasping with pain.

'It's the only way,' I said. 'I think we're in the valley bottom near the Aldersons'. I'm setting out. Tell you what,' I said, struck by a brainwave, 'I'll take some of the witches' hats and drop them on my way. So if I've gone completely the wrong way, people will know which way I went.' Becca looked at me. I don't think she knew what I was talking about. Then she winced in pain. 'Sandro?'

'He's unconscious but he's breathing. And the bleeding seems to have stopped,' I said.

I clutched the pumpkin and the witches' hats and set off. I had gone only a few yards when the car and the pumpkin lights vanished in the fog. I was utterly alone, swallowed up in the vast expanse of whiteness. The weight of the fog seemed to press right into my lungs, making it hard to breathe. There was nothing to take my bearings from. I was a city girl, used to neon and street signs and pavements. But here there was nothing. I could feel panic rising, rising until I wanted to scream. But I didn't. I fought it down. *God helps those who help themselves.* I dropped the first hat. I knew, whatever I did, I must not turn round. I had to keep walking in the same direction, otherwise I could end up walking round in circles. I kept my feet firmly facing the same way. I walked slowly, carefully, my feet slipping out of my party shoes, slithering on stones, sinking in the ruts as I followed the path. It was little more than a narrow stretch of flattened grass with occasional smooth stones. Sometimes I thought I was imagining it, that it wasn't there at all. But I tottered and tripped and slipped on. Occasionally I switched on my mobile, which gave a narrow shaft of clearer light. But I was saving that in case I got somewhere where there was a signal.

I tried to remember how far it was to the farm. No more than a mile, I reckoned. If I was on the right track. Twenty minutes. Yes, twenty minutes on a nice flat path with trainers and in daylight. Not in strappy shoes in fog with only a dim orange glow. Ow! My foot turned over. Pain shot through my ankle. Maybe I should try walking without my shoes. But it was so cold, the stones so sharp and wet. I limped carefully on, glad of Clayton's jacket. But the skirt of the T-shirt dress was now damp with the fog and clung to my legs and their thin tights, now ripped to shreds. I couldn't stop shivering.

But I just had to keep going. There was nothing else to do. Every few steps got me closer. If I was going in the right direction.

A journey of a thousand miles starts with a single step. Arghh. My heel caught in something and I crashed to the ground. Pain jarred through my wrist and up through my shoulder. I sat there for a moment, feeling utterly defeated. A sheep bleated and made my heart race. Its eyes glinted yellow. I was surrounded by these glints of evil yellow light. I gasped and struggled to my feet again, abandoned my shoes, clutched the pumpkin and carried on.

By now I couldn't feel my feet. They were like bricks on the ends of my legs. Solid, heavy, frozen and very difficult to move. Pain shot through my ankles and into my legs. I felt curiously light-headed, remote from it all. I almost hypnotised myself by counting. A mile was around 1,500 metres, wasn't it? And I was taking about three steps to a metre, so that was 4,500 steps. I counted backwards. It was harder; it took concentration. I found I was stuck on 2,378 and couldn't think what came next. But while I worked it out, there were a few more steps made.

I thought my eyes were playing tricks on me. I seemed to have spent my whole life slipping and tripping through the fog on this apology for a path, but now there seemed to be something up ahead. I stopped trying to work out what came after 2,378. 2,278? 2,780? Too difficult. A cluster of shapes loomed out, darker than the fog around them. Buildings? Then a small light spread a dim glow on the surface of the fog. Then there was a questioning bark from a dog, followed by another. Suddenly there were dogs going mad. It was a house. Definitely a house. Lights went on somewhere in the fog. A window inched open. My heart lifted, I could have sung with happiness.

'Anyone there?' I heard. Even muffled in the fog, I recognised it. It was Guy's voice.

'Help!' I yelled as I stumbled towards the door. 'Please help!'

The door opened and, still clutching the last witch's hat and the plastic pumpkin, I collapsed into the Aldersons' back kitchen. For one hysterical moment I wanted to shout 'Trick or treat!' but then managed, 'Home, I'm home.'

Kate and Guy scooped me up and, amazingly, made sense of my burblings. Within seconds, Tom and Guy were out with the quad bike and the Land Rover and torches. Kate loaded them up with blankets and rang 999. I could hear her voice, calm and precise, giving directions, telling them what had happened. How had she managed to translate my rambling gibberish into something so sharp and clear?

She was wrapping me in blankets and lifting me onto a sofa. She coaxed the fire back into life and brought me something hot to drink. I was still shivering. Even though I was warm, I couldn't stop. Now my feet had thawed, the pain was excruciating. Kate held the cup to my lips. Suddenly I hadn't the strength to hold it. Ruth and Zak came down and were given instructions to keep the fire blazing and to make sure I was comfortable, while Kate got dressed and waited for the paramedics and the fire crews to arrive. And she went with them along the dale to find Sandro and Becca.

I'd done it. I'd made it. Help was coming. It was all other people's responsibility now. As I gazed at the very real flames now licking up from the hearth, and as I began to feel the first inkling of their warmth in my shivering body, I gave up and slipped gratefully into a state between semi-consciousness and sleep.

Later, in the ambulance, as we headed down the dale to the hospital, I heard a lot of cars whizz past in the opposite direction.

'Police,' murmured one of the paramedics to his companion, 'and lots of them too. Wonder where they're going at this time of night? Something's up.'

Suddenly, we heard a strange noise, a huge bang, an

249

explosion, followed by another. Groggily, as I lay on the stretcher, I looked through the ambulance windows and I could see in the far distance a bright glow exploding through the blanket of fog and colouring the whole night sky a vivid, burning red, as though the world was on fire; as though the world was ending.

Chapter Twenty-Two

Simeon Maynard was dead. He had died as dramatically as he had lived, in an explosion that had lit up the night sky for miles around. The police racing up the dale were on their way to Ravensike to arrest him on a long list of charges including tax evasion, fraud and money laundering. But he and one of his henchmen had grabbed as much cash and as many of their papers as they could and tried to flee in the helicopter. Witnesses said that as soon as it took off it was swallowed up in the fog. Within seconds there'd been a huge bang. The helicopter had hit power lines and then crashed into the fellside, the resulting flames visible for miles even through the fog. That was the red glow I had seen from the ambulance. They reckoned Maynard had nearly half a million pounds in cash in the helicopter with him. For weeks afterwards, walkers would find scorched fragments of twenty-pound notes fluttering on thorn bushes.

Jake had been right all along about him and his dodgy empire and now his research paid off. His background stories filled the newspapers and it made his name. Flick presented a TV documentary, hastily brought forward to a prime-time spot. That was based on Jake's research too. She did well. They did well.

They'd also managed to speak to people who'd been at

that party. But here they had to be more circumspect. The police might have been after Maynard and had the effects of a helicopter crash to deal with, but they still found time to arrest a couple of footballers and their girlfriends on drug charges. There was also an allegation of rape. I wondered uneasily about the giggling girl being led up the stairs by two men.

Becca and I had plenty of time to read about it as we shared a hospital room for the next week. Becca had a broken arm, a broken shoulder and various other sprains, bruises, wrecked muscles and, to top it off, pneumonia. To my surprise I found that I had escaped with a badly sprained wrist, two sprained ankles, a lot of torn ligaments, numerous cuts, bruises and gashes. And pneumonia.

'Next time you take a midnight hike, please don't do it in bare feet,' said the nurse as she did the dressings. 'You were very brave, but also very stupid and extremely lucky.' I winced and nodded and dutifully swallowed the tablets she was now passing to me. I felt as if an elephant was standing on my chest as a pony kicked me between the shoulders. Every breath was a massive effort.

'I've put your clothes in the cupboard. Well, what's left of them. The dress looks pretty well ruined, but the silk jacket might be all right. Just as well you had that leather jacket or you might not be here at all now.'

I wheezed gratefully.

Then she bent her head down close to mine. 'And I've wrapped that necklace in a paper towel and put it in the pocket of the leather jacket. Make sure you get someone to take it home for you as soon as you can, or it will vanish.'

'Yes, I will, thank you,' I wheezed again, and tried to find a position in which I could breathe.

Sandro had a broken arm, severe concussion, but no pneumonia, and had been wheeled into our room for a few moments before the club had flown him down to London. It had all been very emotional and incoherent as the three of us were in no state for anything at that stage. He was now in a swish private hospital, was doing all right, but wasn't going anywhere in a hurry.

As for Clayton . . . there was no word. In all the reports of the goings-on at Ravensike Lodge, the only mention said that leading goal-scorers Jojo François and Clayton Silver had been at the party but had left early and long before the police had arrived.

I felt curiously detached from it all. Whether that was the disappointment of finding out that Clayton wasn't the man I had thought that he was, or whether it was because of the pneumonia or the drugs, I don't know. All I knew was that I just wanted to be able to get back to some sort of normality.

Kate was brilliant. She had come down to the hospital with me in the ambulance and had the presence of mind to bring some clothes and toiletries with her. She had stayed with me until all the tests had been done, and then gone back up the dale, no doubt done a day's work, cooked a meal for the family, so I could hardly expect her to drive the forty miles back down to the hospital again in the evening.

Becca's mum and dad were here now. They thanked me profusely, tearfully, for my efforts in saving Becca. They had brought me some flowers, some apple juice, some chocolates. I lay back on the bed and thanked them in return. And then they, understandably, concentrated on Becca, hugging her, helping her, making a fuss of her.

It was quite irrational, I know, but I felt out of it. Alone. And I couldn't even leave the room and leave them to it as I just didn't have the energy and my feet were like puffballs.

So I thought I was dreaming when I heard my mum's voice. But suddenly there she was, leaning on a walking stick and Bill, abandoning them both to swoop down and hug me hard.

'My darling girl!' she said. 'My lovely bold brave girl!'

Kate had called them and they had come straight up. Their only delay had been in hiring a car roomy enough for Mum and her plastered leg.

'We just wanted to get to you as soon as possible, to make sure you were all right,' said my mother in between hugs.

We? We? My mother never thought in *we* terms. A little bit of my mind noticed this with some satisfaction as I proceeded – with what breath I had – to tell them all that had happened. As my mother leant forward, anxiously, holding my hand – the one that wasn't sprained – and peering at me intently, Bill looked down at her, indulgently. Something had changed; something had shifted between them.

Mum was talking to me fiercely. 'That was an amazing thing you did,' she was saying, 'brave and determined. I am so proud of you. So very proud of you. And I'm just so glad you're safe.' She was crying and smiling at the same time. I'd never seen her so emotional. Everything was all so unreal.

They were introduced to Becca and her parents. There was much discussion of their daughters and the bad luck of the accident and the good luck of the rescue and my presence of mind etc, etc, etc. And then, just as it seemed as if everyone was going to start crying all over again, Becca's mum said to my mum, 'You're wearing one of our Becca's scarves!'

'Oh yes!' said Mum to Becca, 'are you the girl who made it? I love it, love it. In fact, I wear it nearly all the time. I've never had a scarf like it.'

Becca's parents beamed proudly and my mum smiled happily in return. Then a nurse came in and said, tactfully but firmly, that it was long past visiting time.

'Kate invited us to stay with her, but it's such a long drive, we're booked into a hotel around here,' Mum was saying. 'But we hope to see her before we go back.'

That *we* again. And when the time came for them to go, Mum actually allowed Bill to help her as she manoeuvred up out of the chair.

'We'll be back in the morning,' said Mum, leaning forward on Bill's arm to kiss me goodbye. Bill winked. And I drifted off to sleep, feeling that the world was becoming very strange.

Chapter Twenty-Three

The police came to see us the next day. Two lots. The first, in uniform, wanted to know about the car crash. We explained about the fog and about how Sandro hadn't known the road. The younger policeman nodded. He knew that road well. Easy to get it wrong, especially in the fog, especially when you didn't know the road.

'But Sandro hadn't been drinking!' said Becca anxiously.

'No, miss, we know. The blood tests showed that. Don't worry. It was clearly an accident.' He looked at me.

'You did well, miss. Lucky too. Not a very sensible thing to do when you don't know the area. Even the best of us could get lost in the fog up there.'

'I had to do something.'

'Well, you must have had someone looking after you, that's all I can say. You must have had someone looking after you.'

The second lot of police officers were much harder. A man and a woman in plain clothes. They asked so many questions: Why were we at the party? Who had we gone with? How long had we known them? Did we recognise people there? Did we see Simeon Maynard? Was there anything strange going on?

'There was a row involving Clayton Silver, wasn't there? The man you'd gone with.'

'Yes, but that was nothing much. Just a woman who was very drunk. Clayton didn't react to it at all and then someone took the woman away. There was nothing to it.' (Only, I thought, my utter disillusionment and the total collapse of the idea of Clayton Silver that I had foolishly built up in my head.) 'I'd gone with Clayton, but after the first hour or so, I hadn't spent much time with him. It just seemed easier to leave when I had the chance of a lift.'

'Did you see anything of Simeon Maynard at all?'

I told them of that quick glance I'd had of him scrabbling desperately through papers on his desk.

Then we moved on to the matter of the drugs and I could truthfully say I'd seen no footballers doing anything with drugs. As for the rape . . . I explained I'd seen a girl I didn't know going up the stairs with two men. Was she unwilling? No. But she was drunk.

And so it went on. Had I known Clayton Silver long? Had I seen him with Maynard? Did I know any of the other people at Shadwell? Did I know Bob Brandon, the manager, Terry Hopkins, the assistant? No, no, no again.

I lay back on the pillows, exhausted. I really had tried to help.

'Look, I met Clayton Silver and Alessandro when they walked into The Miners' Arms a few weeks ago. I went to lunch with him, went to a dinner with him in Newcastle and then to the party. It was no big thing. It was just because I happened to be around, that's all. He's not my normal sort of boyfriend and I'm quite sure I'm not the type of woman he normally goes out with. It was just a matter of accident and geography.' Was I trying to convince them or myself?

'Yet he bought you a very expensive necklace?'

How did they know about that?

'And we understand that you were with him during that . . . incident . . . at King's Cross. You were seen running away.'

'I was seen running for a train,' I replied as sharply as my wheezing allowed. 'If you know all about that, then you know it was just a stupid mistake when Clayton's keys got locked in the car.'

They said nothing and I was suddenly nervous, even though I had no reason to be. How much did they know? Had Jake been right about Clayton being involved in something dodgy? I was glad I had nothing to hide. But how lucky that I'd left Ravensike without him. Still, *Tell the truth and shame the Devil.*

'I think Clayton Silver liked the fact that Simeon Maynard poured money into Shadwell. He loved playing with the best people. But apart from that I don't think he had much time for the man. I certainly don't think he was involved in any way with him.'

And I didn't. But then again, I hadn't thought he was the sort of man to walk out on his son, did I? I'd done my bit. Now I wanted to forget all about him.

That, however, proved impossible. Simeon Maynard's death was *big* news. As I slipped in and out of sleep in my hospital bed, Simeon Maynard seemed to fill my head whether I was awake or asleep. The drama of it, the implications of it, the footballing lifestyle, all were analysed until there could simply be no more to say. Then the story moved on. The pictures of Ravensike Lodge and the crash scene vanished as I began to think more about the implications for football in general and Shadwell in particular.

It was hard to avoid news of Clayton Silver and his team-mates. Shadwell had imploded. It was one of England's top clubs, yet it seemed to have been built on sand, or the fortunes of one man, and on his death had collapsed like a pack of cards. I watched it all, fascinated despite myself, unable to summon up the energy to switch the television off.

Jake had been right – of course. It seemed the club had virtually no money. Simeon Maynard's finances were so perilous as to be nonexistent and it would in any case take months to untangle it all. Two of their star players had been charged with drug offences, another with rape. Sandro was in hospital. No one knew what the future held. Or even if the club had a future. In a midweek match they were beaten five nil by a team at the bottom of the table, and one of the players punched an opponent so hard he broke his jaw. The commentators relished their failure. 'A team without hope' was a typical comment. Clayton had apparently played appallingly. 'Tarnished Silver', one paper called him.

There was talk of the club going into receivership, reports and rumours of who – if anyone – would take it over. Already the sports pages were writing obituaries of one of England's most famous and successful clubs.

The more the dreary tales of dodgy dealing and failure unfolded, the gladder I was that I had not got more involved with Clayton Silver, that I had realised his true character just in time.

Which still left the press to deal with. The hospital had been inundated with messages for me, requests for interviews. Some of them wanted the story of the crash and my struggle through the fog – they had already christened me 'The Halloween Heroine'. Others were more interested in my involvement with Clayton as part of the ongoing Simeon Maynard saga.

'I'll have to do something,' I said to Bill. 'It's not fair to make the hospital cope with all this.'

'The easiest way is to give an interview to one person and let them share it,' said Bill.

'I guess so. But which one?' I said, looking at the long list of messages left for me.

'Well, there's an obvious one, really, isn't there?' said Bill.

'You're right.' I reached for the phone.

Jake arrived at the same time as a porter carrying yet more flowers, two huge and identical bouquets, one for me and one for Becca. Becca's message said, 'I miss you so much and hope to see you soon,' while mine said, 'Thank you with all my heart for me and for Becca.' Both were from Sandro.

Becca's mum was nearly as excited as Becca and went bustling off to find more vases, clucking at the extravagance of it all, while Becca leaned against her pillows, reading and re-reading the card, looking suddenly well on the way to recovery as she was wheeled away to the fracture clinic.

In the middle of all this, Jake came in a little awkwardly, clutching a small bunch of flowers. He handed them over and I could only put them down on the locker. Then he saw the enormous bouquet sent by Sandro, as well as others from Mum and Kate and Matty.

'Oh,' he grinned, 'I think I've been outclassed.' Then he rummaged in his jacket pocket, 'But I've brought you these as well,' and he handed over a crumpled paper bag of liquorice sticks. 'I know how much you like them.'

Now I understood why we'd stayed together for nearly two years. He was a nice guy really. Not for me, absolutely not for me, but nice. I leant back on the pillows, held a liquorice stick in my good hand and nibbled contentedly while, in between wheezes, I told him all about it – partly as an ex-boyfriend who still quite liked me and partly as a journalist adding flesh to the story that was going to make his career.

'And to think I thought you weren't safe alone in the house,' he said. 'I never thought you'd be doing a one-woman mountain rescue in the fog.' He looked at me admiringly. 'Even people who know the hills can go round in circles for hours. How on earth did you manage to find the right way?'

'It seemed fairly logical at the time,' I said, remembering that little scrap of ribbon and path that was no more than an occasional smooth stone in the cropped grass. I lay back, quite liking this new sensation of respect and admiration from Jake. A bit late in the day, but still good.

Then we moved on to the party and what had gone on there.

Jake (and Flick I assumed) was preparing more background material for when the inquest verdict had been announced. He was talking about a book too. Ironic, really, that someone like Maynard could make Jake's fortune. I told him about the party, playing down my involvement with Clayton.

'They seemed in a bit of a panic,' I said, describing the scene in Maynard's study.

'Hardly surprising,' said Jake. 'They must have known the police were onto them. That's why they were in such a hurry to get out.'

'Do you think . . . ?' I hesitated to ask. After all, Clayton was nothing to me now, nothing at all, but I still needed to know. 'Do you think Clayton Silver was involved in any way?'

'Silver? No. Not that I can see. The manager, Bob Brandon, now he was in it up to his neck and I think we don't know the half of it yet. But I can't find anything to link Silver with it all, apart from the fact that Maynard liked to have him around, show him off. No doubt he got the odd backhander and perks, like using the helicopter. They all did. But Silver never went to any of Maynard's villas. Brandon and the assistant coach and their families were *always* there. And a couple of players used it – one even had his stag weekend there, all expenses paid. But Silver seemed to keep pretty much out of it. Well, as far as I can see anyway.'

He looked sharply at me. 'Why were you there with Silver anyway?'

'Oh, just to keep Becca company. She was going with Alessandro. And I presume Sandro's not involved?'

'Oh, no. As innocent as a newborn babe, that one.'

'Good. I'm pleased. For Becca.'

'Of course, once all the fall-out's finished and the dust settles, Alessandro might not have a job. Nor might Silver or any of the others. At this rate, I'd be surprised if there's still a football club. But,' he put his notebook back in his pocket, 'it's good to see that you're all right, Tills. I never realised you were such a fighter. Thanks for all this.'

'You're OK. I owe you a favour anyway, or my family does.'

And I explained about Matty being my cousin and how the fantastic picture spreads had all been thanks to his tip-off.

'You mean *you're* related to Foxy?' Jake looked stunned.

'Yes. I only just found out. She's nice, the whole family is. Very normal. Kate – Mrs Alderson who owns the cottage we – I – stayed in, is Foxy's mum.'

Oh, it was wonderful to watch Jake's face as I explained more. As soon as he let me go out of his life, not only do

I turn into a heroine, but I'm a witness to one of the most dramatic stories of the year *and* I'm cousin to a top supermodel. So much for Silly Tilly. Poor Jake. If he'd known that, he might have tried harder to keep me. I would have laughed if it hadn't hurt so much.

'If I think of anything else that will help you with the book, I'll let you know.'

'Any little thing, all adds to the picture.' He was still looking at me, wonderingly, seeing me in a whole new light.

'Thanks for the flowers and the liquorice sticks, Jake. And' – I could afford to be generous now – 'give my love to Flick.'

'Oh. Right, yes I will. Thank you. She'll appreciate that.'

'Bye.'

'Bye.'

I heard his footsteps down the corridor. Then the porter appeared again, almost staggering under a huge arrangement of flowers. They were an extravagant mix of bright bold autumnal colours that seemed to glow and fill up the room.

'You don't want a vase for these, you need a bloomin' greenhouse,' muttered the porter as he looked helplessly for somewhere to put them. While he stood nursing them, like a giant and awkward baby, I fumbled with my good hand and found the card.

'Get well soon. You were brave and determined. And wrong. C.S.'

Good grief. Even when he's sending flowers to my hospital bedside he has to try and score points. And what was with the 'C.S.'? Couldn't he even bring himself to put his name? Was just simply saying 'Clayton' to the girl in the flower shop too much for him? Did he even go to the flower shop? Of course not. Probably got one of his many assistants to do it. I looked at the huge bouquet, nearly dwarfing the porter. Ridiculous. Over the top. Show off. Just like him.

'There's no room in here for those,' I said tersely to the porter. 'Thank you for bringing them but could you take them away please? Perhaps they'd look nice in reception.'

I scrunched up the card and dropped it in the bin.

Slowly, she unwrapped the little parcel he had given her. The packet fell from her hands. Instinctively, she stooped to catch it and as she did so the tissue paper ripped open and a cascade of colour spilled out into the air as velvet ribbons uncurled, unfurled and flared out like the sudden burst of flames, a shock of colour that brightened and lightened the small, sparse room.

Her first thought was that the ribbons – such brilliant cherry-red velvet – would be the perfect trim for her only good dress, that it would lift the fading colour as well as hide the fraying edge.

Her second thought was that such fripperies had no place in the thoughts or the dress of a respectable widow and that they were certainly not the sort of gifts that a travelling photographer should present on such short acquaintance. It was an overfamiliarity. The frames for her sons' photographs were one thing – and even of those she had been unsure – but ribbons! Completely different.

She let them run through her fingers, feeling the sensuous luxury of the velvet, admiring the glow of their colour despite herself.

There was a third thought too. Of herself as a child, standing at her mother's knee by the door of the farmhouse down below. A packman had come across the narrow bridge and her mother had bought needles and thread and buttons from him, and then when the transaction had been completed he had handed her mother some narrow lengths of ribbon, 'Red, the same colour as the bairn's hair,' he'd said. And her mother had smiled and tied up Matilda's hair and her own and they had laughed at how beautiful they were. They had danced a jig up and down the length of the dairy, pretending they were grand ladies at a ball.

Her mother died in childbirth not long after, and her father followed just a few years later, so Matilda had brought up her brothers and sisters. In that time, and since her husband's death, in which she had cared for her family, dug her garden, tended her chickens, helped with the beasts, clipped the sheep, worked for her brother, made butter and cheese, knitted, sewn and kept her children fed and clothed and, above all, God-fearing and respectable. In all that time, unlike many of her neighbours, she had never once had to apply to the parish for relief, although sometimes it was only pride that fed them. She had seen her daughters leave home when they were no more than children, and then seen two of her sons go to the other ends of the earth. And in all those years, no one had ever given her anything as frivolous as ribbons. As she made her way to chapel and avoided the drunken invitations of the miners in the lodging houses, no one had seen how much she would enjoy the chance of pretty things. Were they really so wicked?

Now this photographer, who had walked into her life off a rainy fellside, had gone straight to the heart of something she had almost forgotten about herself in all these years. Yet somehow he had seen it.

She let the velvet of the ribbons run softly through her hands once more, then briskly wound them back, wrapped them in the tissue paper and handed them to the photographer.

'I am very sorry, Mr Peart,' she said. 'I thank you for the frames for the photographs but I am afraid I cannot accept these. They are, I think you would agree, not suitable.'

'Not suitable?'

'As a gift between acquaintances. They are for young lads to give lasses at the fair, not for us, Mr Peart.' She still held the packet out towards him.

But the photographer didn't reach out his hand to take them back.

'When young men buy ribbons for maids it's because they are tokens of affection,' he said. 'We may not be young any more, but we can still feel respect, affection, and even perhaps something greater than that. If you understand me, Mrs Allen.'

They gazed at each other, silently, above the little packet of ribbons. He went on. 'At first my visits here were entirely for the sake of business. But there are other dales and other farms and mines. I confess the frequency of my visits to this particular corner of England has much to do with the conversation and company of its inhabitants, one in particular.'

He looked momentarily uncertain, as Matilda Allen's expression betrayed no reaction to his words, but he gathered his confidence and continued. 'In fact, Mrs Allen, I am taking steps to move my business to this very dale. I have been looking at premises just five miles from here. Stanhope House, perhaps you know it?'

She nodded the tiniest acknowledgement.

'It would provide comfortable accommodation for a man and his occupation. And his family.'

The last three words hung on the air.

'Do I understand you are considering marrying again,

Mr Peart?' asked Matilda Allen quietly, still gazing directly at him. He took a deep breath.

'If you will have me, Mrs Allen. If you will do me the honour of accepting my offer of marriage.'

She looked at him. But for a moment she didn't see him, this middle-aged man with his greying hair and his good tweed suit. Instead she remembered her husband. A tall, solemn young man of high principles, willing to take on her brothers and sisters. He had been a worker, drove a hard bargain but a fair one, had not wasted his money on drink or pleasure but made sure his family were well cared for. It had been a good enough marriage.

But he had never given her ribbons . . .

She realised William Peart was waiting for her to speak. She glanced down at the ribbons in her hand. She knew what she had to say.

'Thank you for your offer, Mr Peart, but I am sorry I cannot accept it.'

'But—' He rushed to say something but she shook her head.

'I have enjoyed your visits. I have learnt a great deal, not just about photography but also of the world. I thank you again for the photograph of me to send to my sons and for the frames to hold their pictures. That was a great kindness. But I fear you still know little of it, really, or how we live.' She gestured to her clothes, her faded heavy skirt, the darned blouse, the patched jacket. 'I am a working woman, Mr Peart. I cannot be of help to you in your business.'

'You could be a companion,' he said eagerly. 'I have had better conversations with you than with many of the men I meet in my travels. It would be a comfort to a man to come home to a wife like you to ease the

*loneliness. You wouldn't need to work. But you could
have the care of some hens, if you wish. No sheep, but
we could have a house cow. There is space enough . . .*

'And your son. He could leave the mine and work for
me. I would train him up in the business. He wouldn't
have to travel to the ends of the earth to make his way.'

He could see the hesitation in her eyes. But then her
mouth firmed.

'I'm sorry, Mr Peart. Your offer is good and kindly
meant and I thank you for it. But you and I live in
different worlds. I can no more live in yours than you
could survive a winter in mine.'

'But Stanhope House . . . it could be the best of both
worlds for us both,' he said eagerly.

'Or make us equally unhappy as we both miss what
we know.'

He was about to say something else, then stopped,
thought for a moment and then said, 'Mrs Allen, I am
sorry. Perhaps my offer was so unexpected that it has
taken you by surprise. May I ask you, please, to consider
it for a little while? I shall return in a few weeks and
ask again. If your answer is still no, then so be it. I shall
not trouble you again, but please give my offer the benefit
of some consideration.'

'I will do that, Mr Peart, because you ask me. I fear
the answer will be the same in a week or a month or a
year, but I cannot stop you coming back to hear me say
so. I do not think I could become a photographer's wife
in Stanhope House. Not even –' and the corners of her
mouth lifted slightly – 'not even with a house cow.'

He gathered his hat, his big cape and went out to the
patient pony and the little cart. Matilda Allen watched
him for a moment. Then, as he turned to look back, she
moved away from the window.

In her hand she still held the packet of ribbons. He hadn't taken them back from her. She put them down on the scrubbed table. A hint of cherry-red velvet glinted through the tissue paper, tempting, tantalizing.

Chapter Twenty-Four

I don't know if you have ever been hugged by an Italian mamma full of gratitude that you have saved her son's life. But trust me, she will squeeze the breath out of you even more than pneumonia will. But it was wonderful. She hugged me. She cried. She hugged Sandro. She cried. She hugged me again. All while my mother tried to make tea.

The Santinis – Sandro, still looking a bit battered, his arm in a very high-tech splint, and his mother Claudia – had come round to my mother's flat, where I was still convalescing, to say thank you. Claudia spoke very little English, though she managed to say 'Thank you, thank you' over and over again while hugging me. She certainly got the message across. Then she handed me a small package. 'A small thank you,' said Sandro, almost shyly. 'My mother chose it herself.'

I unwrapped the package. Inside was the most beautiful gold bracelet, a striking design of elaborate curls and loops – delicate, elegant and unusual. I slipped it onto my wrist. 'It's beautiful. I don't know what to say. Thank you.'

And Claudia hugged me again. My mother, who speaks some Italian, offered everyone tea and cakes. Then she and Claudia sat chatting away, both of them constantly looking towards Sandro and me, as if they could scarcely believe we were there.

'So you're back in training?' I asked Sandro.

'Yes. Just a very little, but every day. That way I will soon get fit again I hope. It is good to be training, good to be outside. But it's not good at the club now. There is no heart, no joy in it. No one knows what will happen.'

It still wasn't certain that Shadwell would survive. If it did, it would certainly be much changed. The minority shareholders had cobbled together some sort of rescue package. But without Maynard's millions, they were desperately short of money. It looked as though they would have to sell a lot of their players in the January transfer window and Shadwell would slide ignominiously out of the Premiership. They hadn't won a game since the day of the Halloween party. They were a team in total disarray. Fighting off administration meant they didn't have a lot of points deducted from them and get relegated. But as it looked as though they would get relegated anyway, it seemed a pretty pointless battle.

Whatever happened, it seemed Shadwell's glory days were gone.

But what did that matter to me? I still felt so cheated by Clayton Silver. After all he had said to me about his father . . .

With so much time on my hands, I'd done a lot of Googling of Clayton, trying to find out more about his son. It was so long ago that the original stories weren't online. There were occasional passing references to the scandal, but nothing that told me exactly what had happened. But there were plenty of other stories about him and various women. None of them seemed to stick around for long. No surprise there, I thought, angry with myself for wasting so much time even thinking about him.

'Clayton is very unhappy, I think,' said Sandro, giving me a careful look.

I shrugged my shoulders, showing it was nothing to me whether Clayton Silver was unhappy or not.

'He is very . . .' Sandro groped for a word. '. . . very encouraging for me. But otherwise I think he is angry. They all are. They don't care. They give up. They go out, they drink, they play cards.'

Two nights earlier he said, there had been a mammoth card game. Clayton had lost tens of thousands of pounds. 'Clayton does not like losing,' said Sandro.

'Looks as though he'll have to get used to it,' I said tersely. 'But not a good time to be throwing lots of money away.'

Sandro nodded. 'We are not sure how long there will be money to pay us. Already so many people have left.'

Behind the scenes the agents were already busy doing their work, ready for the opportunity to transfer players.

'We wait till then, I try and get fit by then. See where I go.'

'Would you mind leaving Shadwell?'

Sandro shrugged. 'It will be good to be at a club that wins.' Then suddenly he cheered up and smiled, his lovely baby-faced smile. 'Becca is much better. She is recovering. We talk every day. When she is better she will meet my mother.' He grinned. 'I think they will like each other.'

'Bound to.'

Catching the sound of Becca's name, Claudia turned to look at Sandro and then back to my mother, clearly asking her what she knew about Becca. I couldn't grasp much of the Italian, but by my mother's tone I reckoned she was giving Becca a cracking character reference.

Claudia and Sandro left after many goodbyes and thank yous and a torrent of Italian that Sandro had given up attempting to translate. When they had gone, my mother leant on her stick for a while as if to catch her breath, and then she reached out and hugged me hard, harder even than Claudia had, harder even than when she was at my hospital bed, harder than I could ever remember her hugging me before.

'Oh, Tilly,' she said, her eyes full of tears, 'I'm sorry.'

'Sorry?' I was completely wrong-footed. I'd never seen my mother like this before. Frankie Flint didn't do tears.

'I'm sorry,' she repeated. 'I think I must have been a bloody awful mother.'

'You weren't! You aren't!' I said, shocked.

'No. After the accident, your father, your brother . . . it was as if I was scared of losing you too. I was too frightened to love you properly.'

'Mum, I know. I understand.'

'I wanted to keep you by my side all the time. I never wanted you to go out to play or to school even in case something happened. I knew that was wrong, so I had to make myself let you go. I know sometimes it seemed as if I didn't care. But I did. Too much. I would come into your room when you were asleep and just watch you. Sometimes, I wouldn't be able to hear you breathing and I would have to touch you just to be sure.'

'I know. I remember.'

'You remember? You knew?'

'Once, I must have been about seven or eight – there was still pink princess paper on my bedroom walls – I woke up and you were kneeling by my bed, stroking my hair. I pretended I was still asleep but you knelt there for ages. All night, perhaps. It made me feel safe.'

'It did? Really?'

'Yes, Mum, really. I know things weren't easy for you and I know you sort of closed yourself down and threw your-self into work. Maybe we weren't like other families' – and I thought with a brief pang about the cheerful, noisy Aldersons – 'but, believe me, I knew I was loved. Always.'

'But when Kate rang and told us about your accident

and I thought that you could have died, and you would never know how much, how very much I loved you, it seemed such a waste of all those years.'

'They weren't wasted, Mum, far from it. You've been terrific. You've built up a fantastic business and you've shown the world you can be successful and principled at the same time – *and* made sure I did my homework. I'm really proud of you. It was pretty cool at school to have a famous mum. Did my street cred no end of good, you know. Anyway,' I said, trying to lighten the suddenly serious tone, 'I can honestly say, hand on heart, that you're the best mother I ever had.'

Mum looked at me and laughed, rubbing her hand under her eyes to wipe away her tears as she did so. 'Well that's all right then, isn't it?' she said. 'And I'm very lucky to have a daughter like you.'

Then both of us, exhausted by emotion and convalescence and the gratitude of Sandro's mother, collapsed back on the sofa in the sitting room. And when Bill came round later with his gourmet version of meals on wheels, he found us sitting on the sofa, with a box of chocolates between us, watching *Gone with the Wind* on one of the movie channels. He looked at us both enquiringly. He could sense a difference in the atmosphere but he was too sensible to ask directly. Instead, he moved the chocolates and sat on the sofa, one arm around each of us, and the three of us watched happily as Clark Gable, my dear, frankly didn't give a damn.

Mmm, a bit more cinnamon, I thought. And a bit more of the perry for the pan and – glug – a bit more for me. I let the mixture simmer for a little while and tasted it again. Yes, that was it. Already it smelt wonderfully Christmassy. Oh, it was good to be back in my own little kitchen, even if it was only a fraction of the size of Mum's. Carefully I poured the mixture over the pears in the waiting dish and popped it into the oven. It would have been so easy to stay with Mum until Christmas and then over Christmas and then . . .

'You go, Tilly,' she had said cheerfully. 'You have to make your own life. And after all, you're only going a few miles. Anyway, your room is always here . . .'

'I know, Mum, I know.' Since her unexpectedly emotional outburst, life had become strangely more relaxed. It was somehow easier to move out again. No guilt. No pressure.

Bill had helped me move my stuff back to the flat – how had I acquired so much stuff in just a few weeks? – and as he dumped the last of my bags in the small sitting room, he perched on the arm of the chair and said, 'Your mum's looking better, isn't she? And not just her ankle.'

'Much,' I said, as I whacked up the heating and filled the kettle. 'She's different somehow. Less driven.'

'I thought I'd ask her – both of you – to come over for Christmas again.'

Every year since he set up his first restaurant alone, he had asked Mum and me to join him and his staff for Christmas dinner. Every year my mum said no.

'Why have you never given up on her, Bill?' I asked as I started putting food away and getting the coffee out. 'Why have you always been there for her?'

'Because I fell for her the moment I saw her walk into the kitchen at Bistro Nineteen,' he said simply. 'It was her first proper job and her shiny new whites were too big and too stiff. But,' he shrugged, 'she fell for your dad and that was that. When your father died, your mum needed someone to look after her. And I thought I was the best person to do that.'

I raised my eyebrows at the thought of my mum needing looking after as she launched her mega-career with single-minded determination. Then – in the middle of spooning the coffee into the cafetière – I suddenly in a flash saw it all again . . .

Mr Cheeseborough, Mum's brilliant accountant and now finance director had come recommended by Bill. The lovely Eileen who was Mum's PA until she retired and Penny took over had worked for Bill. And all that publicity Mum had, all those write-ups in the paper that really got her going . . . 'It was you, wasn't it?' I said, waving the coffee spoon at him. '*You* organised all that publicity for Mum.'

'Journalists have always liked my restaurants,' he said innocently. 'And of course I talk to them, tell them anything that might amuse them, help them fill a few column inches . . . But only in the early years,' he added hastily. 'After that, your mum generated all the publicity she needed herself.'

'And that's when she didn't have so much time for me . . .' I said slowly, remembering all those times I had spent in the warmth and chaos of Bill's kitchens, recalling that it was Bill who had taught me how to slice an onion so I didn't cry, how to make a smooth white sauce, the perfect pastry or chicken stock. Bill who'd always been there when Mum couldn't be.

'I just tried to fill in the gaps she couldn't cope with. The sort of things your dad would have done if he'd still been around. Take some of the load. Give her less to worry about.'

'But there must have been other women. Weren't there?' I remembered one or two. Brisk cheerful women who worked in the kitchens with him and then eventually went off to other restaurants, other chefs, as is the way in the restaurant trade, taking some of his recipes but none of his heart with them. Or if they weren't in the catering business, they found it hard to cope with the hours. Tricky to conduct a relationship when you're working in different time zones.

'Oh, yes. There have been other women. Quite a few here and there. But after a while . . .' He shrugged again. 'Anyway,' he said briskly, as if the conversation was in danger of getting too revealing, 'I shall ask her again if you would both like to join me for Christmas dinner.'

'And this year might, just might, be the year she says yes,' I said, hugging him hard. 'Worth a try, Bill, definitely worth a try.'

And now here I was two days later, trying out recipes. Life was almost back to normal. The human body is truly amazing, I thought, looking at my feet. Just a few weeks ago they had been battered, bruised and bleeding, so horribly swollen that I couldn't walk. And here they were now, all perfect again, with lots of pale pink patches of new skin. If only battered hearts healed as quickly.

I was just clearing up the kitchen when the entry-phone rang. Soon Matty was bursting into my tiny sitting room.

She wore a minute skirt, thick tights, slouchy boots and a huge cashmere sweater under an emerald green trench coat, topped off by one of Becca's scarves. It was her version of London scruffy and she looked, of course, amazing. She was also carrying a huge bunch of flowers. Very striking. Very hand-tied. Very exclusive florist.

'For you,' she said handing them over, 'to say welcome home.'

'Thank you,' I said, admiring their style and also their lovely scent. 'How did you know?'

'I was working round the corner from Bill's Bistro so popped in to say hello and he said you'd vacated the Frankie Flint convalescent home, recuperation wing and force-feeding camp.'

During the weeks I'd been recovering, Matty had been a regular visitor at my mother's flat. She had cheered me up, brought me treats and got on really well with Mum and Bill. She had become part of the family – part of this new family I suddenly seemed to be part of and liked a lot.

'Bill said you were back in your own flat and going back to work. Is that wise? I thought you'd wait till after Christmas. Oooh, lovely smells. Cooking something nice?' She peered into the oven.

'Well, I thought about waiting till after New Year, but that was just putting it off really. If I go in for the next week, I'll have done the tricky bit, got myself sorted, got over all the questions and stuff, so after Christmas I can just go straight back in. And it's pears in mulled perry and they should be ready now. Would you like some?'

'Fantastic, yes, please.'

Carefully I took the dish out of the oven and spooned some out for us both. The flat filled with a lovely steamy, spicy smell.

'Wow. Proper food,' said Matty, 'but just one, please. I'm not running up and down fellsides at the moment.' She tucked in happily. 'Delicious. Nicest thing I've eaten since I was up at home.' She looked longingly at the dish but resolutely refused any more.

'Oh, by the way,' she said, slinging her long skinny legs over the arm of her chair, 'guess who I saw in The Brit last night?'

'Who? And what were you doing in The Brit?' The Brit was an über-trendy bar, theoretically open to all but generally occupied by the ritzy-glitzy set who could afford their ridiculous prices.

'Your footballing friend, Clayton Silver. There was a whole gang of them in there, mainly from Shadwell, getting absolutely smashed. Very loud, very objectionable. Total pains in the arse. No wonder they can't win a match. I'm amazed they can stand up. You are well shot of that one.'

'Yes, I am, aren't I?' I said, shivering as I remembered the

278

Halloween party. 'But come on, who were you with in The Brit?'

'Oh God, Josh Ritchie.'

'You mean Josh Ritchie as in lead singer of Magic Boy? Wow.'

'The very same.' She sighed. 'Would you like me to tell you all about him? Believe me, I can. From his wonderful mother, his distant father, his teachers who didn't understand him, his girlfriends who apparently all thought he was the best thing *ever* in bed, how much he paid for his new house, every single detail of the alterations he's making. By the time we got to his shellfish allergy I had lost the will to live. He was still talking when I called a taxi. I wonder if he's noticed yet that I've gone.'

I was a bit disappointed, having harboured a small passion for Josh Ritchie myself for some years. Is it better to dream about someone and not know them at all? Or to know them and have to face up to the horrible truth? I think I'd need a lot of wine to work that one out. I poured myself a glass.

Anyway . . .' Matty rummaged for a moment in her huge satchel-like bag and triumphantly pulled out a booklet. 'Look at this!'

It was a college prospectus. Excitedly, Matt flipped through the pages and pushed it towards me.

'Photography course?' I asked, astonished, and started to read the details out loud. '"*Professional industry-recognised photographic degree course. Working creatively you will explore a range of photographic genres.*" Hey, Matt, is this really what you want to do? Now?'

'Yes. Absolutely,' said Matt. 'I've always known it's what I want to do and there's no point in putting it off any longer.'

'But you've got a great career having your picture taken, not being on the other side.'

'Yes, but for how long?' said Matt. 'I don't want to do it forever, so I have to have my exit plan sooner or later, and now seems a good time. I can't spend too many more evenings being bored to death by the likes of Josh Ritchie.'

'Yes, but—'

'And I can still do some modelling work. I don't suppose they make students work forty hours a week, do they? I can fit it round classes. And learn from the people I'm working with at the same time. Paid work experience. How good is that?' she said triumphantly.

Suddenly her phone rang. She scrabbled in her bag, flicked her phone open, looked dismissively at the number and then suddenly went pale. Then pink. She half turned away from me to answer it.

'Well, yes. Fine. No, not tomorrow. All day. No, any time. When you can. Yes. But what? Well, why can't you say? Oh, OK. You know where I am, don't you? Right. See you then.'

She snapped her phone shut and looked at me, her face alight. 'That was Dexter,' she said. 'He's coming down to London tomorrow. To see me. He has an idea.'

'What sort of idea?'

'Don't know. He won't say. I've got to wait until tomorrow.'

And my wonderful, confident, successful, no-nonsense cousin looked as excited as a two-year-old.

Matilda was surprised at how often she looked out for him. When she was walking up and down to the farm, which she seemed to be doing more often as her daughter-in-law coped – or didn't cope – with the latest baby, she was always glancing at the track that wound down from the main road, hoping to see the little pony pulling the cart and the photographer with the reins in his hand.

She hadn't realised how much she had enjoyed the

280

glimpses he brought her of another world beyond the dale. She thought of the way he concentrated when he set up the huge camera, and of how kindly he had explained things to the boy. The boy would be up and away soon. The mines were dying. His brother might find a place for him on the farm, but he was filling his own nest with chicks that would need to be fed.

She picked up the packet of ribbons, pushed aside the tissue paper, let the ribbons run through her fingers and remembered the way William Peart had looked at her as he had asked her to marry him.

If she said no to him on his next visit, she knew he would keep to his word and never come up the dale again. Suddenly she found that thought too hard to bear. She went to the door and looked across the fellside to where the road turned down by the chapel, scanning the horizon, looking, hoping to see him coming to hear her answer.

Chapter Twenty-Five

There was something I had to do. It had been weighing on my conscience all the time I'd been in hospital and while I was at my mother's. Creeping into my thoughts every now and then with great big black thud. Yes, the necklace. I had to get rid of the damn thing. My first instinct had been right. I couldn't keep it. I couldn't return it to him again, either. Not again. So now what?

Sadly, no one had stolen it from the hospital cupboard. It would have made life so much easier if they had. Instead, it was still carefully wrapped in an NHS paper towel in the pocket of Clayton's leather jacket. The jacket had been in the back of the hire car from the north to London, dumped in the hall cupboard at Mum's flat, and had now come back to mine. And the necklace was still there.

Perhaps I hoped that if I ignored it, it would go away, or get pinched, or be lost or slide down the back of a seat and be gone forever, not my problem any more.

But it hadn't and it was.

Do you know how difficult it is to get rid of a designer necklace? Dreadfully. And embarrassing. I didn't even want the money. That would make it so much worse. I'd give it to charity, if only I could get rid of it.

At first the jeweller I went to clearly thought I was a

thief. He asked me for a receipt. He asked me how much it had cost. When I said £25,000, he just laughed.

'Well, it was a charity auction,' I said.

'And someone just gave it to you?' he said, doubt dripping from his voice.

'Well, yes, actually, he did,' I replied firmly.

'You see, miss, this is a Theodore Bukala design. Unique. Very desirable. Very expensive. Very traceable.'

'Yes. So?'

'So for a piece like this we would need to be absolutely certain of its provenance.'

'You mean you think I stole it?'

'Of course not!' He put on a convincing air of being shocked. 'We just have to cover ourselves.'

'Look, I just want to get rid of it. But it would be good to get a decent sum for a charity while I was at it.'

'My my, he really isn't a friend any more, is he?'

'No. He is most certainly not.'

'Well, you could always give it direct to a charity. But it's such a distinctive piece they would want to make the most of the publicity over it – about where it came from and why. Could you cope with that?'

'No, probably not,' I said reluctantly, suddenly very tired.

'Have you got ID on you?'

'Yes, driving licence, bank card. I've even got my passport.' He copied all the details.

'We have a client who would like this, so I am in a position to help you out.'

Eventually he wrote me a cheque for £5,000. He would probably sell the necklace for at least £15,000, but I'd gone past caring. I took the cheque and left the shop and tried to forget the memory of Clayton slipping it over my head and kissing my throat as he did so.

As soon as the cheque had cleared, I would divide the

money and send half of it off to one of Mum's pet projects in the rainforests and the other half to the Ted Blake cancer charity. They might as well benefit twice over. That seemed fair.

So that was the necklace gone. But there was still the leather jacket lurking at the back of the wardrobe. Clayton Silver had so many designer clothes I don't suppose he'd even noticed it was missing. I'd drop it in the charity shop next time I was passing. On the other hand, unlike the necklace, he hadn't actually given me the jacket, had he? Better do the decent thing, I suppose. I found the biggest Jiffy bag I could, stuffed the jacket in and posted it back to Clayton.

That was me done with him for good. All links severed.

Chapter Twenty-Six

I was just heading home from the post office – trust me to want to send a jacket back at the busiest time of the year – when my phone rang.

'Tilly! Are you busy? Can you join us? We're having a celebration!'

'Who's us?' I asked Matt, confused.

'Dexter and me.'

'What are you celebrating?' My mind raced through a whole load of different possibilities.

'A joint project. Come over and we'll tell you all about it. We're in Harry's Bar, at the back.'

At first I didn't recognise Dexter. I had forgotten about his new haircut and that he was quite so good looking. He'd also swapped his trademark baggy jumper for a stylish jacket. Very worn, a bit shabby, but still swish. I spotted him and Matty before they noticed me. They were sitting side by side in one of the booths, their heads bent over a notebook. Despite the ten-year age difference, they looked at ease together, well matched and not just because they were the same height with those long legs. It was something about their body language, their expressions as they looked up and spotted me.

Dexter's grin was just as cheerful as always. That hadn't changed. They both stood up to greet me and it suddenly dawned on me that they were now a couple. I wondered if it had yet dawned on them.

'So what's this exciting project then?' I asked as Dexter poured me a glass of wine.

'Look!' said Matty, her eyes bright with enthusiasm as she pushed a small scrap of newspaper towards me. 'Dexter brought me this!'

I looked. It was a small, smudgy advert showing a large dilapidated building with another one, only slightly smaller and slightly less dilapidated, next to it. '*Hartstone chapel and schoolroom.*'

'It's a property advert,' I said. 'It's the chapel opposite the pub.'

'That's right,' said Dexter. 'After leaving it empty all this time, the local authority has finally decided to sell it.'

'So?'

'So I thought I might try and buy it. And it struck me that Matty might want to be in on the deal. That's why I've come down to see her, to talk about it.'

Now I was baffled. 'You want to buy the chapel?' I asked. 'You and Matty?'

Matt nodded, grinning.

'You want to open the chapel again at Hartstone?'

'Yes!'

'Oh.'

I wondered for a moment if I really knew my newfound cousin at all. She was going to reopen a chapel? I mean, I knew they took such things seriously up there on top of the world, but it's not the sort of thing a model usually does with her earnings.

'Not as a chapel, you idiot!' Matty was laughing. 'As a gallery. A photographic gallery. All those photos Dexter's been collecting. All those he's going to take to go with them. They're just piling up in the back of the pub. It's a wonderful

286

project, but absolutely hopeless unless we have somewhere to display the end result. The chapel would be perfect! It's vast and has an upstairs gallery and lovely fancy stonework and huge windows. It would be a wonderful gallery and part of the history of the dale. Ideal!

'Then there's space for a gallery just for Dexter's work. And in the schoolroom next door we could have another gallery with changing exhibitions, so there would always be something new for people to see, and a place for local photographers to exhibit their stuff. And where the education authority built those dormitories and bathrooms and things, we could have a café. What do you think?'

She was so excited, so enthusiastic, her hair in a wild halo around her head, her eyes shining. She looked stunning.

'Well, yes. Fantastic!' I said. 'But are you sure? I mean, can you just do something like that?'

'It's all right,' said Dexter, as he looked sideways at Matty's laughing face. 'I've had unofficial talks with the authorities and we should have no problem. Quite the opposite; in fact we might even get a few grants.'

'Right. And who's going to run it? I mean, what about your work and your degree and stuff?'

Matt rested her chin on her hands, in the process sending waves of her hair rippling over her shoulders. A couple of other customers nudged each other, knowingly. Even in a place as sophisticated as this, Matty looked extraordinary. 'What better project could there be?' she asked.

'Dexter will be up there to see to all the building stuff. But I'm up and down all the time as it is. I guess I'll just be up and down there even more, won't I?' She smiled at Dexter. 'There'll be long holidays, weekends. The course is only three years, after all. Then I'll be a proper photographer, just like Dexter. The perfect partnership.'

The pair of them bubbled with their ideas and their

287

enthusiasm and I was soon as drawn into their plan as they were.

We drank a triumphant toast to the success of the Hartstone Chapel Gallery. And another toast. And another. Thoughts turned to food.

'Sushi, that's what I fancy,' said Dexter, surprisingly. 'Something I can't get at Hartstone.' When we agreed he strode out to find a cab and it struck me that, like Matty, he was just as at home in the streets of London as he was on the high fells of Hartstone.

So the three of us spilled into Matty's favourite sushi bar and kept coming up with more ideas for the chapel that they hadn't even bought yet.

'Keep the blue ceiling!'

'One gallery has *got* to be edgy. Stir it up a bit.'

'Themes – weddings, parties, work!'

'Café. Must do proper food.'

'Cards, posters, books!'

And so it went on. Each suggestion Matt scribbled on the ever-growing list on her notebook.

As I chased the last little bit of nigiri round my bowl I smiled to myself. 'What would Granny Allen say?'

Chapter Twenty-Seven

It had been a good day. I'd had lunch with Polly and Susannah. They'd been great while I was recuperating, popping in and out of Mum's, keeping me up to date with the gossip, taking me out for lunches. Now the party season was in full swing, they were trying to get me out most nights too. But after Halloween, I'd had my fill of parties.

'Ah, we're not grand enough for you these days,' moaned Polly. 'Now you've been mixing with celebs and have got a top model in the family.'

She was grinning widely as she said that, so I knew she didn't mean it. Which is precisely why one day I'd introduce them to Matty. They'd all get on well.

'Anyway, I'll let you off,' Polly was saying. 'You being a heroine and still a bit feeble. But you've *got* to come to my brother's engagement party and we have to squeeze in one more lunch before Christmas.'

How could I refuse? 'I'll have you know I have been in this bar since eleven thirty *just* to make sure of a seat,' said Susannah as I found her in among the bags and parcels of the Christmas shoppers grabbing a drink.

It was good to feel life was getting back to normal. Good to be back at work too.

Everyone had been very kind. We'd agreed I could go in

late and leave early. 'Heroines get special deals,' said my boss. He was really keen on my 'Celebration' idea too.

So now, when Polly and Susannah were trying to persuade me to go shopping with them, I had to refuse.

'Sorry. I'm working. I have a very posh children's party to go to. Though before that,' I realised, as I scrabbled round in my bag, 'I'd better call in at my mum's. I must have left my iPod there.'

We walked down the road together, still chatting happily before going our separate ways. 'Don't forget Jamie's party!' yelled Polly in farewell and I nodded back happily to show that I'd be there. But as I turned off by myself, I felt suddenly down again. Although everything was going well, I still felt – well, a bit adrift, really. As if something wasn't quite right, as if something was missing.

The children's party was part of my 'Celebration' series. I'd mentioned it to Matty and she, of course, knew an actress who was giving an over-the-top birthday party for her four year old; Matt had sorted it for me to go along. If you're going to discover a long-lost cousin, one with a bulging contacts book is just the sort to have.

'Kezia's fine about it,' said Matty breezily. 'Having your picture in a glossy magazine, even over a table of cupcakes, never hurts. And I guess the red-tops will use the pic too.'

The actress's house wasn't far from Mum's flat, so it was easy to call in there on my way. Mum was sitting at the dining table, address book to hand, surrounded by piles of Christmas cards.

'Just doing the last few,' she said.

The room, full of light and warmth and the heavy scent of freesias – Bill's latest offering – was welcoming and familiar. But very different. I still had to get used to the changes in my mother. She and the flat had always carried a slight air of anxiety, as if there was always a great list of work to be got through and no time to play. Now she was making the Christmas cards – previously yet another task to be dealt with as briskly as possible – seem a positive pleasure.

She'd put on a little bit of weight since her accident. Hardly surprising as she normally was never still and a broken ankle does slow you down a bit. And of course Bill had been bringing her all those wonderful meals. She was still enviably slim, but just a little rounded, softer. She'd lost that hardness that I'd noticed that day I'd had lunch with her at the beginning of October.

'You look pretty,' I said, without thinking.

'Pretty?' She looked surprised as she laughed. 'Gosh, it's a long time since anyone called me that.' But she looked pleased. 'Anyway,' she said, 'I have an idea for you.'

While I'd been staying at home, I'd spent a lot of time talking to Mum and Bill about the food producers I'd met up north, raving about the chocolate and the ice creams, the cheeses, the puddings and the proper meat.

'I think we can do more in Frankie's,' she said. 'We should be thinking about British producers. Give them a real alternative to supplying the supermarkets, try and use more local produce, even if they can only supply a few branches. If we have a real network of suppliers, we can cover the lot. I've thought about it before, but it's so tricky and time-consuming, hunting out all the small producers. But you,' she said, giving me one of her fierce looks, 'have already done a lot of the hard work. You've got lots of contacts. Could you find more? What do you think?'

I thought of all the lovely people I'd met who put their heart and soul into producing good-quality stuff. Getting their food into Frankie's would be brilliant for them and brilliant for us too.

'It would be great. Gives them a bigger market and us something different. Win win.'

'Exactly,' said my mother. 'I've had a few thoughts about it, but I wondered if it was something you'd like to take on. Well, think about it, anyway. It's a way of taking Frankie's forward. If you wanted to be involved, that is.' She looked at me, suddenly anxious for my approval.

'I do, yes, definitely,' I said, intrigued by the idea, already thinking of possibilities. My mother was actually asking me for help. What's more I could do it. After the night in the fog I reckoned I could do anything. I could certainly sort out a selection of small producers. 'Yes, I could do that for you,' I said.

'That would be good,' said my mother, smiling, 'a good step into the future.'

'We'll have a proper talk about it. But in the meantime, I have this children's party to go to,' I said, hiding my surprise at her suggestion by making a great show of hunting for my iPod, which I finally found in the fruit bowl.

'It looks cold out there,' Mum said, 'you must wrap up warm. I know it's not far. But I still think it's too soon for you to be out and about.'

'I'm fine, Mum. And I've got my nice warm coat.'

'Well, take a scarf. Here –' and she reached out for the scarf that Becca had made, which was hanging over the back of a chair – 'borrow this. Then I know you'll be nice and cosy.'

'OK, if it keeps you happy.' Anything for a quiet life. 'And I'll definitely think about the small supplier stuff. It's a great idea.'

I pulled on my coat and wrapped Becca's scarf around me. The appliquéd flowers seemed to glow with the scraps of cherry red velvet at their centres. I rushed along the road to the posh party, wondering about the change in my mum, and felt somehow extra warm and safe and looked after.

The plan had been for the photographer and me to get there just before the party started so we could get the birthday girl, Saskia, and her mum and the table of food before the hordes of four-year-olds attacked it.

Kezia had dressed for a photo shoot not a birthday party – skin-tight dress, towering heels and the most amazing make-up. The nanny, who brought Saskia in, was in jeans and flat pumps, hair tied back in a ponytail and definitely ready for action.

The huge room had been turned into a princess's palace. Pink walls, with battlements and distant views and a slide that was a short cut from battlements to basement. The entertainers were setting up in the corner – a handsome prince, a smiley servant and a not-at-all-frightening dragon.

The food was amazing. A cake shaped like a castle, complete with princess on top. There were tiny cakes and savouries in the shapes of crowns, wands, hedgehogs, little white mice, ladybirds, sparkling sovereigns, tiny dragons, biscuits like bracelets. Brilliant stuff. Much too good for four-year-olds. The photographer did lots of pics with the birthday girl and her mother, the table, the castle, the food and the not-very-scary dragon, who kept poking his head in. It was good fun. Kezia was surprisingly down to earth and Saskia posed like a professional which, at four years old, she already was.

The mothers looked marvellous. Whether they were as dressed up as Kezia – and a few of them were – in designer jeans, or just top-to-toe Boden, there were so many flawless complexions, perfect hairstyles.

While the photographer took his pics, I was keeping out of the way in the corner when one of the mothers looked up from shepherding in her two children and said, 'Oh hello, it's Tilly, isn't it?'

I blinked for a minute, trying to place this woman in her

funky red and black spotted skirt and stripy jumper. Then I realised, as she tucked her children's coats under one arm, and accepted a glass of champagne with the other, that it was Nell, wife of Clayton Silver's team-mate Jojo François, whom I'd last seen at Ravensike Lodge on Halloween.

'Better than the last party I saw you at,' she said cheerfully. 'What a nightmare! How *are* you? I heard you were an absolute heroine. Great story. I see you've recovered.'

'Just about,' I said. 'But it wasn't the best night of my life.'

'No, I think we all got out just in time. Even if you didn't actually make it straight home. You were amazing. How on earth did you manage it? In that thick fog. You certainly saved Alessandro and his girlfriend. For which we should all be grateful. Mind you, I don't suppose he'll play at Shadwell again.'

'No?'

'Well, they're going to have to sell most of their players, aren't they? The atmosphere's dreadful. Jojo's been out with an ankle injury for the last three matches and I don't know if that's better or worse – sitting there watching them play dreadfully or playing with a side that hardly wants to be there. Training sessions are a nightmare, everyone's fed up, disillusioned and backbiting – and with no idea what's going to happen next, of course.'

'Yes. I saw Alessandro. He was telling me about it. He's just gone back to a little light training.'

'Probably not much point. Jojo loved that club but he would be happy to leave as soon as he can. He's hoping he might get a transfer to Paris St-Germain after Christmas. Still, you'll have heard enough of this from Clayton.'

'No. I haven't seen Clayton since that night.'

Nell looked surprised, then said, 'Oh, well, that could explain why he's been extra bloody difficult. Absolutely impossible, according to Jojo. And the fans aren't helping. Booing the team doesn't exactly encourage them, does it? And now of course Clayton's lost his licence.'

'Lost his licence? I didn't know.' I had a sinking feeling. I think I knew what was coming next.

'Yes, he was in court yesterday. It's in the papers this morning. Haven't you seen them? He was caught doing over sixty in a thirty zone near King's Cross a few weeks ago. What an idiot! They did him for dangerous driving, so it's a year's ban. Not even his fancy-pants lawyer could get him off. Personally, I think it's amazing that anyone manages to break the speed limit with all the traffic. All he needs really.'

Suddenly I was back in Clayton's car, barrelling along the central reservation, dodging in and out of the bus lanes, screeching underneath the speed cameras. It was stupid to think he would get away with it. Yes, of course he'd been an idiot, but he had been determined that I would catch my train. I remembered his delight as he powered the car in and out of the traffic . . .

'Sorry?' I realised that Nell had asked me a question.

'What are you doing here? You haven't got kids, have you?'

'Oh no. I'm working. *Foodie* magazine? I'm just starting a new series called 'Celebration' – looking at different sorts of celebratory meals. The idea came to me when I was up north at a chapel tea, of all things. Look.'

I knew I was gabbling as I tried not to think of Clayton. I took my phone out of my pocket and showed Nell the photos I'd taken in the chapel, the groaning table, the homemade cakes and the photos and samplers on the wall. *'Judge not that ye be not judged.'* 'So I just thought it would be interesting to do all sorts of different occasions and the food involved.'

'Hey, we've got our local food awards on the show in the New Year and we have a meal afterwards with all the prize-winning stuff. Would that be any use?'

'Brilliant! It would.'

'Here,' Nell rummaged in her purse and produced her card. 'Email me and I'll let you know nearer the time. And if you ever feel like coming on the programme and talking about your heroic rescue mission, we'd love to have you.'

'Well, I might pass on that, if you don't mind. But the local food stuff sounds perfect. Thank you.'

I carefully put the card in my pocket.

'I have to say,' said Nell looking hesitant and then plunging on, 'I have to say that I thought you and Clayton seemed quite good together. Sorry that it hasn't worked out.'

'Yes, well, it was only a couple of meals when he happened to be in the north. No big deal really.'

'That's not what he told Jojo.'

For a moment I longed to ask more, but then remembered the Barbie doll spitting her accusations at Ravensike and Clayton doing nothing to deny them. I shook my head to clear the memory.

'Anyway, he wasn't what he seemed.'

'You're not worried about that silly cow who made the scene at the party, are you? That's old stuff.'

With that the photographer came to ask me something and Nell got grabbed by another mother who was pinning her to the wall and talking at her nonstop. I kept hearing the dreaded phrase 'PTA' and saw Nell looking desperately noncommittal.

The party was soon in full swing. The entertainers had all the children trying to rescue Saskia from the dopey dragon. I never would have realised that twenty little four-year-olds could make quite so much noise.

Eventually we'd got all we came for, the beautiful table looked wrecked and the entertainers led the children back for party games.

I said my goodbyes to Kezia and was just putting on my coat when Nell came out into the hall, a toddler in one hand and a glass of champagne in the other.

'Some of the dads have been watching Sky Sports,' she said, 'and say Shadwell have nearly scored a goal. Not quite, but nearly, which is as good as it gets right now. That should cheer Jojo up a bit. Though, as I say, after January, that might not be anything to do with us any more. Anyway, good to see you again, Tilly. I'll see you at the food awards – if not before.'

'Yes, right. Thank you. Good to see you again.'

I wound Becca's scarf snugly round my neck. 'Nice scarf,' commented Nell, and a couple of the other mothers nodded in agreement. 'A friend made it,' I said.

'It's fun, different,' said one of the mums. 'Does she have a shop? Website?'

'Not yet, but she will do soon,' I said positively and headed for the bus stop.

I sat on the bus, leaning against the steamy windows, looking out at the twinkly lights in the darkness and the people making their way home from their Christmas shopping. My mind was a jumble. Normally, on my way home from a job I'm already writing it up in my head, thinking of that crucial first sentence, from which the whole piece will flow. But today I couldn't. My head was full of Shadwell and what Nell had said. And about Clayton losing his licence. A whole year without his beloved cars. All because I didn't want to miss my train. I had yelled at him to slow down. But he was only doing it for my sake. My mind grew even more confused. The birthday party was muddled up with the chapel tea all those weeks ago in Hartstone Edge.

I reached into my bag for my phone and looked at the picture again. The piled tables, the cakes, the sandwiches, the fruit loaves, the steaming urns and the waiting cups and saucers and the sampler, '*Judge not, that ye be not judged.*'

I was sure that Nell had been about to say something about Clayton and the Barbie girl's accusations. She didn't sound as if she was going to slag him off. 'Old stuff,' she'd said, as if it didn't matter. And she was a mother, so it would matter to her if a bloke had walked out on his responsibilities. She wouldn't dismiss it easily. I felt in my pocket. Yes, her card was still safe there. She'd asked me to email her, hadn't she? Well, I would. And I might just ask her about that Clayton gossip while I was doing so. I mean, it didn't hurt to get the story right, did it?

I got off the bus and walked the ten minutes to my flat, my hands in my coat pockets, my chin tucked down in Becca's scarf.

But when I got to the end of my road, instead of getting my front door key out of my pocket, I don't know what came over me. I didn't even think about it. I hardly missed a beat or altered a step. I just turned round, walked back down the way I'd come, and got back on a bus.

Only this time, the bus was going to Clayton Silver's.

Chapter Twenty-Eight

It was madness, of course. Absolute madness. I didn't know if he would be there. I certainly didn't know if he wanted to see me – though I could make a pretty good guess. I wasn't even totally sure that I wanted to see *him*. I thought I was succeeding in putting him out of my mind, out of my life. But I just felt I had to do this. Why think of asking Nell the truth, when I could just ask Clayton?

The road where he lived seemed spookily quiet. My boot heels clicked and echoed and, even though it was only early evening, I had the feeling that it wasn't just the security cameras that were watching my every move.

Then, of course, I got to those vast electronic gates and they were locked and he wasn't in. The huge house with its wrap-round balconies soared up above me, but apart from a glow from the back of the house – presumably Maria's bit – it was all blackness. I thought of trying the intercom and seeing if Maria would let me in. As I got up close to it, a glaring security light flashed on, dazzling me. I stepped back, and kept carefully out of its target area.

To keep warm, I walked back and forth in front of the gates, back and forth, trying to work out why I was there.

I thought back to Halloween. Of that scene with Barbie shouting at Clayton. She'd been drunk. He'd been so calm. She had been so sure of what she was saying. He hadn't denied it. Maybe it was so ridiculous that he hadn't needed to.

Then I remembered the message on the flowers he'd sent me. Something about my being brave. But wrong. Back and forth. Back and forth.

It was no good. I was getting cold. I didn't dare risk being ill again. Clayton had probably gone straight out with his team-mates, drowning their sorrows. He seemed to be doing a lot of that lately if Matty was right. Of course he wouldn't be coming home. He wouldn't want to be by himself. He'd be out with his mates, picking up women. There were always plenty of women ready and waiting. This had been a totally pointless journey. God knows why I'd done it. Time to go.

I had just made my mind up, when a big car turned off the road and up to the gates, setting off the security lights again. As the gates opened, the passenger window went down. There was a pause while I took a deep breath, walked towards it, shielding my eyes from the dazzle of the security light.

'Tilly Flint?'

'Hello, Clayton.'

'You coming to see me?'

'Yes. If that's all right . . .'

'You'd better come in.'

I followed the car through the gates. Clayton jumped out, yelling 'G'night mate' at the driver, and then motioning me into the house and up into the sitting room with the wonderful Iolo John painting. It seemed a lifetime ago that I'd gone to sleep on one of the orange sofas and Clayton had so carefully placed a duvet over me.

Standing in front of me now, he looked tired. He didn't have his usual starry glow, that gloss of success and self-confidence. Too many late nights out drinking. Too many lost matches. Too many failures at football and cards. Not to mention the driving ban.

'So Tilly, what do you want?' His tone was sharp.

'I just heard about the driving ban. I suppose it was that morning you were taking me for the train?'

He nodded.

'I'm sorry.'

'Don't be. No point. You were yelling at me to slow down.'

'I know, but . . . I've been thinking about you. I needed to clear something up.' I didn't really know how to go on.

Clayton said nothing. All signs of 'Quicksilver', of his sparky, drawly, mischievous conversation, had vanished. He just stood looking at me, waiting. He had, I realised, not offered me a drink, not even a cup of tea, certainly no little cakes. Hadn't even invited me to sit down. So I didn't. This was not a good meeting. But I was here, so I'd better say what I'd come to say.

'That night in Ravensike Lodge.'

'You did well that night. You're OK now?' His voice held the tiniest tiny spark of emotion and I clung to that.

'Ooh, um yes. Oh,' I said, suddenly remembering, 'thank you for the flowers.'

'Glad you got them. But I guess you weren't waiting out in the cold to tell me that. So what is it?'

I couldn't think of what I wanted to say, or how to say it politely, so instead the words just tumbled out. 'That girl, the one who said you were the father of her sister's baby, was she telling the truth?'

'No.'

There was a silence. Then Clayton asked, 'Was there anything else you wanted to know?'

'It was just that she was so *sure*.'

'And even though she was so drunk she couldn't stand,

that she was screaming like a banshee and was also probably stoned out of her skull, you were ready to believe her? Just like that?'

'Well, no. Well, I suppose I mean yes. I was. But I didn't ...' I was beginning to feel as though I might have got something horribly wrong.

Clayton sighed and suddenly I felt so desperately sorry for him and wished I could restore him to his Quicksilver self, with his daft and lively show-off chat.

'I thought we were friends, Tilly,' he said wearily. 'I thought we had something good. I'd never met anyone like you and I talked to you like I've never talked to anyone else. It was special. Then some drunken tart appears out of nowhere and oh yes, in a second you'd rather believe her than me. Hey, I thought you'd got to know me, yeah? You don't know a thing about her. Or her sister. But never mind, you still think she's more reliable than I am. Well great, Tilly. Thanks a lot.'

It would have been so much easier if he'd been angry. But his face was expressionless, his voice almost toneless. He could have been made from wood.

'You had this little place in your brain that said "flash footballer" and you fitted me right in there. Didn't matter what I was really like, did it? You weren't going to bother to find out. All that talking we'd done, just a waste of breath, wasn't it?'

He was right. My face burned. I'd been too quick to decide what he was like, completely ignored what I'd got to know about him, just on the basis of one drunken girl.

'So why was she saying such things? Why should she say them if they weren't true?' My attempt at outrage sounded feeble.

'Oh God, Tilly. Because she's mad? Because she's stoned? Because she just likes causing trouble? Don't ask me, ask *her*. Not that you'd get any sense out of her. Look,' he sighed again, 'if you really want to know, here's the story. Ten years ago, yes, I did have a little thing going with her sister. I was a kid, just making a name for myself. There were lots of women. I was having fun. She was one of them and I saw her for a few weeks, maybe two months. End of.

'Two years later, I'm with Shadwell, yeah?, going great. This woman suddenly appears back on the scene with a baby, tries to tell me I'm his father. But I know I'm not. The dates are sort of right, but only just. And don't tell me I was the only guy she was sleeping with. I'm not that stupid. But she reckoned that because I was the flavour of the month at the time – in the papers, on TV, the lot – that I was an easy touch; that I would just pay up. But I didn't. So I asked for blood tests and such and it was like I thought. The baby wasn't mine.

'Do you really think I would walk away if I thought I had a son? Whatever stupid cow was his mother? No way. I thought you would have known that. I really did – you of all people . . .'

'I did really,' I said. 'Once I had a chance to think about it. I guess that's why I came today. To ask you and to say I'm sorry. You're right, I just leapt to the wrong conclusions. I should never have doubted you.'

'No. You shouldn't.'

'I don't know why I did. And I'm very sorry. I really am. I should have known better, should have known *you* better.'

'Right. OK.'

We were still standing, awkwardly, in this huge ship-like room, looking out at the lights of London.

'Anything else you want to know?'

'No, I guess not. But, I should tell you . . .' Suddenly I didn't want to say what I'd done. 'I sold the necklace.'

He gave me a hard look.

'I sold it for five thousand pounds. I think the man will sell it on for a lot more.' I was gabbling, spoke quickly, anxiously, to tell the story. 'I gave the money to charities. One of my mother's Fairtrade projects and Ted Blake's charity too.'

His expression relaxed and he nodded. 'Right. I'll let you out.' He walked out of the room and down the glorious curving wooden stairs.

'I'm sorry,' I said to his back, 'about the club going through such a hard time. It can't be easy.'

'It's not.'

'How did it go today?'

'We lost of course. But we're getting used to that. Too used.' He shrugged. I could see the ripple of muscles under his jacket. 'We ain't got no players. Nobody gives a toss. Caretaker coach is clueless. No one knows what's going to happen. Half the team will be gone in January. We're playing with kids.' He stopped on the stairs and briefly turned round to me. 'But maybe today we weren't total crap. Maybe there's the makings of a team there. But it's a long way off yet. And it'll all change soon.'

He was opening the front door for me.

'There's just one more thing,' I said, as a blast of cold air swirled in. If this was the last time I was going to see Clayton Silver, I might as well get my two-penn'orth in. 'It's just to say that I really enjoyed the times we spent together,' I said. 'I'm very glad I met you. I just wish I'd had the chance to get to know you better. I hope everything works out in all this mess and that you can get the team back together, or move on, or whatever you want.'

'That it?'

'No.' Deep breath. Last chance. 'You look tired and not particularly healthy. You look as though you're drinking too much and not eating properly and goodness knows what else. I just wish you'd look after yourself properly – or let Maria look after you. I don't understand what's going on in the club, but if everyone's going to be transferred after Christmas, surely you need to be at peak fitness otherwise no one will want you. But for your own sake, mostly. The club may be collapsing around you, but, oh Clayton, you're too good to waste.'

I wanted to shake him, slap him, hug him – get him out of this awful, defeated state. I couldn't bear it. 'Where's Quicksilver?' I was almost shouting now. 'He seems to have vanished when everyone needs him most. The club might be ruined, but you don't have to be ruined with it . . . Don't throw it all away. Please don't.'

I paused for breath, frustrated at my inability to get through to him. 'Have you spoken to Denny? What does he say? He wouldn't think much of the way you're going on, would he?'

Finally, I ran out of steam. All I could say was, 'Take care of yourself. Please.'

Clayton was staring at me impassively. 'Quite finished now, have you?'

'Yes.'

'I'll open the gates for you.'

'Right. Thank you.'

I'd said my bit and much good it had done me, but at least I'd said it. I went out into the dark. The security lights blazed and the huge gates opened out for me. I looked back to wave goodbye at Clayton but he'd already gone in and the door was shut. The gates closed behind me. The light faded. I'd done what I'd come for. I'd said my piece. I'd told the truth and shamed the devil. Ha!

The only truth I knew now – too late – was that I had misjudged Clayton. Somewhere in that hellish Halloween

305

party I had got it horribly wrong. Made the wrong judgements.

Now Clayton was going through a nightmare and I could do nothing to help him. He needed someone to get him through this bleak time. But it wasn't going to be me.

I walked off in search of a bus stop, my chin tucked into the scarf, stamping along the road in a fury with myself.

Chapter Twenty-Nine

Polly's brother's engagement party was OK. I managed fine. There were plenty of people there I knew and they were all pleased to see me. One or two of them, who hadn't seen me since the accident, asked about the Halloween adventures. But I was able to say to them, 'Thanks for asking but I really want to forget about it now.' So I had a few glasses of wine, nibbled some juicy king prawns in chilli dip, and I talked to friends, and danced with a couple of blokes, all very easy and no pressure. I was almost enjoying myself. It was good to be in a party that was just so *normal*.

In the kitchen, talking to Polly's brother about possible wedding dates, I suddenly heard Clayton's name mentioned above my head. I looked up, baffled, and realised that someone had switched on the small flat-screen TV above the microwave.

'Missed the footie results earlier,' said a chap who had been a year or two ahead of me in school. 'Just catching up with the sports news now.'

I looked up at the screen. Three football pundits in sharp suits were sitting in squashy armchairs discussing one of the day's matches.

'Well, it might have been a two-two draw, but it was a real triumph for Shadwell. They can be proud of themselves. Their first point for seven weeks.'

'Their first *goal* for seven weeks,' chirped up another pundit. 'And it was all down to Clayton Silver. He never stopped. He was all over the pitch. He wasn't playing just his own game but everyone else's too. Encouraging, cajoling, shouting – a real captain's game. And boy did it work.'

'Yes,' said the third. 'There was a young team out there tonight – let's face it, all the experienced players are either injured or on remand. The manager and his assistant have gone. Half the backroom staff have left. Dreadful atmosphere at the club, but you'd never guess that from their performance tonight. Silver seemed to inspire those youngsters.'

'Maybe we were all a bit premature in writing off Shadwell.'

'Well, they've still got a mountain to climb, a terrific mountain to climb, but on the evidence of tonight's performance, at least they're in with a chance. Here's what Clayton Silver had to say when our reporter spoke to him after the match . . .'

As they cut to the interview, someone switched off the television, but I felt strangely proud that he'd done so well. I wished I could tell him in person. But he had made it quite clear he didn't want to speak to me again.

I hoped all that praise he was getting from the TV commentators would restore some of the Clayton Silver gloss. I went back to discussing wedding plans with Jamie, and it was as if seeing Clayton doing well had lifted one tiny worry from my shoulders.

Next day I was glancing at the sports pages while I was waiting for the kettle to boil. They were all singing Clayton's praises.

I couldn't go round to see him again. That was an absolute no-no. Maybe I could call? No, too embarrassing. I didn't have his email address. Text? Yes, maybe. But then

I remembered Bill when he set off on his grown-up gap year. He had sent my mother lots of postcards as well as emails. Pretty postcards with funny short messages and drawings on the back. Some of them had almost made her smile before she threw them away.

I found a card – one of a London bus that I meant to send to an American friend – and wondered what to write on it. Finally I drew a little stick man holding up a scarf saying *Shadwell* and just wrote, 'Well done.'

It seemed a bit inadequate. I looked at it. Was it a really stupid thing to do? Would Clayton think I was just being annoying? I went out and posted it quickly, before I could have second thoughts.

Their next match was another draw. I sent another postcard. A London policeman this time. I drew two little stickmen waving their scarves. 'Keep on keeping on!' I wrote.

Clayton probably thought I was mad. But he could always throw the cards in the bin.

For weeks she trod the path between her own house and her son's with an extra briskness. As she tended to her increasingly ailing daughter-in-law, or worked with her son, sometimes she would see someone on horseback or in a pony and trap and her heart would lift. But it was always someone going to the mine about official business. One day the photographer would come back. She knew that. And this time, she knew what she would say to him.

The weather changed in the sudden way it did in the dale. The fog came down. For days it had been so thick that it had seemed to be in the very house, pressing on everyone, making everything heavy with damp. The children were fretting and fractious. Their mother coughed endlessly and their father looked increasingly anxious.

Everything was damp and dark, even at noon. The damp and cold seeped in through the very stones of the house. Carrying a bucket of milk, Matilda splashed across the slurry-covered yard between the cow byre and the kitchen door, her fingers frozen. Not even the very clever photographer could take his pictures when you could barely see across the yard.

Chapter Thirty

It was an excellent Christmas. Mum had actually accepted Bill's invitation to spend it with him at his restaurant. I wasn't as astonished as I might have been. Though at first I felt a bit doubtful as the taxi drove through the nearly empty streets. Probably because Mum had gone very quiet. She stood in front of the bistro door, taking the deep breaths she does when she needs to calm herself. But she was wearing the red cashmere cardigan I'd bought her. She'd declared herself delighted with it, had insisted on wearing it to Bill's. She looked good in it and I was inordinately pleased, even though I could hardly get used to not seeing her in black. The world seemed to be shifting around me.

Suddenly the door flew open and there was Bill, beaming, a paper hat on his head and a sprig of holly tucked into the front of his chef's apron. We could see relief on his face and smell delicious turkey smells from the kitchen and hear jolly choruses of 'God rest ye merry, gentlemen'.

'Happy Christmas!' said Bill, greeting us both with a kiss. 'I'm so pleased you've come at last. Frankie, you look wonderful. Oh and you too, Tilly,' he added hastily.

'Happy Christmas!' I said, handing him over the foodie gifts I'd brought – some of the sloe gin and chocolate-covered sloes I'd found up north – and thinking it odd that Mum hadn't brought him anything.

'Ooh thank you,' he said, weighing up the bottle in his hand. 'This seems interesting. I shall keep it to open later, if I may. In the meantime, let me introduce you.'

There was Ram, a tall Nigerian law student who was washer-up and kitchen porter and whose wife and children were still in Nigeria, Elsie who was tiny and ancient and who'd done Bill's admin since he'd very first set up on his own. Then there was Liz, a waitress who was about forty but looked older and had the sort of face that hinted at a life too dreadful to ask about.

I wondered if it would have been better if Mum and I had stayed at home and had our normal polite and peaceful time without these strangers.

Finally there was Declan: gay, Irish and, once again, between partners, but refusing to show he cared and putting on a sparkling performance.

'Tilly!' he whooped in greeting. 'And this must be the fabulous Frankie! Champagne?'

For the next hour or so he acted as host, master of cere-monies and lord of misrule, while a beaming Bill – refusing all offers of help – came in and out of the kitchen with plates of starters: little smoked salmon nibbles, skewered langoustines, scallops on the tiniest slivers of black pudding. And then the turkey and all the trimmings. And the pudding blazing away like something out of Dickens.

'Ooh, Bill, you're better than Mrs Cratchit!' said Declan, filling our glasses yet again. 'As Tiny Tim said, "God bless us every one!"'

We pulled crackers, told jokes, paid forfeits, drank lots more wine. Ram told us about his young son and the daughter he had not yet seen. Elsie told outrageous stories of her escapades during the war, and flirted with Ram, Declan and Bill equally enthusiastically. Liz said little but smiled quite a lot, which was nice to see. Declan became more outrageous and in the end even my mother began to laugh.

Using the tiny games that had come from the crackers, we played dominoes and snakes and ladders – my mother and Ram being the fiercest competitors of all; sang along to the carols; had chunks of cheese and some tiny mince pies that were delicious. And then coffee and brandy, until we were all too full to move and slumped, smiling, round the table.

We all offered to help Bill clear up, but he refused all offers, until finally he said, 'Well, all right then, Frankie, if you insist,' and the two of them disappeared into the kitchen with much chattering and more laughter. The world felt right. And I wished I hadn't drunk so much because I wanted to know if it really was like that and it wasn't just the wine.

Suddenly it was dark and Bill was making up food parcels for Ram and Elsie, Liz and Declan.

'Look, we're closed till New Year's Eve. You might as well take all this stuff,' he said. And I realised that Bill knew they relied on the free meals they had at the bistro and a week without them would be tricky. He'd also ordered taxis to take them home.

Then there was just Bill and Mum and me. It seemed very quiet after all the laughter earlier. Bill was ripping open the paper from the sloe gin and chocolates.

'Wonderful!' he said, kissing my cheek. 'Just the thing to warm a cold winter's night. Now, I'll just get *your* presents.'

Then Mum said, quite tentatively for her, 'I have a present for you, but it's back at the flat. I thought you might come back with us.'

'Why, yes. Of course. Marvellous,' said Bill, looking stunned. 'What a good idea. Yes. I'd love to. I'll just get a few things . . . call a taxi . . .'

He rushed around in chaotic fashion, talking to himself, looking for things, picking them up, putting them down. He went into the kitchen and produced another massive food parcel, while my mother watched on, amused. Finally, the three of us were in a taxi going back to Mum's flat.

As soon as we were in and settled, he handed me my presents – some perfume, a selection of offbeat travel books and a pair of silly slippers like spotty ladybirds. I sprayed some of the perfume, which was wonderful, enthused over the books and popped my feet in the ladybirds and admired them prodigiously.

'You can't be too grown up, you know,' said Bill. 'It's not good for you,' as I gave him a thank you kiss.

Then Mum went to the Christmas tree and produced a long box, which I had presumed was an emergency box of chocolates in case anyone unexpected turned up. But now I could see it was heavier. She handed it to Bill, who unwrapped it eagerly.

'A chess set!'

'You used to play. I remember you used to play in the old days.' Mum looked uncertain.

But Bill had opened the box and was looking at the pieces. They were made of heavy solid glass, beautifully smooth shapes, wonderful to look at, even if you didn't play chess. They caught the reflection of the Christmas tree lights and bounced them back so that the room was filled with warm, dancing colours.

'There's a wonderful little shop just near the physio's. When I saw that I just thought of you. And it's a thank you, too, for all that you've done while I've been crippled. I don't know that I could have coped without you. I didn't realise . . .'

Her voice tailed off. She looked at Bill hopelessly and I'd

never seen her look so vulnerable. This was Frankie Flint somehow lost for words.

'Thank you,' said Bill, kissing my mother gently, 'it's beautiful.' In exchange he handed over an envelope. My heart sank. Oh no, I thought. Just when my mother has let her emotions show, revealed a bit of herself and actually admitted she has feelings, then Bill was going to reciprocate with a Marks and Sparks voucher. Please no. Let it at least be Waterstone's . . .

Mum was opening the envelope, her face clearly prepared to say a kind, polite 'How nice.' But instead she gasped, looked up at Bill and then back at the paper in her hands.

'I hear,' said Bill, gruffly, 'that the Zanzibar sunshine is just the thing for newly mended ankles.'

'Zanzibar!' I squawked. 'Are you going to Zanzibar?'

'If your mother would like to,' said Bill diffidently. 'I can always cancel.'

'No! I mean yes!' said Mum quickly. 'Bill, I would love to go to Zanzibar. With you.'

At which point I began to believe in Christmas angels and *It's A Wonderful Life*'s Clarence getting his wings. And almost expected Tinkerbell to waft in on a cloud of fairy dust. My mother *loving* to go on holiday? She hates holidays. From the time I was old enough to go with school or with friends, we have never had more than a weekend break in Paris or Rome together – which I always felt she was doing strictly for my educational benefit.

But here she was, next to the Christmas tree, gazing at Bill and agreeing to go to Zanzibar with him. Maybe we'd all had much too much champagne. Maybe my mother had been snatched by aliens.

'It's for the middle of January,' Bill was saying anxiously. 'I thought it would do you good before you got back to work properly.' He looked straight at my mother and

315

grinned. 'Are you really coming? Do you want to? Are you sure?'

'Yes, yes and yes,' replied my mother.

I must have been standing there with my jaw dropping open, because Mum looked at me and said, 'I've been doing a lot of thinking while I've been hopping around. Life's too short to waste. You can't dwell on the past; you have to make the most of now. Seize the day. *Carpe diem*. I'm just so lucky to have had a second chance, and even luckier that Bill never gave up on me. God knows he was entitled to.' She turned to Bill. 'Thank you for looking after me these past months, but more than that, thank you for looking after me all these years – even, *especially* when I didn't want you to. Thank you for never giving up.

'I'm just glad you kept coming back. Zanzibar sounds wonderful.'

'Champagne!' said Bill, as he hugged my mother and then me, kissing us both. 'We must have champagne!'

'Well actually,' said my mother, 'what I'd really love is a cup of tea.'

Next day the fog had lifted as if by magic. The sky was a sharp cold blue and a film of ice covered the water butts. Matilda stretched up to grab the washing line as the wind snapped it up out of her reach. After days of the damp and dark, this dry wind was just what they needed, cold as it was. The children played out in the yard, wrapped up, rosy-cheeked, happily chipping the ice off puddles.

Someone was walking down the track. Matilda looked intently, hopefully, but could soon see it was one of the Calverts who lived in the chaos of the midden-like houses of Bottom Row. This time Calvert didn't look as though he were begging favours, wheedling food for his children.

Instead he looked jaunty, as though he'd had too long in The Miners' Arms.

'Morning, missus,' he said, touching his cap with mock politeness.

She nodded at him, curtly.

'So you won't be having your photographs taken no more then,' he said.

'Will I not?'

Her hand shook as she pegged a thin blanket on the line, refusing to look at Danny Calvert, though she knew he was standing there, hands in his pockets, rocking on his heels, full of himself. She was glad of the battle with the wind, the line, the blanket, the clothes pegs.

'You see, yesterday,' he said, with an air of great importance, 'yesterday I was working for the coroner.'

The coroner . . . The end of the blanket whipped out of her hand. She groped after it, resisting the urge to turn round and demand the information from Calvert. The coroner. Please, God. No . . .

'In the fog, must have been the night before last. Photographic man and his pony and trap went straight over Skutterskelf Edge. Reckoned they'd been there all night. Old Richards had to shoot the pony. Photographer was already dead though. Jim Dinsdale and me got him back up, took him to the Black Bull. He's laid out there now, in the outhouse. Got the cart and pony up too. Cart's not much good for else but firewood. But the coroner gave us some money for our trouble, from the public purse, he said.'

Dan Calvert told his story with a particular relish. 'The photographer took a picture once of our Billy and granddad cutting peat. But he took lots of you, didn't he, missus? Well, he won't be coming back no more, that's for sure.'

317

Matilda fastened the flapping blanket onto the line. Her heart felt as cold as her frozen hands. But she would not let anyone see. Ever.

'He was a good man, Danny Calvert,' she said turning round. 'And if you've not drunk all the coroner's money away, be sure you give some to your Mary so your bairns don't go hungry again.'

One of the grandchildren had fallen and was screaming. She turned back to the yard to pick him up, her long hair falling in its plait over her shoulder. She tried not to think of the photographer lying cold at the bottom of Skutterskelf Edge with the ruins of his cart and cameras scattered around him. All night, in the fog.

She tried not to think of his kindness or the solidness of his presence in her small house. Of the sense of possibilities . . .

Now he would never know that she had changed her mind; that she wanted to be his wife. They had never got their second chance. Too late.

Work. There was always work. Plenty of that to distract her. She set her shoulders as she carried her grandson back into the house and took up her many tasks. When she saw the pack of ribbons sitting on the shelf, for one moment she was tempted to hurl them in the fire, let the flames destroy them as her hopes had been destroyed. But even as she went to throw them, she stopped, wrapped them carefully back up in the tissue paper and pushed them to the back of a drawer. Waste not, want not. Some day someone might need those ribbons.

Chapter Thirty-One

Carefully, I filled in all the space on one side of the card with little stick men waving flags and sort of jumping up and down. Lots of little speech bubbles too, saying 'Hooray!' or '2-1'.

Yes, Shadwell had won a match, their first since Halloween, and it was now late January. I'd been trying to do some work on the computer, but I kept clicking on to the sports sites to keep track of the match. I was excited enough when I thought it was going to be a draw, but when Clayton scored the winning goal, I cheered out loud. And now I was sending him another postcard. The last.

I'd sent him a card after every match since the day I'd been to see him. As he wouldn't talk to me, it was the only way I could get through to him, to try somehow to keep him going. I'd drawn little stick figures, with mottoes – that 'Keep on keeping on' when they'd managed a draw, or 'Nil illegitimus carborundum,' when they'd lost again. Now they'd won, he wouldn't need that any more.

I drew carefully, trying to make each little figure slightly different, trying to fit in as many as I could. On the radio, there was a phone-in about the match. Yes, I was listening to a football phone-in. Sad or what? Even though Shadwell had won, the fans weren't happy. They knew that the top players were all likely to be sold. JoJo was, as Nell predicted, already off to Paris St-Germain. The players involved in the rape allegations had had their charges dropped and were off to Middlesbrough and Hull. Sandro was probably going to either Chelsea or Manchester United. Becca said that Sandro didn't know yet, but I knew she was just pleased he was still going to be in England. 'It's all agents talking to agents. I don't understand it and I'm not sure Sandro does,' she'd said when I'd spoken to her the night before.

As for Clayton, the fans on the phone-in seemed certain he was going to follow in the path of David Beckham and go to one of the American clubs. Lots of money and glamour for his last year or two at the top. I wondered if he'd like that. It would be very filmstarry and probably a lot more fun than turning out with whoever was going to be left at Shadwell.

'Turn up with your boots and you'll get a game, there'll be so few players left,' said one caller. Another urged the club to give up, go into administration, accept the ten-point penalty and relegation and start again from the lower league.

'It's too late now. Why prolong the agony?' he asked, which seemed a bit defeatist. But probably realistic.

But Clayton didn't think it was too late. He was still trying hard.

Mum and Bill were having a good time in Zanzibar. I had the texts and the pictures to prove it. That broken ankle – or something – certainly seemed to have changed Mum's outlook. I picked up my phone and clicked again on the picture she'd sent: the two of them sitting at a café table in the sunshine, the sea a vivid blue behind them. I remembered that photo of my parents and me and my little brother all those years ago and I felt a small pang for the father I could hardly remember and a huge rush of relief that my mother and Bill could be so happy.

Becca had got her website up and running. While her arm had been strapped up, she'd thought up all sorts of new designs and got her mum, her aunties and her cousins to knit them for her as she couldn't wait to see them. Now she had a team of knitters, a real cottage industry, and the scarves were flying out – helped by Matty being pictured wearing one. Never hurts to have a top model looking stunning in something you've made.

As for Matty, she was bubbling over. She and Dexter had bought the old chapel and she was spending nearly as much time up at Hartstone as she was in London – with the exception of work in enviable places such as New Zealand. Dexter had assembled a team of architects and designers and was just waiting for the official planning permission to come through before getting on with it. Matt and Dexter had spent days together sorting out just what they wanted in it and how it could be done, discussing, arguing, laughing.

'It's great,' said Becca. 'He's going round with this huge grin on his face. All he talks about is Matty and the chapel gallery. And all Matt talks about is the chapel gallery and Dexter. She's been in love with him since she was about twelve years old. She was devastated when he got married. But it's fantastic that they've got a second chance, isn't it?'

'Fantastic,' I agreed, thinking about Matt and Dexter, Mum and Bill, and wondering if I would ever get a second chance. But it was too late for me and Clayton. Much too late.

Finally, I couldn't fit a single more matchstick figure onto the postcard. The effect looked quite good, though – a whole crowd of cheering fans.

I looked at my drawing on the postcard. If I wrote Clayton's address quite small, I could put more of the cheering figures spilling onto that side of the card too. I carried on, drawing carefully, reluctant to finish it, reluctant to let him go.

There, that was it. I couldn't squash another figure on anywhere. I stuck a stamp on it and went straight round to the postbox to send it off.

That was me done with Clayton Silver. The End.

I went back to my flat and made myself a bacon sandwich – all in the line of work. I was well on with the database of small producers for Frankie's. I was really enjoying creating it, even though it was hard work. Every specialist sausage maker or cake or biscuit baker recommended another two or three. I talked to people who ran farm shops and farmers' markets and food fairs. There was so much going on. I already had plans about which producers I could go and visit. In the meantime, I was having a very jolly time ordering samples for taste tests. Chill boxes of goodies kept turning up at the flat. The bacon had been that morning's delivery. It had real flavour, didn't shrink when you cooked it and grilled to the most delicious crispness. Who needs gourmet meals when you can have the perfect bacon sandwich? There was some lemon cake too, for pudding. I could smell the tantalizing, sharp tang of the lemons. Purely research, you understand. I was actually knee deep in notes as well as crumbs and I wanted to get the first draft of a plan ready by the time Mum came back from Zanzibar.

A few months ago the mere idea would have sent me into a panic, but now I knew I could do it. I'd stayed in the cottage on Hartstone Edge on my own. I'd got help for Alessandro and Becca when the car crashed. I could do things, I realised. I could do things. I settled down to work.

A few evenings later I was testing chocolate made by two former archaeologists living in the Yorkshire Dales – rich and dark and flavoured with ginger, strong coffee or the wonderful light taste of fresh raspberries – when Matt rang.

'You stay in too much,' she said. 'I'm going to a fish-and-chip-shop opening tonight. Do you want to come?'

'A fish-and-chip-shop opening?' I said, licking the last of the chocolate crumbs off my fingers. The raspberry version had been particularly good.

'Yeah. Well, very upmarket fish and chips, of course. Terry Wotsisname – one of those cockney geezer actors – reckons we're all getting too into foreign food so wants to restore the good old British chippie.'

'No, I don't think so, Matt, but thanks. I'm not sure it's my sort of thing.'

'Yes it is,' said Matt firmly, 'most definitely. No excuses. Trust me. Anyway, it's food, isn't it? It might give you an idea for a feature. And I promise not to go on too much about the chapel gallery, though I *must* tell you about Dexter's latest idea. He's only – no, I'll tell you when I see you. Anyway, fish and chips might be fun. Wear jeans.'

And she was gone. Matt was right. It was better than working all the time. Or even eating chocolate. And Matt was a force of nature, anyway.

So I dug out my favourite jeans, a pair of boots, a bright stripy top and my gold bracelet from Sandro's mum. I wondered who was wearing the wonderful silver and amber necklace now, but that was nothing to do with me any more. There was a ring at the bell. I ran downstairs and got into the back of Matty's car.

We were stuck at traffic lights for ages. While her driver drummed his fingers on the steering wheel, Matty was telling me the latest about the plans for the chapel. It all had to go to a planning committee.

'Dexter's got a brilliant architect on it, so we're sure the council will agree. It will have to be better than letting it sit empty and fall down. The survey was good. Structurally it's pretty sound. Most of the damage is just cosmetic and it shouldn't take us long . . . Tilly, are you listening?'

'Yes, of course.' Matty followed my gaze. We were stuck outside a newsagent. An old newspaper bill said, 'Quicksilver works magic for Shadwell.'

'I wonder how he is,' I said. 'The last time I saw him, he looked dreadful. Ill, tired, defeated. I misjudged him, you know. I got it all wrong about him walking off from his son.'

'I know.'

'You know?'

'Yes. I've been asking round. There was no truth in it at all. The woman was as mad as a fish and as sly as a snake. Now there's an interesting animal. No, Clayton Silver might be a typical flash footballer, but he didn't abandon any son.'

'No. I got it totally wrong. He's not even a flash footballer. I just decided that he was and then made everything he said and did fit. By the time I realised I'd got it all wrong, it was too late. I tried to tell him. But it was no good. The damage was done.'

I felt sad and wistful for what might have been. But Matty was having none of that. 'Oh, it's never too late,' she said cheerfully. 'Look, I thought it was too late when Dexter went off to Manchester and got married when I was sixteen. And he hadn't even registered that I existed, except as a kid who followed him around. End of the world, I was sure. But it wasn't, was it? Because there he is, back at Hartstone, just older and wiser.'

'Old and wise enough to realise he needs a successful model as business partner and maybe something more?'

'Precisely,' said Matt, smiling happily. 'So who knows? Even Clayton Silver might get old and wise one day. Even you . . .'

I was just trying to work out what she meant when the

car stopped and she leapt out. She was wearing a pair of impossibly skinny jeans that looked as though they'd been sprayed on, plus little boots with heels so high they must have taken her to well over six foot six. I ambled in behind her, knowing no one would notice me in her shadow.

Fish and chip shop? This place was so far up itself that . . . no, let's not go there. There was lots of champagne, of course. And the fish and chips were served in tiny little cones wrapped in newspaper. But not any old newspaper. Oh no. This was specially printed newspaper full of splendid reviews of all the shows that Terry, the cockney geezer owner, had been in. Very authentic. They do that all the time down the Mile End Road. The vinegar was balsamic. The mushy peas were tiny, minted and pureed, and the tomato ketchup was handmade, organic, sun-blushed, probably made by the light of a waxing moon by a score of young virgins – but, frankly, it didn't taste as good as Heinz's. OK, the fish was good, very good – tiny little pieces in the lightest of tempura batter. But in portions the size of a fingernail.

Even so, at least half the guests weren't eating anything. I swear one of the skinniest actresses I've ever seen spent all evening with the same chip, holding it seductively against her bottom lip while she fluttered her eyelashes alluringly at anyone who mattered.

There was lots of air-kissing and screeching. And people taking pictures. I loved the way Matty looked as though she were too busy talking to people to take any notice of the camera, but I also noticed that she seemed to know just when a camera was near and very subtly pose for it. That's what made her good, I suppose. Among the other guests were restaurant reviewers, actresses, and lots of people who were famous on account of being well known. It was all quite fun to watch.

I tucked myself in a corner that was out of the way but from which I could see the main room. I had my little cone of chips – about five of them – and was just stabbing the last one into the remains of the tomato sauce when I had that funny feeling you get when you know someone's looking at you. I looked up.

There, on the other side of the room, under a picture of a lobster, was Clayton.

My insides lurched. He was gazing at me through the crowd of minor celebs. Just looking. There seemed to be no expression on his face at all.

He'd been the last person I expected to see. Yet, on reflection, it was the sort of event he was quite likely to be at. Wasn't he a friend of the cockney actor who owned it? Vague memories surfaced of them both in Shadwell scarves.

And then suddenly it dawned on me. Matt knew! She'd known he would be here. That's why she was determined to get me here too. She knew I'd got it wrong about Clayton and was trying to put it right. I looked around the room in a panic for her. She seemed to have vanished. But Clayton was still watching me.

Suddenly all those little cards I'd sent him seemed ridiculous. Pathetic. Why on earth had I done that? I remembered how cold he'd been with me when I'd gone round to his house, the disdain he'd shown me. Well, he wasn't going to get a chance to do that again. No way.

I crumpled up my empty chips cone and placed it on one of the counters that was Formica pretending to be marble. Though, actually, knowing this place, it was probably marble pretending to be Formica. I slid round behind a group of men who were either rugby players or club bouncers – in any case nice and big and solid. From there I thought I might be able to work my way behind a group of vaguely familiar blondes and out into the street.

No. Clayton had moved round. I wasn't sure if he'd seen me, but he was definitely blocking my way. I ducked down out of sight. A food critic from one of the glossy Sunday supplements looked down his aristocratic nose at me. I smiled feebly and crept past him on bent legs. There was a corridor. I went along it. LADIES. Hooray. Clayton couldn't follow me in there. I nipped in, shut the door and wondered what to do next.

I remembered the first time I'd seen Matty, leaping from the Ladies at Club Balaika. I eyed up the possibilities. The window was narrow and covered in bars. Even if I could get through it, I'd struggle to reach it. I was neither as tall, nor as slim, nor as supple as my cousin. Still, I'd just wait here for a while. Clayton wouldn't stay long, I was sure.

People came and went. Each time they did I leant towards the mirror and did my eye make-up. My mascara has never looked so good. Finally, when I thought the coast was clear, I went out cautiously. To the left the corridor led back to the restaurant, but to the right there was an emergency exit. Thank you, God! I pressed down on the bar and escaped into the cold January night. Straight into the arms of a waiting figure.

'Aargggh!' I screamed.

'Hello, Miss Tilly,' said a deep, familiar voice. 'What kept you?'

'Clayton. What are you doing?' I shouted at him. 'You scared the living daylights out of me!'

With that there was a flash of camera lights. A couple of photographers had heard the noise and come to investigate. That made me even crosser. 'Clayton, will you just let go of me, please? And tell them to go away.'

He loosened his grip but still held my hands. I couldn't escape.

'I just wanted to talk to you,' he said. 'And I had the idea you were trying to avoid me, which would be a shame, a real shame.'

The lights of the cameras flashed again. We both turned and glared at the photographers.

'Look, I'm sorry about those cards,' I gabbled. 'They were just a bit of fun. I didn't mean to annoy you. I was just worried that you seemed so low and I was scared that you might just waste everything and I didn't want you to do anything stupid and it was just to sort of encourage you really and to—'

He kissed me, gently, slowly. 'I know. I know why you sent them and I loved them. I really loved them.'

'You did?'

'Yeah. They made me smile.'

'Really?'

'Yeah, really. And right then there wasn't a whole lot to smile about.'

He kissed me again. The camera lights flashed like fireworks.

'Will you not do that, please?' I said, rather primly.

He stepped back and grinned. Even in the orange light from the streetlamp and the yellow gleam from the back rooms of the restaurant, I could see that Clayton Silver was restored to his old self. His eyes look tired, older somehow, but the bounce, the confidence, the grin and the gloss were back. I wanted to grin back because I was just so pleased to see him like that.

The photographers, having decided we weren't going to have a punch-up or a slanging match, got bored and went back to the fish and chips and celebs.

'Come on,' said Clayton, and led me quickly down the side of the restaurant until we were out in another street, far away from the fuss. He slowed down. We were walking past big houses in quiet streets.

'I'm glad you were here tonight,' he said. 'Saved me ringing you.'

'You were going to ring me?'

'Yeah. I liked those little cards and messages. They were sort of cool. Didn't want them to stop.'

'Oh. I . . . I didn't know . . . I wasn't sure if you'd just throw them away. If you'd even look at them.'

'The fans were booing us. The papers were calling us worse than shite. Half the staff had left the club. Message boards were making out I was some sort of international drug dealer or gun smuggler or terrorist or rapist. And that was just the good stuff. We were a laughing stock.'

For a moment he looked angry. I remembered how he hated to be made a fool of, hated to be a loser.

'Then, in the middle of all that, there'd be a silly little postcard with a drawing and stupid message on it. And they made me laugh. It got so that after every match I was looking for that little drawing to come through the letter box, because then I knew there was someone on my side. And, for the last few months, I've certainly needed someone on my side.'

'I'm sorry, still sorry, about not believing you, about believing that crazy woman.'

'Yeah, well. It was a strange night anyway. I should never have taken you to that party. Should never have gone myself. I've been to enough Maynard parties to know the score. But we always went along with it. He was paying the bills. Well, we thought he was. So he made fools of us too in the end. Though he paid a pretty harsh price for it.

'But that night was weird, even by Maynard's standards. So maybe it was easy to get hold of the wrong idea. Still, I thought it was a cool thing to do to come round and see me and say so.'

'Did you? You didn't seem very pleased!' I remembered his blankness, his utter lack of emotion.

'Well, it was a pretty bad time. Absolutely rock bottom. But yeah, it was good you came. And you were worried about me. That was good. I didn't have anybody worrying about me. Things started changing after you'd been round.'

'No. They'd already started changing that day. Remember? You'd had a good match. You scored a point.'

'But it was easier after you'd been round.'

'Really?'

'Yeah. It made a difference. A big difference. And you told me off. Gave me a right bollocking, you did. That was great. No one else bothered to do that. Just you. Until Denny – he rang and gave me a right going-over. My so-called mates just wanted to get pissed, which made things worse. And the women, well, they didn't want to know. They thought I was a loser and kept well clear. I thought you were the same.

'I thought that maybe, after all, you were just a girl who wanted a footballer and would stay away when things got bad.'

'It wasn't like that at all!'

'No. I know.'

'Anyway, you're not a loser. The team's still there. They might be kids, but they're doing all right, aren't they? Everyone says you're inspiring them. A brilliant, inspirational captain, they say.'

Clayton laughed. 'Hey, girl, you been reading the back pages?'

'Well, yes, when it's about you . . . I needed to know you were OK. And you're more than OK.'

'Thank you.'

Somehow, by now, we were holding hands.

'So where are you off to? Someone said you might be going to the States?' and I had a sudden pang.

'Well, Miss Tilly, that's the interesting bit. I might not be going anywhere. I might stay just where I am.'

'What, stay with Shadwell? Even though they've hardly got any money and might even go down?'

'We're not going down. I'm not going to let us.' He gripped my hand tightly.

'But you always said that you liked playing with the best! That losing wasn't an option. That's why you put up with Maynard.'

'Yeah, well. Maybe I think differently now. Look, I could go to one of the clubs in the States. They've been making offers. My agent is getting excited. But you know what, in the States, football's a game for girls, little girls. Everyone else watches baseball or American football – you know, those big guys so padded up they can't hardly move. They don't take football, proper football, seriously. It's just like, I don't know, like we think of ice-skating or something. Yeah, they'd give me a lot of money. But I've got a lot of money. More would be nice, but not to . . .' He waved his arms round in the air, groping for the right words.

'. . . not to be thought of as girly?' I laughed.

'No! Well, yeah, maybe. But you've got to be somewhere where they care about it – like, really care, haven't you?' He looked defensive for a moment and then suddenly passionate.

'At the end of last year, everyone said we were rubbish. We *were* rubbish, total crap. Everyone playing was either a kid or an old man or stoned out of their skulls still. The manager and his mate went before the club could sack them – or the police got them – and we were left with the assistant's assistant. But it came together, yeah? It began working. We started to play like we'd kicked a ball before, like we even knew what we were doing.'

'That was because of you.'

'Yeah, maybe. I got so angry with them I was yelling and shouting and then trying to explain things to the kids, trying to make them see what we had to do. And yeah, it might work. It might work.'

'And you want to stay and see if you can make it happen?'

Clayton stopped and looked at me and said, 'Yes. I guess I do.'

'More than going to the States and getting the film-star treatment and lots more money?'

'Yeah,' he grinned. 'But what's the point of all that money if no one's talking about you or reading about you and cheering? Or calling you rubbish when you do badly? Or sending you postcards with little drawings on?'

I hugged him fiercely. 'I think it's a terrific idea. Really terrific. Just that you're even thinking about it is great. It'll be bloody difficult, though.'

'Yeah, well, that's what makes it interesting, doesn't it? I guess we'll see what happens, when everyone's finished doing deals.'

By now we'd walked down as far as the river and carried on wandering alongside it, the streetlights reflecting on the ripples. A police launch roared past and I shivered.

'You warm enough? Here.' And Clayton put his jacket over me, a beautifully soft leather jacket with the shadowy stripy lining.

'It's the same jacket!' I said. 'The one I wore on Halloween night in the fog.'

'I hope it kept you warm.'

'It was about all that did.' I shivered at the memory. 'I was frozen and soaked as it was. Without the jacket I would have had it.'

'I'm glad it helped to look after you. Really. It's one of my favourites and I didn't know where it was. Until this parcel arrives on my doorstep. It was good to get it back, but you could have written a note . . . You were great that night. What you did was amazing.'

I breathed in the scent of the jacket. It smelt wonderfully of leather and equally wonderfully of Clayton. It didn't smell of fog any more.

'I didn't feel amazing. I was terrified. I kept falling over. All I had was the light of that plastic pumpkin.' I started to tell him all about it and suddenly it seemed funny. A story we could laugh about. Especially now that we knew Alessandro and Becca were fine, absolutely fine.

'Well, you were so brave and determined. I'm glad I helped. Or rather my jacket did.'

'You did.'

We ambled along, arms round each other. 'Clayton . . .'

'Mmm?'

'You know when we went up near Newcastle in the helicopter to that posh hotel?'

'Yeah.'

'You know those men you met . . .'

'Yeah.'

'What was that all about?'

'Why?' He took his arm from my shoulder and danced round to face me, trying to look serious, but struggling to keep the laugh out of his voice. 'Do you think it was something dodgy? Something criminal? Do you think they were going to pay me wodges of cash to throw a match? Do you think it was a Chinese betting scam? That I was going to take a backhander for something?'

'No! Well, at the time, perhaps I might have thought something like that, to be absolutely honest,' I said slowly. 'But not now, I don't. No. Now I know you wouldn't do anything like that. I'm sure you wouldn't.'

'Sure?'

'Yes.'

'Positive?'

'Yes.'

'Just as well,' he said, and hooted with laughter, 'because they were sponsors, wanted to use me to sell their toothpaste.' He bared his teeth in a horrid grin. 'And now,' he laughed, 'they've run away and don't want anything to do with me because Shadwell is in the mire. But next season it will be different. Next season we will be TRIUMPHANT and they will come crawling back to me and I will tell them where to stick their toothpaste – minty freshness and all!' And he laughed and danced me round. 'Next year Shadwell will be back. Clayton Silver will be back. And,' he paused, 'I hope you will be with me. Will you?'

'I will.' I said. I didn't even have to think about it. 'Yes. I will.'

'You're not going to run out on me again? Hide away?'

'No.'

'Because I have great plans, Tilly Flint. And they'll all go much better if you're there with me.'

He swirled me round and took me in his arms and kissed me.

'I love you, Miss Tilly,' he said.

'And I love you, Clayton Silver,' I said, and realised I did, that I'd loved him for a long time, only I had been determined not to accept it. Since the night I'd gone round to his flat and seen him so down and depressed, a little bit of my heart had been with him ever since. Suddenly it all seemed so simple.

We stood smiling, laughing. Some lads came along the pavement on bikes whooping and calling at us. We laughed right back at them. Everything seemed easy, obvious. And right. Clayton held my face in his hands and looked at me almost in wonder. Then kissed me, long and slow. The streetlight formed a sort of halo round us. I pressed myself closer to him, breathing in the smell, the taste of him.

'Try again?' he said. 'It's not too late?'

'Never too late.'

'And you've got no trains to catch early in the morning?'

'Absolutely not,' I said.

'And you're not going to go to sleep on my sofa?'

'That's up to you . . .'

'Then it's time to go home,' he said, reaching round me, kissing me and scrabbling in his jacket pocket for his phone to call a car. As he pulled the phone out, so a tiny piece of material came out with it. The tiny scrap of velvet I had managed to tug off the tree all those months ago, the velvet that had helped me find my way through the fog. It must have stayed trapped in the bottom of the pocket where I had pushed it on that awful night.

Now it fluttered high in the air and seemed to glow in the light of the streetlamp. I reached out and caught it and tucked it safely into the pocket of my jeans as Clayton bent down and took me in his arms again.

'This is the beginning, Miss Tilly,' he said. 'Just the beginning.'

Chapter Thirty-Two

The chapel looked wonderful. It had been cleaned, repaired, restored and once again stood grey and imposing and solid against the harsh background of the dale.

Inside it soared upwards to a blue and gold ceiling. Deep arched windows let in shafts of summer sun, bouncing off the newly painted white walls and filling the vast space with light.

'And look at *this*,' said Matty triumphantly as she picked out one of the photos in the centre of a display.

'It's you!' I said.

'No, Miss Tilly, it's you!' said Clayton.

'Good grief,' said my mother, 'it's Kate.'

We all looked again. The photograph showed a tall, strong-faced woman standing in a fellside garden on a hot summer's day. She stood upright, gazing calmly, steadily at the camera. Even in the faded black and white you could see the sunburn on her face and arms. And a long lock of hair had come loose and curled down around her throat. She seemed unable to do anything about it, as she was standing in the doorway carrying a heavy enamel jug in both hands.

'Is she actually smiling at the camera?' I asked.

'Looks like it, doesn't it?' said Matty, her eyes swarming over the pictures, taking in every detail. 'But it isn't Mum.

It's Granny Allen. As we've never seen her before. Amazing. Really amazing.'

'Where did the picture come from?' I wanted to know.

'Some old chap brought it in. It was in a bundle in an old house that had been a photographer's studio. There are more, too, but we need to do some work on them before we can show them. But they're all her and they're all completely different from any others of her. All by the same photographer. Goodness knows why they were kept. Or why they were so different. I've no idea.'

I looked at the expression in the last picture. Of Matilda Allen's half-smile, the amused glance. That smile wasn't for the camera, that smile was for the photographer.

'Oh, I don't know,' I said, suddenly seeing Granny Allen in a totally new light. 'I think we can make a good guess.'

The band played, the sun shone, the ladies of the chapel and the WI staggered back and forth with plates piled high with home-baked cakes and quiches, pies and pastries, tarts and trifles, sausages and sandwiches, cheeses and chicken legs, buns and biscuits.

Becca was dashing between The Miners' Arms and the chapel, helping where she could. As she nipped over to the chapel with a tray full of extra cutlery, I could hear her babbling to herself in Italian. She was off with Sandro a few days later to stay with his mother and sister for a few weeks.

'Oh, help. I'll never make a good impression. My Italian's still pathetic,' she fretted.

'Even with all that one-to-one tuition?' I grinned.

'Oh, don't! I'm sure he's taught me things that are quite unsuitable to say to his mother,' Becca wailed, bustling off with the cutlery.

Elsewhere, Alessandro and Clayton were signing autographs

and chatting to groups of football fans. Matty was being filmed for a TV special. Dexter was talking enthusiastically to a girl from a colour supplement, and hordes of people were oohing and aaahing over their family pictures. Goodness knows when there had last been so many people at Hartstone.

An American was gazing intently at the photographs. 'We've got a picture of Granny Allen back home,' he said. 'She was my great-great-great grandmother, but she looks real fierce in her photo, with her Bible. Not like this. Hey,' he said suddenly, looking at us. 'You guys must be my relations. Some sort of cousins.'

Before long he was organizing us for a photograph. There was Matty and Dexter, Mum and Bill, me and Clayton, Becca and Sandro, laughing in the old chapel against a background of photographs. The sun streamed in and people milled about, eating, drinking and enjoying themselves.

'I wonder,' said Matty, wrapping her arms round Dexter and kissing him happily. 'I wonder what Granny Allen would say.'

My mum smiled and looked around. 'I think she'd say she'd done a pretty good job, wouldn't you?'

Epilogue

TEAGUE–FLINT: On 1 November at Chelsea Register Office, William Teague to Francesca Flint, nee Thwaite.

IN A MOVE that's come as little surprise, Clayton Silver has been appointed player-manager of Shadwell, the club that was left in disarray with the sudden death of their former chairman last year and the consequent financial chaos. After the bumper sale of players in January, Silver (31) is credited with making a team of the few players who remained and keeping them in the Premiership. His career with Shadwell started . . .

British Television Association Awards. *Factual programmes. Jake Shaw and Felicity Staveley for Knowing the Score, an investigation into the murky world of former football club owner and businessman Simeon Maynard.*

As the nights draw in, cheer up the dark days of autumn with the latest in Becca Guy's fun and stunning collection of scarves, as seen tucked under some of the most famous chins in town. (Did you spot fabulous Foxy in one last week?) When not knitting up north, Becca is otherwise known as the fiancée of Chelsea striker Alessandro Santini. This is a WAG who's very much her own boss, but we hear there are plans for two weddings – one in England and one in Italy – next summer.

TOP MODEL FOXY is swapping one side of the camera for another as she plans to go back to school. Foxy, or, to give her her Sunday name, Matilda Alderson, is going back to college this autumn to study photography. 'It's what I'd always planned to do, it's just that I've got a bit sidetracked in the last few years,' said the stunning redhead. 'I shall probably still do the occasional assignment, but now I really want to learn to take pictures of my own, and modelling will very much take second place to that.'

If she needs any help or advice, Foxy can always turn to any number of the fashion industry's top snappers, many of whom rate her as their favourite model. But she might prefer to ask partner Dexter Metcalfe, himself a respected photographer, with whom she recently opened the intriguing Hartstone Chapel Gallery in the high Pennines.

Footballers were out in force on Saturday when Shadwell's player-manager, Clayton Silver, married Tilly Flint in a very traditional wedding. Best man was Denny Sharpe, manager of Silver's first club. The bride was given away by her stepfather, restaurateur Bill Teague. Tilly, a former food journalist, has recently joined her mother 'Fairtrade' Frankie Flint to bring new ideas and a new approach to England's favourite coffee bars. The bride wore a simple but stunning silk dress, and carried a bouquet tied with cherry-red velvet ribbons.

Tilly's Recipes

Tilly's cooking is not a matter of exact science and like all good recipes these need personal adjustments until they become your own.

Sloe Gin

Sloes picked in October, ideally after a first frost
Cheap strong gin (The monks used supermarket own brand 40%)
Empty gin bottle or something similar
Approximately 4oz of sugar

You don't need to wash the sloes, but if you really feel you must, then make sure they are absolutely dry before you use them. Using a big darning needle or fork, prick the sloes all over, so the gin can get in and the juice can get out, and put them in the empty gin bottle until it's half full. Add the sugar. Add the gin right up to the top of the bottle. Shake it gently to dissolve the sugar.

Put it in a dark cupboard and for the first week or two, give it a few rotations every day or so. At Christmas, strain it and decant into another bottle. Perfect in a hip flask on bracing winter walks.

Lemon Scallops and Angel Hair Spaghetti

Scallops – around 3 per person for a starter
Angel hair spaghetti or any fine pasta
Olive oil
Butter
Lemon
Crème fraiche
Small glass of white wine
Salt and pepper
Fresh parsley/chives

Melt a blob of butter in a pan and grate the lemon rind into it. Add the wine and let it simmer until it's reduced. Stir in the crème fraiche and a good squeeze of lemon juice. Add salt and pepper to taste.

Put the pasta in boiling, salted water. While it's cooking, heat the olive oil in a pan. Dry the scallops and cook them for around a minute each side.

Drain the pasta and arrange on plates. Pour on the sauce – not too much, you don't want it too gloopy – place the scallops on top and decorate with the green herbs and lemon rind.

Braised Herby Lamb with Root Vegetables

Vegetable oil
Lamb shanks
Pearl barley
Rosemary
Thyme
Mint jelly
Any root vegetables – potatoes, swede, parsnips, onions, leeks – chopped in to big chunks. Whole shallots are good too

Water
Seasoning

Cover the bottom of a big ovenproof dish with a good layer of vegetables and the pearl barley. Add a dollop of mint jelly and stir round.

Fry the lamb shanks in the oil for five minutes or so until they're golden on all sides. Put them on the layer of vegetables. Add the water, seasoning and herbs. Cover with a right fitting lid or tin foil. Put in a low to moderate oven for around two hours.

Tilly's Poached Pears in Cider

4 pears such as Comice
½ – ¾ pint of good strong cider or perry
2 big tablespoonfuls of soft brown sugar – depending on how dry the cider is add a dash of orange juice
A cinnamon stick, cloves, and a scraping of nutmeg

Stir the sugar, orange juice and cider together in a big pan and simmer gently for a few minutes.

Peel the pears. You can leave them whole with their stalks on, which looks pretty, but they are less messy to eat if you slice them in half and take the pips out. Put in an oven proof dish.

Put the cinnamon stick and cloves in a bit of muslin in the dish, add the scrape of nutmeg. Pour the cider mixture over the top and put in a moderate oven for 45 minutes or so, until the pears have absorbed a lot of the mixture.

Serve hot or cold. For extra indulgence, whip up a dash of Calvados into some thick cream to top.

What's next?

Tell us the name of an author you love

| Sharon Griffiths | Go |

and we'll find your next great book.

www.bookarmy.com